MW01067802

Against Her Will

Peter Martin

Dedicated to my wife whose invaluable help made this novel possible.

Also by Peter Martin

Against Her Will
Missing -Dead or Alive
A Dangerous Secret
A Means to an End
In the Face of Adversity (Coming July 2019)

"But sometimes, when she'd be all by herself, walking home late in the evening on a crowded street she'd be afraid of her own shadow following her..."
— *Sanhita Baruah*

Chapter 1

A HAND TOUCHED DONNA'S ARM AS SHE WALKED PAST. She shuddered slightly, then heard a familiar posh almost public school voice calling her name. David Wallace, her boss. Her eyes closed for a second, and she muttered, oh no, under her breath.

'Got a minute?' he asked, raising his eyebrows expectantly.

'Sure David – is there a problem?' Her heart sank as she glanced up at the clock behind him. It was already ten past five. Why did he always do this just as she was about to leave?

'Yeah - it's this customer report of yours. We need to have a chat about the analysis you've made. One or two of the trends you've shown seem a little unusual, to say the least.'

'OK, let me get my notes,' she said with a frown.

'Bring them to my office, would you?'

Gritting her teeth, she realized what this would mean. A dissection of her whole analysis, bit by bit; which knowing David, would probably tear two weeks' work to shreds.

She went back to her desk to fetch the necessary paperwork, cursing him for doing this to her yet again. The realisation of how meticulous he was made her fear the chances of leaving before six o'clock were virtually nil. Just what she didn't need when she was supposed to be going out with Blake at seven-thirty to celebrate their forthcoming engagement.

David gave a little smile on her return, making her cringe.

'Pull up a chair, Donna.'

She sat down, paperwork in front of her, and proceeded to try to clarify her analysis.

Every minute detail had to be explained, so determined was he to find out exactly what she'd done. All the figures had been checked and rechecked, so there couldn't be a mistake in the analysis – could there? As time passed her nerves began to fray.

Her fingers drummed on his desk, and she almost felt like crying, as David droned on and on, with no apparent conception of how late it was. The clock on the wall struck six-fifteen. The man wouldn't shut up. It seemed like he didn't want to go home. Which wasn't surprising, considering he lived on his own and appeared to live and breathe work, expecting everyone else to do the same.

Ever since he'd interviewed her for the Statistical Analyst job, two years ago, she'd noticed his keen interest in her work. Obviously having seen something beyond her supposed beauty. But now she suspected this interest was more than just work orientated.

To his credit, he knew his subject inside out, but when he found a couple of little errors that changed her analysis completely, she almost died with shock. How stupid must she have looked right in front of him? God knows what he thought.

Finally he stood up and smiled faintly, much to her relief. 'All right Donna, let's call it a day, shall we? Thanks for staying behind, I really appreciate it.'

'Sorry I messed up.' She gathered up her papers as she rose.

'Think nothing of it. We all make mistakes, don't we? Even me, believe it or not. Have a good night.' He gave her a warm smile, then hesitated as if he was about to say something else. But he didn't. Nevertheless, she felt slightly uncomfortable, as on occasions she'd caught him gazing at her. If ever he'd asked her out – heaven forbid - she'd die! Thank goodness he didn't, she thought as she made to leave.

'Donna!' His voice was loud and made her jump and turn round. 'Can I give you a lift?'

The colour on her face began to change to red again. 'Er... well...'

'It's on my way home – honestly.' He stared at her with a slight grin on his face.

'No, it's all right, but thanks anyway.' She quickened her pace, almost running towards the main office door.

'Oh come on, Donna - ' he shouted after her, but she didn't stop. Didn't dare. Or was she overreacting to his friendly gesture?

Making her way hurriedly down the corridor, she reached the lift, pressed the button, and waited for it to arrive. It seemed to take forever – her heart thumped against her chest, fearing she'd miss her train. At last the lift arrived. Once she was inside, she drummed her nails on the chrome handrail as the floors ticked away, took out her phone and tried to get in touch with Blake, but couldn't get through to him. Damn.

Finally, the doors slid open, Donna rushed through, still annoyed at herself for being late.

When she got out of the building, she was surprised to see how dark it was. Then she heard the sound of someone's footsteps clattering behind her. Oh my God, was somebody following her? But when she glanced round there was no one there. Then walking on, she heard it again. She closed her eyes for a second, and sighed, thinking she was getting paranoid, then quickened her step, intent on getting to the station as quickly as possible.

This was all David's fault – for not being willing to accept the fact she didn't want a lift and making her feel on edge. When people got overfriendly, she felt uncomfortable and embarrassed. Why they thought her attractive, she found it hard to work out, even though she'd been told this from an early age. There'd always been remarks about her slender figure and turquoise eyes.

As she walked at a brisk pace, she looked at her watch, wondering if it might be possible to make the six forty-five train back to their flat. That would leave her half an hour to get ready, but it'd be a close run thing.

She crossed the main road, hurrying towards the subway, glad the sound of footsteps seemed to have gone. Hopefully, whoever it was had given up, or maybe she'd imagined it.

Dusk was fast approaching, the streets were deserted and grey. A spot of rain pricked her forehead. She pulled her jacket together and hurried to the mouth of the subway where the muffled words to `Let it Be` rang out. The entrance looked empty and dim apart from the busker sitting cross-legged on the pavement. His out of tune guitar sounded so bad it made his voice sound good. Donna smiled to herself as her heels clicked on the concrete.

Although walking through this subway made her a little nervous, she was in a hurry. No way did she want to be late for the meal. Blake would think... she didn't know what he'd think. Sometimes he had problems dealing with other men liking her, no matter how many times she reassured him. But the idea he might consider David Wallace a rival was too ridiculous for words.

If only she could contact Blake, it wouldn't matter. She pressed the keypad on her mobile again, intending to let him know she was running late, but his phone still seemed to be switched off. Shit.

At the end of the subway, she saw a figure standing there, his head covered by a hood. As he coughed, a hand appeared in front of his face. The lights above him were bright, but Donna didn't look his way until he suddenly spoke.

'Got the time darling?' His muffled words made her jump.

He sounded young. There was a strange sweet smell close by, that made her want to puke and quickly get by.

It was six-forty, leaving her five minutes to get to the station.

'Nearly quarter to seven,' she mumbled, scurrying past.

As she hurried on out of the subway towards Dexford train station, suddenly, out of nowhere, an arm bent and tightened round her neck, and she was dragged into a long narrow alley, that stank of stale pee and uncollected garbage. She started gurgling at once, finding it almost impossible to scream or breathe, when a gloved hand closed around her nose and mouth. Terror spread through her body as she panicked and struggled to get free. Was this a mugging or something much worse? Oh my God, don't hit me, she prayed. Best give him whatever she had, and hope he'd let her go.

He pulled her to one side and into one of the nearby derelict buildings, then yanked her up by her long blond hair. A fist thumped into her stomach, causing her to crumple and gasp in pain.

Wild large eyes glared at her through a balaclava helmet.

He snarled and gave out a high-pitched chuckle as if he enjoyed frightening her like this.

'Oh no... please leave me … alone. Take whatever you want… but please don't hurt me,' she begged, pushing her handbag towards him. She tried to get up but was still in his grasp, his hand gripping her arm so tightly she winced in pain.

'Stuff your bloody money – pretty lady,' he hissed in a strange gruff voice.

All a tremble, she pleaded for mercy. Ignoring this, the man smashed his fist into her face. Warm blood trickled down her nose. She whimpered, before striking her again several times in the ribs, and on the chin. The pain was so excruciating, she could hardly draw breath.

She battled desperately to get up from the filthy debris filled floor to run. But he was too quick, and caught her by her coat, forcing her back onto the ground. Soon he was on top of her, kissing her roughly about the face as she tried to avoid his horrible greasy lips. His gloved hands clutched her breasts hard, making her clench her teeth and whine in agony. He ripped her blouse open. Buttons flew off in all directions.

Donna sobbed, shockwaves of hysteria surged through her. Oh God, if only someone would help her. This was unbearable, unreal - was he really going to do this to her. Surely not? How she wished Blake were here. Please... oh sweet Jesus... help me, she thought. She'd rather die than have this happen. How could this monster violate her like this?

In her desperation, she raked his arm with her fingernails, and went to gouge his eyes, but his hand grasped hers, wrenching it back with such force that she wept in agony. The man laughed hideously at her futile efforts to stop him. He was so strong, and well able do whatever he wanted to her. She was simply too weak to prevent it. Please God, make him stop.

Suddenly he moved his hand away, towards his own body, and fumbled with the zip of his trousers. She tried desperately to wriggle free, but he caught hold of her ripped blouse, and slapped her on the face with the back of his hand. Her nose went numb, and she tasted her own coppery blood. She tried to raise her head, but he pressed his body down hard almost suffocating her.

As he continued, she closed her eyes, trying to shut out the horror of what was happening to her. Unable to defend herself in any way, she lay there passively, wanting it over as quickly as possible. But it seemed to go on forever. And the pain deep inside was torture, like some hot blunt instrument splitting her in two. She felt his balaclava clad face close to her own, spit from his mouth trickled onto her cheek. There remained a foul pungent sickly smell about him that repulsed her.

Finally, he uttered a great groan of exquisite pleasure, stopped, and giggled. Donna shuddered, lying prostrate on the ground.

He got to his feet, breathing in deeply, and stared down at her. 'How does it feel? Bitch! Not so pretty now, are you, eh?' He growled.

Cold eyes stared at her; and widened with desire again making Donna's heart flutter with dread. Her mouth flooded with sour saliva and bile come up through her throat. He began to kick her in the stomach, her legs, face, just about anywhere – and when he'd finished, he looked down at her and gave out a high-pitched laugh that almost sounded like a hyena. That same vile odour remained on him, and then he was gone.

She remained on the ground, hardly able to move, relief at being alive passed quickly. She needed to cover herself up. Her whole face began to swell up like a balloon - in fact she hurt all over and found it difficult to breathe. Her private area was deadened by what he'd done. Dear God – she felt so sick and unclean. Why had this happened to her? If only she could wake up from this horrible dream.

It took some time, but at last she staggered to her feet, wrapping what was left of her clothing tightly around her. Leaning against the wall, unsteadily she stumbled forward out of the building.

When she heard what sounded like a gang of youths approaching, her heart lifted, in the hope they might assist her. They looked across at her, some of them giggling, while others preferred to look the other way.

'Please... help me,' she begged, but in reply they made lewd remarks, before walking past. Weeping, she found their behaviour incredible.

Donna didn't see the man whose arms she fell into. She glimpsed a grey beard, and a woman with her mouth gaping open.

'Oh my God!' the man exclaimed. 'What on earth...?'

'I...I...' she whispered, tears streaming down her blood soaked face.

'Harold – she's been attacked. Look at her face and clothes. Oh you poor thing. Quickly - call the police and an ambulance!' the woman shouted, covering Donna with her coat. She placed an arm round her and guided her out to a nearby bench. Donna heard Harold mumble something into his mobile phone.

She shook with ague, her body aching all over. As she glanced up, a crowd of people had gathered, talking, staring as if she was some kind of freak show. Why did they have to gawp at her in that way? She just wanted them to go away and leave her in peace.

Soon after hearing the sirens, Donna saw the flashing lights. The ambulance stopped close to where she was sitting. Two figures dressed in green uniforms emerged and rushed through the crowd to her. One, bent down and put an arm round her, and introducing herself as Anne, a paramedic, began to talk to her, but Donna couldn't take in what was being said. Finally Anne helped Donna up and guided her towards the ambulance, then assisted her to climb inside.

Lying down, Donna was relieved when the doors closed and the vehicle left the scene of the attack. After what only seemed a few minutes, they arrived at Dexford General Hospital.

From there she was taken to her own room, where she was undressed and examined by a female doctor.

After they'd patched her up, they allowed her to wash herself in a shower, which she did over and over again in a valiant attempt to rid herself of the filth all over her.

Once she was in bed and had taken the sedative the doctor had prescribed to relax her, she drifted in and out of sleep, waking intermittently with vivid visions of the man's evil eyes and the wicked laugh behind his balaclava helmet.

Sometime later she got up and went to the en-suite bathroom, and staring at herself in the mirror, she sobbed at her swollen face and bandaged nose. This brought it all back to her, and again terror swept over her. That horrible man had made her feel cheap and used. She'd never be the same again, and wanted to die.

Back in her room, resting on top of the bed, she kept her eyes closed, wishing the pain would go away. The sound of someone entering the room caused her to open her puffed up eyes, to see a plump policewoman with a round face, rosy cheeks and an easy smile, standing before her.

'Hallo Donna.' Her voice was soft, her large grey eyes widening with concern and compassion. 'I'm Jill Meadows, Dexford police. Sorry to disturb you, at a time like this. I know you need to get some rest and it's late, but I just wondered if you felt up to answering a few questions, about what happened to you.'

Donna didn't answer, she just wanted to be left alone.

'So how are you?' Jill asked.

She burst into tears.

The police woman reached out to touch her hand, but Donna pulled back in a flash.

'Look, I can see you're upset. You have every right to be. But you'll be fine, no one can hurt you now. And I promise we'll be working day and night to find the man who did this to you. But to do that we need your help. I realise how difficult this is, but important to know exactly what happened while it's still fresh in your mind - I believe it could make a huge difference. Could you try do that for me?'

She didn't respond.

'Please, Donna. I appreciate you've been through a terrifying ordeal, but it's vital you tell us whatever you can. Come on try -

for me and all the other girls out there, who are at risk until he's caught.'

'I... I can't talk about it.' She shook her head rigorously, breathing in and out deeply.

'I know you don't want to, my dear, but if you try really hard you can – believe me. There's no point in bottling this up inside. Tell me about what he did. Or his next victim might not live to tell the tale. Is that what you want?'

She began to shake violently, biting down hard on her bottom lip. Jill Meadows was right. She had to talk about this, but it was so horrific, so humiliating; she felt too ashamed to say anything.

'How about a drink?' Jill asked finally. After a few seconds silence Donna nodded.

'What do you fancy?'

'Anything. Water…'

Jill poured her a glass of water from the jug on her bedside table. Donna took a small sip, then gave it to Jill to put back on the table.

'You will get over this – but of course it will take time. You're young and strong, so your injuries will heal quickly. But what you've experienced can have devastating effects, mentally as well as physically - you'll need counselling from someone specially trained in rape trauma.'

Donna pulled a face and shook her head.

'I bet a girl like you must have lots of admirers.' Jill seemed to be trying a different approach.

She didn't even want to think about that.

'You have a boyfriend?'

She nodded timidly.

'Thought so. His name's Blake, isn't it?'

'Yes.'

'Hey, that's a nice name. He's a bit of a hunk, I noticed.'

'You think so?' Donna mumbled, unable to look Jill directly in the eye.

'Really good looking – shame I'm not ten years younger.'

She gave a slight smile, but this small talk did nothing to calm her down, instead it made her nervous. She felt herself going hot.

'Been going together long?'

'Five years,' she sighed still without looking at the police woman.

'That's a long time for someone so young. What - were you childhood sweethearts?'

She shrugged her shoulders.

'That's sweet. You'll be glad to know he's waiting outside with your mum and dad.'

She creased up, suddenly afraid again. 'I don't want them to know... everything.'

'I realise that, but remember they love you dearly, so they'll be very sympathetic and understanding. And can give you all the love and support you need right now.'

'But it was degrading and I feel so dirty.'

'There's no reason for you to feel like that - honestly. You couldn't have done any more than you did, and in the circumstances, I think you were very brave.'

'We were going out... to celebrate our engagement. Blake must have thought I'd stood him up,' she blurted out, biting down on a fingernail.

'Oh dear – that's a shame! Well, he knows you didn't stand him up now. He's been worried sick – I can't tell you how relieved he is that you're still alive, and out of danger.'

'He'll go spare if he finds out the truth.' She turned away to bury her face in her hands. 'Oh God, what have I done to deserve this?' She wept softly.

'Nothing, love. You were just in the wrong place at the wrong time. Listen, I don't like to keep on at you, but I have to ask you again about what happened. Come on now - just take your time – I've got all night if need be. Let's start with when you finished work tonight, shall we?' Jill said, a notebook in her hand ready.

Donna closed her eyes and started to tremble; she didn't want to do this, but it seemed she had no choice. It was so demeaning having to reveal all the intimate details, but Jill was so patient and supportive, Donna got through the ordeal. And once she began to open up, she was able to tell Jill everything she could remember.

It came tumbling out. All the unthinkable disgusting things that vile man had done to her. She was distraught at times, but could describe everything in great detail except for his appearance.

'Thank you Donna, it takes a lot of guts to speak about this. I'm very proud of you.' She smiled at her when it was all over. 'Forensics are going through your clothes right now, and we've taken samples of what's under your fingernails and from your vagina. Hopefully, if they can get his DNA, it'll be on file. I'll arrange for a police artist to come and sit with you in the morning, so we can get an idea of what he looks like. Is that all right, love?'

'I... I didn't get a good look at him. He wore some sort of mask, a balaclava I think it was; I only saw his piercing eyes. But I... I can't even tell you what colour they were, because it was dark, and I was so frightened.'

'Doesn't matter – like I said, any of these tiny details might come to you in time. Remember even without a description, it's possible we might find evidence from the samples we've taken. It may not be as difficult as you imagine.'

The very thought of having something of his in her body, something that might grow into... Oh sweet Jesus, hoping to God the morning after pill she'd taken earlier had worked. The alternative didn't bear thinking about.

'Right then – maybe it's time I left you in peace. You've got more than enough to cope with right now. In the morning I'll get all this typed up, you can read through it and sign it if you're happy. I'll speak to you later then, love. I expect you'd like to see your family now. They've been waiting for quite a while.'

'What – yes.' She twitched nervously.

How could she face them? They'd want her to tell them about it. And what about Blake? If only she could let him take her in his arms and make all the pain go away. But she didn't think that was possible. And neither did she want him or anyone else seeing her smashed up face and body. Yet it seemed she had to.

She nodded.

'OK. Now, if you need me any time, night or day, call this number. It's my direct line.' Jill gave her a card. Then just before leaving, she hugged Donna, who wanted to cry again.

As she lay there, she began to breathe erratically, panicking over having to face her family. She couldn't prevent herself from shaking. Oh God, would she ever stop being afraid?

Chapter 2

A SHORT TIME LATER, DONNA LOOKED UP TO SEE THE DOOR TO HER ROOM OPENING. A stout jolly looking black nurse came in first, all smiles, followed by her parents and her soon-to-be fiancé. She blinked nervously when she saw them, and her heart began to pound. She could hardly bear to look at them.

Her mum was a tall, thin, wiry woman with long bleached hair and pale complexion. Her face was heavily made up; eyes clear blue. She held Donna's dad's hand tightly. He was a couple of inches shorter but sturdy, bald, with a black moustache, and wore jeans and tee shirt. Several heart shaped tattoos covered his arms.

Behind him was Blake, tall and slim, with short black hair, he constantly displayed a shadow of a beard on his face. Tufts of his body hair peeked out of his opened necked white shirt. He was olive skinned and had dark brown eyes.

Donna closed her eyes, not wanting to speak to them.

She heard chairs scrapping along the floor as they were brought to the side of her bed.

The atmosphere was tense with emotion, and she sensed her family staring at her battered face.

Everyone was quiet, frightened to say anything, as tears trickled down her cheeks. She opened her eyes at last to the sound of her mother's voice. 'Oh my poor darling. Just look what that monster's done to you!'

Donna cringed and wished she could hide her face. Instead she wept uncontrollably.

'Don't cry love.' Her mum got up from the chair and held out her arms.

Donna started to shake and drew back from her mum, unable to stand any more of this right now.

'They ought to string him up when they catch him,' her dad growled.

Donna's mum sat reluctantly back down in her chair. 'No one's safe out on their own these days. Makes you wonder what the world's coming to.'

'I'll kill the bastard, if I ever catch hold of him,' Blake said angrily.

'Did you get a good look at him, love?' Her mum asked.

Donna shook her head, her face creased up in pain.

She glimpsed Blake moving off his chair to sit on the bed. He attempted to put his arm around her, but the very thought of it made her recoil from his touch.

'No, please don't!'

Blake's face dropped. Donna didn't want to talk yet, let alone have any physical contact with him. She wanted him to understand, but wasn't sure he would.

'Sorry love,' was all he said, before backing off to his seat.

'Donna, don't get upset, Blake didn't mean anything.'

'I don't want to be touched, mum.'

Finally, she sank back down into her bed, and turned her face away from them.

'Please don't be like this,' her dad said. 'We only want to help, sweetheart.'

'Did he take anything from you?' Blake suddenly asked.

She started to sob again, her tears staining and wetting the pillow.

'Talk to us Donna. Tell us what happened.'

Slowly, she moved her face towards her mum. 'I can't. I just want to forget about it, but every time I close my eyes, I keep seeing him hitting me.' She tightened her fists and put them defensively in front of her face.

'All right, let her be, love – now's not the time,' her dad said.

'But she's our daughter – have you seen what that scum's done to our beautiful little girl? Her face - ' She dabbed her own eyes with a tissue.

Blake looked forlorn. No one spoke for a while, then at last her dad said, 'Perhaps we ought to go. We'll come back tomorrow Donna, when you're a little better, but ring us any time you like, if you need us.'

She didn't react to his remarks, but felt their eyes glued on her.

'You staying a little longer, Blake?' Donna's mum asked, while her dad beckoned his wife to hurry up.

Blake didn't respond to this, but chose to remain in his seat. Perhaps he wasn't sure what was expected of him.

'You take care of yourself now,' her dad said.

She didn't say goodbye to her parents as they left; couldn't even look at them or at Blake either, who sat there in silence, obviously wondering what he should do next.

After what seemed an eternity, he finally spoke, 'You don't mind if I stay, do you?'

She shrugged her shoulders.

'When you didn't turn up at the flat, I got really scared. I didn't know what to think. I wondered if you'd changed your mind about me. You have no idea how beautiful you are, and how many other guys fancy you.'

Blake and his ridiculous insecurities again. She wasn't listening. Why couldn't he understand what she was going through?

When he took hold of her hand, straight away she pulled it away from him. He frowned.

'You want to know what really happened, Blake? He... he didn't just attack me... he... ' and bit by bit it came out, about all the unspeakable things the foul man had done to her and how sickened she was by the vile actions. Blake listened, staring at her with shock, and obvious disbelief. His eyes widened, and his mouth tightened with anger.

When she'd finished, he looked down at the ground, shaking his head; then she watched him wring his hands tightly together. She waited for him to say something - but he was silent!

'Maybe now you have some idea why I didn't want you to touch me.'

With a glazed look in his eyes and through clenched teeth, he said, 'You never ought to have stopped late. That Wallace bloke has got a lot to answer for. And why didn't you phone me? I would have picked you up – and then this wouldn't have happened.'

'Because your bloody phone was switched off.'

What... ' he began, looking puzzled, but she didn't let him finish.

'What's the matter? Don't you believe me?'

'Of course I do. Look, I'm your boyfriend, for Christ's sake. I love you and I want to help – so please don't give me a hard time over this.'

'He frightened the shit out of me.' He might have killed me, she thought. Easy as snapping a twig.

Blake got up and moved towards her again, but she jumped back like a startled rabbit, and held out her hands to stop him.

A sad scowl appeared on his face. 'But what he did hasn't got anything to do with me.'

'Maybe not. You still don't understand, do you, Blake? Sorry, but I can't bear you to touch me, right now.'

'Donna - you're not thinking straight.'

'They made me take a pill - so I won't be pregnant with that maniac's child?'

His eyes widened again, showing up the creases in his forehead.

'And look at my face. Not quite your beautiful girl any more, am I? Why did he single me out for God's sake? What did I ever do to him?'

'Nothing, I realise that. He probably did it because he couldn't have you any other way. But I'll tell you one thing, I'll fucking strangle the bastard, if I catch hold of him.' He balled up a fist and banged it into his other hand.

'Well, how will you do that? I don't even know what he looks like. I never saw his face. He wore a balaclava helmet so it's impossible.'

'No it isn't, Donna. Something about him will have stuck in your memory, for sure. Like how tall he was, his build, if he was black or white. And if he spoke, you might even guess his age. And by his accent whether he was local or not. The police will be onto that and lots of other things… like matching his DNA for instance…'

But she wasn't listening to what he was saying and was instead drawn back into that dreadful alley again. Why in God's name did I have to work late?

'Did you hear what I said? You have to be positive in this.'

She gave him a half-ironic smile.

'So how long are they keeping you here?'

'I don't know. No one's said. They've taken some X-rays and done other tests. They'll probably come to a decision in the morning.'

'The flat will be so empty without you. I'll miss you like crazy.'

She put her hand over her eyes. You'll miss me, Blake. Is that the only thing you can say? She needed something else from him, wasn't sure what – comfort and silence, perhaps. Total silence. Couldn't he give her that much?

'I wish they'd let me stay here with you, Donna.'

She moaned quietly.

Blake sat there for a while longer, not saying much else. Neither did she. An unfamiliar atmosphere grew between them, an uncertainty, a cloud of confusion; as if they'd become estranged. Like two people on the edge of breaking up.

He rose, shrugged, made to touch her again, then let his arm fall to his side.

'I'd better go now – it's getting late. See you tomorrow - Ok.'

If he really loved her, he'd insist on being allowed to stay as long as possible. But maybe she didn't want him to linger in this room with her any longer – she didn't know.

He backed toward the door. 'Night, love.'

She glanced at him for a second, but didn't answer.

She was glad he'd gone, yet part of her wanted him to stay. Her mind was in turmoil and she hurt all over. Staring into space trying not to think of her predicament, she imagined herself being somebody else in another place, away from this room. She didn't hear the door open nor did she see someone approach her bed.

'Donna.' It was a male voice, her doctor by the sound of it.

Her mouth opened, but no words came out.

'Would you like something to help you sleep?' he said.

She nodded faintly, which he obviously took to mean yes. He gave her a couple of tablets with a glass of water. She took them, then lay back on her bed. Slowly she felt herself slipping further down in the bed. Her eyes were heavy; her last images were of the concerned look on the doctor's face.

Restless sleep followed. She dreamt of the man who'd raped her, that he'd come to the flat intent on finishing the job. But Blake had burst in on him. There'd been a terrible fight, and Blake ended up with a beating worse than her own. And Donna could do nothing to help him. She cried out in agony before waking with a jolt. For the first few seconds she was very disorientated, then came the realisation of where she was.

And as the early morning light seeped through the window blinds, it allowed her to see even more of her surroundings. The agony she was in was almost too much to stand - how did you live through this and come out the other side?

With great difficulty she got out of bed, and shuffled towards the door as the pain from her ribs was intense. She observed the hospital in full swing, nurses and doctors going about their business, tending the sick. The smell of disinfectant lingered in the atmosphere, and sensing the anxiety of those who waited fretfully for the outcome of operations', she began to tremble with dread.

Suddenly came the urge to run away, to get out of this awful place, and she would have too, if she hadn't felt so weak and tired. Instead, she had to go back to rest on top of her bed.

Lying there, she wondered if the swelling on her face had gone down. The night before she'd been shocked to see her puffed up eyes, one of which she still couldn't see out of properly. Touching each of them gently, they felt just as bad. She must look ugly, and half wanted to remain this way, to retain a measure of anonymity. And become a plain Jane, who never got looked at twice, instead of an object for men to crave.

But it was Blake's reaction that worried her the most. He seemed unable to deal with the situation. She needed him to be strong, but maybe something in him had changed too, because of what had happened. What if he didn't care about her anymore?

Before the attack, he couldn't keep his eyes or hands off her. Yet, now she feared he'd no longer want her, and dreaded life without him.

◇◇◇

A little later, a nurse brought her a light breakfast, but she had difficulty in eating it due to her stitched lip. Afterwards, a doctor, a kind looking man with a warm smile, came over to see her.

'How are you feeling this morning Donna?'

'All right,' she lied.

'We've had the results of your blood tests. All negative, thankfully. But you have four broken ribs, which we've bandaged, so I suggest you take it easy for a while so the bones get a chance to knit together again. Your face is badly bruised, but I assure you that should heal within week or two without any scarring. It looks a lot worse than it really is... honestly – so don't worry. Oh and by the way, I've written to your GP advising him to arrange for you to see a counsellor to help you come to terms with your ordeal. I imagine he'll contact you, once you get out of here.'

'When can I go home?' she said.

'Soon. But you'll need several weeks rest before you even consider going back to work.'

Donna looked up at the doctor anxiously. 'How will I ever get over this?'

'That's a difficult question to answer. It all depends on the individual, and whilst you'll never forget what happened, I honestly think you can get through this in time. No one's saying it's going to be easy, but it's amazing how resilient people are when they need to be. And if the police do manage to catch this man quickly, before he does any more damage, it'll be a huge weight off your mind.'

'I'll never relax until they do.'

'You will, I'm sure with your family's support. This wasn't your fault, Donna– it was a random attack – a case of being in the wrong place at the wrong time. You're lucky to be alive, very lucky indeed.' He smiled warmly at her. 'Now if there's any other way I can help, you only have to ask. And remember there are lots of specially trained people and organisations out there, should you need them. Most times, you just need to pick up the phone. You take care now.'

She nodded, but didn't think anyone could put this right.

Chapter 3

THEY TOLD HER BLAKE WAS WITH A CUSTOMER WHEN SHE PHONED TO ASK HIM TO PICK HER UP FROM THE HOSPITAL. So, she left a message, telling him she was ready to go home. With luck he wouldn't be too long.

She sat in the easy chair by her bed, suitcase beside her, waiting for him to come. Her dark sunglasses covered most of her face.

After about half an hour she looked outside and noticed it had started to rain, which just about summed up her mood. When there was no sign of him, she began to feel on edge.

It must have been another fifteen minutes before she saw him ambling towards her, apparently without a care in the world. How dare he be so insensitive?

'Ready to go?' he asked her, without even apologising.

Feeling dejected she replied, 'I am. So where have you been until now?'

'Oh, I got stuck in traffic – and then I couldn't find a place to park. It was horrendous.'

'Blake, I've been sitting here for ages. People keep looking at me strangely, probably wondering what I'm doing here.'

'Sorry love, but I couldn't do much about it,' he protested.

She gave him a dirty look annoyed by his pathetic excuses. Her feelings of vulnerability and insecurity started to heighten again, and there he was acting as if being late didn't matter. But to her it did... very much.

They walked out of the hospital together, but she sauntered slowly, stooping like an old woman, waving away all his offers of help. When he walked briskly on ahead of her, it seemed like they didn't know one another.

All the way home, she was on tenterhooks, and his attempts to make conversation were met with stony silence.

Their flat was in a sedate suburb of Dexford. Blake parked the car outside the four-storey block of flats. Theirs was on the ground floor. He went in first, through the small hallway into the living room, which led through to the kitchen. On the back wall, above the bookcase hung a framed photograph of Donna in her cap and gown, and directly underneath it the certificate for her First Class Mathematics Degree, her proudest moment. Further along the hall were two bedrooms; and sandwiched in between was the bathroom. All tastefully laid out with expensive fixtures and fittings.

She shrugged aside Blake's attempt to help her take off her coat, then went to the bathroom to freshen up. Removing her dark glasses, she surveyed herself in the mirror that took up one wall of the room, and didn't like what she saw. The facial injuries remained almost unaltered. Her skin seemed pale. There was a haggard look about her, which she thought had aged her ten years. She cursed herself for not being able to give a good description of him, but it was no use. No matter how hard she tried, nothing came to mind, except the putrid smell of him and that strange laugh of his. The man had disguised himself too well.

At last, with her dark glasses back on, she came out, sat down on the white leather settee, a little way from Blake watching the Sports News on TV.

'All right, love?' He smiled. 'There's a drink on the table if you want it.'

'Thanks.'

She took a sip, but didn't enjoy the hot chocolate even though normally it was her favourite drink.

Blake kept glancing at her with nervous concern. But no matter how hard he tried to strike up a conversation, it seemed he was fighting a losing battle.

She sat staring at the screen, not seeing the action in front of her. And guessed Blake wasn't sure what to make of her. Well, she wouldn't say any more about her ordeal, and certainly not for his benefit. She didn't even want to think about it. And as long as he didn't mention the subject, she'd be all right.

After a while, Blake got up and said, 'So what you want for tea?'

'Anything,' she said in a disinterested tone of voice.

'How about a steak and kidney pie out of the freezer?'

'Sure - whatever.'

Obviously wishing she'd show a little more enthusiasm, he went away to prepare the meal. Sadly she couldn't motivate herself for anything.

Later he put the plate in front of her, and watched while she ate. Despite the appetising smell of the meal, she wasn't hungry.

She ate slowly, and when Blake finished before her, he was quick to say, 'Look love, if you're not hungry, just leave it.'

'Sorry.' She put down her knife and fork.

His lips formed a straight line of disappointment, but he didn't say anything.

'I'll sit here for a while, if you don't mind. Leave the TV on – all right?'

'Sure, no problem. It's up to you, love.'

He washed up, and although he didn't complain, Donna could tell he wasn't happy. Well, she had more pressing things to worry over than his bruised pride. Like where her attacker was hiding. And if the police were any nearer catching him, after her almost non-existent description of him. They'd told her there were no matches on the police database to the DNA samples they'd taken. It seemed hopeless.

She wondered how many others he'd attacked; how many more he'd beaten and raped, and was filled with a sudden rage. He was out there now, probably planning another assault. Maybe he looked ordinary, the kind of guy no one paid attention to, another anonymous nobody, but he was very dangerous and capable of anything. These thoughts made her feel very vulnerable and afraid.

Half an hour later, Blake sat down next to her, a glum expression on his face. No doubt fed up of this situation. He kept glancing at her again as if he hoped she'd talk to him.

'Blake, what the hell's the matter with you now?' She turned to face him in an almost aggressive manner.

'Nothing, I'm concerned about you - that's all.'

'I'll be fine, Blake. I... I just need some time...'

'All right, all right... I can see that. But I do worry over you, you must realise that.'

'Well... I'm all right,' Tears had welled up in her eyes. He tried to put his arms around her but she moved back from him. 'Please don't touch me, I've already told you I can't stand that... right now.'

With a hurt look on his face, he said, 'Sorry.'

They didn't speak after that, the only sound came from the television. Around ten o'clock feeling tired, she got up off the sofa and sighed. 'Think I'm going to bed now,' she informed him.

'Ok, I'll come as well.'

In the bathroom, with difficulty she changed into her nightwear, and left the room wearing a full length red dressing gown. She got into bed, while Blake went into the bathroom, hoping to be asleep by the time he'd finished. But no. After only a few minutes she heard the door open; and dreaded what he might do next.

He got in beside her and at once tried to snuggle up to her. She froze, then pushed him away with her elbow.

'Oh for God's sake – what now?' He said as if she'd given him an electric shock.

'Please Blake. I've already told you not to touch me.'

'All right, suit yourself,' he sighed, swiftly moving to own his part of the bed.

He remained quiet after that. She sensed his impatience.

They lay apart for a few minutes. He yawned and stretched out, before turning onto his side with his back to her, which made her tremble with anger. She pulled back the covers to get out of bed, struggled into her dressing gown, then walked to the spare room, and got into the single bed. And prayed Blake wouldn't follow, but within a couple minutes he did.

'Hey come on - surely, you're not going to sleep in here tonight.'

'Well, I'm not sleeping with you – that's for sure...'

He rolled his eyes. 'Donna - I didn't do anything. All right, so you're upset, but I only wanted to show you some affection. I love you, always will do, no matter what happens. And I'm doing my level best for God's sake, so why are you being so hostile to me?'

'Just go, will you!' She got out of the bed to push him towards the door with as much force as she could despite her injuries. His attitude stank. Anyone would think he was the only person hurt in this.

Chapter 4

DONNA HAD BEEN AWAKE A LONG TIME, WHEN SHE HEARD BLAKE MOVING ABOUT IN THEIR BEDROOM. Maybe he'd woke early too, and before long, there was a knock at the bedroom door. He popped his head round the door, an uncomfortable, embarrassed look on his face. Obviously having trouble dealing with the situation.

'What is it, Blake?'

On entering the room still wearing his dressing gown, he blushed. 'I wanted to apologise over how I acted last night.'

'Oh,' she whispered, trying hard to stop her feelings from getting the better of her 'It doesn't matter.'

'But it does. I was totally out of order. It was inexcusable.' He said coming over to sit on the bed.

'I'm sorry, but I can't sleep with you right now.'

His eyes filled with tears and he looked to the ground. 'Ok. I can live with that.... I was just making breakfast. Do you want some?'

Raising her eyebrows at him, she pushed herself slowly up to a sitting position. 'No thanks. I'm not hungry. Now if you're finished, I'd like to get dressed.'

He moved out of the way, holding up his hands, and disappeared, probably to the kitchen, thinking about his stomach as usual.

She didn't do much that morning, except to keep the television switched on, but her mind was somewhere else.

Blake read a book until mid-afternoon, when he suddenly put it to one side, got up and walked to the hall, then came back wearing his denim jacket.

'Thought I'd go shopping. Do you want to come?'

'What - looking like this? You've got to be joking, haven't you?'

'Ok, suit yourself - see you later then.' And with that off he went.

Donna felt insecure again, and couldn't believe he'd leave her alone in the flat. She scampered to the window, saw him get into his car, and drive off without even glancing back. She bit her lip and burst into tears.

Her head ached so much she took two aspirins and lay down in the spare bedroom. In the vain hope of ridding herself of her headache, she closed her eyes and hoped to drop off to sleep; but also wished Blake would hurry back.

Just as she was dozing, the buzzer to the flat rang loudly startling her. Fear of opening the door crept through her veins. Who could it be? She was shaking when she switched on the intercom. Was that heavy breathing she heard in the background? Oh my God, what if the rapist had decided to track her down?

'Miss Donna Askey?'

'Yes.'

'Flowers for you, madam.'

'Oh, just a minute,' she replied, petrified by this unexpected interruption. Her heart beat faster, as she visualised so many different things. Did the attacker's voice sound like this?

Hurriedly, she rushed over to the window, and looked out. A florists van was indeed outside with the logo *'Say it with Flowers.'* She saw a youth with long black hair and a cap covering most of his face. Then just before she moved away, she noticed his jacket sporting the very same logo.

Nervously she told him to leave the flowers outside. Then returned to the window and watched him walk away and drive off. When the van disappeared out of sight, she ventured to the entrance to the flats, opened the outside door, picked up the bouquet, and returned inside, hurriedly locking herself in again.

She couldn't imagine who'd sent them. Maybe they were a macabre gift from the rapist, who had somehow found out where she lived. Then she saw the card, which said - *'From all your friends and colleagues at Bluethorn.'*

Relief ran through her body. What a nice gesture, she thought. It almost brought a tear to her eye, but then she gasped, realising it meant they must know about the attack. What if they'd found out that she'd been raped too? How horrifying, the very thought of facing them when she eventually went back to work filled her with dread.

Taking the flowers out of their cellophane wrapping, she cut and arranged them into several vases, and placed them around the room.

A 'Get Well Soon' card signed by everyone came with the bouquet; and there were even a few messages that under normal circumstances would have made her smile. Very nice of them, but she didn't need all this fuss. If she did ever find the courage to go back, she prayed they'd leave her in peace and not bombard her with questions about her ordeal.

She sat down on the sofa anxiously waiting for Blake to return from his shopping trip, still worrying about the flower deliveryman. Maybe she was getting paranoid.

Two hours later the front she heard the door open. 'It's only me'. And she breathed a great sigh of relief. But what had he been doing all this time?

He came into the living room carrying several bags, containing mainly food - trust him to think about his stomach again.

'What have you been doing – buying the whole bloody shop?' she asked, her eyes blinking fast as if she was about to cry again.

A look of astonishment came on his face at this, but all he said was, 'Actually, I was looking for a present for you. Only I wasn't sure what to get. Here, I thought this might cheer you up.'

He gave her a bag. She looked inside; saw a pretty pink silk blouse with a bow.

'It... it's very nice.' Tears flooded into her eyes. Having taken it out of the bag, she held it against her. It was gorgeous.

'Why don't you try it on?'

'I will later.' She gave him an uneasy smile.

He returned her smile, then went into the kitchen to put away all the food he'd bought, coming back a few minutes later with two cups of tea. As he sat down beside her, she noticed him looking around the room at the flowers.

'Hey - those are nice. They from anybody I know?'

'Bluethorn sent them.'

'That's decent of them. And a card too. You must be pleased they're thinking about you. Those guys have a high opinion of you, Donna. When you go back they'll welcome you with open arms – no question about it.'

Donna blushed red with embarrassment. Her eyes widened and she shook her head slightly. 'There's no way I'm going back there, Blake. Someone's told them why I'm away by now, and probably that I was raped. I'll never be able to look them in the eye again. They'll always doubt me – think I asked for it, seeing as I'm supposed to be so bloody attractive, or that I gave that guy some encouragement.'

'Come on, why would they think that? And besides they'll never find out the whole truth anyway. The only people who know are the police, the doctors and me. None of them would ever come into contact with Bluethorn. Donna, you're starting to get paranoid now.'

She ignored his last remark.

'How about going out for a meal afterwards, love? Save us cooking?'

She shook her head. 'I'll give it a miss. It's not as though I'm very good company right now.'

'Shall I get the dinner on?'

'I'm not hungry. Do yourself something if you want – I'll have something later.'

'It's not worth it - just for one.'

Rubbing his face and eyes with his hands, he sat there looking irritated.

The tension rose within her again. He was hungry. Just like he always was.

'Get yourself a takeaway if you're that hungry. You look like you could do with feeding up.'

His eyes lit up momentarily. 'Ok, I will - I'll bring you a bag chips back, if you want,' he offered.

'I've already said I'll have something later. How many times do I have to tell you? Just get whatever you want and leave it at that – all right!' She disliked herself for having raised her voice, but how was she supposed to behave around him? She wanted some peace.

He shot her a dirty glance, took a long breath, before storming out in a temper, slamming the front door shut. Obviously hurt by her cutting remarks. Well, she couldn't help it. He'd never understand what she was going through. Maybe she was difficult to live with right now, but he needed to be more tolerant and considerate. It looked like he didn't have it in him to handle this.

It felt as if she'd lost everything dear to her. Tears ran down her face again, and wouldn't stop. Her head ached and she was so depressed; she kept walking up and down the room, hugging herself with her arms. A terrible fear came into her stomach, that Blake no longer loved her any more. Because of that maniac, he would regard her as soiled goods. She still wanted him badly; her heart yearned for him. But as soon as he moved close to her, there was nothing she could do to show him any affection. She panicked. What if she couldn't overcome this? He'd leave her for someone else and then what would she do.

Later, sitting on the settee, her legs tucked under her, she stared at the television; unable to take in anything on the screen. Surely, he wouldn't be out long. He was only getting himself a takeaway after all.

She began to get tetchy, constantly flicking channels in the vain hope of finding something of interest. Unfortunately, there was nothing. In the end, she switched it off and threw the remote on the floor in frustration.

She walked across to their hi-fi, put on a CD by her favourite artist Nelly Furtado; and sat back, hoping the music would relax her. Yet within minutes, this too got on her nerves. She turned it off, unable to get that cutting look on Blake's face off her mind.

The time passed slowly, and still he didn't come back - perhaps he'd gone to the pub for a drink, to calm himself down. After an hour and a half she became frantic. Then she heard a noise, like a pebble hitting the window. She got up from the sofa and raced over to see what it was. Pulling back the curtain she looked outside, her breathing erratic. There were a clump trees nearby, and she thought she saw a figure running away. Oh my God, she whispered. Was this him again? She rushed to the door, to make sure it was locked, and pushed the deadlocks across. The only way he'd get in would be by breaking it down. She sat down, sighed with relief, but realised every little thing was spooking her something terrible.

1

Chapter 5

JUST AFTER NINE O'CLOCK, WHEN IT SEEMED AS IF HE'D BEEN GONE FOREVER, THERE WAS A BANG AT THE FRONT DOOR. She jumped out of her seat on hearing her name called; pulling her hand through her long hair, wondering... shaking from tip to toe.

'It's Blake, let me in. Come on Donna – what's going on?'

There was no spy-hole, so she had to put the door on the latch, having undone the deadbolts.

It was Blake. She could have cried, but didn't want him to see how hysterical she was, so she looked to the ground and let him in without a word.

'What's with all the locks?' he asked with an odd look on his face.

'I... I just thought... you were him... that man... ' She sniffed back the tears that threatened.

'Come on love – get a grip. There's no way he'd find out where you live. He doesn't even know your name, so it's impossible. One or both of us has to go out sometime. You can't stop in the flat forever, and if you won't come with me, what other choice do I have?' He put down the plastic bag that smelt of fried chicken and chips.

She shrugged her shoulders.

'Sorry I took so long - I needed a bit of fresh air. Being stuck in this flat all day is doing my head in.'

When he sat down, she smelt the faint aroma of sweet cider on his breath. 'Was getting some fresh air, via the pub?'

'I just had a small one.'

'I bet you did.'

'I've got plenty of chicken and chips if you want some.'

'All right, but I'm still not very hungry.'

She sat by him, and as he opened the paper, he allowed her to take a few of the greasy salt laden chips, that were normally delicious. Tonight however, to her, they tasted bland and soggy.

Blake was ravenous. He finished his tea in no time at all, and even took back a few of the chips Donna left.

She didn't want to talk, was still unnerved, so they watched television in relative silence.

'Look Donna, sorry I flew off the handle at you earlier on. I was acting like an idiot again.'

'It doesn't matter,' she said morosely.

'But it does to me. I know I need to control my temper better, after what you've been through. I should've realised you can't help how you are right now. I'm trying so hard, and when I can't make any difference, I get frustrated. I didn't mean to hurt you - you've been hurt enough already, haven't you? But this rape thing is affecting me too. This is hard to cope with, isn't it love?'

'Hard for you to cope with. Well how the hell do you think it is for me? You're just cheesed off because you can't have sex – that's what this is all about, isn't it?' she shouted at him.

'No, that's not true. It's the everyday things, like holding your hand, touching you, kissing you and so on. I find it hard to take when I've done nothing wrong. What happened to you was horrible, but I'm not the same as him – and never will be.'

'Well, most other men are. They all want to get inside my knickers. And deep down, you're the same. So what happens if this goes on for weeks or maybe even months? You'll get a little bit frustrated - won't you Blake? Because sex is always on your mind. What then? Going to rape me as well, are you? Or will you go elsewhere for your carnal pleasures.'

'Donna, you're going way over the top here. I'm not like that. No matter how long it takes, I'll never lay a finger on you without your consent – I promise. Nor would I look at another woman,' he boasted as if he really meant it.

A likely story, she thought. She pulled a sour face; convinced he hadn't the strength of character to carry this through. But she prayed he would.

They both sat there for a time, not speaking much. Donna felt restless. So, she got up saying she was going to bed and went to the spare room as before. As soon as she got into bed, Blake came up to the doorway, with that same feeling-sorry-for-himself expression on his face.

'Night then, Donna.' He stood there, obviously wanting her to change her mind.

His plight did have an effect on her. She felt for him, longed to make it up to him, even though it was impossible right now, and said, 'Listen; is there any chance of you getting a few days off in the next couple of weeks? We could go away for a break, spend a little time together. What do you think?' She was thinking out aloud.

'I'd love to, but how can I? I've already got the rest of this week off, but it's pandemonium at our place. How about in a few weeks' time when things have quietened down a bit? Or will you be back at work by then?'

'I haven't got a clue. I've never been raped before, so I've no idea how long it takes to get over these things.'

'What about the engagement meal we'd planned. Why don't we rearrange it?'

Donna felt tense again. 'For God's sake Blake, stop pressurising me. I can't get my head straight right now.'

'Sorry, you're right of course. Best leave it for now then – ok?'

'I think about what happened to me all the time. I can't get it out of my mind.'

'I wish there was something I could do to help, but I can't – can I?'

'You can stop losing your temper, Blake, and try to be patient with me for once in your life.'

'I'm sorry,' he sighed, shaking his head.

He left then, looking as despondent as before, wanting it seemed, to put all the wrongs right. She imagined he went back to their king-size bed, which she'd previously loved to share with him. The single bed was cold, and she used to like to cuddle up close to him. But no matter how much she wanted to, she could no longer do that, not after that madman had virtually destroyed everything she had.

<><><>

There was no way Donna could go back to work in her present state. Instead she and Blake spent the rest of the week in the company of counsellors, doctors and police - each an ordeal in itself. As expected, her suggestion of going away with Blake slipped by, without anything else being said or done. Donna was hurt, but thought it was pointless anyway, with their relationship almost buckling under the strain. And at present, she preferred to stay indoors. It was bad enough people staring at her when she supposedly looked beautiful. Now she looked ugly it was ten times worse.

The situation with Blake remained tense too. Although he accepted her conditions, Donna remembered how important the physical part of their relationship was to him. Sooner or later, it would get to him.

When he went back to work the next week, she visited her parents, to avoid being left on her own. It was either that or nothing. She was never comfortable in their company as it reminded her of her unhappy childhood, but she had nowhere else to go.

◇◇◇

The week after Blake returned to work, late on the Friday afternoon, the phone rang. Donna picked it up without thinking about who it might be.

'Hi Donna, Dave Wallace here. Sorry to bother you at a time like this – 'he began.

Donna's heart stopped for a split second, her face began to burn. This was just the person she didn't want to speak to.

'Hello Dave.'

'I wondered how you're feeling right now?'

'Err... I'm still not very well. I get anxious over every little thing even though I'm on tablets to calm me down. And I can't go out on my own without being frightened to death.'

'That's understandable, after what you've been through. Anyway, would you mind if I popped round to see you sometime next week? I'd like to discuss a few things; maybe draw up a plan of action to get you back to work. Of course, if you're not up to it at present, that's not a problem. We could review your situation again in two weeks' time, if you like. What do you think?'

She'd have to let him come at some stage, although the thought of seeing him sickened her. But she wanted to get it over with, and then she could forget about it.

'Well... come if you want. My face should have almost healed by then – hopefully.'

'That's wonderful, Donna. Glad to hear you're taking the first step. In my experience that's always the hardest part, but once you have, everything will seem that little bit easier. Look forward to seeing you,' he said, in a relieved tone of voice. They then arranged a time for him to come and visit.

As soon as she put the phone down she began to tremble. Was she doing the right thing, in allowing him to see her on his own? What if he started acting like that madman? What if he tried it on with her too? There'd be no escape. But he wasn't like that. Ok, so he probably fancied her, but surely he wouldn't do anything to her.

When Blake came home from work that night, she asked him what he thought she should do.

'Well, that's a good question. He'll try to get you to go back to work even if you're not ready yet. So, don't let him bully you. If you've got a doctor's note, there's nothing he can do.'

'I know. They want me back, that's obvious. If he tries to persuade me, I'll say I'm not well enough yet. After all I'm not indispensable.'

'Quite true. You'll have to go eventually, but go back too soon, and you'll end up in a worse state than you are now. It's your call, but whatever you decide, I'll back you.'

She smiled at him for that, relieved at his support.

During the rest of the week, Donna couldn't get the meeting with Dave Wallace off her mind. Normally a fair man, but with a reputation for getting things done, he was very astute and clever. If he could find a way to persuade her to go back, he would, she thought.

She didn't want him to come. If he asked her any questions, how truthful should she be? She wasn't sure.

When the day came, she woke early and was eating her breakfast before Blake got up. If only he could be there at the flat with her, but that wasn't possible. She'd be on her own, and although she might have asked her mum and dad, they never wanted her work at Bluethorn and would only cause trouble for her.

Dave was her boss; he'd only do what was in his best interests. She could face him, she said to herself during the day. This was purely an informal meeting after all. Nothing to be concerned over. Dave would be nice to her – he had to be; and everything would pass off amicably.

If her parents were easier to talk to, she'd have confided in them about Dave and lots of other things. But they never listened to her and had always tried to exploit her. She'd coped with that and having plenty of men lust after her. After all none of them had ever harmed her physically. Only her attacker had taken this to an extreme. Unfortunately that was all it had needed to turn her life upside down.

When the buzz of the bell finally came, she almost jumped ten feet in the air. Dithering like a dog, she answered the intercom.

'Hello, Dave Wallace here. I've come for our meeting. Is that ok?'

'Hi Dave, I'll let you in.' She hoped he wouldn't notice how anxious she was.

As he stood in front of the door, she saw he was just his normal self; plump, early thirties, wearing a pinstriped suit. His ginger hair swept back failing to conceal his impending baldness. Small intrusive brown eyes observed her. When he spoke, Donna could see his brilliant white false front tooth, which he'd once told her he'd had fitted after an accident playing rugby.

'Hello Donna,' he said with a static smile on his face.

'Come in Dave.'

He followed her to the living room, where they sat at opposite ends of the settee. He declined her offer of a drink – it seemed he wanted to get on with matters at hand.

'So how are you?'

'Oh, you know. As well as can be expected, I suppose.'

'I see you still have a little bruising around your eyes. That guy must have given you one hell of a beating.'

'He did.' A sudden self-consciousness came over her, and she touched around her eyes with her fingers.

'I imagine you've seen your doctor recently?'

'I have. He's told me it'll take a while for me to get well again.'

'Obviously. You're on medication?'

'Yes, I'm on anti-depressants to help calm me down. But that's only taking the edge off my anxiety.'

'You might need to be on a higher dose.'

'I'm on the highest dose already. But they take a few weeks to get in your system – so I'm told.'

'So how often are you seeing your doctor?'

'Once a week, but I expect he'll reduce that once I start to get better.' She watched him take notes of the conversation they were having and wondered exactly what he was writing down.

'So you've no idea when you're likely to be back at work? You must understand I'm not trying to push you in any way. However, it's company policy to encourage employees to come back as soon as they are able. In fact, we'll give you all the support you need. So how do you feel about that?'

'How do you think I feel?' Donna's anger rose within her ready to bubble over like an active volcano. 'You haven't got a clue, have you? I've been through hell. I suppose you know he raped me as well as beating me black and blue. You think about how horrific and terrifying that is – if you can.'

He winced with shock, then said, 'I can't and I'm sorry. And no, I wasn't aware he'd raped you. But no matter what happened,

I'm sure you have the strength of character to make a full recovery. You mustn't let this one incident destroy your life –'

'Just go Dave? I can see you're the same as all men.'

'Donna, for God's sake –'

'Leave me alone.'

'All right, I'll talk to you at a later date, when you're in a better frame of mind.' And with that a blotchy redness rose up into his face.

'Yes, I think you better had.'

Coughing uncomfortably, and getting up from his seat he said 'Please send in your doctor's notes promptly, it will make things a little easier. I'll ring you in a few weeks to see how you are. Ok?'

'Of course.'

'Take care of yourself Donna, we'd really love to see you back. It would be tragic if you couldn't return to work - but please understand there's no pressure on you whatsoever.'

'At the moment the idea of coming back and facing everyone at work fills me with dread.'

'I feel so sorry for you. But I assure you we're all thinking about you, and personally I look forward to seeing you soon. You're a very intelligent girl – in my opinion there's no limit to how far you can go with Bluethorn. Don't you forget that. I'll be in touch,' he said with a hint of a smile.

She nodded as he left the room.

As soon as he'd gone, Donna began to weep; quietly at first, then louder and louder until it became a hideous wail. There was a glass of pop on the coffee table, which she picked up and smashed against the wall in despair. She pushed the table over, then began throwing anything she could find, and pulled over all the furniture, before finally slowly sinking down onto her knees, sobbing like a baby. Lying on the carpet with her arms about her head she closed her eyes, wanting all the pain and humiliation to go away. But it wouldn't.

She came to her senses when she heard the sound of the front door opening and Blake calling her name. When he came in, his eyes fixed on her with concern.

'Donna, what's wrong?' he asked her softly.

She shook her head, turned away from him.

'What's happened now? The flat looks like a bomb's hit it? And why are you lying on the floor, for God's sake?'

'I... I just freaked out. Don't know what came over me, but I couldn't stop myself.'

'But why?'

'Because... because Dave my boss was here... And I couldn't cope. I panicked and let it slip about being raped – I thought he knew already. And now he's had it confirmed, they'll all be gossiping about it. There's no way can I go back there now.'

'He won't tell them anything, love - honestly. He'd get the sack if he did. What you told him was strictly confidential.'

'And who could prove it was him? They'll say they don't know where it came from and that I egged that monster on. When I'm better, I have to get another job,' she insisted, looking jittery once more.

Blake held out his hand to help her up, but she didn't take it.

'Come on, don't be like this. Something weird is happening to you – you need to get this checked out. Anyway we'd better start clearing up this mess.'

She moved towards the window, looked out and shuddered again. 'That's the same as me, a complete mess.' She laughed, waving her arms about, turning her mascara streaked face back to him.

'Don't say that,' Blake sighed looking sad.

'Why not, it's the truth? All because of that vile man - dirty, filthy stinking animal - putting his hands all over me. I can't stand it anymore.'

'But that was only one man. It doesn't mean every man's the same as him. There are lots of good men about, and only a few bad ones. The same goes with women, there's good and bad.'

What did he know? It wasn't the same for him.

'Yes, well even the bad women don't go around attacking and raping folks. I'm sick of men ogling me, making suggestive remarks. I've had enough, I'm a human being after all, not a piece of meat,' she ranted, as her whole miserable life came spilling out.

Blake looked calm; Donna wondered how long before he lost control.

'You're very special – you should be flattered by all the attention you get. Millions of women would give anything to be like you.'

'Oh sure they would. Well, I don't want to look like me. I want to be ordinary, the same as everyone else. And you're like all the others. You only want me for sex.' She pointed a finger at him accusingly.

'I don't love honestly. If that was true, I'm not doing very well out of it, am I? How long have we been going together now? Four years, is it? I seem to remember we waited over a year before we slept together. And we're getting engaged. Supposed to be getting married in a year or two as well – so how can you accuse me of that?'

Donna mumbled at him under her breath. It didn't matter what he said, she couldn't stop thinking as she did.

'I'm not arguing about this any longer. I'm going to get this flat back to normal, and if you had any sense, you'd help me,' he said.

Her eyes were brimming full of tears again. She walked over to the spare room, went in and slammed the door shut behind her.

She lay on her back on the top of the bed, feeling so depressed, as if she had nothing to live for in the future. All that remained was more misery and pain. Everything she'd achieved so far meant nothing. Her Mathematics degree, her Statistical Analyst job, her family, friends and most especially Blake, were meaningless to her now. She wanted none of it, but couldn't work out what could take its place – if anything.

Blake was moving about in the living room, by the sound of it, doing the vacuuming. After about half an hour, silence descended on the flat. How long before he disturbed her again, she wondered? Within minutes he knocked lightly on the door before entering.

Donna glanced at his exasperated figure.

'Well, I've done the best I can, but there are a few broken things that can't be mended. Come out now if you want.'

She looked up at him. 'Any reason why I should?'

'Yes, there's every reason. Mainly because I've spent a lot of time and effort clearing up what you've trashed. I hope you've got your frustrations out of your system or else it's going to cost us a small fortune.'

She got up, and walked soulfully into the living room, which he had so meticulously cleaned up. She stood still for a few seconds, realising all the trouble he'd gone to. Then looked into Blake's harassed eyes.

'I'm so sorry,' she blubbered.

When he walked over to her, she went surprisingly into his arms, sobbing her poor little heart out, grateful this time to have his strong arms wrapped around her. But before long in a panic she pulled herself free from him again.

'All right?' His eyes widened with shock.

'What am I going to do Blake? Please tell me.'

'I don't know. Try to get over this, I suppose – they say time is usually a good healer – don't they? You mustn't let that fruitcake get to you – he's done enough damage already – you want to let him ruin the rest of your life as well?'

'I'm not sure I can get over it.' She was shaking. 'The harder I try the worse I get.'

'Go and see your doctor again, perhaps this time he'll put you in touch with a psychiatrist, or some help group for rape victims. Pick up the phone – it's not that difficult is it?'

'He gave me tablets the last time. They're useless.'

'Come on, these pills can be really effective if you give them a chance. Don't forget, you've only been taking them for a week or two.'

'I'm not relying on pills for the rest of my life, and I don't intend discussing what happened with a group of strangers. Before long the whole world will know. Thanks but no thanks. You're a real help, Blake, a proper Dear Deirdre aren't you?' She glared at him, then strode off back to her room, leaving Blake probably wondering what she'd turned into.

She lay back on her bed, eyes closed, worrying over how she'd ever get herself well again. It was going to be a long painful process – that was for sure.

Chapter 6

AFTER FALLING ASLEEP QUICKLY THAT NIGHT, SHE FOUND HERSELF AWAKE EARLY AGAIN. In the semi-darkness, she could just make out it was four am. She sat up in bed, feeling very jittery, her stomach churned. Unable to stand it any longer, she got up, pulled on her dressing gown which hung on the wardrobe door, and made for the living room.

There she turned on the light switch, found the remote control and waited for the television to come on. She sat on the sofa with her legs underneath her bottom, breathing erratically. When the TV came to life, she kept the volume down low, so as not to wake Blake. Hoping to find something that might hold her attention, she flicked through the channels but found nothing of interest, and in her frustration switched it off.

Next, she looked through a pile of discarded old magazines and newspapers kept underneath the coffee table, and skimmed through each one, without really reading what she saw. By the time she'd done that, she found only half an hour had elapsed. How slow time went when you were enjoying yourself, she thought miserably.

Suddenly feeling very fidgety and agitated, she got up from her seat, and walked from one end of the room to the other, over and over again, arms folded, in a desperate attempt to rid herself of the awful anxiety feelings present in her stomach. After about fifteen minutes, she stopped herself, went back to the sofa, but although she lay down almost over-tired, she was too het up for sleep.

She needed to keep her mind active and off the attack. There were bits of fluff and dust on the carpet that Blake had missed and therefore needed cleaning. The vacuum cleaner was in a small cupboard just inside the front door.

The noise might wake Blake, but that couldn't be helped. If there was a job that needed doing, she'd do it, sooner rather than later.

She was about to switch on the hoover, when Blake appeared in the doorway, wearing only his boxer shorts.

'What the fuck are you doing now, Donna?' he wanted to know, yawning.

'A spot of cleaning.'

'You what? At this time of the morning – I only did it last night. Have you gone nuts or something? I hope you realise I have to get ready for work in another hour or so.'

She frowned, her hands quivering.

'You've got the whole day to do that – I need my sleep!'

'I was awake and noticed the carpet was still dirty. I thought I'd –'

'Well don't!' His eyes were ablaze with fury.

He turned round; and stormed back to their bedroom; banging the door shut, a probable futile attempt to keep out the noise should she switch on the hoover.

A sharp stab of pain went through her body. Blake's insensitivity had hit her hard. She wanted to cry, and struggled hard not to. No point in letting know he'd hurt her feelings. He should have been more understanding and make allowances for her behaviour. But no, he had to lose his temper. Did he really care for her as he'd always said? Perhaps everything he'd told her was a pack of lies? Getting engaged no longer seemed a very good idea.

Cleaning was out for now. Fear of another altercation swayed her into returning to the spare room. As soon she slipped underneath the bedclothes, everything began going round in her head. The rape replayed itself repeatedly in her thoughts like a record stuck in a groove – and those dreadful images wouldn't go away. And now Blake's attitude was adding to what had, and was, happening to her.

There was no point in lying there closing her eyes and hoping for the best because it wouldn't happen. Within a few minutes, she sat up again, switched on the bedside lamp and found out a book from the bookshelf next to the bed. One of her favourites, '*To Kill a Mockingbird*' by Harper Lee.

She started to read, and at first, it took her mind off things, but then suddenly she was jolted by the alarm going off in the next room. Blake groaned loudly as he got out of bed, forcing her to stay put.

As he went about the business of getting ready for work, she wondered if he'd come in to her to say goodbye before he left. He didn't. She was relieved, but also upset that he should be so callus.

So what could she do with her day? Maybe the housework, shopping, or perhaps bake a cake – she didn't know.

In truth, she didn't feel like doing anything. Nor did she want to stay in the flat alone either; because she was frightened. That left only a visit to her parents. Even though she had patched up her differences with them, their relationship was far from easy.

When she arrived on their doorstep later that morning, they were surprised, but also glad to see her. She hugged them both, but couldn't stop herself from weeping again, her tears finding their way onto her father's shirt. He pulled her back.

'Still not very well, Donna,' he commented. 'Come and tell us all about it.'

Arm around her, concern in his eyes, he guided her into the living room, while her mother went in the kitchen to make them a cup of tea. Donna moaned, inwardly, looking around the room at the countless photographs of her displayed on the walls; in fact, in every available space. All taken in such a way as to emphasise her supposed beauty, which had been apparent to her parents from an early age since she'd won the Pears Baby of the Year Award.

She remembered how proud they were of her, and how much they'd encouraged her to become a model and an actress when she was older. She'd been a child protégé, appearing in many television commercials for soap powder, and cereals; and they'd made a tidy bit of money out of her in the process.

When against their wishes she turned her back on acting, modelling and show business in general, they'd been bitterly disappointed. Despite their opposition she found success through sheer determination via another avenue - Mathematics.

Her parents had always known she was clever - she'd shown that at primary school when in arithmetic she'd been way ahead of everyone else. Yet they were forever reiterating the fact that she'd make more money exploiting her looks rather than her brains. However, her enthusiasm for Mathematics never waned. She attained a place at University, and exceeded all expectations by gaining a first class honours degree. By then she'd put an end to modelling once and for all.

While appreciating what she'd achieved, her mother still secretly yearned for her to be in show business, but any hope of this was shattered when Donna was offered a job as a Statistical Analyst at Bluethorn. Although the job was well paid, it was nothing to what she would have earned in a successful modelling career. It all came down what to what gave her the most satisfaction. And until now working at Bluethorn had fulfilled her completely and she'd made a success of it.

As they sat either side of her, listening intently she said, 'I don't know what to do, or where to turn.'

They looked shocked and surprised as she revealed the full extent of her attack, including the rape, which she'd been too ashamed to speak of. Each put an arm around her, hugging and kissing her when she broke down once more amid a flood of tears.

'Donna, go and see the doctor, and tell him what you're going through,' her mother said.

'I did, but he didn't seem to want to listen. He said these feelings will pass and offered me more medication. And that counsellor isn't much better. She listens, but all she suggests is group therapy. But I don't want other people knowing my business. And then there's everything else. I've started sleeping in the spare bedroom because I can't bear to be in the same bed as Blake. I've put him through hell. On top of all that there's work. I don't know what my boss thought when he came round. I probably haven't got a job there now even if I could face going.'

'Don't be silly,' her father said. 'He'll realise you're not your normal self and make allowances. And I think Blake's bearing up as well as he can. As long as he's tolerant, and I know he will be, you'll be fine.'

'I don't want to be like this, but I can't stop myself. I long to be back to normal, but that will never happen.' Sobbing, she dabbed her eyes with a tissue.

'That bastard has got a lot to answer for. I'd like to know what the police are doing. They don't seem to have many leads. The sooner they catch him, the better we'll all feel,' her father said breathing in deeply.

'Oh sure we will. But what about Donna? She might feel safer, but ultimately it won't bring back the old Donna, will it?'

'If they catch him…' Donna's voice was shaky. 'I want him to suffer, like he's made me suffer. Yet even that's too good for him. And if they send him to prison, he'll be let out in no time, while I've got to live with this for the rest of my life.'

'It doesn't have to be like that Donna,' her mother insisted. 'You'll get over this. No point in letting this low life ruin your life – you're bigger and better than that. Rise above it. Bad things happen to everyone at some time in their lives. Although we never forget them, we have to carry on, and learn from our experiences, don't you agree?'

Donna regarded her mother with a fixed stare, seemingly dismissing rape as something to recover from easily – as if she'd broken a leg or had a bout of the flu. The same as when they forced her to act in commercials when she hadn't wanted to. One time Donna had run away and hidden in the garden shed, only to be scolded and given a slap round the face when her mother found her.

'You'll get better from this Donna,' her father added staring at her, obviously trying to encourage her. 'You're a fighter, always have been ever since you were little. You need time to come to terms with what happened. They say it's the best healer there is. And they're right. When I lost my dad, your Granddad, ten years ago, I'd loved him so dearly I thought I'd never get over it. For weeks if not months, I was an emotional wreck, but little by little with each passing day, gradually I was able to cope with it.

'You know what I'd do if I were you. Get yourself back to work. Once you're with friends and colleagues with your mind occupied, the pain should start to ease.'

'You're joking dad, I can't do that now. They all know about the rape – it slipped out when Dave came to see me. He's bound to tell someone and before long, it'll be the talk of the place. Can you imagine what it'll be like, knowing they've been talking about me behind my back? They'll stare at me like an animal in a zoo and make snide remarks. I can't face that.' She screwed up her eyes as if she was in intense pain.

'Well, leave Bluethorn if you want,' her mother suggested. 'There's plenty of other things you could do – and for a lot more money too.'

Donna's hand gripped hold of the pad of her seat; she found it hard to believe what she was hearing. 'Oh yes, and we all know what that would be, don't we? I'd rather die than go back to that.'

Her mum visibly jumped at this, then narrowed her eyes at Donna.

'Never mind that now,' her father said, his face full of concern. 'It's important for you to get well again, then everything else will follow. Why don't you and Blake go away for a few days? That might take your mind off things.'

Remembering when previously she'd suggested a short holiday only to be rebuffed by Blake, she smiled, wondering if perhaps this time would be different.

'Maybe I will, dad. I'm not good company right now, and we had a bit of a row before I came out.'

'Nothing serious, I hope,' her mother asked, her face dropping slightly again.

'No, but – '

'Well, it's up to you, love,' her dad said.

However, the more she thought about a holiday together, the more convinced she became that it was a good idea. With that decision made, she relaxed a little more. By the time she left, she was in better spirits, and almost looked forward to returning to the flat. She must make an effort, or risk losing him. That on top of the rape, would finish her off.

As soon as she got back, she set about cooking him a Shepherds' Pie, easy to prepare but also one of his favourites.

He came back at his usual time and went straight into the kitchen, looking rather tired.

'Something smells nice,' he remarked.

'It's only Shepherd's Pie.'

'My favourite. Great – I'm absolutely starving.'

She smiled, her eyes sparkling with this comment.

'Go and change, it'll be ready for you when you come back.'

As they ate their tea in front of the television, Blake told her about his day at work, and his problems with a certain large customer who'd gone overdrawn. Donna didn't mind him talking shop, but felt guilty as she was giving more thought to how she might approach the subject of going on holiday.

'I was wondering... ' she began later, massaging the back of her neck. 'What you thought about going away for a few days. I don't mean anywhere exotic, just a trip to the coast or the country. We need some time together, Blake.'

He pulled a face, which quite surprised her. 'Much as I'd love to Donna, I've explained how it is at the moment. It's impossible to get any leave, especially as I've only recently had a week off.'

Donna's mouth dropped open with shock. She'd been convinced he'd jump at the chance this time, and could get the days off, if he'd wanted.

'Come on Blake, meet me halfway. This is important for both of us. What comes first, your girlfriend or your work?'

He squirmed uncomfortably in his seat. 'Surely it could wait a while. I might stand a better chance at the end of the holiday season... all right?'

She clenched her teeth angrily and looked away.

'Damn it Donna, don't get stroppy with me. Look, I need to watch what I'm doing, or it could damage my prospects for the future. There's no need for me to tell you how important that is, with us planning to wed within a couple of years. Especially if you can't go back to work yet.'

'Oh thanks a lot. Trust you to think about money, at a time like this.' In her anger she picked up a cushion and threw it at his face.

He caught it with some difficulty. 'Well, somebody's got to think about it, seeing as you'll be off work for the foreseeable future.'

'I can't help being traumatised. And besides I am still on full pay.'

'Yes, but that'll run out eventually and then what? Sick pay? That won't go far towards paying the bills, will it? You need to do something. You're on a very high salary. Somehow, get yourself together and back to work, or you can kiss goodbye to that nice expensive house we were looking at a few weeks ago.'

Her eyes seemed to bulge out of their sockets. 'Piss off, will you, Blake.'

She got off her seat and stormed off to the bathroom. Flopping down onto the toilet with her hand over her eyes, she convulsed into a fit of tears.

She didn't want to talk to him again and decided he probably didn't want to talk to her either by the looks of it. They remained apart for the rest of the night.

The next morning, although she woke early she stayed in the spare room once more. He didn't shout goodbye as he normally would before he left; but in truth she wouldn't have answered him anyway.

All this made Donna even more depressed. There didn't seem any point in getting up. It wasn't until mid-morning that she got out of bed. And then she just hung around the flat lethargically.

The time seemed to pass so slowly. With nothing to do and nowhere to go, it was driving her crazy. She couldn't face visiting her parents after yesterday, with them constantly fussing over her, and her mum forever hinting for her to return to modelling.

When Blake came home from work the flat was in a shambles, the sink was full of unwashed crockery and items of clothing were strewn over the floor and furniture. The look on Donna's face suggested she didn't care.

He sat down with a deep sigh, taking in the scene before him.

'So how are you feeling now?' he asked.

'How do you think I feel?'

'Look, I'm sorry about last night. I was out of order. I should have considered your feelings. So I spoke to HR and asked if I could have a week or even two or three days off. Luckily, Alex Cross cancelled his week's holiday, and they agreed I could take that week, in a fortnight's time, if you can wait until then.' He breathed in deeply, obviously in the hope that this met with her approval.

A slight smile came across Donna's face. Her heart flipped. All he'd done and said before, was almost forgotten.

'So where do you want to go?'

'I'm don't mind. I'd dismissed the whole idea after you said you couldn't get the time off.'

'Well, think about it again now,' he urged her.

She scratched the back of her head, her eyes looked upwards for inspiration. 'I don't know. I can't. Why don't you surprise me?'

'I might do that.' He grinned like a Cheshire cat. 'But you need to look after yourself because no matter how long the holiday is, we still have to get on with our lives afterwards – don't we?'

'I know but it's very difficult to carry on as nothing's happened.'

'Well, maybe this holiday will be the beginning of your recovery.'

Her mood lifted and even when she told him she hadn't cooked any dinner he didn't seem to mind. He even suggested they went out instead.

Donna's mood had improved by the next morning. A visit to the doctor's was imminent that day. He wanted to see how she was progressing, renew her sick note if need be.

Sitting down opposite him, on the edge of her seat, she looked down rather than at him. He had a quiet soothing voice, which did calm her a little. He asked her how she felt.

'I'm still very anxious most of the time. And I get these horrible feelings in my stomach – butterflies, and I can't seem to get rid of them. I don't sleep well and nearly always wake early, but I don't know, maybe a shade better than I was.'

'Mm, you do sound a little more positive than before. Obviously, it will be a slow process, but you'll find as time passes you will gradually improve. Are the tablets I've given you helping?'

'A bit.'

'I see. In the coming weeks they will start to kick in more. But don't be afraid to tell me they're not working as well as they should - all right? There are lots of other anti-depressants on the market; we can easily change them for another type if these don't suit you.'

'My boyfriend and I are going on holiday very soon, and then all being well, I'd like to talk to you about going back to work.' She exhaled deeply.

'Oh really – that's good. But are you sure you're well enough? Remember, what happened to you is very serious and traumatic. And it will be some weeks yet before you feel the full benefit of your medication. I strongly advise you to think very carefully about this. I'm sure your employers will be considerate even if you do need a few more weeks off. Come and see me when you return from your holiday and if you still feel ready, we'll discuss it further then.'

She wanted to try to go back to work for Blake's sake, especially after he'd managed to get time off for the holiday. All she hoped was that everything didn't go terribly wrong while they were away.

All through the next week, although she still couldn't sleep with him, her frame of mind continued to improve. He seemed to accept what she told him and said he was still pondering over where to take her on holiday. She began to look forward to something again.

As the day got nearer, she felt sick and was a little off her food again, but put this down to worrying over the holiday. However one thing kept nagging at her and the longer these symptoms continued the more anxious she became. Then two days before the holiday, she realised something had to be done.

When the doctor confirmed she was pregnant she couldn't believe it. It was by far the worst possible scenario. And how should she deal with this? Discreetly on her own, so no one would be any the wiser; or did she tell Blake and hope for the best? In truth she knew her conscience would make her confide in him. How would he react? Well, she would soon find out.

She decided to mention it as soon as he got in from work that day before she lost her nerve.

When he came into the living room she felt embarrassed, her stomach fluttered as she tried to pluck up the courage to break the news.

She could barely look at him when she spoke. 'Blake, we need to talk?'

His expression was one of surprise. A half-smile formed on his face as she finally looked sombrely at him.

He sat down beside her gazing straight into her eyes. 'What's on your mind, love?'

'Blake, there's no easy way to tell you this... sorry... but I'm pregnant.' Her face was suddenly contorted up in pain.

'You what? How can you be? We haven't done anything since... it's impossible unless you've been ... ' His hand clenched his thigh tightly as obviously he thought about the implications.

The colour drained from his face as his eyes widened with anger. He'd jumped to the wrong conclusion. How could he think she'd slept with someone else after all he'd been living with her through this nightmare? Surely, he'd see that if she couldn't sleep with him, she couldn't sleep with anybody. And the other possibility didn't bear thinking about.

'I haven't been with another man if that's what you think. How could I after being raped?' She was hurt he'd even considered such a thing.

'So how else could you be…?' he began, and then he stopped in mid-sentence, as if it suddenly dawned on him. 'They gave you a morning after pill at the hospital, didn't they?'

'They did.' She wiped the sweat from her brow with the back of her hand. 'Either I was already pregnant, or the pill didn't work.'

Shaking his head, he said, 'I don't believe this.'

'How the hell do you think I feel?'

'So what are you going to do about it?'

'I… I don't know…'

'You're not going to have it – are you? The rapist's kid.' He turned his face away in disgust.

'It's not the baby's fault. It didn't ask to be conceived. Did it? Anyway, who's to say it isn't yours. It's not as though we didn't have sex before the attack.'

'Yes, but we'll never know that until the kid's born. No, I'm not having that. Get rid of it – and the sooner the better.' He talked as if there was a monster in Donna's belly.

Everything she'd feared seemed to be happening in the matter of a few seconds. There was so much anger on his face and it appeared he'd never accept the baby, but he hadn't given himself time to come to terms with this. It was hopeless. She broke down and buried her face in her hands. Tears seeped through her fingers. She sensed this would mark the end of their relationship.

He remained where he was; made no attempt to touch her. Then pushed a tissue towards her. She took it, blew her nose, and peered at him through bleary tearful eyes; noticing the guilty expression on his face – perhaps he realised his immediate rejection of her baby was wrong.

'Come on now Donna. This isn't the end of the world, you know. Far from it. It's a little setback – that's all. Once you've come to your senses, you'll see it's the only thing to do. You'll get over it, and then slowly everything will get back to normal.'

'You really think so. This is my baby's life we're talking about here,' she said, lightly stroking her stomach.

As he frowned; she realised it would be difficult to change his mind if his initial reaction was anything to go by.

'I can't kill my own child.' She put her arms defensively round her middle.

'It's not even a baby yet, it's just a tiny fetus. If you don't, it'll be the biggest mistake of your life,' he said going red in the face.

It looked as if he wouldn't budge on this. He'd go on and on until she did what he wanted. Maybe this time she wouldn't shift either. And why the hell should she? Because what had it to do with him? It was her body, so it was up to her. She could do as she wished.

'I'll do what's best for me and my baby, Blake. You can take your bruised ego and shove it as far as I'm concerned.' She pushed him away in anger.

'Hey, my opinion ought to count for something. We're supposed to be getting married, remember.'

'So you keep telling me.' She got up from the settee.

'For God's sake Donna, stop going on, will you? At least think about it for a few days.'

'That's precisely what you haven't done. As for me, I can't stop thinking about it – first someone rapes me, and now I may be pregnant with his child; or the baby could be yours. But it's also my baby, so ultimately it's my call, despite what you or anyone else says.' She began to walk away from him.

'Donna! That's exactly why you should have an abortion. There's plenty of time for kids, later on when we're ready,' he insisted moving to follow her to the spare room, her normal refuge lately.

Turning to face him she pushed him to one side once again 'I never want to speak to you again. Leave me alone.'

After she'd slammed the door in his face, she put all her weight against it, expecting him to try to force his way in. But it wasn't necessary. Perhaps he'd given up or just didn't care.

Chapter 7

OVER THE NEXT WEEK, THEY HAD LITTLE TO SAY TO EACH OTHER. She assumed he'd cancelled the holiday because it was never mentioned again. When he was around she stayed in her room, and when he wasn't she lounged about the flat, not doing very much. Her predicament constantly played on her mind. What could she do about it? If Blake didn't want her, all she had left was to confide in her parents. But if she did that, they'd say the same as Blake, and insist she terminate the pregnancy. What she needed was an unbiased opinion and only her doctor came to mind.

So, a couple of days later, she sat nervously in front of him, rubbing her nose every so often, as he looked at his notes. There was a slight tremor in her voice as she told him what had happened.

He seemed strangely unmoved, as if this happened frequently, which surely it didn't; and sitting back in his chair, sighing quietly before speaking he said, 'Well, this is rather an unfortunate set of circumstances. I can understand why you're in a dilemma. But I can't make your mind up for you; you have to come to a decision yourself, or with your family's help. Of course, if you have the child and your boyfriend's not the father, it may cause problems between you and him. Then again he might take to the child. I'm sure you must have considered the options – abortion, adoption etc, but as I've said you should do what's best for you and your child.'

'I can't decide what to do. I did want to have the child,' she said touching her stomach gently. 'But I may have to look after it on my own.'

'Family and friends will rally around, I'm sure. Most do in a crisis. If you do need help, whatever you decide, we can provide it,' the doctor assured her in a very impartial way, which irritated Donna, as she wanted someone to tell her what to do. But he couldn't do that. This left her feeling let down and still in a quandary.

As she walked back to the flat, and for days afterwards, she went from one decision to another, constantly changing her mind. Finally, she knew what she had to do and as he'd promised, the doctor made the arrangements.

On the morning of the termination it all seemed to be done in a matter of fact way. The doctor asked if she was sure about having an abortion and she nodded tearfully. When she returned home, she rested, but she forgot the time. As soon as Blake came back from work, she jumped when he slammed the door, but hadn't the energy to avoid him, and besides maybe they wouldn't fight now.

He looked mildly surprised to see her there, and at once she felt flutters in her stomach. Before sitting down, without a word, he put his suit jacket on the arm of the settee and his briefcase on the floor beside him. Then he spoke.

'Drink?'

'Thanks,' she replied, her heart pounding with expectation.

He came back into the living room five minutes later with two mugs of tea, which he left on the coffee table in front of them.

Donna picked up her mug, took a sip, and then put it down again.

'Very nice.' She glanced at his handsome face that looked as boyish and as appealing as ever. 'You always did know how to make a great brew.'

'Practice makes perfect.' He sat back on the settee, yawning from another seemingly tiring day. 'So, how's it going?'

'All right. Getting by, I suppose. Yourself?' Her bottom lip quivered.

'The same...'he began, but stopped in mid-sentence when Donna took his hand. He looked amazed as this had hardly happened at all since the attack.

'Blake, I've got something to tell you.' She squeezed his hand.

'Funny you should say that, because I've got something to tell you as well.' He didn't return her gesture of affection.

'I promise you, you'll find my news is much more important than yours.'

'Ok, fire away then.'

'I… I had an abortion this morning like you wanted.' She smiled uneasily, hoping everything would be all right now - and long as he didn't ask to sleep with her, she'd be fine.

His large blue eyes widened with surprise. 'Well, I'm sure you did the right thing.'

'I'm devastated about it, that's for sure, but I couldn't bring that baby into the world, knowing it wouldn't get the love it deserved.' A tear of regret trickled down her cheek.

'That's true. I admire you for having the courage to do it.'

'So are you happy now? It was the most difficult thing I've ever done. It's bloody awful, I can tell you – something I never want to go through again.'

He gave an ironic snort, which puzzled Donna, then said, 'Knowing how you are these days, I'd say that's nigh on impossible anyway.'

'And what's that supposed to mean?' She turned towards him.

'Nothing.'

'You're trying to say I'm frigid, aren't you? Why, you ignorant bastard,' she snarled, her face now beaded with perspiration.

Blake looked embarrassed; he blushed, shifting his neck in the collar of his shirt uncomfortably. 'Well, yes I suppose I am, at the moment, although I'm sure it's not permanent.'

'You patronising pig,' she screamed, hitting him across the cheek with a slap so loud next door might have heard it. 'Don't you dare talk to me like that again or I will definitely never let you touch me again.'

As he stroked his cheek, which must have stung painfully, he replied, 'Perhaps I don't want to touch you again, anyway.'

Donna's jaw dropped open. How dare he say this after she'd just had an abortion specifically for him? Perhaps he was still angry at her for not letting him touch her. But what did he expect? A maniac had raped her, beat her up and left her for dead.

'And what do you mean by that?'

'What do you think I mean? You're making me out to be the villain in this. I didn't rape you – he did. I have the right to feelings and needs the same as anyone else. Have you any idea how I feel when you keep pushing me away, even if I so much as dare to try to hold your hand? And will having an abortion make any difference to that? I doubt it. You've got to stop taking your problems out on me – all right.' He nodded at her, moving his eyebrows up.

Donna was shaking furiously, trying hard not to shed any more tears for him. She realised then any feelings he had for her had vanished; if they'd ever been there in the first place. She turned away from him and went back to the spare room.

Flopping down on the bed, she was devastated over Blake's reaction to the abortion. She'd killed her own child for him – for God's sake. The pain she felt oozed out of her. She could do nothing to stem the tide and hated herself for what she'd done. No one would ever want her again because she'd been raped and was now frigid. That's what Blake thought anyway.

Sometime later she managed to pull herself together, and finally dried her tear-stained face with a wad of tissues. She sat up on the bed, looking into space.

When all of a sudden the front door banged shut, she got up, opened the bedroom door, and walked across to the living room window just in time to see him get into his car. He drove his red Ford Fiesta off at high speed. He wouldn't be back for a while, she surmised. But where would he go? Out with friends to get drunk perhaps – or maybe even out on the pull? Unless he'd already found someone else and that's what he hadn't told her. She tried not to think about it because it would send her off into even more turmoil. Overwhelmed by his reaction, she couldn't understand why he was doing this to her. Many times in the past he'd gone out of his way for her, but now he'd changed completely. All because the physical side of their relationship had gone.

But despite this, she wished he'd hurry up. She felt so alone without his presence in the flat, even if they were at loggerheads. With him there she'd feel safe, especially with her attacker still at large.

The longer he was away the more on edge she got. She panicked despite how he'd treated her. What if he didn't come back? What would she do? True, she could have her pick of men; but he'd been the only one to treat her as an equal, and not a sex object to conquer. Until now. All right, so she'd changed of late, but he had too. And if she could overcome her fears, shouldn't he at least meet her halfway?

By midnight, she convinced herself he wouldn't be coming back. If he was spending the night with another woman, she couldn't forgive that. Not ever.

Getting up from the settee, she made her way to the bathroom for a quick shower. She'd been told to take it easy for the rest of the day and although she should have been in bed hours ago, she was too wound up to sleep. But she couldn't stay up forever.

She lay quietly on the bed in the spare bedroom wanting to shut the whole world out of her life, but sleep wasn't going to come easily, with Blake still not home. Perhaps he'd got himself into trouble because of how upset he was – she even blamed herself for his behaviour.

It was deadly quiet in the flat. Lying there tossing and turning, sweat pouring out of her, she felt all alone, as if no one cared about her, except for what they could get out of her.

Only a little while later, she was jolted awake by Blake's noisy entrance at the front door. Her heart beat faster with sheer relief; but also fear. He hadn't left her after all. She heard him rummaging about, first in the living room by the sound of it, then in the kitchen. He was humming, perhaps in a much better mood than when he'd gone out. Thank God, so long as he was in a good mood for the right reasons. However, she didn't intend venturing out of her room until the morning.

Then came the sound of the bathroom door locking. Followed by water splashing, as he gargled his throat, which she found vaguely amusing. But her relief soon changed when suddenly the door to the room burst open. The light from the other rooms filtered through, causing it to be in a sort of semi-darkness, as she opened her eyes.

'Donna!' he shouted at the top of his voice. The bellowing of his rich baritone voice reverberated round the room.

She started to shake, smelling the faint odour of stale beer on him - and saw the glazed look in his eyes. He was in fact still angry and very drunk.

He spoke through gritted teeth and said, 'Donna, I want you out of that bed. And back where you belong.' He switched on the light.

She narrowed her eyes until she grew accustomed to the light. Sitting up in bed, moving back, she feared what he might do to her in his present state. 'Leave me alone Blake. You're drunk; go and sleep it off.'

'Leave you alone!' he shouted at her. 'I've left you alone for long enough. I won't tell you again - get into our bed.'

She shook her head vigorously.

He bent over towards her, making her gasp with fright as he pulled back the covers of her bed. She was wearing only a flimsy nightdress to cover her modesty. Visions of what had happened on that awful night returned to her, her whole body vibrated with terror, wondering what he intended next.

He breathed heavily, almost hoarse in his rasping. 'Have you got the faintest idea what you do to me? You, the most beautiful creature I've ever set my eyes on. Never in my wildest dreams did I think I'd get it together with you. But now just when I thought you were mine you tell me I'm not to touch you anymore. That's fucking evil, wicked, that's what it is.'

She said nothing. Shivered not from the cold, but through dread. He'd never been like this with her before.

He reached out, his hand clenching the top of her nightdress, and pulled at, then ripped it from her body, leaving her wearing only a pair of skimpy knickers. Gasping in shock, she covered herself with her arms.

'I want you so badly,' he growled, his eyes widening, giving him a manic expression that frightened her. 'More than anything in the world. You're tormenting me, you wicked bitch.'

'No, no, no, please.' She moved further up the bed, but knew there was no escape. 'Blake; I've just had an abortion, for God's sake. I can't –'

'You can and you will, you cow. I don't believe that man raped you – it's an excuse to ditch me for somcone else. Well, I will take what is rightfully mine.' He looked at her as if she was dirt.

'You're no better than the man who raped me – no, you're worse. I loved you, and I thought you loved me!' she shouted, her arms tightening around her body.

She whimpered, then began to cry - it was as if the whole male population were out to destroy her because she wouldn't give herself to them.

Blake stopped suddenly. Froze in mid-flight, looked at her strangely, then his head dropped forward, and he collapsed in front of her in a heap on the bed.

She screamed and screamed until her throat was hoarse from it, hurriedly pushing him off. With the tension released, she was too petrified to do anything else. Saliva dribbled from her mouth onto her arms. She wondered if anyone had heard her.

Even though he lay there in a drunken stupor, dead to the world, she still hated being in the same room as him. If he woke up, there was no telling what he might do. She moved off the bed, pulled on her dressing gown, and with difficulty, grabbing hold of his arms, struggled to pull him out of her room and back into his own. There she left him on the floor, closing the door behind him.

She realised then, that there was no alternative but to leave as soon as possible. She got dressed; gathered all her clothing and belongings from around the flat to pack into a large suitcase, which she pulled down from the top of her wardrobe. Back in the confines of her room, she pushed a chest of draws against the door, placing the luggage on top, hoping if he woke in the night, it would stop him from getting in.

It was out of the question to leave the flat this early in the morning – no taxis or buses would be running. So she lay on her bed with the light on staring at the door, praying he wouldn't try to force his way in.

If only there was someone she could phone, but who would believe Blake had almost tried to rape her? The police would treat it as a domestic issue and wouldn't want to get involved. As for her parents, unless he did something unspeakable, she didn't want them to know.

This was all too much to cope with. Blake had forced her to relive her nightmare all over again – and now she was certain she'd never trust him or any other man again.

She must have been lying there on the bed for hours it seemed, when she suddenly realised the new day was coming; beams of light filtered through her curtains. Then came the noise of activity from the other bedroom, of someone retching over and over again. Her heart leapt, fear returned. Blake getting rid of whatever he'd drunk the previous night. It made her feel sick and disgusted at his uncouth antics. To her now all men were pigs.

As the minutes ticked by, she listened intently to what was going on in their bedroom. It sounded as if he was trying to clean up something from the carpet. He must have made a right mess. But that was the least of her worries.

The chest of draws remained in front of the door and she moved the bed next to it to make doubly sure he couldn't get in. She was determined to keep them there until he'd gone.

Fortunately, luck was on her side. He didn't attempt to enter her room. Instead, he continued to rummage about for a long time, so much so she thought he'd end up being late for work.

After much stomping about, the front door of the flat slammed shut, as did the outside door to the building. From this, she deduced he'd actually gone. After a few minutes, she decided to try to move the chest of draws and bed away from the door. It was difficult to move them easily, but eventually she got the door open with just enough room to allow her to get by. She squeezed past, making her way into the living room, where looking through the window, she was just in time to see his car travelling down the road.

A strong smell of disinfectant and stale sick lingered in the air. It turned her stomach. She sighed to herself, thinking about the life she might have had to face with him. It seemed she'd had a lucky escape, but the alternative, the prospect of an uncertain future, filled her with despair.

Last night's deplorable behaviour had made her realise he wasn't the man she thought he was, and marrying him was out of the question. If she did she'd face a life of hell. Perhaps he had been drunk, and wouldn't remember what he'd done. But that wasn't the point. The point was, even in a drunken state, he had the intent. What if it happened again? No, now she'd ever feel safe with him again.

Sadly for her, she had no one to turn to. No friends who might take her in. The only option left was her mum and dad. Her last and only resort. From as far back as she could remember she'd never been happy living with them. True, they'd never physically beat her, but they'd made her life a misery in lots of other ways. How well she remembered them shouting and screaming at her whenever she refused to go on a film set, or to strut about on the catwalk. Things she could forgive but never forget - but right now she was in a tight spot and had no other choice.

When she was ready, she phoned for a taxi. The taxi driver beeped his horn as soon as he got there. She struggled out of the flat with her luggage onto the pavement, glad when he got out to help her.

As the taxi moved off, she didn't even look back at what had been her first home of her own. All the memories remained, and although they made her feel sick, it was impossible to forget the happy times they'd shared. But the events of the past few weeks overshadowed this, and now there was no going back.

The taxi driver made for the address he'd been given, to the suburb of Dexford, where her parents lived. It would be difficult to live with them but there was no alternative. It wouldn't be forever, only until she could get back on her feet again. But how long that would   take,   she   didn't   know.

Chapter 8

SHE SHOULD HAVE PHONED TO LET THEM KNOW WHAT HAD HAPPENED, BUT SHE'D FELT TOO ASHAMED AND HURT. It was probably best to tell them about it when she got there. She knew they'd welcome her back with open arms, but how difficult would it be for her to get away once they had her in their clutches. Unless she could get herself back to work they would try to manipulate her once again. The only consolation was that she was safer there than at the flat with Blake.

As the taxi pulled up outside her parent's house, Donna saw her father's stocky figure in the garden, on his knees weeding the borders surrounding the lawn. His stomach flopped over his grey trousers; and as he looked up, he smiled and waved, seeing her get out of the taxi. The driver took out her large suitcase and various other bags and put them down on the pavement. She gave him a twenty pound note and told him to keep the change. He drove off, leaving her surrounded by luggage.

Her father got up suddenly and walked briskly towards her, obviously realising something was amiss. When Donna attempted to pick up the suitcases, he waved her aside, and lifted the largest up himself.

'What's going on love?' he asked her, his eyes full of concern.

She shook her head, not intending to say anything yet. Picked up her other bags and followed him towards the front door. The door opened even before they got there.

Donna's mother stood just inside the doorway, no doubt sensing trouble.

'What on earth's the matter?' she asked, although she must have had a good idea by the amount of luggage her daughter had.

Eyes full of tears, she strode past her mother into the house, without saying a word. And after putting the bags down in the hall, she went into the living room, to sit down on the armchair close to the fire. She looked down at the carpet, aware both her parents were staring at her. But they didn't speak.

'I'll get us a drink, shall I?' Her mother said finally.

Donna burst into tears, forcing her father to rush over to her to take her hand and squeeze it gently. He stared at her with angst, then handed her a tissue from the box on the coffee table. She blew her nose and wiped her eyes. 'Thanks dad.'

Her mother came back with two cups of tea, handing one to Donna. She took a sip, tasting whisky, a ploy she suspected to calm her down a little, and then put her cup down by the fire grate.

'Want to talk about it now, love?' her father asked in a quiet soothing voice.

Donna glanced at both of them, biting her bottom lip, moving about uncomfortably in her seat. It was no good; no point in holding it back any longer.

'I've left him.' The pain of it had already taken its toll by virtue of her red blood-shot eyes.

'But why? I thought you were happy with him. You'd even set a date for the wedding, hadn't you?' Donna's mother said in exasperation.

'You'd better tell us what this is all about, Donna. If he's hurt you - he'll wish he hadn't – especially after what you've been through recently.' Her father balled up and squeezed his fist.

So leaving out the worst bits, like Blake almost trying to rape her, she told them exactly what had happened. Including the abortion, which she'd planned to keep from them, but what did it matter now?

'This is unbelievable.' Her mum said, shaking her head. 'I never dreamed Blake was like that.'

'Everybody has fights Donna. You've both been through a lot – isn't there any way you can patch things up?'

'It's gone too far for that dad. He hasn't been the same since I came out of the hospital, and gradually he's got worse.'

'Well all I can say is, it's despicable. Looks like you're best rid of him,' her mum said.

'Maybe I am, but that doesn't make me feel any better. Sorry, but I had nowhere else to go.' Frantically she rubbed her eyes.

'You can stay here as long as you like – that goes without saying. There'll always be a home for you here. Won't there Joe?'

'Of course. It'll be so nice to have you around us again,' he agreed.

'Thanks mum, dad – I just wish it hadn't come to this.'

'Never mind that, you're back home alive and well, and that's all that matters,' her mother said.

'I'll only stay until I find a place of my own.'

'There's no need for that – stay for as long as you like. So let's hear no more about it - all right?' her father said.

Donna nodded, bravely trying to smile but the smile never reached her eyes. 'Can I have my own old room back?'

'Course you can - with pleasure,' he beamed with a grin.

Later she took the lighter bags upstairs, her father struggled behind with the large suitcase, which he left on the floor just inside the bedroom.

'Thanks dad.' She went easily into his arms, hugged by the man who'd always been the one steadying influence in her life.

'It's great to have you home. I'm so sorry this had to happen, I know how much you thought of him.'

'Mind if I unpack my stuff now. I'll be down later – all right?'

'Sure, take your time, love. You know where we are if you need us,' he winked at her, like he used to when she was a kid.

A strange sense of relief came over her when he'd gone. Sitting on the bed, she looked around, seeing it much the same as ever, littered with pictures of her, first as a child actress, the sweet as sugar little girl in television commercials. Then later as a model for some of the country's biggest catalogues, and finally a beauty queen, narrowly failing to become Miss England twice, and Miss United Kingdom once. Many said she looked stunning in whatever pose she was photographed, although she insisted she was far from perfect.

As she stared at each of these photos in turn, considering what she had just been through, it made her physically sick – perhaps this was rubbing salt into her wounds.

But the picture that made her most proud was the one on the dressing table, of her graduation, a truly happy moment, her only real achievement so far. It had given her the confidence to believe there was nothing she couldn't attain if she put her mind to it.

It took a while to put everything back in the wardrobe and as she did this she reflected on her terrible ordeal and her future at

Bluethorn – it was proving so incredibly difficult to come to terms with. Her job as a Financial Analyst had initially filled her with excitement, as had her relationship with Blake, but now both had all but slipped from her grasp. And if she didn't have them – what did she have?

Once she'd finished unpacking, she sat on the bed suddenly depressed again – and right back where she started.

The reality of coming back home hit her. She couldn't help fearing her parents would try to control her life and push her into changing her career. And remembered only too well the incessant pressure they'd placed her under to be model and an actress. How she'd found the courage to stand up to her mother and embark on a degree course in Mathematics she would never know. Although her mum seemed pleased when Donna graduated, Donna was certain she still longed for her to do something else.

There had been trouble too when she moved out to buy a flat with Blake. A big mistake, they said. She was too young. He was wrong for her and so on. Well, they'd been proved right. The 'I told you so' scenario was like a kick in the teeth. She felt vulnerable and was again forced to be much too dependent on them. Another nightmare for her, almost as bad as having to face work again, with all of them knowing she'd been raped.

Finally, with a big sigh, she realised the time had come to speak to her parents, or else they'd wonder what was going on. Reluctantly she got up and traipsed downstairs.

Walking into the living room, she saw them sitting down together, an old photograph album open on her mother's lap; full of pictures of her from when she was a little girl and first thrust into the limelight.

Donna sat opposite them in her dad's armchair wondering what her mum was up to now.

As her father sat puffing pungent smoke from his pipe, he wore a contented smile. He smoked because it helped him relax, he said. But the smell always made her want to puke. She realised nothing had changed, her mum as ever the driving force, trying to control situations in her daughter's life.

'Ah Donna. We couldn't think where you'd got to – I guess you wanted a little time to yourself?'

'Something like that mother.' She folded her arms nervously across her chest.

'Why don't you sit between us? I was just leafing through these beautiful pictures of you when you were younger. Come and look, see if you remember, eh?'

Donna cringed, although she tried hard not to let them see. This was all she needed, but there was no way out.

It took a few seconds before Donna forced herself to sit between them. Everything was so familiar, the smell of tobacco mingled with her mother's over-powering lily of the valley perfume, almost making her retch.

As she watched and listened, her mother looked through the albums, admiring every snap of her daughter as she went on. Donna had only been back a couple hours, and already reminders of the past were being put in front of her; in fact, it seemed the number of photographs and amount of memorabilia around the house had increased tenfold. At the moment she realized there was no escape from her mother's obsession; the only way was to listen and let it go over her head. Then make up her own mind without involving them.

'If I were you Donna, I'd get onto the Estate Agents about selling the flat. Then when it's sold, be sure you get your share so you can start afresh. The sooner the better, don't you think... eh Joe?'

'Yes. Get what you're entitled to.' He took the pipe out of his mouth, to relight it as it had gone out. 'And how about getting back to work?'

She felt the colour drain from her face. 'Maybe, I'm not sure. My note expires in two weeks. I need to talk it over with my doctor.'

'Well, if I were in your shoes I'd do something before then. Or you'll get too much of a liking for staying at home. And the longer you're away, the harder it'll be to go back.'

'Yes, dad but –'

'Joe,' her mother interrupted, with eyes staring at him with disapproval. 'Leave the poor girl alone. Can't you see how upset she is? Over that terrifying ordeal. And everything that's followed. You don't get over something like that in a few weeks – it can take months if not longer.'

Her father moved his black bushy eyebrows up in exasperation. 'I'm not stupid. I'm trying to help the kid - that's all. We don't want her wasting away here all day – do we?'

'She won't be wasting away here, as you put it, darling. You don't know what you're talking about as usual. What she needs is to relax and rest - convalesce, I think is the right term.' She nodded her head to emphasise her point.

'All right, I realise she's in need of a lot of counselling and support, but it'll do her good to get back to normality again. All she'll do here is sit and ponder over it – and make herself worse.'

'Don't you understand anything about what she's been through?' her mother retorted angrily.

'Stop it! Stop it! Both of you. I want some peace and quiet. I don't need you two bickering over me, so just let it drop, will you?' She glared at each of them in turn. I'll handle this in my own way, she thought, no matter what they say.

'Of course, it's up to you my dear,' her mother said.

'I wasn't pressurising you either, Donna. I was trying to help – honestly.'

'I know you were dad. I'm sorry; it's just that everything's getting me down right now.' She nervously bit her thumbnail, emphasising her current state of mind.

'We understand,' her mother said. 'Don't take any notice of us – I just wish there was something we could do, that's all – I really do.'

Donna began to breathe erratically again; felt like crying but somehow stopped herself. And wished to God, they'd leave her alone.

'I'm going out for a walk, I need some fresh air. You don't mind, do you?'

'Of course not. And if you want our company, you only have to say.'

'No, it's all right mum, I'll be fine. I want to be on my own for a bit.'

'Ok Donna. You be careful, and don't stay out too long eh.' There was deep concern on her father's weathered face.

'I won't.'

She got up from her seat, found out a warm sheepskin coat and black scarf, which she'd just unpacked, and having shouted goodbye to her parents, she ventured outside.

The weather was chilly and a cold wind blew her golden hair everywhere. As the wintery sun was just going down, she shivered, hurrying towards the busy road. Then turned right heading for the small shopping precinct which consisted of four shops, a cafe and a pub, where normally plenty of people would be about. Unfortunately, at this time of day the shops would soon be closing, so she carried on walking a little further, out of her comfort zone. She made her way towards a grassed area leading to Dexford Country Park, and found the cold icy wind made her shiver despite her warm coat.

There was a car park close by, and a picnic area with wooden benches and tables. Surprisingly lots of people were about, some walking their dogs, others just trudged around the park together, most took no notice of her. She sat quietly on a bench by herself, looking out at the scenery, pondering over going back to work. An ordeal she didn't think she could face.

Suddenly hearing the sound of a twig breaking close by, her heart leapt. She gripped the bottom of the bench, looked round, and in the distance thought she saw a dark figure moving about, before disappearing off into the trees. People round her seemed oblivious of this and provided little comfort.

For a few seconds Donna couldn't think straight, panic engulfed her. Her eyes darted all over the place trying to see where the man had gone. She was overwhelmed by a terrible fear, and imagined this figure was her attacker stalking her, waiting to strike again. Cold sweat poured out of her, and she had difficulty breathing. She wanted to scream but couldn't. And felt the need to get out of there quickly before anything happened. Moving off the bench, she made a run for it, not noticing or even caring what anyone thought. Out of the picnic area, and past the shopping precinct, she didn't slow until she reached the outskirts of the estate where her parents lived.

When she got to her destination, she paused and leaned against a lamppost, to get her breath back, constantly looking behind her in case the madman had followed and found out where she now lived. Some minutes later when she was fairly sure he wasn't loitering out there, she began to breathe normally again. No point in telling her parents what was going through her mind though.

She walked up the drive, but went round to the back of the house, by way of the kitchen. Through the window she saw her mother standing in front of the sink. When Donna came in, she glanced across, no doubt curious of her daughter's whereabouts.

'Feel any better now?'

'Not really.'

Her mother put the palm of her hand to Donna's cheek. 'Cold isn't it? Hope you haven't caught a chill out there.'

'Don't worry, this coat is lovely and warm.'

'You ought to try to pull yourself together now. I know you've had a horrid time these past few weeks, but now you must make the effort to get yourself well again. Don't forget, you've got so much going for you. You're young, still the most beautiful girl I've ever seen, and I'm not just saying that because you're my daughter. You could have any boy you wanted, achieve almost anything if you put your mind to it. There's no reason to throw it all away on account of one horrible man.' Her mother looked at her admiringly, with the glint of a tear in her eye. 'You've been blessed with a gift from God, love. Use that advantage to help you. Blake may have broken your heart, but there'll be a hundred more waiting in the wings to take his place – believe me.'

'Mum, don't keep harping on about stuff. I've heard that so many times, and I'm sick to death of hearing it.' She took off her coat, hurriedly throwing it over a chair.

'But if you do go back to work, your male colleagues especially, and some of the women too, will flock round you, wanting to help all they can. It'll be a piece of cake.' She smiled, ignoring her daughter's last remark.

'I don't think so. Because I'm not sure I can. I don't want them whispering about me behind my back, and laughing at me. I'll feel like walking out.'

Donna's mother lifted her chin up. 'You mustn't let yourself think like that. It'll only tarnish your life even further if you allow it to. You're just the same person inside as you were before.'

She moved away from her mum, certain she wasn't the same person. And never would be again. 'Mum, I don't need a lecture. I'll cope, all right. I'm going to my room now.'

'Of course, darling. I'll come up later to see how you are.'

'Mum - I'm a big girl now.' Donna spoke slightly sarcastically, which her mother didn't seem to notice.

She was so tired after everything that had gone on. It felt comfortable in the room where she'd lived for all but one of her twenty-two years. She lay back on her single bed, knowing she'd still miss not having Blake around. Best not think about what had happened at the end to spoil their beautiful relationship - better to remember the good times.

She was devastated that it had gone wrong, as at one stage she'd been certain she'd spend the rest of her life with him. Would she eventually find happiness elsewhere? She didn't know nor care at present. But in the meantime, what would she do on her own?

Of course, at home she was safe, and she did have some feelings for her parents, despite what they'd done to her. Yet after only one day with them, they were already driving her mad. They irritated her, with their constant mollycoddling; and their incessant references about her looks, and how this would allow her to do whatever she wanted. Donna hated this. Didn't they realise what mattered was the person you really were inside? After all looks didn't last forever.

To Donna, staying with her parents indefinitely was not an option. Sooner or later she had to stand on her own two feet, because the way her mother's mind was working, the pressure to return to a modelling career would soon be relentless, and be difficult to deal with. If she couldn't go back to her present job, she was adamant eventually her future would only lie in a career in Mathematics in some other shape or form.

Dropping off to sleep that night, she dreamt of her attacker and what he'd done to her; and woke up wringing wet with sweat, thoughts of him raping her, still clear in her mind. In her dream she remembered crying out for help but as before no one came.

Suddenly she sat up in bed, her nightdress sticking to her, soaked with perspiration. Was there nothing she could do to rid herself of these demons? It frightened her even to go to sleep. She faced an unbearable life, it seemed, whether awake or asleep.

<><><>

The following week she made an appointment to see her doctor again, in the hope he could give her a bit of advice. And decided not to tell her parents as she didn't want them to worry or be too involved in her life.

In the end, it was rather a pointless exercise. Although sympathetic, he didn't offer anything new. He suggested, once again, seeing another counsellor to help her cope with her return to work. He was about as good as her mum and dad and left her feeling on her own in this.

When she agreed to go back to work in a week's time, she was given a prescription and a note for her employers saying she was fit for work but with restrictions. He also gave her a week's supply of tablets to help her anxiety while she was at work. If they were anything like her other tablets, she didn't think they'd help, but she didn't tell the doctor this.

She returned home half an hour later and was met by her mother in the hall. 'Donna, David Wallace phoned. He wanted to know how you are. I said you'd phone him back.'

'Oh no, I don't want to speak to him.'

'Well, that's up to you. I'm only passing on the message.'

'I know.'

'So are you going to return his call or what?'

'Suppose I'll have to.' She wondered how he knew she'd moved back in with her parents. It had to be Blake.

With shaking hands, she picked up the phone and dialed David's number. Nervously and with hurried words she spoke with him, mentioning her visit to the doctor, and her proposed return to work the following week. To his credit, despite what had happened during their previous meeting, he seemed genuinely thrilled and surprised. He told her he'd prepared a revised rehabilitation programme allowing her to work a few hours at a time, which was along the lines the doctor had suggested, and assured her she wouldn't be pushed her into doing anything until she was ready. But she still felt uneasy about facing everyone.

Putting the phone down, she breathed out slowly, glad that was over. Soon she had to return to work, and there she'd face an even bigger ordeal.

The tablets she took did little except to take the edge off her anxiety, and as the day approached, the butterflies in her stomach increased steadily. She found it difficult to sleep and became agitated, which added to the tense atmosphere at home. Her father was more sympathetic to Donna's problems but said little when her mother continually alluded to the idea of Donna returning to modelling. Donna felt like screaming, but instead she sulked and smoldered with anger.

That first week she was due to work from ten until one o'clock on Tuesday and Thursday. Surely, she could manage that.

The night before was particularly bad, feelings of nausea increased, and that in turn led to panic attacks, highlighting how difficult this would be. She was tossing and turning for what seemed like an eternity, and eventually decided to get up.

Having visited the bathroom, and taken a tablet to help her get through the day, she went downstairs to find her father sitting at the breakfast table, a bowl of cereals in front of him. He looked surprised to see her.

'You're up early aren't you love?'

'I couldn't sleep, dad.' She rubbed her eyes and yawned.

'Well, that's understandable. You'll be all right once you get there. Just get through today, and you'll be over the worst,' he told her, touching her hand across the table.

She sniffed back tears that threatened to come, moving her head back. 'I'm not sure I can do this, dad.'

He looked concerned. 'Darling, you'll be fine. At least try or you'll never know, will you?'

Donna shook her head. He went over to her, put his hand on her shoulder.

'Look, listen to me. You have to rise above what happened to you. If you give in to it now, it'll be twice as hard the next time.' He was obviously trying to encourage her, and added, 'So promise me you'll give it your best shot.'

She nodded reluctantly.

As previously arranged, when the time came, her father got up to give her a lift. 'Ready then?'

'Suppose so.' Her stomach turned over once again.

She looked across at her mother sitting there quietly, smiling sadly at her. 'Take care now, Donna, and if you don't feel well come home. Remember there are plenty of other jobs out there if this one doesn't work out.'

'Oh sure, thanks a bundle, mum, that's exactly what I don't want.' What sort of incentive was that? Perhaps all the incentive she needed.

She was dressed in a new grey pin-striped suit, and a cream blouse. Her face, made up delicately, was framed by her shoulder length blond hair. According to her parents, she looked breath taking, although she felt anything but.

She said goodbye to her mother on the doorstep before getting into her father's blue Ford Mondeo. As they drove off, she turned to see her mum waving.

The journey into work was quiet, save for her father's small talk, obviously trying to keep her mind off what was to come. But she didn't listen to half he said because so much was going around in her head. Then before she knew it, they were outside the Bluethorn building.

'Thanks for the lift, dad.'

'Good luck and don't worry. You'll be ok,' he said to her reassuringly.

There were tears in her eyes as she turned away from the car, and hoped he didn't notice this.

'Pick you up at one o'clock,' he shouted before he drove off.

The sun was shining as she walked into the building where she'd worked for the past eighteen months. She'd been happy here too until the attack. Now as petrified as on her first day, she entered the lift and pressed the button for the sixth floor. She was in the lift on her own, waiting anxiously for it to reach its destination.

As soon as the lift opened, she saw Vanessa the receptionist, who'd known Donna since she'd started with the company.

'Hallo Donna!' she exclaimed all smiles. 'How brilliant to see you back.'

Donna felt colour coming to her cheeks. 'Would you phone David Wallace, tell him I'm here?'

'Of course. Won't keep you a moment.'

Vanessa picked up the phone and dialled through to David. Donna meanwhile, stood awkwardly in front of Vanessa's desk, legs turning to jelly. The extra tablet she'd taken that morning didn't appear to be working, so she took deep breaths in an effort to calm herself down.

'He'll be out in a minute,' Vanessa said staring at her, probably noticing how nervous and afraid she looked. 'So how have you been keeping? Been off for a while, haven't you? The place hasn't been the same without you.'

'Really,' Donna said with an embarrassing smile. How she wished Vanessa would stop rambling on; it made her feel even more nervous.

At last, David Wallace came bounding towards her, what remained of his ginger hair flapping all over the place, his face alive with pleasure at seeing her.

'Donna, you made it.' He shook hands with her. 'So glad you're back. We can't afford to be without people of your calibre, you know.'

'Thanks David, that means a lot to me.' Trying hard not to feel emotional as they went through to the cloakroom, she hung up her coat.

The office area was open plan; there were around a dozen people, most of whom she knew, busy tapping away at their computers as David walked her through.

'As you can see Donna, nothing much has changed. Everything is more or less as it was, except for one or two personnel. Business is brisk I might add as you would expect. Come on, we thought you'd like your old desk back.'

'Thanks David, that's very thoughtful of you.' And they made their way around to it.

As she walked across the office, she saw a couple of her old colleagues looking up to greet her. Her heartbeat increased, and she began to feel giddy on seeing the banner on the far wall 'WELCOME BACK DONNA'. This little gesture made her the centre of attention when she wanted as little fuss as possible.

She wanted to crawl in a hole somewhere and hide, but that was impossible. A lot of her work mates shouted hallo and said how nice it was to see her back. Donna acknowledged them as best as she could. Already she was feeling very much on show. David gestured for her to go through to his office, just behind where she normally worked. He closed the door and she sat opposite him.

As he observed her, she began to shake.

'Right Donna, first of all there are a few formalities we need to go through. If you've got your return to work form, we can then confirm your rehabilitation programme. Once that's done, we'll get onto the work you'll be doing…'

Donna found it difficult to take everything in. She barely looked at David as he spoke and only realised she had to sign something when he pushed it in front of her.

'Right, if you're ready, I'll take you across to Claire, who's been doing your job since you've been away.' He stood up, lifted up his arm to guide her out of his office to where Claire was sitting.

'Claire, this is Donna,' he said politely.

'Ah, new recruit eh,' Claire joked.

Donna tried to smile. 'Not exactly.'

'Claire, if you could just familiarise Donna with what you do. Obviously she already knows most of it, but there may be one or two things that have changed since she's been away.'

'Of course. Great to see you, Donna. Why don't you pull up a chair?' Claire said shaking her thick auburn hair back. She appeared to be wearing contact lenses, which made her eyes squint now and again.

Donna found a seat and watched as Claire guided her through what she was familiar with already. Claire was friendly enough and didn't pry, only asking her if she was better. They talked a little about what had gone on since Donna had been away.

As the morning passed, Donna began to realise how difficult it would be to get back into the job that at one time she'd done almost without thinking. She found it so hard to concentrate, constantly imagining they were all staring her. With a feeling of awkwardness, she stumbled on her words when spoken to, and sensed they didn't know how to approach her either.

It seemed to be a constant battle to remain at her desk, and on two occasions she had to go to the toilet to be sick. The morning dragged. Then at eleven-thirty Claire told her the daily team meeting was scheduled for fifteen minutes time. Donna didn't think she could face this and suddenly felt faint.

David Wallace took the meeting as usual. He began by mentioning Donna straightaway. 'As you're all aware, today we welcome Donna back to the team after a lengthy absence. I'm sure I speak for everyone when I say it's lovely to see you back, Donna. You've been sorely missed, and I know we'll all give you the support you need to get into the swing of things again.'

They clapped for her, and she felt all their eyes on her, but she just couldn't find any words to say to them, and instead peered down at the floor humiliated. Her face was burning and how she stopped herself from leaving the room she didn't know.

Finally, when the meeting dispersed, still feeling nauseated, she couldn't stand it any longer. Time to get out of this awful place, and without saying anything, she went to her desk next to Claire's, picked up her handbag and dashed out. The cloakroom and toilets were in the same direction, so anyone noticing her wouldn't suspect a thing. Putting on her coat, and scanning her pass at the door, she walked towards the lift. Vanessa looked up, and must have seen her distressed face but didn't say a word. Once she was in the lift, Donna wasn't sure how she felt, the initial relief was soon replaced by a sense of failure. But she couldn't stop herself. Obviously, she wasn't in any fit state for work yet.

Chapter 9

AS SOON AS SHE WAS OUT OF THE STUFFY BLUETHORN
BUILDING, DONNA CLOSED HER EYES AND BREATHED
IN THE FRESH AIR. Turning around and looking up at her place
of work, she couldn't stop herself from sobbing over what she'd
just done. She ought to go back in there before it was too late, but
couldn't pluck up the courage.

Walking away, she eventually ended up at Dexford's Shopping
Centre, heading towards a bus stop to wait for a bus, to take her
back to her parent's house.

It didn't take long for one to arrive. She fumbled in her purse
for the right change, before making her way up the stairs to an
empty seat away from the other passengers, in case she felt
emotional again. Fifteen minutes later she got off at a stop only a
few yards from the house. It was twelve-thirty, half an hour before
her father was due to pick her up from Bluethorn.

He'd just finished washing his car, and was wiping the sweat
from his brow with the back of his hand, when he glanced up and
saw Donna's troubled face.

'What's this?' he asked her. 'I thought you weren't coming out
until one o'clock. You should have phoned - I'd have picked you
up.'

'It doesn't matter dad. I'm perfectly capable of getting myself
home.' She walked past without looking at him.

'Hang on a minute, love. You sure you're all right?'

'Couldn't be better.'

'Come on Donna, what's happened now?' He went over to her and grabbed her arm.

'What do you care? Let go of me, will you?' She wrenched it free.

She was aware of him following her into the house. How she wished he'd leave her alone – wasn't it enough that she'd had to walk out of work, without having him pester her as well?

Donna went straight upstairs to her room, without going in to the living room to see her mother, and closed the door behind her. As soon as she sat down on the bed she broke down, sobbing gently, head in hands.

Before long, there was a knock on the door. She sighed wondering what now.

'Donna – why are you upset? Please can we come in?' It was her mum this time, putting on her concerned-for-Donna voice.

'Please go away. I want to be on my own,' she answered, amid her tears.

'Please let us help. Tell us what all this is about. You're worrying us to death again,' her father added in a troubled voice.

'I can't.'

'Darling, we're staying out here until you say we can come in – you hear me? Even if it takes all night,' he told her stubbornly.

She closed her eyes momentarily, wishing they'd leave her in peace, before getting off the bed to open the door to them. Then lying down again, she put her hands underneath the back of her head, and stared up at the ceiling. They both sat down on the edge of the bed and remained silent. It appeared they wanted her to make the first move.

'I had to come home,' she said after a few minutes.

'Whatever for? You told us you felt better and wanted to go back,' her mum said.

'I thought I was ready, but I was wrong. It was horrible,' she explained, moving up to sit up against the headboard, before telling them about the 'Welcome Back' banner and everything else that had happened. Everyone had been nice to her she told them, but she couldn't handle being the centre of attention, and kept getting the impression they were all talking about her. This she couldn't take.

'Why don't I phone David Wallace, and explain why you had to leave. He might let you come back again at a later date, when you feel better,' her mother suggested.

Donna looked up at her, knowing full well what she was up to. The option to go back wasn't there any longer and didn't her mum know it. Donna bunched her hands until the whites of her knuckles were showing, wanting so much to scream. Instead, she just shook her head vigorously.

'I'm not going back there, mum, I can't cope with it, not with them knowing about what happened to me. I prayed I could, and I tried really hard, but I can't.'

They went to her, putting their arms around her, holding her tightly hoping to comfort her. But she didn't want sympathy, she wanted to feel better, be normal again, but didn't know how.

'So, what are you going to do now? Maybe you ought to see that doctor again,' her father suggested.

'He can't do anything but pump me with pills that won't do any good. I haven't a clue what the answer is. But I'm leaving Bluethorn. I'd rather die than go back there.'

'All right, if that's what you think is best. Obviously, we have our opinions, and you can listen to our advice if you want, but at the end of the day it's up to you. It's your life after all,' her mother said.

'But I won't have a job. And I don't have Blake either. In fact thanks to that monster, I've lost everything.' She stroked her thick hair with the back of her hand.

'You'll always have us, love. And when you're well again, you'll get another job easily. You're bound to with your qualifications,' her dad added, patting her hand.

'Come on now Joe, let's go downstairs, we're crowding her space. Let Donna think this through herself. We're here if you need us, darling. Anything we can do, you only have to ask.'

Donna didn't react to this. She didn't care what they did. Her future was uncertain - but what did that matter? Nothing seemed to matter anymore.

'Mum, dad,' she whispered. 'I'm so sorry to put you through this.'

'Don't be silly,' her father said. 'We understand. You can't help it, but that's not your fault. That maniac is to blame, he who the police don't seem to be able to find.'

'They'll never find him dad, because I couldn't give a good description of what he looks like or anything about him. It's hopeless.'

She guessed they'd taken the hint, because they got up quietly and left, closing the door softly behind them. Thank God, she thought. It was best if she dealt with her problems in her own way.

At six o'clock she went downstairs to have an evening meal with them, but returned to her room almost as soon as she'd finished eating.

It had been an extremely stressful day and although she dropped off to sleep quickly, she spent a restless night, floating from one bad dream to another. From her unhappy childhood to her troubles with Blake, and of course the horrific attack. It was as if all the men in her life were fighting against her, wanting her for their own ends.

When she woke the next morning, she felt drained by the bad things that kept happening to her - and couldn't see the point in getting up; there was nothing to get up for anyway - so she remained in bed, lying there dozing wondering when or if her parents would interrupt her misery.

Finally, the door to her bedroom opened, squeaking slightly. Her mother standing there stony faced as if she had something on her mind. But remembering back to when she was younger, she knew her mother never liked her to lie in, thinking it an idle occupation. Yet, what did she expect after the events of the last few months?

'Sorry to disturb you, but dinner's ready if you'd care to join us.'

'I'm not hungry right now. I'll have something later.'

Her mother blinked rapidly seeming not to know what to make of this. They stared at each other for a few seconds.

'Well if you're sure. But remember you have to eat no matter how miserable you feel. No one can live without food.'

'I'm not stupid, mum!' She shouted causing her mother to flinch.

Looking surprised by the sound of her daughter's voice she replied 'We're beside ourselves worrying over you Donna, we really are. You can't carry on like this. God knows where you'll end up.'

'And what's that supposed to mean?'

'Nothing. I'm only saying…'

'Well don't. If I had somewhere else to go, I would – believe me. I'm only here as long as I have to be. So you needn't worry. Once I'm gone, you'll no longer be burdened with my troubles – will you?'

'Don't be ridiculous. Whether you're here or not, we'll still be just as concerned,' her mother replied angrily, leaving the room and the door wide open.

Donna frowned. Why should she be bothered with them, especially her mother? Maybe she should use them, as they'd always used her. Then she breathed out with relief, glad to be on her own again. Perhaps it was her present muddled state of mind, but they were driving her crazy. The thought of spending an indefinite amount of time here, filled her with dismay. When she'd moved in with Blake, it had been like a breath of fresh air. At last, she'd had the freedom to do what she'd craved for, without interference or manipulation. But now that relationship was over, and she couldn't face going to work, or being with her parents. It was back to square one again. As she continually thought in this irrational way, her head spun.

Her only solace for the rest of the day, was to remain in her bedroom, first reading a book and then watching television, with not a peep out of her mum or dad. She was in no mood to speak to anyone although she guessed one of them would show their face eventually.

The television was still on; she lay back on her bed intermittently dozing every now and again, until a quiet knock at the door brought her back to reality. She whispered 'oh no' and hoped it would be her father. At least he listened to her with an open mind, even if he did eventually side with her mother most of the time.

When the door opened she was relieved to see it was indeed him, his face troubled but also stern. He gave a serious smile.

'Mind if I sit down love? I brought you something to eat and drink - you must be starving. It's five-thirty and you haven't eaten a thing all day.'

He had a tray containing a plate of ham and cheese sandwiches and a bottle of fizzy pop, which he placed on the table by the bed.

'Maybe just a little,' she admitted.

'Well, that's a start I suppose. You tuck in now.'

Donna looked up at him, pangs of hunger hit her nostrils. She picked up a sandwich and began to eat it slowly. Despite not wanting to appear too keen, she ate most of the food.

'Any better now?'

'Not really. Not as hungry perhaps, but I still feel so low. I don't know what's the wrong with me? You can't begin to imagine, dad.'

'I don't suppose I can. By the way, David Wallace phoned. He wanted to know how you are. I told him you're ill again. He was very nice about it; said he wanted us to keep him informed. He'll take you back love, which isn't surprising considering your qualifications and abilities. They still have a very high opinion of you. Just get another note from your doctor, and David will let you go back whenever you're ready.'

Her father seemed pleased by David Wallace's sympathetic attitude.

But she felt a jolt in her stomach, as panic rushed through her once more. Tears formed in her eyes and she shook her head from side to side.

'Please Donna; this is your career we're talking about here. Don't throw it away over what happened to you. That's plain stupid.'

'You don't know what that monster did to me, dad. He raped and beat me and took away my self-respect. I thought I was going to die. And when I found out I was pregnant and had an abortion, not knowing whose baby it was, I was devastated. I have to live with the fact that I killed by own baby and that it might have been Blake's child. I'll never forget that until the day I die. And now I can't face work, because they know why I was off sick, and are judging me. It's too much to take.'

Her father cleared his throat, then scratched the back of his head, as if he was trying to weigh up the options. 'All right,

Donna. Perhaps it's better if you do leave Bluethorn. There'll be plenty of other jobs to apply for. So when you get over this, look for something else.'

'Stop it! Stop it!' she screamed her teeth clenched together in agony. 'I don't want to talk about it anymore. Just leave me alone.'

'Come on now Donna...'

She got up from her bed and literally pushed him away in an effort to make him leave the room. 'Go away. I'll sort it out myself – like I always have. No need for you or mum to keep badgering me.'

'All right... all right,' he said, his eyebrows raising to reveal the deep creases in his brow. 'If that's what you want, that's what you'll get, young lady.'

On leaving the room, he slammed the door in temper, which brought about waves of guilt, as she realised how badly she'd treated him when he wasn't to blame. She was over reacting and not dealing with her problems in a rational way. He hadn't liked her attitude and guessed he'd soon be telling her mother what had gone on. But what the hell.

◇◇◇

Once again the following morning, she stayed cosseted away in her room, only leaving to make herself something to eat and drink, at which time her parents made pathetic pleas to her. They went on and on nagging her, but she was determined, and said very little in an effort not to lose control.

As the days passed, they seemed to get the message and left her alone. She spent the time doing nothing except to read magazines or watch television. And then she lost interest in caring about her appearance – she didn't wash as much as normal or even brush her teeth. Her hair was unkempt and greasy and her face lacked its usual makeup. She just couldn't get herself out of the trap she'd fallen into. It was as if her resolve to make her own decisions and not listen to her parents, had shut her mind to any sense of reason. Her room became the only place where she could get some peace. When her doctor visited Donna refused to answer his questions and sent the poor man packing.

Days turned into weeks and arrangements were made for another counsellor to visit her, but she had no intention of responding to him and his stupid questions. There wasn't much to live for now anyway. So what was the point in getting better?

Her parents would move heaven and earth to help her as they saw fit, but any advice or help from them would be a ploy to get her round to their way of thinking. How long it would be before they meddled she didn't know, but she would be prepared?

When it came, though the timing was unexpected, the rest wasn't. It was early in the morning, she'd been woken by the milkman rattling his crates of milk, and was now sitting up watching her portable television. A gentle knock on the door, was followed by her mum and dad and the doctor of all people, all having serious sombre expressions on their faces. Donna only glanced at them, before staring down at the carpet, her hair covering her face so no one could see the expression on it.

Her mother who so far had been subdued spoke. 'Donna, I'm sorry, but this has gone on long enough. You can't carry on like this. You must co-operate with the doctor before it's too late.'

She didn't even bother looking at them knowing her mother's patronising voice so well and also the condescending look she'd have on her face.

Moaning loudly, she didn't care much what they did or said. They couldn't force her to do anything against her will. If she didn't want to co-operate with the doctor, she wouldn't. She'd hear what he said, but that didn't mean she had to oblige him with a response.

He sat down on the bottom of the bed beside her, while her parents remained standing, obviously keen to see what was happening, but staying in the background.

'So how are you, Donna?' he asked her in a deep melodic voice.

She didn't speak, and shrugged her shoulders.

'Not very well I see. Which isn't surprising given what you've been through lately.'

Donna gave an ironic snort that summed up her current mood.

'Please allow us to help you. Your parents are worried sick. I appreciate you're not fit for work yet, but somehow you must try to get yourself well again. I realise how hard it is for you, but with your family's support, you can do it. Make an effort to go out, find an interest, anything you that will stimulate you, and help you regain your confidence. In the meantime, might I recommend we increase your medication, as obviously your current dosage isn't working as well as it should. And finally, I'd like to ask you a pointed question. Please don't be offended... but do you ever have any thoughts about self-harm?' The dour expression already on his face remained unchanged.

Her mouth puckered out, she glanced at him for a second, then shrugged her shoulders again.

'Donna, I want to help you, as do your parents but if you won't talk to us, there's nothing we can do.'

She could feel his eyes almost burning into her. She didn't reply. Her anger was rising. How dare they get the doctor out without her permission? If she wanted help, she'd ask for it.

'We've talked about counselling before? I know you've seen several counsellors already, but didn't find the sessions very satisfactory. Well, I could put you in touch with someone more specialised with people in your situation. The person I have in mind was also attacked at roughly your age, so she knows something of what you're going through.'

She glowered at him. 'How many times do I have to say it? Leave me alone. I don't want your fucking help or anybody else's either. You're all making me ten times worse. You hear me?' Her face appeared twisted and tormented.

'Please don't be like this,' her mother said, sniffing back tears, meant to emphasise her concern.

Donna stared at them all. She felt like screaming, throwing things, anything that would make them go away. Then she broke down again, but when her mother went to her aid, she pushed her with such force that her mother staggered back against the door.

There was silence in the room, all of them seemingly shocked by Donna's actions. She wished they would react, because she wanted to scratch their eyes out, as she would have done to that monster given half the chance.

'I'll make out a prescription for you, and an appointment for you to see this counsellor. Naturally, we can't make you to do anything if you don't want to, but I urge you to take my advice, or your recovery may be even more difficult and prolonged.' The doctor handed Donna's mother the prescription.

And with that, they left Donna alone in her room. Hearing her father thanking the doctor for coming, as they went downstairs together, she could imagine what they were saying and that she wouldn't like it. All right, so maybe she was at the low ebb but the way they kept on at her, meant she'd never get herself right.

Cold sweat trickled down her back, then she became restless too. She wanted to get out of bed and run far away from her problems - from her life in fact. Go where no one would ever find her to start a new life. And she might still do that if things didn't improve.

Chapter 10

FROM HER ROOM SHE COULD STILL HEAR THEIR MUMBLINGS. A haughty laugh came from the doctor, then the front door closed and he was gone. Donna knew her parents would be back upstairs soon enough and didn't look forward to that.

It wasn't long before they returned, walking straight in to sit on the bed beside her. She noticed how serious they looked as if they were really concerned.

'Donna, you have to pull yourself together, for your own sake as well as ours,' her mother began, with watery eyes.

'We were devastated when we found out you'd been raped, but what's happened since is even worse. Splitting up with Blake, the abortion and now this business at work. And all you do is mope around up here, twiddling your thumbs. What's got into you, love?' Her dad looked deep into her eyes, shaking his head, obviously wishing someone could talk sense into her.

'Nothing. I don't need this – and I can't help the way I feel.'

'No, but you can't expect us to sit here while your life goes down the pan.' Her mother leaned over to put a hand on her shoulder. Donna flinched. 'You're still very young; with your whole life ahead of you. There's so much you could do if only you realised it. It's heart breaking to see you like this.'

She slid down into the bed, closed her eyes, and covered her ears with her hands to drown out whatever they were about to say. She hoped they'd get the message, as it was all she could think of to make them go away.

After a little while she was aware of them getting off the bed. Then she moved her hands from her ears and opened her eyes to see the door to her room closing. Thank God for that, she thought and turned onto her side and drifted off to sleep.

She woke to the sound of someone swishing back the curtains to allow in the light. Moving over onto her back, and with squinting eyes she saw her mother's determined face in front of her, obviously in a very black mood. She was always apprehensive when her mother was like this.

Before long Donna felt herself being pulled out of bed by the arms.

'Come on young lady, up you get. Before he went the doctor said not to let you lie around all morning in bed, feeling sorry for yourself. All right, everybody knows you've had a terrible experience, but that's over now - time to get off your backside and start living your life again. And if you can't do it by yourself, we'll do it for you. Now – I won't tell you twice.' It was an order.

'You can't do this. Piss off and leave me alone, will you?' It wasn't the first time she'd sworn at her mum, but on this occasion she seemed incensed by it.

Donna saw her mother raise her hand, but didn't expect the slap she got across her cheek. It stung painfully and made her gasp. 'Wash your mouth out, young lady. Don't you ever talk to me like that again – you hear? You will get up now whether you like it or not. Or do I have to drag you by the scruff of the neck into the bathroom myself, as I did when you were a kid? Come on, what's it to be? And when you've had something to eat, we're going out to fetch your prescription and then you're coming shopping with us. No argument. I'm through pussyfooting with you.'

'And what if I won't go?'

'You're coming. End of story. We're getting you some new clothes.'

'I don't need anything.'

'You do. You need them so you can be presentable when you go to interviews.'

'Interviews?'

'Yes, interviews for jobs. If you're not going back to Bluethorn, you'll have to find something else. It won't be difficult with your qualifications. You were the one who wanted to get a degree, weren't you? I know there's not much you can't turn your hand to, be it beauty or brains. So now let's see you prove it.'

Donna found out some clothes, all the time glaring at her mother, and headed for the bathroom, still feeling the stinging pain of the slap. Her mum meant business that was for sure and was still waiting outside the door when she came out.

The two of them came downstairs together, and went into the kitchen, where Donna's father was already sitting, reading his newspaper.

As she sat opposite her dad to eat a bowl of cereal, looking over his spectacles he said, 'I gather we're going shopping?'

'That's what mum's said.'

'Good. You need something to wear, to make you look nice again. So that you'll stand out from everyone else at your interviews. Then you'll be halfway towards getting another job.'

'Dad, even if that were true, I wouldn't want it to be that way. If I get a job, it'll be through ability, rather than because I happen to be pretty.' She got up and put her cereal bowl in the sink.

'But you'd be a fool not to try to look your best. First impressions count for a lot.'

'I don't need this from either of you.' She started to move towards the door.

'Sit down!' her mother bellowed. 'You'll make the effort if I have to push you all the way myself.'

Feeling tearful again, she clasped her hands together before speaking, 'I can't do anything anymore. My confidence is shattered, and everywhere I go I keep imaging that man is out there waiting for me.'

'Darling, he's not. He doesn't know who you are, or where you live or worked. He won't even remember what you look like.'

'Your father's right, you'll be with us, love, all the time we're out shopping. We won't leave you alone for a minute.'

'I'm not sure. Don't want you spending all your money on me. I'll have some of my own one day, and then I can buy all the clothes I want myself.'

'Donna, we have money sitting in a bank account doing nothing. Your mother and I can't think of anyone we'd rather spend it on than you. Now, not another word. We'll have a browse around the shops and see what happens – all right?'

She hadn't the energy to argue any further.

The morning was cool, dry and sunny but windy. For Donna it was the first time she'd been out since the day of the Bluethorn incident. She shivered and was glad when she got into the car.

Dexford Shopping Centre beckoned. Normally a place she relished visiting with all its boutiques and designer shops, but today she didn't care and was only doing this because of the pressure her parents were putting on her.

They stopped outside every clothes shop they came across, pointing to this and that in the window, hoping to encourage Donna to go inside. But she pulled a face, or shook her head as if she wasn't interested.

Her parents never lost their cool however, even when they saw how stubborn Donna was trying to be. It was only when they went inside a large department store to buy her dad a new coat that Donna looked at a few of the dresses situated close by.

'Why don't you try one on?' her mum encouraged, looking across at her.

Donna jumped slightly, bit her lip, suddenly feeling embarrassed, but then saw a turquoise chiffon dress that was rather nice. Normally she would have gone for it like a shot, but right now...

She took it off the rack, stared at it for a few seconds.

'Go on, what have you got to lose,' her dad said.

The more she thought about it, the more tempted she became. Without looking at them she went into the changing room with the dress.

The old yearnings for nice pretty clothes didn't quite return, but perhaps it wouldn't hurt if she tried this one on. There would be no obligation whatsoever to buy. As she stared at herself in the mirror, even she had to admit, the dress was very fetching. However she wouldn't parade about in it in front of her parents, and didn't care what they thought.

She was undecided, her eyes darting all over the place as she attempted to make up her mind. Back in she went to the mirror for another look. Surely, it wouldn't hurt – would it? She'd pay them back later.

Out she came, and without looking at her parents said, 'I'll have the dress, that's if it's all right with you?'

'That's fine,' her father said with a hint of a smile.

Once she started, there was no stopping her, and going from shop to shop, she eventually settled on a grey suit and a cream silk blouse, in addition to the turquoise dress.

On the way home she said, 'I'll pay you back.'

'And how will you do that?' her mother asked.

She hesitated. 'I don't know, but I will.'

'Anyway, I'm glad you got something. All we need to do now is to find you somewhere to wear them,' her father said glancing in his mirror at her as he drove.

'We'll have to get ourselves invited to a few parties, go out more often too. And you, young lady should reacquaint yourself with a few of your old friends, the ones you dropped for Blake. Or make new friends when we go out,' her mother added.

'Don't worry Donna. Just take it at your own pace. Why don't you ring up a few people like Clare or Felicity – you were really close to them before you met up with Blake – weren't you?' her dad said.

Donna sighed to herself. Felt nauseous even to consider such a thing.

Her dad continued, 'I can't help telling you this, but you'll look sensational in all your new clothes. Just think, if you can look great, when you're at your lowest ebb, imagine how you'll be when you're at your best?'

She let out a quiet gasp. He was getting as bad as her mother. Would they never give it a rest?

'I'm not interested. I won't wear those clothes, nor will I go to any parties or meet up with any of my stupid old friends. They'll all know about it too -'

'Not that again. But how can they? There was nothing in the papers or the local news, there's no way –'

'They'll find out, dad. Word gets around. I can imagine them now, hey… I hear some guy raped Donna… and so it goes on and on. You don't know what it's like out there in the big wide world.'

'It's no good talking to you,' her mother said. 'You can't tell me the whole of Dexford know about the rape. Anyway if you won't go out or socialise, find yourself another job. And if you can't get a job you want, do what you do best. You'd walk into something in no time. All right, so you're a little older but over the next five or ten years you could make a fortune and then after that, you could do whatever you choose.'

'How can you even think I'd want to go back to that?' A single tear trickled down the side of her face.

'Donna, you haven't much choice? If you can't do what you're trained for, what you did before is the only answer. Smile nicely at the camera and you'll have it made. That's not too difficult, now is it?'

'You never give up; mother, do you? Even when I'm ill. How can you sink so low?'

'Someday you'll learn, Donna. I realise you're uncomfortable modelling in front of people or cameras. But darling, your mother's right, you don't have to do much except to walk casually from one end of the stage to the other. It's easy money if you look at it logically.'

Her mother looking serious joined in. 'And love, as you're no longer earning, think very carefully about your options. Unemployment or sickness benefit isn't much and won't last forever. And then what will you do?'

Donna's face filled with torment and anguish. Coming back home had been a big mistake. And now there was no way out.

'I won't do it, no matter what you threaten,' she blurted out, feeling like she was looking death in the eye.

'You have to do something. Everyone's in the same boat - they have no choice either. Not many things are certain in this life, but we all have to pay the bills. Whether we've been raped or not.'

What a heartless thing to say? And coming from her dad, made it seem even worse.

'Anyway, tonight we're getting you out of the house. The three of us are going to dine out at *'Rossi's'*, that new Italian restaurant off Dexford High Street. Very posh and expensive, your father says. You can put on that new turquoise dress of yours, doll yourself up. All right?'

She began to tremble, the very idea of going out with her parents was bringing on an anxiety attack.

As soon as they arrived home, Donna stormed out of the car with her shopping, making her way to the front door. She opened it with her key.

'So where you going now?' her mother shouted after her.

'To my room –'

'Fine, but don't you forget we're going out tonight. You be ready on time – all right?' her father said following her into the house.

'I'm not going.'

Her mother and father looked at one another with despair.

'We'll call you when... ' her father began but Donna was half way up the stairs and didn't hear the end of the sentence.

Slamming the bedroom door shut, she threw her new clothes onto the bed as if they were bits of rubbish. Then switched on her hi-fi and played heavy rock music loudly, knowing this would irritate her parents. Surprisingly, she never heard another peep out of them. Thank goodness for small mercies, she thought.

Perhaps they meant well by insisting she should go out, but they didn't understand what an ordeal it would be for her. Whilst people had often been complimentary towards her, in her present state she couldn't bear anyone looking at her, especially men, even if they were only admiring glances. Ever since the attack she wanted to fade into the background. This was building up to another crisis; she felt it coming on because as long as she lived she would never pursue a career in modelling.

Having sat on the bed for a while, she took the clothes out of their bags; and hung them in her wardrobe without looking at them. Then she lay back down, put the earphones in her ears and into her hi-fi, and closed her eyes to block out the world outside. Yet even this was no good, with thoughts of her parents floating around in her mind, she felt tense and her breathing came in great bursts, as she remembered the anger on their faces when they returned home. It was as if her mother had staged the whole affair, by spending money on new clothes so that she could dress up and be noticed.

However, a little time later, the inevitable happened, she went on a guilt trip that wouldn't go away, and pulling out her earphones, walked over to the wardrobe, took out her new dress and placed it on the bed. She would go out with them, but only this once, she decided. Finally, she went for a shower, then hurriedly returned to her room to get dressed.

She began to apply make-up, and as she glanced at herself in the mirror, stopped for a second, wishing so desperately that Blake had been the person to take her away from this. But no, he'd let her down badly, at a time when she'd needed him most. Now she had nothing to take his place.

In the middle of this, someone called her. Turning her hi-fi down, and poking her head around the bedroom door, she saw her mother shouting from the bottom of the stairs.

'Donna! Are you getting yourself ready to go out or not? Time is moving on. Your dad's booked a table for seven o'clock - and it's almost six-fifteen now.'

'All right, all right, I'll be down in a minute.' She screwed up her eyes in frustration at her mother's attitude - it went against the grain to give in to her mother's wishes. But she felt compelled after they'd just spent all that money.

'Good, don't be too long now.'

With that Donna closed the door.

How she wished there was a way out, but there wasn't and although she had to go this time, she wouldn't give in again. So she finished making-up, meticulous around the eyes, mouth and cheeks. Round her neck she wore a solid gold twisted necklace, given to her by her father on the occasion of her twenty-first birthday.

After combing her thick shiny hair, and glancing in the full-length mirror on the door of her wardrobe, she felt a little ill at ease, knowing what would be said when she went downstairs – how she hated all those sorts of compliments.

The clock struck six-thirty when she opened the bedroom door and walked down the stairs to the living room, where they were waiting for her.

She saw the delighted painted smiles on their faces, their eyes alive with pleasure at the sight of her.

'Oh Donna, you look absolutely gorgeous,' her mother commented in a proud voice. 'Even better than before University and Mathematics took over your life. I can see you on the cover of any top fashion magazine.'

'Incredible.' Her father agreed as he went over to embrace her. 'You'll certainly turn a few heads tonight.'

'Well, that's ok if you want to turn heads. But I don't!' Donna was embarrassed, rolled her eyes, then her cheeks began to burn, as she stared at the clock on the wall behind her parents. She'd noticed briefly that they were dressed for the part and wondered whose benefit it was for.

'Ready for the off?' her mother asked staring directly at Donna, making her tremble slightly.

'If I have to.'

'Right, let's go. I want us all to enjoy ourselves tonight. And not think about anything else – understand Donna?'

'Well, father, that's up to you two, seeing as you're the ones who keep referring to my possible return to a modelling career – which I didn't want as a child and I certainly don't want now!'

'Let's call a truce, shall we?' It seemed strange that her mother saw it that way, as a ceasefire in this battle between them, when all Donna was fighting was an illness, and the right to choose the life she wished to lead. She wasn't well enough to socialise, in fact the pressure she'd be under tonight in trying to mix with other people would make her even more withdrawn.

She said little on the journey there, and although they tried to bring her into the conversation, she wasn't listening and only mumbled yes and no every now and then.

Having parked around the corner from *'Rossi's'*, they walked the short distance to the restaurant, an impressive blue-bricked building. As soon as they entered the brightly lit reception area, they were greeted by an olive-skinned man, with slicked back dark hair. Despite his pristine appearance, he smiled warmly and shook hands with all of them.

He beckoned them with his hand, escorting them to a table at the back of the restaurant, away from the spotlight, private yet relaxing. Donna sat facing her parents with her back to the rest of the diners, feeling nervous and afraid as a waiter brought the menus to them. Her father asked them what they wanted to order and in the end they all decided on a chicken pasta with cheese and tomatoes in a herby sauce.

Donna wasn't particularly hungry, yet found the food and drink very palatable. Had it not been for the company, she might have even liked the place. As it was she found herself continually *'clock watching'*, wanting only for the night to end.

As they sat eating their meal, she listened to them reminiscing about when she was a little girl. It seemed after each mouthful her mother took, the conversation went from her modelling career, back to her childhood fame, to parading on the catwalk as a beauty queen. It was like listening to a recording from years back and went against the truce her mum had supposedly called. It brought back bad memories when she'd rebelled against their wishes in any way she could. She remembered cutting up her outfits and pretending to be ill, hiding in places to avoid being in the limelight. Once she almost starved herself, until finally the penny dropped for her parents, but this time it wouldn't get that far – because she didn't intend going through that again. Sadly, their demeanor only added to her misery.

Sitting there quietly Donna sensed there seemed a smugness to her mother's attitude tonight, as if she was getting her own way or was perhaps pleased with herself. In fact, there was an aura about her parents actions, that made her feel vulnerable and threatened. Were they trying to corner her into doing something else? Or was this leading up to something more? After all she'd been through this so many times before. She couldn't allow that to happen, and would rather walk the streets, or even end it all if there was no other way out.

And as they talked about Donna's achievements with pride and admiration, there was little mention of her university degree. Her teeth almost crunched together, her hands clammy as panic set in. Little thought had been given to the lasting effects of the events of the last few months. They reiterated time and time again how a career in modelling was short and there would be ample time to take up mathematics again later – rambling on as if she wasn't there.

She'd had enough, and might have thrown another tantrum had not a middle-aged couple suddenly appeared at their table. Donna recognised the woman at once, heavily made up, with short auburn hair wearing a lot of jewelry - rings on every finger. Priscilla Evans, the famous fashion designer. Donna was startled, as it dawned on her what the new clothes, the meal, and talk of her appearance were all about.

'Well, hallo there!' Priscilla exclaimed in her posh cultured voice, loud but affectionate. 'Fancy seeing you here loves. Joe, Beryl - how delightful. It's been such an age since we last met. And Donna too. Well might I say you are looking lovelier than ever, darling?'

'Hallo Donna, Joe, Beryl,' the man said. He had an abundance of jet-black hair that seemed to cover most of his face, sprouting down his nose, and out of his ears.

They all smiled at each other, but this meeting brought uncomfortable flashback memories to Donna.

'Good to see you again Mrs Evans,' Donna remarked.

'Priscilla, James – why don't you pull up a chair and join us. We'd love to hear your news - it has to be all of four years since we last saw you,' Donna's mum said.

'Oh, we couldn't possibly intrude on what must be a family gathering.' Priscilla's smile revealed a large set of brilliant white teeth in the process.

'Not at all, you wouldn't be. We'd be honoured if you'd join us as our guests,' Donna's dad said, getting up from his seat to fetch two chairs from nearby tables.

'Well, in that case, we'd love to.' Priscilla laughed in a horsey way.

While Priscilla and James waited for their meals to arrive, Donna was forced to listen to them talk about the latest news in the fashion industry. She wasn't interested; although fashion conscious, she was just as happy wearing jeans and a top. Feeling awkward, she couldn't believe this was happening.

'So what are you up to these days, darling?' Priscilla asked Donna. 'I sincerely hope you got that degree you gave up your modelling career for.'

'I did.' She was quite surprised that Priscilla should ask her this, or even remember it. So, she started to talk about her graduation and job as a Statistical Analyst, omitting to tell them that at present she was unemployed.

'Very impressive Donna. I'm glad you've achieved your ambition. It's a shame you can't combine it with the modelling. You could have gone right to the top, darling.'

'I wouldn't say that.'

'Believe it, my dear. I for one will never forget the impact you made before. You were so photogenic – the camera loved you and always will. If you ever decide to take up modelling again, I'd definitely take you under my wing. Couldn't you consider working part-time in your day job? It's not too late you know,' Priscilla said staring at her.

'I'm sorry, that's not possible. I'm not interested in anything like that now.'

'How old are you, Donna?'

'Twenty-two.'

'Well, you're not even in your prime yet. With your face and figure, if you look after yourself properly, you could go on well into your thirties. And the money you could earn, why I'd say within five years you'd be a millionaire.'

'Oh really –'

'Yes, really. I imagine your job is a good one, but somewhere down the line, you have to ask yourself about your earning potential elsewhere. Wouldn't it be nice to be financially independent for the rest of your life? Then you'd be able to pick and choose what to do in the future.'

Donna shook her head angrily.

'The trouble with my daughter is, she's never realised how lucky she is. And as you're well aware, in the past it has helped her to be successful, but not only in the field of modelling. When she was a little girl, she could act a bit too. I know it was only in commercials and bit parts in the odd children's serial, but her character always came shining through. She was the little girl everyone loved and thought was so sweet. There wasn't anything she couldn't turn her hand to.'

'Mum – you're talking rubbish again.'

'Don't be so modest. God gave you a gift, so you'd be foolish not to make use of that –don't you think Priscilla?'

'Absolutely!'

'There you are, you've heard it from the horse's mouth. If that doesn't convince you, nothing will,' Donna's mother said.

'Tell you what I'll do. How about if I arrange for you to have a photo session, with Alan Nicholls, our top fashion photographer, who I seem to remember, you've posed for before, some years ago. You could model a succession of my latest designs – that would help bring you to the attention of lots of people. I'll show the photographs to a few people in the loop. You'll be a sensation, my dear. So how about early Saturday afternoon? A day when you're not at work. Alan has a studio in Rochester, a tiny village about twenty miles from here. What do you think Donna?' Priscilla said raising her plucked eyebrows expectantly.

Donna was dumbstruck. Where had all this come from? She'd been suspicious from the start. But it was too much of a coincidence that Priscilla had *'accidentally'* been at the restaurant at the same time as them. This was hard to comprehend but typical of her parents to resort to something like this. And for the time being Donna decided to keep quiet. But when she did open her mouth, nothing came out. There were tears in her eyes.

Her mother put an arm around her and said, 'She'll be fine. She's a little emotional at the moment – having recently split from her boyfriend.'

'Oh, I didn't know.'

'Looks like she needs something to bring her out of it – and returning to modelling could be just the thing,' her father said.

Donna didn't agree with any of this, but was so distraught, she let it lie.

The rest of the evening passed in a blur. Donna watched her parents suck up to Priscilla, obviously thrilled about her proposed return to modelling. It seemed all they were interested in was making money out of her.

As Priscilla and James got up to leave, they both remarked on how they looked forward to hearing about the photoshoot on Saturday. Everyone seemed happy but Donna. The very thought of posing for the photographs and everything it entailed filled her with trepidation.

She didn't know why her courage had suddenly failed her again, why she'd meekly said nothing. And to make matters worse all the way home from the restaurant, her parents talked about nothing else but this new adventure. As her heart beat faster, she felt an anxiety attack coming on. Somehow, she had to find a way out of this before it was too late. She put her head against the back seat to relax herself, and breathed in and out slowly, closing her eyes.

As they turned into their street her mother glanced back and asked, 'Tired are you, Donna?'

'Just a little, think I'll go to bed.'

'Don't blame you, love,' her father said. 'It's been an eventful day, hasn't it? But at least now you've got a chance of pulling yourself out of the hole you're in. You should have every reason to be optimistic about the future.'

'I don't want to go...' Donna mumbled holding her elbows with her hands.

'Oh, come now love. It's only a photo session, even if it is with one of the top fashion photographers in the country. What possible harm can that do? You won't be on your own, your father and I will be there to help you. No need to worry about a thing.'

Fidgeting uncomfortably, she said, 'How many times do I have to tell you, I don't want to do any more modelling.'

'Of course you do. It's what you've been destined for all your life – and it's about time you realised that,' her mother said.

Donna shook her head at them as if she thought they were mad. 'You'll regret this, just like the last time.'

'No we won't, because once you get there you'll be in your element.'

She wasn't listening to them. The car had barely stopped when she swung her legs out of the door, dashed into the house and ran directly upstairs to the safety of her room. At this point she realised she'd have to go through with the photo session, but by God after that she would fight by whatever means she had at her disposal to get away from these two people who'd ruined her life. It was a do or die situation now.

Chapter 11

THE SMALL VILLAGE OF ROCHESTER SAT NESTLED IN A PICTURESQUE VALLEY SURROUNDED BY HILLS OF DIFFERENT SHADES OF GREEN.

As their Mondeo estate came into the main street, it slowed down, passing a small cluster of gift shops and finally an antique centre, before coming to a halt outside a white washed building. A sign above the building in large italic letters read *'Alan Nicholls Photographic Studios'*. The three-storey building was old, perhaps late Victorian, tall with square windows, possibly with living quarters above.

As they got out of the car, Donna noticed quaint residential dwellings dotted on the hillside, and observed how peaceful this little hamlet seemed; there was a sleepy atmosphere about the place. She shivered, surprised by how cool and windy it was outside, despite the sun - it would be good to get inside to the warm.

A bell rang when her father opened the door to the Studio; he stood aside for his wife and daughter to enter first. Almost at once they recognised Alan Nicholls, standing behind the counter, a mobile phone to his ear. With his hand he indicated for them to take a seat.

He was a skinny man with slicked back brown hair, a pock marked face and wore green trousers and a white shirt. Donna remembered as a child, how his different coloured eyes had spooked her. But she also recalled him being a humorous man, very good at putting his subjects at ease.

Nevertheless she felt anything but at ease in such plush surroundings. And seeing the walls adorned with photographs of beautiful models wearing exquisite fashion items added to her anxiety.

Instead of sitting down, she preferred to lean against the counter, her back to Alan, while her mother and father sat chatting to one another, mainly about the famous women who'd graced these studios. When she heard them say they thought she'd outshine them all, she squirmed with embarrassment.

Impatient to get the ordeal over with as quickly as possible, Donna tried to imagine what clothes Alan would want her to model, knowing if any were too revealing, she would almost certainly walk out.

At last, with his head leaning slightly to the right, his phone call ended, and a huge smile came across his face, his eyes focusing on Donna momentarily, as he put his phone away. When he spoke, it was in a deep mellow voice that belied his thin scrawny features.

'Hallo there, nice to meet you all,' he said, lifting up the counter to go across to them.

After greeting her parents, he went over to Donna, taking her hand in both of his, making her cringe.

'It's good to meet you again my dear after all this time. Donna, you're looking more beautiful than ever. Priscilla's been telling me all about how successful you've been at University and in your job. It's so refreshing to see someone as attractive as you, having some of the old grey matter as well. Why don't you come on through? Then we can get the shoot started as soon as possible.'

The studio was dark apart from one corner, set up as a mock beach, and lit by spotlights. The photographic equipment stood close by, ready for Alan to use.

As they sat down, Donna caught a glimpse of a door marked 'Changing Room', adding to her unease.

Alan pulled up a chair to sit directly in front of them, and at once focused his eyes on Donna, studying her at close quarters. She disliked being scrutinised in this way and hated being on show. However, Alan's smoothing voice calmed her down a little.

'Well, well, I must say my dear.' He stroked the back of his neck with his hand. 'You do have the most delightful face. A wonderful bone structure too, clear blue eyes and thick blond hair. How could I ever forget what a perfect model you are? And if I remember correctly the camera loves you. You know, you're a photographer's dream. And what a fine figure you still have. I can't wait to take a few pictures of you – and dare I say it, but they'll be absolutely sensational.'

'See what did I tell you?' Her mother beamed with pride. 'If a photographer of Alan's standing tells you that, you have to believe it.'

Donna felt on edge - these ridiculous compliments didn't help. She quivered like a jelly inside and out. Why did they have to keep doing this to her? Couldn't they see how it was affecting her? Perhaps the pound signs in front of their eyes were obscuring the view.

Then she realised her father was glancing at her, concern in his eyes. 'Don't worry darling. I know you're nervous, but I promise you, you'll be fine. Alan is a master at making people feel comfortable – you must remember that. Which is the reason why he's so successful at getting the best out of his models. And don't forget we'll be here all the time, so you have nothing to fear.'

Smiling reassuringly at his subject, and sitting up straight, Alan said, 'Right then Donna, if you're ready – let's begin. If you'd like to go into the changing rooms, you'll notice all the clothes I have in mind for you to wear are on hangers. Put on whatever you fancy, anything you think you might feel good in. Then let's take a look at you before I start taking the pictures – how does that sound?'

'All right.' But feeling unsure of herself, she looked towards her parents for support, hating the idea of having to pose for these shots. She worried over who'd be allowed to see them. What if the man who raped her saw them and found out who she was. Dear God, he'd come after her again for sure.

'Would you like me to go in with you, help you sort out something to wear?'

'No, no, I'll be all right mum.' She scurried towards the changing room.

'You sure? It's no trouble - honestly,' she shouted after her, but Donna was already inside and had closed the door behind her.

'Don't fret Beryl – leave her be. Let her do this on her own.'

Donna was glad her father had made this remark, but it didn't make her feel much better. She didn't want to do this, and they were still ignoring her pleas. This showed they hadn't learnt their lesson and that this was just for their own selfish ends.

She looked at all the outfits Alan had ready for her. There were many different styles, dresses, tops, trousers, skirts, evening gowns, swimsuits; all the garments had in common was that they were made of the best materials and styled to the highest standards. The quality of the cloth, and the bright colours of yellow, blue, red, plain and patterned, impressed Donna; they must have cost a fortune to make. But touching the clothes and seeing those strange designs, made her realise she wouldn't want to wear or buy any of them.

For a while, she stood there as if momentarily frozen in time. What was she going to do, that was the question? When she hated the thought of posing for these stupid pictures.

In the end the answer came to her without much trouble. She couldn't go through with it, wouldn't do this, not for her parents, herself or for anyone.

Then looking in the mirror she noticed a fire-exit door. Turning round she saw a long metal rail bolted into the top of the doorframe and also into the floor. In the middle was a bar with a sign above *'Push Bar to Open'*. Dare she push it? There was nothing to lose, everything to gain. She gave the metal bar a hefty shove with both hands. The door disengaged and daylight flooded into the changing area.

She walked out into the sunshine, trembling as the cold wind hit her. This was the back of the building on what appeared to be a car park. Behind the grey tarmac were fields filled with yellow corn, and beyond that trees that might be the beginning of a forest or wood. She just wanted to get as far away from the Studio as possible.

Walking over the tarmac, she headed towards the cornfield. As she stepped into the field, she jumped at the sound of her mother's shrill voice.

'Donna! Donna! Where on earth are you going?'

Donna quickened her pace to run further into the cornfield as the commotion going on behind her seemed to be getting closer.

'Please stop, Donna,' her father's deep voice boomed, but his tone was softer and almost pleading rather than threatening.

This caused her run faster, but the corn was quite high, and she found it extremely restrictive to get through. She noticed a clearing to the right and breathing heavily made a dash in that direction.

Several voices were now shouting her; it seemed like the whole of the village were in pursuit. As she came out of the cornfield on to a dirt track, which led to a road, she glanced back to see they weren't far behind.

Sprinting as if her life depended on it, she might have got away too, but for a car travelling towards her. She jumped out of the way just as the car passed, but slipped onto her right knee and cried out in pain. Regaining her composure, she looked up to see her father and Alan coming over to her. It was no good, she couldn't go on and had to resign herself to defeat. As she got to her feet, her dad grabbed hold of her arm.

'Donna – what the hell are you doing? – damn it!' he exclaimed shaking his head at her.

'Nothing – let me go,' she cried trying to wriggle free, but he was too strong for her.

'For God's sake, what are you running away from?'

She glared at him, her eyes full of hate, as tears ran down her face.

'I'm not doing this. And you can't make me.' The tone of her voice determined and defiant.

'You're joking - aren't you? Why ever not?'

'Because…. Because… I can't – that's all.'

'Don't be ridiculous. You're nervous, feeling low. But it'll pass, I promise you. Come on; let's get you back in there. Sorry about this Alan – she's just a bit anxious, that's all.'

Alan nodded, although the expression on his face showed irritation and disbelief; obviously seeing what her parents couldn't.

'I won't go through with this. And that's final!' She widened her eyes at her dad and then at Alan who gave no sign of emotion.

Just then her mother came striding towards them, her face like thunder. As soon as she reached her, she slapped Donna across the cheek, so hard it sounded like a whip cracking. Donna winced from the sting of it, but glared back in defiance. She wanted to hit her back but stopped herself just in time. Instead, she stroked her reddening cheek.

'How dare you show us up like this in front of Alan? One of the foremost photographers in the country. You've humiliated us. We'll be a laughing stock. If this ever gets out, no one will photograph you again. Talk about tantrums. Alan, I'm so sorry about this. Please, you must forgive my headstrong daughter.'

Raising his eyebrows he said, 'You all need to go home and give your daughter some space. And if she doesn't want to do this, for God's sake listen to her. I seem to remember she's always been nervous about posing for photographs, and if that's still the case, it will never work. Mind you, I get the feeling there's more to this than just nerves.'

And at that he walked off.

Donna didn't speak. This was their own fault, for not even considering their daughter's needs.

Her mother finally spoke. 'When I think about all the trouble I've gone to for you. I did this because I knew you couldn't face going back to work. I thought it would be a way to get you back into doing something useful again. It could have made you rich. Young lady, it's about time you stopped feeling sorry for yourself. This has got out of control. Start to live again before it's too late.'

'How can I? And besides, what's the point? You never listen to me anyway – I'm banging my head against a brick wall. Why the hell do you think I didn't want to eat all those years ago, why I hated every minute of being in those stupid adverts? Don't you ever ask yourselves that? No, I don't suppose you do.'

'Well, you haven't got a cat in hell's chance of being a model now. Or anything else for that matter, the way you're behaving. I hope you're satisfied, my girl.'

Donna shrugged her shoulders. 'See if I care. No wonder I left home to live with Blake. I couldn't wait to get away from you and your stupid obsessions about my looks. And if I'd known what was coming, I'd have found somewhere else to stay - even being out on the streets is better than this.'

'All right Donna, that's enough,' her father said quietly but with some authority. 'We're going home. Let's have no more of this in public.'

She wanted to get away from them, but he had her by the arm and wouldn't let go. He was hurting her. She started to struggle.

'For God's sake, stop it. You want the whole world to know what's going on here.'

'Let me go then.'

'And what happens if he does let you go, young lady? You'll make a run for it – and then what will become of you?'

'You can't treat me like this. I'm twenty-two years of age – an adult, for Christ's sake. You've no right, no right at all.'

'You'll be treated like an adult when you act like one.'

She ignored her mother's comments, but then had the humiliation of her father dragging her along as he walked back to the car, parked by the side of Alan's studio.

As Donna's mother opened the car door, her husband bundled Donna safely in the back. After putting the child locks on the doors they got in the front, intent it seemed, on getting to Dexford as quickly as possible.

During the journey home Donna was silent, staring out of the window, but she didn't take in the scenery. Her parents seemed calm and impassive.

By the time they arrived home, the weather had turned to rain and was pouring down in torrents along the gutters, making all of them rush to the front door, which Donna's father hurriedly opened. Donna was in first, running for the safety of her bedroom. Although she wanted to cry, she sniffed away the tears before they came. Lay on her bed, all curled up with her arms over her eyes. She'd never been so unhappy and didn't know how to free herself of it. That one indescribable act of terror had triggered everything wrong in her life, a life that was now in free fall.

Although she'd been at her wits end, she should have known better than to move back in with her parents. It should have been obvious what they'd do, once they knew she couldn't return to work. There was only one way out and that was to leave. But where could she go? That was the problem. And how? She had a little money saved up, and was due to half of the flat she and Blake had shared, but unless she could support herself, she was done for.

A light knock at her door, brought her back to reality. Her heart sank; she sighed, wanting to ignore them. They were pathetic really. The door opened without any invitation from her. In came her father, looking weary and slightly round shouldered, almost as if he had the world's problems on them.

'Your mother and I would like a word, downstairs if you don't mind,' he said simply raising his head slightly.

Donna looked up at him, a look of exasperation forming on her face. She didn't want or need this. It seemed like her life was moving from one crisis to another, each worse than the last.

'Oh no, please dad –'

'Yes Donna. Together, we have to sort out your life. You can't carry on like this.'

Donna would have jumped out of the bedroom window if she'd had the courage, but she hadn't. There was nowhere else to go but with her father. She went first, with him following closely behind. Although he was by no means as domineering and controlling as her mum, when it came to it, his allegiance always lay with his wife.

Her mother was sitting on the settee when they came into the living room. She seemed sad, her head was down; Donna thought she'd visibly aged. The fine wrinkles around her eyes and mouth looked more pronounced than before.

'Why don't you sit down?' her mother pointed to the armchair opposite.

Donna did as she asked, despite feeling uncomfortable about it, and with both of them facing her, as if she was on trial for some terrible crime. At this point it became obvious something was simmering below the surface and that soon this would come out.

'We have to talk. Your father and I are extremely concerned about you. We know what a harrowing experience you had, and we realise we can't begin to imagine what your ordeal was like. But that was months ago now – isn't it about time you started to come to terms with it? Your bruises have healed and you look as good as new, and although your mental scars may take a little longer to fade, that will improve in time. What we're so concerned about now is how you've suddenly gone to pieces and let your life fall apart. I mean since you were attacked, you've split with Blake, lost your job, and now this latest fiasco at Alan Nicholls's studio - it's getting steadily worse. Your dad and I are worried sick over where this will all end.'

Her father took over then. 'As for Blake, I think you're best shut of the creep. I always had doubts about him even though I could never pin down exactly what it was. I'm glad you found out about him before you got wed.'

'Your dad's right, perhaps all things considered he did you a favour. And to be honest we're not too upset you left Bluethorn either because you've far too good for that place. Obviously, you have a gift for Mathematics, which you'll use to your advantage someday, when you're a little older.'

'That's why it was so disappointing to see you react the way you did at Alan Nicholl's studio,' her father said looking in her direction, but Donna couldn't meet his gaze, and felt herself colouring amid all the patronising going on. 'Your mother went to a lot of trouble to arrange this shoot with Alan, who, so Priscilla tells us, very rarely photographs anyone not signed up with an agency. We're doing our best for you, trying to give you an avenue to get your life back on track. But now after that calamity earlier, this opportunity has gone right out of the window. It's all very sad.'

Once again her mother took over. 'So where do you go from here? Do you have any idea yourself? Or are you planning to sit around the house all day, wasting away to nothing? It's about time you got off your bum and did something positive.'

Donna looked over their heads at a picture on the wall, a landscape painting, the only picture in the room not to contain her. She could feel them staring, and wanted to close her eyes to shut them out - but that wasn't possible. She tried to ignore them. Why shouldn't she? They only heard what they wanted to hear anyway.

'Donna! We're talking to you. Have you nothing to say for yourself?' Her father asked. 'Come on love, you of all people with your impressive university education ought to be able to tell us something.'

She wouldn't be bullied by them. This was how they normally acted in this type of situation, when she'd been unwilling to do as they wanted. It had been the same at University – they'd pressurised her into carrying on modelling during the holidays.

'Well, if you can't come to a decision yourself, we'll do it for you,' her mother said. 'We've made a few enquiries over the past few weeks. I know you've been prescribed anti-depressants by your own GP, as well as seeing a psychiatrist since the attack. So there's only one alternative and that's to arrange for you to see someone privately. We made enquiries some weeks ago, and found a psychoanalyst we thought might help, but we've been waiting a while to see how you progressed. Apparently he's one of the best in his field. We suggest you see him twice a week, so that you can be put on an extensive therapy programme that ought to get to the root of your problems, and hopefully on the road to recovery.'

Donna's face dropped. She wouldn't see anyone else, no matter what it cost.

'Perhaps we could arrange your first session sometime next week, here at the house,' her father bullishly said.

Donna jumped up from where she was sitting and made straight for the living room door.

'Come back here this instant!' her mother yelled after her.

But she ignored their pleas. Neither of her parents followed her. They let her go, probably hoping she'd calm down eventually. Thank God, they didn't follow, she thought. Yet again she slammed her bedroom door shut, flopped down on the bed, and sank her fist down into her pillow in frustration and anger, then buried her face in the same pillow and cried with despair. All this constant pressure was too much. Wouldn't it be better if she wasn't around anymore? Maybe her parents would be happy then.

The pain of taking her own life might be bad at first. But afterwards there would be a great release into a better world than this.

Chapter 12

NO ONE CAME TO HER ROOM THAT NIGHT. Donna no longer cared what they did or didn't do. Unable to sleep, she sat up in bed thinking mainly of her parent's fixation over wanting her to be rich and famous. But why was this so important to them? As if money and stardom was everything. Nobody could buy happiness. What was the point in being able to buy anything you wanted if no one loved you for yourself? All things considered, looks meant nothing. All right, so it was wonderful to be attractive, but nobody remained like that forever. People changed for better or for worse, but as the years passed, it would certainly to be for the worse. And what people looked like had no bearing on what they were really like inside.

Getting up to switch on the light, she gazed at herself in the mirror on the wardrobe door. She looked at herself objectively and trying to be self-critical, stared at her own face devoid of any make up. Unremarkable, she thought. She had two eyes, two ears, a nose, a mouth, creamy white smooth skin the same as everyone else except in slightly different dimensions and shades of colour. She couldn't change any of these things except to enhance them with the application of make-up. As far as she was aware, there was only one thing she could change herself and that was her hair. At present it was thick, lush and worn loose halfway down her back. The colour of corn. What if... she thought, pulling her hair away from her face – oh well maybe not... but then again... why not? What had she got to lose?

Moving away from the wardrobe door to the chest of draws by her bed, she reached for her lady shave which lay in the bottom draw. After a few moment's hesitation, she plugged it in and proceeded to drag the cutting edge over the top of her head. The whirring noise made her excitement more intense, as repeatedly she moved the machine across her scalp, back, front and sides until after about ten minutes the job was done.

Next, she pushed the shaver over her eyebrows, under her arms, across her arms and legs and even in her most private of places. Finally, when there wasn't a strand of hair left on her whole body, she turned back to the mirror to inspect the results – she was as bald as a coot. No chance of being a model now, she smirked to herself.

Her hair lay thick on the carpet, and lying on the bed, she felt so much better over what she'd done to herself. What a pleasure it would be to see the looks on her parents' tiny obsessed faces.

In the morning, she woke up late having almost forgotten about the enormity of her actions. Eventually there was a knock on her door; her father asked to come in.

'Yes,' she said in a disinterested voice.

He poked his head round the door. 'We wondered if you wanted something to – ' he stopped in mid-sentence, obviously having seen what she'd done to herself. He looked as if he'd had the shock of his life and appeared mortified.

'What's the matter dad? Seen a ghost, have you?' she grinned, sitting up quickly to give him a proper view of her bald head in all its glory.

'Oh my God – what have you done?' he muttered to himself with some unease and concern.

'I decided I needed a haircut, and seeing as I can't earn any money myself, thought I'd save you and mum a few quid. I mean you keep going on about me being a model, so I suppose even like this any agency is bound to jump at the chance to hire me. Isn't that so, dad?' A demented smile came on her face.

'What's made you do such a stupid sick thing? This is sheer madness, my girl.'

'Is it dad? Perhaps that's because I am mad.'

'I don't know what your mother will make of this. She'll go absolutely spare,' he said shaking his head in a dejected fashion.

'Maybe she will, but there's not much she can do about it, is there dad? Unless she wants to get some glue and stick it back on.' She laughed as if she was mildly deranged.

'This isn't funny Donna.'

'Isn't it? Well I think it is. And I'm not frightened what she says any more. She can go to hell as far as I'm concerned.'

His face was grim, his left eye twitched ever so slightly as it always did when he was under stress or worried over something. He turned around and walked out of the room. Only a few minutes later Donna heard them both stomping up the stairs.

On entering the bedroom, her mum screamed, then burst into tears at the sight before her. Her father put an arm about his wife's shoulders to comfort her, but Donna guessed there was no feeling better for them in the wake of what she'd done. Only time could put it right, but it would be a very long time - that was for sure.

'What's the point of this?' she asked shuddering.

'I fancied a new haircut – literally. How do you like the new me, mother? Does it make me any prettier, or even sexy perhaps?'

'You've ruined yourself – you idiot. How dare you?'

'I won't be going on any more photo assignments will I, mum? Although you never know, maybe I could start a new fashion trend, the bald sexy look. Like Sinead O'Connor. What do you reckon?' She grinned once more.

'It'll grow back, so it's a rather stupid exercise. Just the actions of a pathetic selfish girl.'

'Oh well, that might be true, but I'll still be able to turn a few heads, but for the wrong reasons. That'll scupper a few of your plans, eh mum?'

'Do you really think that's what I want? Sorry to disappoint you but I've always had your welfare at heart. There are ways and means young lady, like wigs for instance, if need be.'

'Perhaps in a strange way, this could be for the best anyway,' her father butted in. 'By the time it's grown back, she should be feeling more like her normal self.'

'Oh really? And if you think that person who you're paying loads of money, will make any difference – you're wrong,' Donna said.

'The sooner you see this therapist, the better,' her mother said. 'We need to find out what's going on in that pretty little head of yours - and quickly.'

'I want to go out somewhere,' Donna suddenly said, feeling her smooth pate with her hand.

'I don't think so. In your present condition, it's out of the question,' her father said seriously.

'Why ever not? You've always wanted me to get noticed – haven't you?'

'Shut up Donna! Your father's right. Don't you dare do anything like this again – do you hear me?'

'I hear you. But I won't be told what to do any more. It's my life and I'll live it how I like – and there's nothing you can do to stop me.'

Looking shocked by this unusual outburst, her mother was visibly shaking, and turned to her husband. 'I can't take much more of this.'

'There's something wrong with her, love. She needs help, help we're no longer capable of giving.'

Donna was aware of the distress on her parents' ashen faces. They were obviously unsure about how to deal with the situation. Well, they'd brought it on themselves for treating her the way they had. And she'd continue to make them pay, no matter what it cost her.

'So are you going to let me go out, or do I have to go without your permission, mommy and daddy,' she mimicked.

'If you do, your mother or I will come with you. There's no telling what you might get up to in your present state.'

'Maybe next time I'll cut myself again, you know, right across this pretty little face of mine. Get even less admiring looks then, won't I?'

'It won't happen, Donna, believe me, your father's right. We'll watch you twenty four hours a day if we have to.'

'Going to hold my hand when I want the toilet to do my number ones and number two's, are you?'

'If need be, I will,' her mother said.

'Get yourself washed and dressed. Your mother will go out with you to make sure you don't come to any harm.'

Donna pulled a face but didn't try to stop her mum from taking her to the bathroom. She locked the door behind her and stared at herself in the mirror. How strange, she thought, I'm almost like a hardened criminal, caged for a hideous crime. But in reality she was far from that and actually felt very vulnerable and afraid.

Wearing a light blue polo neck jumper and dark blue jeans, she came out of the bathroom and went downstairs with her mother close behind.

Before they left the house, Donna's mum told her husband they were going out, but that they wouldn't be long.

As they walked down the road, Donna shivered despite wearing a sheepskin coat and a woolly hat, which supposedly would hide her bald head. She almost wished she hadn't suggested their outing. After walking through the park, they found shelter on a bench beneath a huge oak tree.

There seemed lots of people about, surprisingly, walking their dogs or just out to enjoy the scenery. How she would have loved to have taken her hat off in front of them and seen their reactions. But then again maybe not – it might have given her mother a heart attack, more's the pity.

After only a few minutes, they found it was much too cold to sit around for long, and decided to make their way home. If she'd got somewhere to go, Donna would have made a run for it, but she hadn't. Best resign herself to the inevitable, she thought as they walked up the drive to the house.

She spent the rest of the day watching television and reading, and come dinner time only picked at her food, much to her parents' dismay.

As the day wore on, she just wanted to be alone in her bedroom, but they were adamant she couldn't be trusted. Consequently, her mood got lower and lower. In fact, it wouldn't have surprised her if they'd tried to strap her to the bed. This was like being in prison, she thought angrily.

In the end, they allowed Donna to go up to her room but with her mother, who sat warmly wrapped in a blanket, comfortably seated in front of the door, to stop Donna from leaving the room.

She hated every minute of this pathetic treatment and longed for freedom to come. All she needed was patience, she told herself, as before long their guard would be down, and then an opportunity to escape would present itself.

In the early hours of the morning, Donna lay in her bed still awake, anger rising with each passing minute.

After what seemed like forever, her mum stopped fidgeting in the chair. She was still, and Donna heard soft rhythmic breathing, that occasionally produced a tiny snore. Time to get up.

Slipping on her dressing gown, she tip-toed quietly towards where her mother was fast asleep. It would be difficult to get by without disturbing her, but she'd give it her best shot. She took in a deep breath, and very tentatively squeezed past the back of the chair.

Her heartbeat increased as she went across the landing, sensing that maybe she should take this chance to run away. But then suddenly she was overwhelmed with the realisation that her attacker might be out there waiting for her to make a wrong move, at a time when she'd be on her own – the perfect time to seize her again.

All these frightening thoughts caused her to panic, and wiping a tear away with the sleeve of her dressing gown, she could see her freedom slipping away. She thought about what the future held for her, as she walked downstairs - only more misery with her parents, who would stop at nothing to get her to do what they wanted.

This expensive therapist was the latest thing. If they thought she was going to let the man brainwash her into doing as he asked, they were wrong. Well, she wouldn't even look at him let alone talk to him. For Donna, this was the last straw. Maybe shaving her hair off was dramatic, but now they were in for an even bigger shock. Something spectacular that would make them sit up and take notice.

From the hall, she made her way towards the kitchen. Went inside, closed the door quietly, switched on the light, and walked over to the draws and cupboards. She knew exactly what she was after, and opening the top draw to the right of the sink, found the kitchen utensils and cutlery.

Donna took a few of the knives out of the draw and went to the living room. Sitting down on the sofa with them, she stared at each one, from the small paring knife, to the steak knife, then the bread knife and finally a carving knife. She tested each for its degree of sharpness. The two small knives weren't very sharp at all, but the carving knife and the bread knife were razor sharp, capable of slicing through muscle, skin and maybe even bone with the utmost of ease.

Donna shut her eyes for a few seconds, concentrating, trying to imagine what it would be like. Of course, extremely painful, but perhaps a pain she could stand? And what about the blood? Would there be lots? That depended on the part of the body selected. She wasn't sure of the answers to these questions, but there was only one way to find out.

She gripped the handle of the carving knife very tightly, then keeping her eyes rigidly shut, and clenching her teeth, she dragged the knife across her wrist. She was frightened of the pain, but the torment she'd gone through these past few weeks had to be worse. Holding her breath, and creasing up her face, she dug in as deep as she could with the knife, and then changing hands, she slashed into the other wrist as hard as she was able. The pain was excruciating, much worse than she'd expected. The initial unbearable pain passed, but the throbbing in her wrists intensified, and holding up her arms she felt the blood oozing out of the wounds and trickling down. This was the only way out. From now on life would be unbearable, and with nowhere else to go, and no job or money there seemed no alternative.

It was a struggle to get up from the settee, and she staggered towards the bookcase to steady herself, only she overbalanced and pulled it down to the ground with a crash.

She lay lifeless on the floor, sobbing to herself, when the living room door flew open. There looking up, she saw her parents standing before her, eyes agog with disbelief and shock.

Donna drifted in and out of consciousness, aware that her father cradling her in his arms, while her mother spoke frantically on the phone. Before long darkness overwhelmed her.

◇◇◇

Donna's eyes fluttered open. She had a sense of being in a bed, in a white room with a window to the left of her. After looking around, she became aware of her arms, which were throbbing unmercifully, then saw the bandages around each wrist – the result of her own actions. And as the memories came flooding back, she realised all her efforts had been in vain. She hadn't achieved her goal – if that was indeed what she wanted - she didn't really know herself. Again, she closed her eyes, before the sound of someone's voice abruptly woke her.

'Donna,' a female voice whispered in a nervous tone.

'Are you all right love?' a male voice asked.

Donna opened her eyes to see her mum and dad, sitting at the side of the bed, their faces white with shock and worry. At once, she looked away from them and began to cry.

'Please go away, leave me alone. Haven't you done enough?' She wept.

'Donna, can't you tell us why you did this,' her dad said.

'Were we really so bad to you, that you had to resort to such an extreme measure?' her mother asked. 'Whatever we did, we did in your best interests. You can't blame us for that, surely.'

She continued to sob quietly. 'I just want to...I don't want to live anymore.'

'You won't be allowed to hurt yourself again,' her father told her.

'No, no, no,' she whimpered, wanting to bang her fists against the mattress, but she could barely lift them.

Within two or three minutes, this caused a nurse to come into the room, followed by a doctor, and seeing the patient's distressed state looked towards her parents.

'Please Mr and Mrs Askey, try not to upset her. She's being watched twenty-four hours a day. There's no chance of her coming to any harm.'

'I can't understand why she's behaving like this, doctor.' Her dad shook his head aimlessly. 'What's wrong with her?'

'You only care... about money,' Donna said.

'That's not true Donna, and you know it. All your father and I have ever wanted is to help you get well again after your terrible attack. We thought modelling was the best way to do that, and would help take your mind off it.'

Donna gave a little shake of her head. Tiredness overwhelmed her, but also she was very frightened and confused. All she wanted was some peace.

'It's all right Donna,' the doctor assured her. 'No one's going to force you to do anything – you're safe here. No need to be frightened any more. We're here to make you better – and that's all. There's no reason for you to hurt yourself again – and waste such a precious young life. Rest assured all of us, your parents included will be working very hard to help you recover.'

'That's right Donna. We're all rooting for you,' her mum said with tears in her eyes. 'And we don't care what job you do even if it's not modelling.'

'I don't believe that.'

'It's true what your mum says. We're devastated over what's happened to you during the last few months.'

'Too late for that now.'

'But…' Donna's mum protested bending over to take hold of her arm, but her husband gently pulled her away.

'Sorry Mr and Mrs Askey, but it's best if you leave now. She's getting distressed again.'

Donna saw them look at each other, and act as if they didn't want to go, but they had to.

After kissing her brow, and promising to visit again, her parents reluctantly said goodbye. Donna's stomach turned over once they'd gone, making her feel very lonely here in the hospital. The nurses constantly smiled at her, trying to put her at ease, but that didn't help.

And then to top it all, when she looked up at the ceiling, she noticed what looked like a camera in the ceiling. With shock, she turned her head away, the idea of being scrutinised filled her with loathing.

She wondered what these people made of her, seeing her head devoid of hair, and knowing she'd tried to take her own life. Was she a head case for wanting to do this? And how she'd gone about it was one of the worst possible ways. Maybe other people would have coped better than her following the attack, but they'd probably have had the support of their family and friends – wouldn't they? Whereas she had no one. She was still alive, but had no idea where this left her.

Chapter 13

THREE DAYS LATER AT ELEVEN O' CLOCK IN THE MORNING, DONNA SAT IN A DIMLY LIT OFFICE OPPOSITE DOCTOR REYNOLDS, THE PSYCHIATRIST ASSIGNED TO HER. A woman with short grey hair, who appeared to be of small build, probably in her late fifties; she was studying a file, no doubt Donna's case history, and every now and then glanced up.

Donna sat quietly waiting for the doctor to speak and noticed how plain and unattractive the GP looked, obviously a spinster married to her job, but then saw a wedding ring on her finger, indicating someone must have found her worthy.

The longer the silence continued the more uncomfortable Donna became, she began to shift uneasily in her seat and wondered what the doctor was going to say.

When the doctor finally spoke, her voice was deep and soothing almost bordering on masculine for such a small woman.

'So Donna, how are you after your little ordeal?' A faint smile came on her face.

'I'm all right.' Was the reply in a very off-hand way.

'I see your wrists are starting to heal up nicely.' She raised her eyebrows above the gold-rimmed spectacles she was wearing.

Donna looked at her wrists. The bandages were gone, and soon the scabs would start to come off. 'Yes, thank you.' She nervously touched the top of her head. Her hair was slowly starting to grow back as well, although she still looked a little like someone out of a sci-fi movie.

'Glad to see your hair is getting back in shape too. Whatever made you decide to shave it all off, my dear?'

A giggle came from behind her hand at this. 'I don't know - I wanted to see how I would look.'

'You sure that's the only reason?'

'Maybe, although I might have been trying to get back at mum and dad. I got sick of them telling me how pretty I am. When they saw the new me, they weren't amused.'

'There's nothing wrong with being told how attractive you are. Most people would love to be complimented like that.'

'They wouldn't if they heard it time and time again, non-stop. In the end I couldn't listen to it any longer.'

'Do you know why you cut your wrists? Was it a cry for help or did you really intend killing yourself?'

'How the hell should I know? They got on my nerves that much over me shaving my hair off, and then wouldn't let me out of their sight. So when I got the chance I decided to show them exactly what I could do, if I wanted.'

'I see,' the doctor said, sitting back in her chair, obviously pondering over what she had to deal with here. 'I imagine this must be connected to when you were attacked and raped. Is that correct?'

Donna shrugged her shoulders, but was unable to look the doctor in the eye. Colour began to rise on her cheeks.

'I gather ever since then you've struggled to cope with life. I hear you broke up with your boyfriend and have had to give up your job as well.'

'Been talking to mommy and daddy, I see?'

'Yes, of course I have. They're extremely worried over you, Donna.'

'Only because of the money.'

'Money?'

'The money they'd make out of me as a model. But I won't do it, not now not ever. Did they tell you about the photo shoot they tried to force me into?'

'No they didn't.'

'Well, they secretly arranged for us to bump into old friends of theirs, who just happen to be in the fashion business. They'd already set up a photo shoot with a top photographer behind my back. I couldn't understand why they'd do that.'

'Well, we need to talk about how to rebuild your life, but I agree they should have asked you first, in fact no one should be forced into doing something they don't want to do.'

'I don't know if I'll ever be able to go back to work or have a relationship with anyone – because the thought of someone touching me disgusts me. I wish I didn't have to wake up in the morning, and I wish there was somewhere I could go to get rid of these horrible feelings.' Tears trickled down her cheeks once more.

'There is nowhere like that, my dear. You have so much to be grateful for, lots to look forward to, and most of your life is still ahead of you. How terribly sad it would be, if you'd succeeded in ending it all.'

The doctor seemed genuine, but she had no chance of making Donna feel any better. She could pump her with more pills and give her as much counselling as she liked, but it wouldn't make a heap of difference.

'I don't want to keep being like this. If this is it, there's no point in living. I feel worthless. I wish that man had killed me, because this is a living death.' She sniffed back more tears.

'You must stop thinking so negatively. I admit, it will be difficult, but I'm sure you have the strength of character to get over this. You need to be shown certain techniques, about thinking positively, and of having the correct perception of what people think of you. There are several one to one therapy sessions we can go through over the next few weeks.'

Donna shook her head, wringing her hands together, frightened of what this woman had planned for her.

'No need to panic my dear, there's no one behind you with a whip, ordering you about. But if you don't do something to help yourself, you'll never get any better.'

'I wish I was someone else, leading an ordinary life.'

'How can you say that? You should be grateful for what you're blessed with. When I think of all the people in the world worse off than you, those horrible deformed bodies, people stricken with cancer and other terrible illnesses.'

'You think so. That's all right for you to say, but if I'd been an ordinary girl that man would never have raped me. My mum and dad wouldn't have tried to force me to be a model either, and I wouldn't have been harassed by so many horrible men.'

'Not only that, but you've very intelligent with it. A first class honours degree in Mathematics is a fantastic achievement.'

'Yes, but where has it got me?'

'It can still get you anywhere you want. It's up to you, my dear.'

'It's up to me, is it? Try telling that to my parents. Well, I intend doing what I want in the future, without any interference from them.'

'Perhaps they were only trying to help.'

Donna had had enough of this. She didn't want to listen to this doctor who seemed to sound just like her mother. Scraping the chair across the floor, she got up from her seat.

'I want out of here. I'm not staying any longer.'

'Donna, listen to me. We can't let you out, not until you're well again. You're a danger to yourself in your present state of mind.'

Donna saw red. This was her life, she would do whatever she wished, and no one could stop her. The doctor remained in her chair, a dour expression on her face, and as Donna opened the door, she was confronted by two male nurses, who quickly restrained her by grabbing hold of her arms. She felt at their mercy, as she had been with the rapist, unable to move. Terror swept over her.

'Let me go!' she screamed wriggling about with all the strength she could muster, but they were much too strong for her. 'Bastards – all of you.'

'Donna, I'm sorry to have to tell you this, but you're to be taken to a different hospital that specialises in cases like yours. There you'll get all the care and attention you need. Having tried to commit suicide once, we'd be failing in our duty of care, if we allowed you to leave, and you subsequently tried to kill yourself again and died. You'll be under strict supervision at all times, but once you start to recover from your illness, you will of course be given more freedom.'

'Call yourself a doctor – you can go to hell! I'm not a loony!' Donna screamed at the top of her voice.

At this Doctor Reynolds actually winced, as the two male nurses took her away. She wondered if her parents knew what was going on, or if they'd instigated this. There was no way of knowing. She felt like a criminal as they escorted her to the ambulance.

'Come along now, love,' one of the nurses said. 'You'll be much happier where you're going. It's like a holiday camp with all mod cons, so you can't help but get better. No need to worry – you'll be out of there in no time at all.'

'Oh sure I will,' she replied ironically getting into the back of the ambulance, fearing once they got her into this hospital, she'd never come out.

A female nurse travelled with her; she constantly smiled and acted at being pleasant. But what good was that Donna thought, agonising over what was to come.

Fifteen minutes later, the ambulance stopped. The driver got out and walked round to open the back doors. It seemed they had arrived at their destination.

Peering outside, she was stunned to see a sign in front of the building 'Grangemore Manor Asylum'. Immediately she shuddered, as this seemed to be a place for the mentally insane, and the idea of being classed as a 'lunatic' scared her to death.

Getting out of the vehicle, she stepped onto the gravel driveway leading up to what appeared to be the front entrance to the hospital. A red-bricked building resembling an old Georgian country house, the sort that had once belonged to titled gentry in a time long gone. This became more apparent when they walked over the large patterned tiled floor in the hallway.

She was taken down a long corridor to Room twenty-two. The nurse accompanying her opened the door and allowed her to go in.

'All right Donna; this will be your home for the foreseeable future. As you can see, it's very comfortable. You have a television, your own private bathroom, a DVD player, access to books, music CD's and so on. There's even a little fridge where you can keep certain foodstuffs. You'll have access to all the facilities here, including a swimming pool, gym, a TV room and a cafeteria.'

Donna shrugged her shoulders, feeling as if she was in a prison, and in all but name she was.

'And there's a large wardrobe for you. We'll have some of your clothes brought over, although, all being well you shouldn't need too many. Hopefully you'll only be here for a short while.'

Donna didn't take much notice of what was said. She meekly went into her room with her meagre belongings. Put them on the bed, sat down and looked up at the nurse.

'Of course, you'll be under supervision around the clock, and although you'll have the run of the place, the main Hospital entrance and exits are locked at night. That's for your own safety and of course we don't want you running out on us, now do we?' Now if there's anything you need, just ring the bell by the side of your bed and someone will attend to you - see you later,' the nurse smiled.

Donna didn't even acknowledge her - as the door closed she was glad the woman had gone.

The room itself was plain but comfortable, but seeing the bars at the window, brought a tiny flutter to her stomach. Even more so when she noticed a small bulb like object in the corner of the ceiling peering down at her; perhaps again like the hospital she'd just come from, this was a camera, she couldn't be sure. It came as a shock to her, but maybe it was to be expected after what she'd done.

She got up and walked across to the bathroom, which on inspection seemed the only place affording any privacy - although surprisingly there was no lock on the door. She shook her head and walked back into the other room. Looking up at the camera or whatever it was, she could have sworn it was moving, watching in case she... just what did they think she'd do? How on earth had her life come to this? She didn't know.

This was unbelievable. She'd only been there a few minutes and already she felt they were spying on her. She felt so mad, banged her fists down on the bed, lay down on her stomach, and cried in sheer frustration, wondering what was coming next – and if there could be anything worse. If there was a way to end it all, she would have – but in this room and place, it seemed impossible.

She hated the feeling of being penned up, it only added to the sensation of fear, which always seemed to be with her.

'Please God, let me out of here,' she begged but it appeared no one was listening to her pleas.

Eventually, she stopped crying, realising this wasn't helping her predicament. She turned onto her side, closed her eyes and pulled an arm up to cover her face. If only this relentless anxiety would leave her. But it seemed this would never happen. All she could do was to lie there and let time pass, in an effort to calm herself down and perhaps go to sleep. However, sleep wouldn't come.

Unaware of what time it was, although daylight remained, she jumped slightly at the sound of someone opening the door. A very serious looking Doctor Reynolds came in without knocking; she gave a slight hint of a smile in her patient's direction. After closing the door she sat down on the bed, smoothing down her skirt.

'Hallo Donna. How are you feeling? Have you managed to rest?'

'Yeah, I suppose.' She spoke solemnly.

'And how do you like it here? Think you'll be able to settle in all right?'

'Haven't got much choice, have I?' This patronising woman was beginning to irritate her, almost as much as her parents had.

'Come on, I'll take you out for an hour. Seeing as it's after teatime, I imagine you must be hungry. We'll go down to the canteen, and get you a decent meal, as good as anything in a restaurant - and for you it's free. They're doing Shepherd's Pie followed by Apple Crumble, which I'm told you like as well.'

'Oh really - well I'm not hungry,' Donna retorted cutting her eyes at the doctor. If they thought she was going to make it easy for them then they could think again. She was going to stage a protest any way she knew how and not eating seemed to fit the bill! After all it had worked in the past when she was a teenager and wanted to avoid posing as a beauty queen. But eventually she had given in to her cravings for food. Perhaps this time she was made of sterner stuff.

'It's no good being like that - not eating won't help you get better. Be a shame to let the meal go to waste, after all the trouble we've gone to -'

'Well, I never asked anyone to cook me anything.'

'Come along.' She beckoned with her arm. 'Once you've got a good meal inside you, you'll feel a whole lot better.'

'I don't think so.' Donna shook her head and pulled a face.

'OK, it's up to you. I'm hungry myself, so you'll just have to watch me instead, won't you? But you can always change your mind, any time you want.'

Donna stayed put while Doctor Reynolds got to her feet and stood there waiting for some response from her patient.

'You know I could have a couple of nurses bring you down to the canteen with me, so I'd advise you to come quietly.'

'This is like being in fucking Wormwood Scrubs,' she complained getting up slowly. Doctor Reynolds opened the door, allowing her patient to strut out, head held high. The doctor struggled to keep up with her, which Donna guessed she didn't like.

They walked down a corridor, past other rooms from where strange noises and cries could be heard. At the end of the corridor were double doors, which the doctor pushed open – obviously the dining room which contained about a dozen tables each with four chairs. It was completely empty, save for one lady wearing a white uniform at the counter waiting to serve the food.

The doctor picked up a tray, and encouraged Donna to do the same, but she shook her head, mouthing – no! Ignoring this gesture, Doctor Reynolds went on to ask the kitchen assistant for a portion of chips, baked beans, a Shepherd's Pie, and a cup of coffee.

'Sure you won't have anything?' She said over her shoulder to Donna, sitting at a table a few feet away, sulking.

'No, thank you.' However, she found the mouth-watering aromas of the kitchen almost impossible to resist. Even more so when the doctor came back to sit opposite her. Donna just rivalled her nose up at the food, but couldn't help looking at the doctor.

'Sure you don't want something to eat?' she said chewing her food slowly before moving on to the next bit.

'I already told you I'm not hungry. Why don't you listen to me? Like I said before, you're just like my mum and dad. No wonder I freaked out.'

'I promise, I'll always listen to you, that's my job. It's what I'm paid for. To hear every word you say, because I need to understand your condition in order to help you get well again.'

Donna felt uncomfortable sitting there in front of the doctor and wanted to go back to her room.

Doctor Reynolds finished her meal and drank her coffee before sitting back in her chair. 'That was very nice. I think you find the food here is really excellent.'

'I bet it is. I'm just not hungry – how many times do I have to repeat myself? And besides it doesn't matter how good the food is, it's not going to make me like it here – is it?'

The doctor dabbed her mouth with her serviette. 'Look, if you want to take that attitude – fine. But you're going to have to accept you'll be here until you can convince us you won't try to harm yourself again. You need to have a good hard look at yourself, and think about how lucky you are compared with a lot of people. Ok, I realise you've been through a harrowing experience, but you can recover from it if you really want to. The choice is yours.'

'Can I go back to my room now?'

'If that's what you want. It's nice to get out though, isn't it? Just think if you co-operate and try to get yourself well again, there may be lots more trips like these. In fact I could even extend them in time.'

Donna gave her a sickly smile as they made their way out of the canteen. Walking back down the corridor together, Donna realised she could have made a run for it, but quickly dismissed this notion - it felt so cold and she had nowhere to go once she was outside anyway.

'We're going to have lots of talks, you and I. I really want to get to the root of your problems, and with your co-operation hopefully, I'll get you out of here a lot sooner than you think. However, I can only guide you - in the end you have to do this yourself.'

Donna didn't care what happened. She just existed from hour to hour. What did it matter anymore? Her parents were behind this, she was sure of it; and had known it right from the start. This was just a ploy to get her back into modelling, but it would never come off. The trouble now was her pangs of hunger were getting worse. Her willpower wouldn't last much longer, but if she succumbed, Doctor Reynolds would consider it a small victory.

They arrived at Donna's room. 'Ahh, well here we are again. Nice rooms, aren't they? I said they were very comfortable, didn't I?' Doctor Reynolds said as she opened the door. 'Oh by the way, I took the liberty of getting some sandwiches brought up for you, in case you get peckish in the night. You take care now.'

Donna pulled a face just as the doctor closed the door and left her to it. The sandwiches, on a plate by her bed, looked very appetising. She closed her eyes, realising just how hungry she was, and wished she could have thrown the sandwiches on the floor, but instead grabbed them and ate them hungrily as if she hadn't eaten for a week. Then went to the bathroom sink and drank water greedily by cupping her hands.

Later when she went to bed she felt a failure, and cried herself to sleep. Her instinct to survive had driven her to give in to her cravings for food.

The next morning, Donna pretended to be asleep, when the door to her room opened, and the doctor entered coughing loudly. She gently shook Donna by the arm, and called her name. On opening her eyes, she noticed the smugness on the doctor's face and guessed she must have seen the empty plate.

'Glad you've finally seen sense.'

Donna said nothing, but instead stared up at the ceiling feeling ashamed of her lack of control.

'This is the first step, you know.'

'Oh yeah, tell me about it.'

'The tablets and my therapy will only work if you look after yourself. By this I mean you should eat well, exercise lots and take enough rest and sleep which will in turn lead to a healthier body and mind. Obviously, there will still be many obstacles to overcome, but once you start to take care of yourself properly, I'll feel much more positive about your recovery.'

Donna felt so despondent, and was powerless to do anything about it. And as if to rub salt in her wounds, the doctor looked so pleased with herself; so certain she could help in the recovery process, now that Donna had given in to living again. Maybe it was best to let the woman think that. But she'd only have to drop her guard for a minute, and Donna would set about doing something even more dramatic. And how would the good doctor feel then?

Chapter 14

SLOWLY, DONNA GOT USED TO THE ROUTINE OF HER EXISTENCE IN THE HOSPITAL. But she hated the intrusion into her privacy, and felt it was a case of big brother gone mad, watching her every move. All right, she deserved to be on suicide watch, but resented constantly being monitored, and was so frustrated she couldn't do anything to stop it. Maybe if she tried to act normally, they would relax their restrictions on her, but as of yet there was no sign of that.

Doctor Reynolds seemed pleased with her progress, as following this first concession, Donna ate well, did whatever was asked of her and acted like a model patient. As her hair grew back, they encouraged her to take more pride in her appearance. She had her hair cut fashionably once it was long enough, and wore make up and clothes that were modern. Donna guessed the doctor was keeping her parents informed about the good progress she was supposedly making during their weekly confabs – but what would they say if they knew what was really going on inside her head? They'd be so shocked. Well, they were never going to find out.

Gradually with more progress came more freedom. She was allowed to walk through the Hospital grounds as well as being given the run of the Hospital itself, as long as a member of staff accompanied her. She ate with other patients and staff, and was even visited by her parents on occasions, an ordeal she got through but could have done without. All Doctor Reynolds insisted on was confinement to her room every evening. However, they told her, should her recovery continue, that too may be relaxed.

In truth, Donna didn't feel any better. Her mood was lower than ever - she suffered from palpitations at night, and yearned for the opportunity to either break free or find some other release.

As the weeks passed she was allowed time in the garden alone for longer and longer periods - it wouldn't be long before an opportunity would come.

<><><>

It was a particularly beautiful hot summer's day in the middle of June, the sky clear, but a slight breeze cooled the temperatures.

She sat on a bench immediately outside the main building. The wind blew through her short pixie style hair, her pose stiff, the expression on her face bland and lacking emotion. The weather caused her to reminisce of times long gone, spent with Blake and friends, when her life had been simple and carefree; a time when harming herself had never entered her head.

Having had permission to stay in the garden for an hour, she knew they wouldn't come to fetch her yet a while. So after a short time, with no exact plan in mind, she went back inside – then she'd just go where her feet took her.

On entering the building, she walked through the reception area amongst patients and staff, some of whom openly acknowledged her with smiles and words, never giving her a thought as they were used to seeing her around.

That first bit had been easy, it gave her greater confidence. She smiled to herself, breathing in deeply as she continued on her way.

Adrenaline pumped through her veins; her hands were shaking slightly, and felt hot and clammy. Could she actually go through with this? With her desire so great, she guessed she could. And the release from life would be so wonderful and pure – the best feeling in the world.

She walked down a corridor past various rooms until she came to the lift. Pressed the button to call for it and within a couple of minutes the door pinged open. To her relief, when two nurses got out, the lift was empty. Once inside, as the doors shut, she selected button four for the top floor and waited for the lift to reach its destination.

The lift clicked at the fourth floor, and the doors opened. Donna got out immediately and after about twenty paces noticed a doorway to the left marked Staff Only. Trying the handle she was surprised to find it was open. It led to a dimly lit hallway, at the end of which was a flight of stairs. Her heart was thumping in her chest as she hastily climbed the stairs, where at the top was another door. As she tentatively opened it she was confronted with what must be the air conditioning area. Huge fans hummed away, and large silver coloured metal ducts stuck out, their purpose she couldn't fathom. There was another door directly in front of her, which she guessed had to lead outside. Walking towards it, she felt pleased no one was about or had tried to stop her.

The door creaked slightly as she turned the handle, but to her amazement, it opened. As the bright sunshine hit her full in the face she screwed up her eyes. Bowing her head, she stepped out onto the flat roof, where going round its perimeter was a metal rail about four feet high.

Walking over to the railings she took in the views from this height. The grey buildings of Dexford town stood in front, and in the distance was an impressive view of green hilly countryside which also skirted the town. Everything looked so different from up here, she'd never realised there were so many trees or how beautiful the landscape was.

Touching the rail she was surprised to find how hot the sun had made it. As she pulled her hand away she laughed. It made her feel dizzy and light-headed, as if nothing else mattered.

Glancing down, seeing the figures below going about their daily business, unaware of her intentions, she wondered what sort of lives they led. Nothing like the life she was forced to suffer and was destined to endure forever - unless she did something about it?

Peering at the rail, she spat on part of it to make sure it wasn't too hot, then wiped it with her sleeve. She raised herself up and over the rail to sit on it, her feet dangling, and hands gripping tightly.

Could anyone down there see her, she wondered? Maybe she should try to attract their attention, and raising her hand shouted loudly, 'Hey, you lot down there!'

Within a few seconds, several figures lifted their heads to look up. Donna was able to see the shocked frightened looks on their faces as they gathered in small groups. It reminded her of the audiences she used to hate facing during her modelling days. Well, maybe this time she wanted them all to see her most dramatic performance.

Then hearing all those people shouting up to her, she took a deep breath, and hanging on to the rail, stood up unsure of what she wanted to do. In that spit-second she heard her name being called. 'Donna.' It was a whisper of a voice.

She turned her head to see a young man with short jet-black hair, and the blue shadow of a beard on his face. He wore a white top and pants, which made her realise at once that he was a member of staff.

'Piss off - and leave me alone,' she screamed at him, flecks of spit coming out of her mouth in her passion.

'Donna, I want to help you. I know what you're thinking about doing, but believe me you couldn't be more wrong. For a girl like you, it would be tragic. And for what? Nobody's worth dying for, babe.'

'How do you know my name?' she shouted.

'I've seen you about. People have mentioned you.'

'I don't want to live. You don't understand.'

'Look, everybody feels like that at some time in their lives. But that doesn't mean we have to do something about it. We get help and somehow get through it. This won't solve anything, except to cause grief and pain to the loved ones you'd leave behind. Is that what you really want?'

'No one cares about me.'

'How can you say that? There's no way that's true.'

'It is,' she insisted, her eyes widening with anger.

'Well, I care about you for a start. Think I'd be up here talking to you if I didn't? How's it going to make me feel if you jump and splatter yourself all over the pavement like a bag of squashed tomatoes? I'd have nightmares about it for years to come, and so would a lot of those people down there watching you. You want to do that to people who've never done you any harm?'

'You don't know what happened to me.'

'You're right I don't. But you're not on your own, you know. Other people go through hell; yet somehow they come out the other side. There are millions of folks worse off than you - you haven't got the faintest idea. Tell you what I'll do, since you're that keen to jump, why not let me do it instead? See how you like it.' And with that, quick as a flash, he whisked himself over the rail to sit on it a few feet away from her, the same as she had.

Donna was horrified, her heart jumped, her eyes wild and threatening.

'Don't you dare come any closer, or I swear I'll...'she said raising up her hand to stop him.

'Don't worry; I'm not coming any closer. But I might just jump off myself. Then you can look at me down there dead. Fancy that, would you?' He was breathing in and out deeply, sweat dripped off the end of his nose.

Donna suddenly didn't know what to think. He was bluffing – wasn't he?

'I mean it, babe.' He let go of the rail, balanced himself with his arms outstretched, then stood up, leaning back against the rail. As the breeze stiffened, he wavered slightly.

'Please no. Don't do it!' She stared at him in disbelief.

'Well, get back over the rail then, before I fall.'

'All right, all right,' she scowled, climbing quickly over to the other side of the rail. But then once she was safe, he stumbled. She gasped with shock unable to move, transfixed by the situation as now the tables had turned. His one hand had just about managed to grab the rail in time. As she looked on, his teeth were clenched; it took all his strength to move his other hand back onto the rail, and pull himself back up onto the ledge. Then having rested for a few seconds, he climbed back over to where Donna was standing.

His breathing was deep and rapid, and he was visibly shaking, eyes fixed on Donna, clearly thinking about their dice with death. As she came to her senses the shame of it tormented her, and if he'd fallen, oh my God that would have been on her conscience forever. It just didn't bear thinking about.

'I'm so sorry,' she said simply, unable to look him straight in the eye.

'It's all right. My own fault. I've always been too clumsy for my own good. The main thing is that I managed to stop you from jumping - thank goodness.'

'You were very brave,' she said feeling the colour coming back to her face.

'Stupid, more like.'

'You saved my life.'

'Maybe, maybe not. You didn't want to jump anyway; or you would have already done it, whether I'd been there or not. Like most people who find life hard to cope with, this was just a cry for help.'

'You think so?' She took in a deep breath as her anger rose again.

'I certainly do.'

'So you're an expert on these sort of matters, are you?'

'Let's just say, you're not the first suicide attempt I've come across in this place. I've seen the successful attempts and the unsuccessful attempts, and I'm telling you; you don't want to hear about the unsuccessful attempts; and how it left them. They all wished they hadn't done it. Thank God I got you to pull out at the last minute.'

She felt uncomfortable all of a sudden.

'Come on, let's get you inside. You're soaked with sweat, and you need a change of clothing.' He guided her towards the door, his left arm draped around her shoulder. They went into the room containing the air conditioning apparatus.

Donna walked with the young man, who appeared to be limping slightly, and wondered if he'd just hurt himself, but was afraid to ask in case she'd been the cause of it, amongst other things.

'I'm Evan by the way,' he said introducing himself, giving her a warm smile. His light-blue eyes, reminiscent of Paul Newman, the actor, lit up. She quivered a little.

'Are you Welsh, Evan?'

'I don't know, maybe there was a link a long time ago. It was my dad's name. These days my family are all Dexford born and bred.'

'And what else do you do here besides saving potential suicides?'

'I'm a male nurse, and I'm so glad I was in the right place at the right time.'

'That's not very butch.' She grimaced as he pressed the button for the lift.

'Maybe not, but it's a very satisfying job, even if it is a bit hair-raising at times.'

The lift door opened. They got in.

She smiled.

'Feel a bit better now?'

'You mean will I pull another stunt like that again? Don't know. All I do know is that now I'll be on suicide watch again. Back to square one.'

When the lift reached the ground floor, the door opened to Doctor Reynolds and two nurses, who were waiting to take her patient off Evan's hands. Donna glanced at Evan. He seemed nice she thought, but what did that matter, since all she had to look forward to now was withdrawn privileges and more supervision of her activities. He guided her out of the lift towards Doctor Reynolds who looked so relieved to see her back safely. Donna knew if she had jumped, the blame would have been put squarely on the doctor's shoulders for allowing her too much freedom before she was ready.

Evan waved as he left to carry on with his own duties, which she'd so rudely interrupted.

'Donna – why on earth did you do this? After all your treatment has been going so well' Doctor Reynolds asked, taking hold of her arm.

'I don't know, do I?'

They walked quietly down the corridor until they reached Donna's room. Once inside the doctor sat on a chair beside her bed.

'I can't understand why you did it? Your progress has been really good, and I was so optimistic about discharging you into your parents care for a short while very soon. But now you've thrown away all the good work by this stupid stunt. Words fail me,' She stared straight at Donna waiting for a reply.

'Don't know why I did it. I didn't feel very well and when I was on the roof, I felt as free as a bird, without a care in the world. I know I've had a lot of help from you and your staff, but I don't seem to be able to get on with my life, and I find it hard to know where to start.'

'Well, you won't do it by carrying on like this. Don't you realise we had to bring you here for your own safety. You were a danger to yourself, and it seems to me, you still are. Anyone would think you wanted to stay here. Why if young Evan hadn't been there to stop you, you might not be alive now.'

'I know that. I didn't expect him to do what he did. And I didn't want him to be hurt on account of me.'

'He was very brave. I saw what he did up there. Saved you without any regard to himself. You should be very grateful. My heart was in my mouth when he slipped and nearly fell off.'

Donna's shoulders sagged and as she thought about what might have happened to Evan, her stomach turned over.

'He made me see I was wrong, that to die that way or be seriously injured would have been horrendous.'

'I agree. I've seen the end products of some of these suicide attempts and believe me you never forget the horror of it. I'd have hated you to end up like that. And imagine how your parents would have felt, and everyone else here at the Hospital.'

Donna shut her eyes, frowning deeply at her own stupidity. Now it would be forever before they allowed her out on her own again. She almost wished she'd gone through with it, until she thought back to what Evan had said.

'I'm all right now doctor, no need to worry over me. I've learnt my lesson, I'll never do anything like it again – I promise.' She turned to face the doctor, pleading with her, hoping not to be treated as she was when she'd first come into the Hospital.

'No, I'm sorry but we can't trust you at the moment. But you can earn that trust back, make a real effort to get yourself well again, then who knows what might happen.' The Doctor squeezed her arm reassuringly as if to let her know she wasn't completely shutting the door in her face.

'It's incredibly hard. I feel so sad and lonely most of the time – and I don't know how to get myself out of it.'

'Nobody ever said it was going to be easy. There are so few people of your own age here, which makes it all the more difficult. But maybe you should try to get involved more, join in with some of the activities even if the people are a bit older than you.'

'Don't know about that. I'm not very good company these days. They'd soon get bored with me.'

'Well, maybe they will, maybe they won't. But unless you try, you'll never know –will you?'

Donna conceded Doctor Reynolds had a point. But really, she had no interest in any of the other head cases residing here. Even though she was probably one of them herself. Only one person came to mind. And that was Evan. She'd noticed that he was quite good looking in a rough sort of way. Yet she feared him too, as she did all the other members of the male population. But surely, he couldn't be all bad, not after what he'd just done to save her life. He wouldn't harm her – it wouldn't make sense.

Much later that night lying awake in bed she thought about Evan, remembering what he'd done for her. There was something different about him, that made him a cut above all the other people she'd met recently. Maybe it wouldn't hurt if he wanted to get to know her a little better, just so she had someone to talk to. They seemed on the same wave length, roughly the same age and maybe he might understand some of what she'd gone through.

He had a nice boyish smile that was kind of cheeky. And his light blue eyes looked genuinely caring. She felt strangely drawn to him and that concerned her. Part of her hoped he'd stay away, but the other part wanted to see him again. Surely, it couldn't be just gratitude that made her like him.

She found it strange that he was a male nurse – to look at him he didn't seem the type. Yet to be able to trust a man again, would be a great achievement in itself.

Chapter 15

THE NEXT DAY DONNA SAT OPPOSITE DOCTOR REYNOLDS IN HER OFFICE, DREADING WHAT WAS TO COME. It was inevitable really.

'I'm sorry Donna, but obviously you won't be allowed to go on any more unsupervised trips for the time being.'

Her mouth dropped open. 'What if I promise not to do anything like it again?'

Shaking her head the doctor replied, 'Sorry, but that's not good enough. You tried to hoodwink us once already, and it almost worked. From now on we'll have to watch you more closely, and you'll only be able to go out when you're accompanied by someone else.'

Donna pulled a face. Maybe she'd made a mistake to attempt suicide on the roof of the building. Or then again maybe she should have gone through with it. Damn Evan, she thought to herself. He'd convinced her there was always hope – but now she doubted his words, as she realised what sort of life they'd force her to lead.

Back in her room, she spent the rest of the morning reading a book by Wilbur Smith, an African adventure and surprised herself by being able to stick with it. After lunch, she watched an old film on the television, a western starring Kirk Douglas.

Later, she had her usual hour-long therapy session with Doctor Reynolds, trying to lecture her on the meaning of life and ways of lifting her self-esteem. She understood the principles of positive thinking and of trying to suppress negative thoughts, but theory was all very well; putting this into practice was another thing altogether. Towards the end of the session Donna's mind began to waiver, which the doctor seemed to pick up on, as she ended the interview prematurely much to her patient's relief.

For most of the rest of the day, Donna couldn't stop thinking about Evan. In fact she had to concede to herself that she found him attractive, and that frightened her. What if he started to like her too? But surely that would never happen. He was probably married with children, or had a steady girlfriend. It wouldn't even cross his mind.

Suddenly while she lay on her bed trying to read, out of the corner of her eye she noticed someone standing in the doorway. It was Evan. He wore a long coat over jeans and blue tee shirt - obviously off duty. He was smiling, and looked genuinely curious at what she was doing.

'Hi-ya,' he began. 'Just thought I'd come to see how you are.'

'Oh, thanks,' she said stiffening slightly, feeling herself blush which was embarrassing and annoying.

'All right if I come in for a couple of minutes?'

'Yes, so long as it is only for a few minutes. I'm tired and I need to rest. But sit down if you want.' She pointed to the end of the bed.

He seemed uncomfortable as he sat there, looking tongue-tied. It appeared it would be up to her to break the ice.

'Busy day?' she asked him.

'Yeah, a bit. You know what it's like.'

'Can't be very pleasant having to deal with all the nut cases in here – people like me.' Donna was unable to look him in the eye, and wished her blushing would subside.

'They're not all nut cases. Just ordinary people like yourself, who are ill and need help. Mind you, it can be pretty scary at times, especially when they try to throw themselves off the top of a building.' He took in a deep breath.

'Talking about me again, are you?'

'Sure I am. But you're not the only one. It's amazing what lengths some folks will go to. You never get used to it, you know. You grow hardened to it, but it doesn't get any easier.'

'I can well imagine.' She visualised a scene of herself being in a room of mentally-ill people, but somehow didn't class herself as one of them. 'I could never do what you do. Even the smell of disinfectant makes me feel sick.'

He laughed revealing a perfect set of white teeth. 'You seem in better spirits than yesterday.'

'Oh sure, a bundle of laughs, me. Especially as from now on it's me and my shadow for the foreseeable future.'

'Well, if you will try to jump off the roof, what do you expect,' The corners of his mouth moved upwards and his eyes seemed to be laughing. 'Seriously though, I'm at a loss to understand why someone like you should want to do that. You look really pretty apart from that tomboy haircut of yours.'

Donna moved her pillow to stand it up behind her, so that she could get more comfortable. She touched her hair, which though styled very short was slowly getting back to normal. 'Self-inflicted, I'm afraid.'

'How's that?'

'Had a bit of a brainstorm. I wanted to see what I'd look like bald. Trying to outdo Britney Spears I think.'

'It's a good job it's not permanent, or you'd be called a few names.'

'What do I care. There're worse things in life.'

'Well, it'll grow back eventually,' he smiled stroking his strong jaw as if he was contemplating something. 'So, you want to tell me what all this is about?'

'There's nothing to tell.' She turned away from him.

'Come on Donna, who are you trying to kid?'

'Perhaps I don't want to talk about it.'

'Well, that's your prerogative, but it usually helps if you share your problems with someone.'

'God, you sound like Doctor Reynolds. What, has she sent you here to soften me up, get me to talk to you after I wouldn't speak to her?' She stared at him now to see how he'd react.

He just smiled, then got up from the bed. 'If that's what you think, maybe I should go.'

'No, wait.' Surprising herself with the speed of her reply.

'All right, so are you going to tell me what's bugging you – or not? Must have been pretty drastic for you to shave your head, and then to try suicide... twice, isn't it?'

She sighed and frowned, moving again to adjust her pillow.

'Obviously you were very distressed. But even with that short hair, anyone would have to be blind not to notice how good you look. That sort of gives you a head start on everyone else. I'll bet you get loads of guys queuing up to chat you up. So why on earth did you do it?'

'That's got nothing to do with you – and besides I don't want lots of guys trying to chat me up.'

'Come on. If I were in your shoes, I'd feel pretty damn good about myself.'

'Oh shut up, will you?' Covering her ears with her hands, she continued. 'I'm sick of people saying that, and thinking I've got an advantage over everyone else. Just keep your mouth shut, will you? And change the bloody record or you can leave - right now.'

'All right, all right.' He held up his big hands in protest. 'I'm sorry.'

After a couple of minutes, she removed her hands from her ears. There were tears in her eyes. He made to go to her, but she flinched, moving away from him, her eyes full of terror.

'Look, if I've offended you... I apologise. Anyway, perhaps you're right, I'd better get going, I have to get home for my tea. Mum doesn't like to be kept waiting, let me tell you.'

'Good, you'll be better off there, rather than stopping here talking to a sicko like me.'

'I don't think so babe, and I would like to come and see you again, if you'll let me. Although I don't suppose you'll want me too now. But you will get well again and when you do it would make a big difference to me, having helped you in some small way.' He moved over to stand by the door.

'I'm never going to get better. And one of these days when somebody's guard is down, I might just try to do it again and this time I'll succeed.' She sniffed, wiping the tears away with her fingers.

'You don't mean that. All right so you're feeling low right now, but you won't always feel this bad – someday soon you'll start to get well. And that's when you can use what you have in abundance to... help ... you...' But as soon as he'd uttered the words he realised he'd said the wrong thing, and quietly swore under his breath.

She literally shook with anger. 'I know what you're insinuating. Right that's it. Fuck off Evan. My parents used to keep saying that and it drove me mad. You're no better than them. Don't bother coming again, because I won't talk to you.'

She couldn't look at him after that.

'Look, I'm sorry if I put my foot in it again. I didn't mean anything...'

She covered her ears again, determined not to remove her hands until he'd gone. After several minutes had passed she looked up to see if he was still there, and to her relief he'd gone. Thank God.

The very idea that he might see her in the same way as her parents made her blood boil. She even considered that he was in league with them. She wouldn't put it past them. Perhaps he'd stay away from now on – because he was only making matters worse.

Over the next few days there was no sign of him. But she grew annoyed with herself, as a tiny part of her actually wished he had come to see her. Maybe he'd taken the hint. On reflection she admitted it would be nice to have someone care about her welfare - after all he had already put himself in danger on her account. And in her mind's eye she saw him stumble on the edge of the roof – and shuddered.

It was lunchtime a week later, Donna was sitting on a bench in the grounds of the hospital, with a nurse, when she saw Evan walk across the road towards them. Wearing the same black coat as before, it looked as if he was just coming in to work. Thinking he would probably pass them by, she was surprised when he stopped directly in front of them. Donna bowed her head, and looked in the other direction, intent on ignoring him. When he spoke, however, it wasn't to her.

'Tracey, mind if I take over for a while. I'll bring Donna back to her room in say about half an hour.'

'Something wrong? Or do you have some sort of vested interest in her?' Tracey asked, perhaps a little annoyed by Evan's intervention.

'Sort of. I'm the guy who prevented her from jumping off the top of the building - remember. So ever since then, I've sort of looked out for her.'

'Ah well, be my guest. I could do with a break anyway,' Tracey said before departing from the scene.

Evan sat down, and keeping a little distance between them, turned to face her, looking worried and on edge. 'Nice day, isn't it Donna? Warm and sunny – too nice to be in a drab hospital like this eh?'

Donna nodded, smoothed her hair, and looked at him out of the corner of her eye.

Sadness showed in his clear blue eyes as he said. 'Look, I don't want to be where I'm not wanted. If you like I'll take you back to your room?'

She'd noticed the hurt in his voice. 'No, it's all right. I suppose I'll have to put up with you, won't I? Stopping in that blasted room is driving me nuts.'

He gave her a slight smile, then opened a packet of crisps and started crunching away, which really irritated her. 'Sorry I haven't been to see you before now, but I've been off work the past week with the flu.'

'Oh really, I never even noticed.' She lied.

'Look, I wanted to give you something by way of an apology for the other night, for upsetting you, like that.' He cleared his throat, looking down to the ground momentarily.

Donna's heart raced slightly, hoping he hadn't spent a lot of money on her. That would be so embarrassing. Her face reddened yet again.

She turned her head towards him, saw him rummaging about in his coat pocket. From that, she guessed it had to be something small. Opening his hand she saw a little plastic bag embossed with a logo which looked to be from a High Street Jeweler's shop. She was horrified but took it from him, feeling nervous. Opening the bag, she gasped, then looked up at him, almost lost for words, and pulled out a packet of wine gums. This astonished then angered her before suddenly she saw the funny side. Trying to suppress a grin she covered her mouth with the bag of sweets.

'I suppose you think that's funny?'

'Well, everyone likes wine gums - don't they?' he said with an air of innocence on his face.

'Yes, but –'

'I don't know what you were expecting, but I thought it best to get something small that I know you like rather than wasting money on something you might hate.'

'As a matter of fact I do like them.' She smiled, popping a yellow one into her mouth.

'Well, at least I made you smile.'

'Maybe you did, but it won't work a second time.' She grinned, offering him the bag of sweets. He took one from the bag.

'We'll see about that, Donna. So how have you been keeping since last we met?'

'How do you think? And now you've turned up again like a bad penny, I feel twice as bad.'

'Oh, sorry about that. I was only trying to be friendly and get you to laugh.' He looked hurt again.

'Don't worry, only joking.' She shook her head as she popped another wine gum in her mouth.

'So what does 'the doc' say? I can see she's put certain restrictions on you, which is quite understandable - so do you have someone watch you twenty-four hours a day?'

'Looks like it. There's not even a lock on the bathroom door. I did think about sticking my head down the toilet bowl and drowning myself, only I can't squeeze it down because the bowl's too small. Don't worry though, I'll think of something else. I'm a clever girl when I want to be.'

'No doubt.'

'The doctor says it'll be a while before I'm allowed out on my own again. I'll just have to be very patient - won't I?'

'Maybe that's where I could help...' he began putting his hand to his chin as if deep in thought.

'Well, unless you've got some influence over Dr Reynolds, I'd say that'll be rather difficult.'

He raised his eyebrows. 'We'll see about that. What if I was to offer to take you out with me? I feel sure she'd agree. She'd trust me seeing as I'm the one that stopped you from jumping. Why don't I give it a go? It'd make your life a bit more bearable, if you can put up with me, that is.'

'You're joking, aren't you? I think I'd rather stop in my room or walk around the grounds with Tracey.' She gave him a slight smile.

'OK, suit yourself babe. No one can say I didn't try.' He shrugged his shoulders.

'And besides, what's in it for you?'

'Nothing. Sure, I'd like to get to know you a bit better, see what makes you tick - but that's only so I can help you get well.'

'You really think I'd tell you anything?'

'I don't know. That's up to you. But I'm a good listener.'

'A nosy parker, more like,' she said, smiling at him in a sarcastic way.

'Well think about it, and in the meantime I'll have a word with 'the doc' – OK?'

'Please yourself.'

'Anyway, it's time we got back. I'm due to start work now and the nurses will be wondering where you are.'

They walked back into the hospital together, and Evan took her back to her room. The thought of going back sickened her, but there was nowhere else she was allowed to go.

'I'll be seeing you then, Donna.'

'In your dreams Evan.' She pulled a face, still not sure whether or not she wanted to go with him.

Sitting back on the bed in her room she couldn't stop thinking about Evan's suggestion. Could he do what he had said, and even if he could, what was he really after? If he was after anything more than friendship he'd be in for a nasty shock! Maybe he had saved her life, but in doing that, might he try to take advantage of her and meddle with her fragile feelings? Well, not if she could help it. Yet though she was wary of him, he was constantly on her mind.

Chapter 16

FOR OVER A WEEK, THERE WAS NO SIGN OF EVAN. She wondered if he'd had second thoughts, or had been unsuccessful in persuading 'the doc', as he referred to her, to allow her this one small privilege. She started to think harshly of him, for playing such a cruel trick, but on the other hand, she'd hardly given him the impression she wanted to go.

Then unexpectedly at the end of one of their hourly sessions, Dr Reynolds came up with a revelation.

'Oh by the way, Donna.' She peered at her over gold-rimmed spectacles. 'You know Evan, the young nurse who helped you a couple of weeks ago. Well he came to see me. He tells me you've become quite friendly, and asked me what I thought about him taking you out for a few hours sometime next week.'

Donna's jaw dropped. She never dreamed he'd really do it. She moved uncomfortably in her seat, feeling a little embarrassed. What could she say to that? On the one hand... but on the other...

'I wouldn't say we're friends, acquaintances, more like. We've spoken once or twice because he's been worried about me.'

'So would you like to spend a little time out with him or not?' Dr Reynolds asked moving her eyebrows upwards in anticipation of an answer.

'Don't know. I haven't given it much thought. Because I wasn't sure if he'd ask you or not. You mean you'd allow it?'

Sitting back in her chair, she took her glasses off, and looking straight back at Donna said, 'Yes, I think that would be in order.

Evan is a good nurse, very responsible and trustworthy. But I've instructed him not to let you out of his sight. So it's up to you.'

The corners of Donna's mouth moved upwards to form a little smile. For some reason she suddenly wanted to go.

'I take it you'd like to go?'

'You don't know how good it will be to get out in the fresh air for a little while, away from this place. It'll be like being released from prison.'

'Look, I've told you enough times you're not in prison. You only have these restrictions placed on you because of your own actions. We have a duty of care to protect you from yourself. Make a real effort to get yourself well, and you could still leave here sooner than you think.'

Donna laughed ironically. She didn't think she'd ever get out of here and wasn't sure she wanted to anyway, not if it meant going to live with her parents again, and shuddered at the thought.

<><><>

It had been arranged for Evan to take Donna out on his day off which was a Saturday. With the agreement of Dr Reynolds, he planned a visit to Dexford Town Centre or if the weather was good a drive into the surrounding countryside.

When the day of the outing arrived, the skies were clear blue and it looked as if the hot sunny weather would continue for the foreseeable future. Donna was dressed in leggings and a short-sleeved lilac tee-shirt, and although she was quite excited she decided to keep her make up to a minimum, not wanting him to get the wrong idea.

It seemed she'd been waiting for an age, when there was a quiet knock on the door to her room. Then looking up there he was in the doorway. Wearing chinos and a grey top, he was dressed quite differently from when he was at work. His black hair was gelled and spiked in the middle, in fact she thought he was quite trendy.

'Ready then?' he asked her.

'As ready as I'll ever be.'

As they walked out of the hospital side by side, Donna was at once aware of the limp he had. She'd noticed it before but hadn't said anything to him and was still wondering if he'd injured himself saving her life.

They made their way across to where his car was parked, and as he was opening the car door, she couldn't stop her inquisitiveness from getting the better of her, and asked, 'Have you done something to your leg?'

'What – Oh, I had an accident some years ago at work, and it was that bad I've never been able to walk properly since. I can't run very quickly either, but at least I've not been left a cripple which is something to be thankful for.' He slapped his thigh with his hand.

He got into the car, and opened the passenger side door for her. The injury to his leg still quite intrigued her.

'So how did it happen?'

Looking a little irritated by her persistent questioning, he answered. 'Playing football. A player came in hard to tackle me. I slipped and turned my ankle and broke it in two places. You wouldn't believe how bad the pain was.'

And as they drove off Donna said, 'I can imagine, but I thought you said you did it at work, yet just then you said you did it playing football.'

'Yes, well football was my work before I became a nurse. I was a professional footballer.'

'You're joking!'

'No, I'm not. I played for Ashfield Rovers, who if you know anything about football were at the time in the Championship, one step below the Premiership. I was nineteen when it happened and had just broken through to the first team. It was only my sixth game and it finished my career before it even got started.'

She saw him go full up, and felt for him. 'You must have been devastated.'

'I was - absolutely shattered. Not being able to play the game I loved so much was sheer torture. The day they told me I'd never play again was the worst day of my life.'

'How awful for you.'

'Yeah...well. So where would you like to go? I don't know what you think about stately homes with large picturesque gardens. But there's one about half an hour away from here. Seaford Hall Gardens is four hundred years old I'm told. It has a wonderful collection of antiques and the grounds are superb.'

She'd never given it a thought, had never heard of the place, but it didn't matter to her where they went. 'If you say it's good, it has to be.'

The house was situated in a beautiful area of countryside and as they approached the hall it was obvious the grounds were well cared for and immaculately kept. Evan stopped the car a time or two so that Donna could take it all in. It was impressive but not the sort of place she would have chosen to visit, yet what could she say. It was best to try to enjoy herself, since he'd gone out of his way to entertain her.

At last, Evan drove the car onto the car park, situated next to the Great Hall. The building was grey stone, half-timbered in places and covered in ivy, but what impressed Donna was how well it had been maintained. Inside was even better, with old oak furniture in all the rooms, wooden floors and enormous fire places. The rooms were made up to look as they had in the seventeenth century, when the civil war had been at its zenith.

Although Donna hadn't a great love for history, she did enjoy looking round the old house, trying to imagine what life must have been like all those years ago.

After their tour of the house, they sat on a bench in the middle of a row of conifers and recently cut hedges. It was pleasant in the shade as the weather was hot and the sun scorching. In previous years she'd always had a suntan, but living in the hospital, meant there was little opportunity to sunbathe. Now she didn't care whether she sunbathed or not.

'Well, this is very pleasant,' Evan commented stretching his arms and legs having finished the cheese salad sandwiches he'd bought them earlier on.

'Wonderful,' she said nodding to him, taking in the smell of freshly cut grass.

'Hope you weren't too bored - I didn't know quite where to take you.' He blinked his eyes a little more than normal.

'I enjoyed every minute Evan - it was very sweet of you to bring me here.'

'Thank God for that. I was a bit worried. Listen – would you like to come back to my house once we've finished here? Mum said to tell you, you're welcome to join us for dinner. It'll be nothing elaborate – I promise you.'

'You've got to be kidding – haven't you? I hardly know you, let alone your family. They'll think I'm your prospective girlfriend.'

'No, they won't, because I've already told them you're just a friend and a patient who needs a bit of cheering up.'

'Oh really. Did you tell your mum I was the mad woman who keeps trying to top herself?' She replied bitterly, her mouth quivering with emotion.

'I didn't tell them anything of the sort. All I said was that you're really nice, but that you're going through a rough time – no more than that. I'm not allowed to discuss your case with anyone. But I did tell them I'd try to persuade you to come, so they'll be disappointed if you don't.'

She frowned. Was he up to something? Yet she had to try to trust him, perhaps he'd done this with the best of intentions. In that case, and if it was only for an hour or so, she might as well agree to go.

'All right! All right, I'll come.' She drummed her fingers on the bench. 'Just don't expect too much of me – that's all.'

'I won't and neither will they. Just be your normal self and you'll be fine. I know they'll take to you straightaway.'

'I wouldn't be too sure of that.'

A little time later, they decided to walk back to the car.

'I would have liked to have taken you somewhere else, but time is getting on, so we'd better go back to my house now. Perhaps I can take you out again some other time.'

She nodded her head, but didn't say anything. Although she didn't tell him, she just wanted to get this ordeal with his family over, as soon as possible.

Donna wasn't familiar with the area of Dexford they drove through, but could see it wasn't a select area. Harvest Road where he lived was narrow with red-bricked semi-detached properties either side. They might have been built in the fifties or sixties, she thought.

He stopped the car outside number 23, a house in the middle of the left side of the street. It looked a little let go, but nothing a good lick of paint wouldn't cure. The garden was a bit wild too; she couldn't help wondering why it was in this state, but again didn't say anything to Evan about it. There were a few children playing hopscotch and skipping in the street, which took Donna back to her childhood. She smiled at them on getting out of the car.

As they approached the door, she began to tremble, not knowing what to expect from these people who she'd never met before. Still, it would be over soon enough, she kept telling herself.

Evan opened the door with his key, allowing her to go in first. The aroma of homemade cakes, vanilla and chocolate hit her at once and made her feel hungry.

'Something smells nice, not on my account, I hope,' Donna said.

'No, of course not. Mum's always cooking something, cakes are her specialty. In particular, Sponge Cakes, Swiss Rolls, and God knows what else. You name it and she can bake it.'

He squeezed her arm, then led her into the living room, where Donna saw two people sitting down. One was old, maybe mid-sixties with short grey hair; the same light blue eyes as Evan, in fact she looked much like Evan too, but was plump with a double chin – obviously his mum. There was some knitting on her lap, and from the warm smile on her face Donna knew she was welcome in this house.

The other person sitting opposite was a young girl, obviously Evan's sister. When she first glanced at her, Donna's heart flipped with horror; as although one side of the girl's face was normal and quite pretty, the other side was almost completely covered by a large growth, hideous and lumpy with blue veins running all over it. Donna almost had to look away, she had never seen anything so disturbing in her life, so much so that it made her pause for thought, and feel like crying. Yet the girl appeared to be acting normally, as if there was nothing wrong. The most annoying part was that Evan hadn't prepared her for this, had never said a word in fact, unless this was at his sister's request.

'This is Theresa, my sister,' Evan said, introducing her. 'And of course my mum is sitting opposite her.'

Donna shook hands with both of them, and with much sincerity said, 'I'm very pleased to meet you Theresa…Mrs Lacey.'

'You were right about her, son. She is indeed very pretty.'

'I bet loads of guys fancy you, don't they Donna?' Theresa said, the good part of her face forcing a smile, which looked genuine without any form of animosity.

Donna didn't react except for feeling embarrassed and blushing slightly. 'I don't know about that. Maybe - but it can be annoying, when they won't leave you alone.'

'Don't say that Donna. You could have them eating out of your hand, get them to do whatever you want.' Theresa's one eyebrow rose in confirmation of her observations.

'Oh, sure I could, but I wouldn't want to anyway. I want people to like me for who I am rather than as a dumb blond. It wouldn't be right.'

'Good for you, Donna.' Theresa nodded as if she was impressed.

'Anyway both of you, stop standing around like spare parts and come and sit down.' Mrs Lacey raised her arm to beckon them to their seats. Evan sat in between his mother and sister, while Donna was glad to sit in the armchair opposite.

'I hope you're hungry, Donna, because I've made lots to eat.'

'Oh, I am, Mrs Lacey, your son has made me walk my socks off today.' She put her tongue against her cheek, which made it puff out a little as she smiled.

'So how long before we can eat?' Evan asked, rubbing his hands together.

'Not long, you've got time to freshen up if you want,' his mother suggested.

He nodded and they both got up. Donna was glad of the respite.

In the hall, he turned to her. 'You go first; the bathroom is the first door on the left, at the top of the stairs.'

Donna nodded, took a deep breath, shut her eyes for a minute, then looking at Evan said, 'I feel so sorry for Theresa. I had no idea. Why didn't you tell me about her before we got here?' She reached out and squeezed his wrist. 'I might have been horrified at the prospect, but I'd still have come.'

'I couldn't take that chance. I know it's awful about Theresa, but underneath it all, she's the same as everyone else. You'd be surprised how normal she is despite what she has.'

'It makes me feel incredibly sad. Is there nothing the doctors can do?' With moist eyes she looked into space, feeling so guilty.

'Apparently not. She has a type of facial cancer that's slow growing but also inoperable. The doctors now think she may only have months to live.' Evan swallowed hard, obviously as his emotions came to the fore.

'I can't believe that. She's so young.'

'I know, it's tearing mum and me apart too. You should have seen her pretty face before the cancer took hold. She'd have given you a run for your money. But she's a credit to the family and very brave. Never complains and always looks on the bright side of things. To be honest, I don't know how she does it.'

'I don't think I could cope with it either.'

'Well, to her life is precious, so she intends to saviour every minute she has left.'

'Good for her.' As she rushed upstairs to the bathroom she felt so bad about trying to take her own life. The feelings of inferiority and shame came to the fore. Maybe it should have been her and not

Theresa in this dreadful predicament. If the tables were turned Donna had no doubt in her mind that, with Theresa's zest for life and strength of mind, she would have dealt with the attack and everything it brought more adeptly.

'All right?' Evan asked her when she came out of the bathroom.

'Yes, still a little nervous, but I'll be fine.'

As soon as they went back into the living room, Donna smelt the aromas of freshly cooked chicken, and perhaps sage and onion stuffing.

They walked towards the dining room table at the end of the room. Evan's mother sat at the head of the table, with Theresa opposite. Donna and Evan occupied the other two places. The meal had already been served and was in front of them.

'Well tuck in everybody,' Evan's mother encouraged them picking up her own knife and fork. Everyone else followed her lead. At first, it appeared no one knew quite what to say, and Donna sensed an atmosphere.

For her this was so nerve-racking – she kept feeling herself go hot and got the impression they were staring at her. She tried not to look at Theresa, who was having trouble getting food into her mouth, and several times dropped some back onto the plate and even onto the tablecloth. Donna felt so sorry for her, but Theresa never batted an eyelid, and continued as if nothing had happened.

Perhaps Theresa had sensed the atmosphere in the room too, as she suddenly looked up and said, 'So Donna, have you ever entered any beauty contests or done any modelling?'

Donna jumped slightly. Why did Theresa have to bring up the one subject she hated talking about the most? It was going to take all her strength of character not to lose her temper over it. And it would spoil an otherwise perfect morning.

'My parents used to enter me for beauty contests, but it always went against the grain. I can't stand horrible old men gawping at me.'

'Oh I don't mind people looking at me,' Theresa smiled. 'I bet you never thought you'd hear me say that, what with my face, eh. In fact, I find it so amusing. Out of the corner of my eye, I see them staring and trying not to look but it's so obvious. But if I let it get to me I'll never go out of the house, and in a way, it's given me strength of character not to let other people bring me down.'

Donna smiled and listened intently to her.

'It's not going to stop me doing what I want to do. I've always been very musical you know – I play the piano, the violin, the keyboard and I write my own music,' she boasted with pride.

'It must be wonderful to have a talent like that. I'd love to hear you play some time.'

'Oh I don't think you would. It's not the sort of music people our age enjoy. I wouldn't want to bore you.'

'You wouldn't - honestly. I'm very interested,' Donna insisted, her eyes sparkling in anticipation. 'Perhaps when we've finished our meal you'll play for us?'

Theresa looked towards Evan and her mother for encouragement, appearing unsure of what to do, but she was urged on by both of them.

'Theresa – I'll just telephone the hospital to let them know we are going to be a bit late, then I'll fetch your keyboard from upstairs, shall I?' Evan said, when they had finished their meal.

Within a few minutes he returned carrying a large keyboard. He unfolded the metal legs and placed the instrument in front of the piano stool which he reached for from under the table, before plugging the keyboard into the mains.

'So what are you going to play for us sis?'

'Oh, a few tunes you might know and a few others you won't.'

She got up from the table to move slowly to the piano stool, and making herself comfortable, adjusted the keyboard so it was just the right height. She looked up at them all, smiling, but her hands were shaking slightly. They were small delicate hands with long fingers.

First came the classical tunes that were played to perfection with much emotion. Then as she became more confident, she announced she would play her own tunes, which sounded as good, if not better, than the well-known ones.

For Donna this was so moving, it left her speechless. To see such a talented and accomplished musician at the peak of her ability despite her condition, was in her opinion a miracle. She could only sit back and admire her.

After about half an hour, Theresa began to look tired and so her mother suggested she should stop playing. Evan looked sad but must have been relieved, as he wouldn't have wanted her to overexert herself. Donna was in awe of the scene she had just witnessed. If only her own parents had been the same, and listened when she didn't want to be in the public eye.

Theresa smiled in appreciation, looking particularly at Donna whom it seemed she wanted to impress. Donna had no idea why, after all, who was she? Just a neurotic woman who'd attempted suicide twice. Although Theresa wouldn't have known about that.

Evan glanced at his watch. It was late, time to get back to the hospital, or he'd have 'the doc' wondering where they were.

'Right Donna, I suppose we'd better go. Or else they'll be thinking something's happened. And you know them – they'll soon get their knickers in a twist.'

'Do come again soon, Donna,' Evan's mum said with the same warm smile as before.

'That's very kind of you Mrs Lacey.'

'Hope you get well soon, Donna,' Theresa said, her good side seeming to look genuine, her eyebrow rising expectantly. 'And yes please come and visit us again. I know looking at me will probably give you nightmares, but I promise you there's a real person underneath all this. It'd be great to have someone of my own age to talk to.'

Donna smiled, feeling a little embarrassed but also honoured that they should take to her in this way.

'Your appearance won't give me nightmares, love; on the contrary you're an inspiration to me. The talent you have is quite amazing. I know your disfigurement is there, but I don't see it. To me you're incredible.' Donna bent over to kiss her on the unsightly side of her face, which caused Theresa to gasp slightly but hug Donna in return.

In the end after all her fears about coming to this house, she felt rather sad to say goodbye.

They were quiet on the way back to the hospital, locked in their own personal thoughts. It wasn't until they walked through the corridors towards Donna's room, that she felt it was time to talk to Evan.

'Do you just have the one sister, Evan?'

'No more sisters, but I do have a brother.' He smiled.

'Really, younger or older?'

'Older by a couple of years. Cole is in the army, so we don't see very much of him these days. He's in Germany right now, but he's going to Afghanistan very shortly. We're all really worried about what's going to happen to him over there,' he sighed deeply.

'Your mother seems to have had a lot of worry – hasn't she?' As they came to her room, Evan opened the door for her.

'Don't all mothers. Mum's had her fair share, perhaps more than most,' he replied, his lips in a straight line, as if he himself had been guilty of something in the past. But didn't elaborate.

'Thanks for taking me out today, and for introducing me to your family. I enjoyed it, and I must admit it puts my own stupid problems into perspective,' she said as she entered her room.

'I didn't do it for that. Just wanted you to meet them and be friends. Sorry I didn't tell you about Theresa - hope it hasn't put you off coming to visit us again.' He looked sad, standing at the door, his eyes dropping slightly to the ground.

'No, not at all. Just wish there was something I could do to help her.'

'I know. But there's nothing anyone can do. Except to try to make her last few months as happy as possible. I've no idea how mum's coping. You know, it's only been a couple of years since we lost my dad to cancer as well, and that was incredibly painful, watching him slowly die. So now it's happening to Theresa, it's going to cut us up even more.' Evan suddenly heaved with emotion. A deep frown formed on his handsome face.

'I feel for you Evan.'

'Anyway enough of my troubles – don't want you feeling sorry for me, babe. So is it all right to take you out again if 'the doc' allows it?'

'Yes, it's done me good to get out.'

'Good, I think it'll help your therapy no end. See you around then - I'll be in touch.' He turned, giving her a mock salute with his hand.

Donna smiled, closing her eyes once he'd gone, realising she'd just had the most enjoyable day since she didn't know when, but as for the future, it was impossible to predict.

Chapter 17

THAT NIGHT DONNA LAY AWAKE THINKING ABOUT HER TIME WITH EVAN. It had been so pleasant, and then at his house, meeting the family and what happened there had been totally unexpected. Of course what stood out in her mind was Theresa. At first, like everyone, she'd been shaken by the sight of her, but then once she'd got talking to Theresa, her opinion had changed completely.

The time spent with this lovely family had made Donna's own troubles seem insignificant and forced her to pause for thought. Maybe this was what Evan, in conjunction with Dr Reynolds had intended – but whatever their intention, it had certainly helped, and now whenever she felt low she would try to think about Theresa's plight.

The following morning, at their next session, Dr Reynolds seemed keen to find out how Donna's first outing had gone, and looking at her over gold-rimmed spectacles, asked, 'So how did you get on?'

'Oh, all right. Not too bad at all.'

'Good, glad to hear it, my dear.' There was a hint of a smile on her heavily wrinkled face. 'You know if young Evan is willing, I see no reason why he can't take you out again, so long as he stays with you at all times, and keeps us informed about your movements.'

'Thanks doctor. I'll think about it. I suppose you know about Theresa, his sister?' Donna couldn't help but mention.

'Yes, it's terrible to see that happen to such a lovely girl. But I can't help but admire her spirit. And from what I hear she never complains or feels sorry for herself. She's an example to us all.'

Donna smiled still feeling a little guilty about what she'd done, perhaps she'd over-reacted to the events of the last few months, but to be fair to herself she believed any woman would have been severally traumatised in some way or another.

'Mind you, Evan's family have had a lot to contend with over the past few years. Not only has Theresa suffered, but Evan himself has had his fair share of problems. He was a very talented footballer you know, but then he had a bad injury breaking his ankle in several places. He was on crutches for over a year, and even now, you may have noticed he walks with a limp. Unsurprisingly, it finished his career.'

'He told me about his accident, but not much else.' Donna stared at the Doctor pointedly.

'Perhaps that's why he took it upon himself to try to help you like he did.'

'I might not be here now if it hadn't been for him. I was at the end of my tether, and still am at times.'

'I know you are, my dear. But that's not all Evan has had to contend with. For a long time, his father suffered dreadfully with stomach cancer, then died about two years ago. And I think there may have been some trouble with his brother as well, but obviously I can't go into the details.' She nodded as if to bring home the point.

'How come you know all this about him and his family? And why are you telling me all of these things anyway?' Donna asked eyeing the doctor suspiciously.

'I've told you, because I thought you might be interested. I just wanted you to know, that you're not on your own – lots of people have gone through worse than you, and still come out the other side.'

'I know, I'm not stupid. Maybe it's not such a good idea that I get to know them after all, not with my track record. OK, he's a nice guy but now that you've told me those things about him and his family, I'm not sure I want to add to their problems.'

Doctor Reynolds tutted. 'Donna, you wouldn't be, but I gather you enjoyed your time out with Evan.'

At that Donna felt her anger rising, she leaned over onto the desk. 'Trying to act as a matchmaker, are you doctor? As well as being a shrink of many talents.'

'You should know it's not appropriate for a nurse to have a relationship with a patient. Look, I'm just trying to do a job the same as anybody else, but I can only help people who genuinely want to be helped. If they don't, then there's nothing I can do. I just thought with Evan's help, I might get you to see that you have much to live for in the future.'

'Oh spare me all the clap-trap. You don't have a clue, do you? You and your devious little tricks. I bet you thought you'd seen through me, well you haven't. I don't know if I want to see you anymore.' She suddenly jumped up from her seat. 'I can't just turn my feelings on and off like a tap.'

'I know you can't. Don't be ridiculous. I'm not scheming or playing tricks, I know you're genuinely ill and I intend to see this case through no matter what it takes. Your parents are paying me a lot of money to help you and that's just what I'm going to do.'

'Doctor Reynolds, I'd like to be taken to my room now please. I have nothing more to say to you.'

'Of course, if that's what you want,' the doctor said without showing any emotion on her face.

In the confines of her room, she sensed the familiar feelings of anxiety and panic starting to kick in. The urge to hurt herself once more was strong, but with everything that had gone on yesterday and thinking of Theresa she resisted the temptation, and slowly but surely began to return to normal. Calming down, she worried that she'd been too hard on the doctor and should maybe apologise - perhaps tomorrow, if the chance arose. In the meantime, trying to put it to the back of her mind she switched on the television, and watched some ridiculous quiz. It didn't really interest her, but it certainly beat staring at four grey walls.

Whilst watching this, she thought about various things in her life and what the doctor had just said. And about how nice it would be, to be free to go wherever she liked. She wanted to get better, and hated the thought of remaining in hospital, but even though they could stop her making further suicide attempts, there was very little they could do to take away the fear which remained inside her. The memory of the rape and the dread that one day her attacker would hurt her again were vivid and frightening.

By the end of the day she had more or less made up her mind to go with Evan for another outing, so long as he didn't try to get involved with her. So when, a few days later, he paid her a visit she was quite pleased to see him. It was late evening, he had his coat on, obviously having just finished work.

'Hi Donna. I've only come to see how you are and ask if you'd like to go out with me again like before.' His lips were poised tentatively.

'I don't know, Evan. I don't want you getting the wrong idea about me.'

'Come on – I'm not likely to, am I? You think I'd try to take advantage of a girl like you. No way. Besides, it wouldn't be ethical, with you being a patient and me a nurse. All I want to do is to help you get better, and out of this place. Sure, I want to be your friend rather than your enemy - but that's all, I promise you.' As he said this he looked quite serious and earnest.

'All right, I believe you. OK, now we've got that cleared up, I'd be delighted to come.'

'Brilliant.' He was beaming all over his face. 'So what about tomorrow? The weather's supposed to be a bit cooler although still dry. How about a drive into the country? Bodwick Green is only about twenty miles away. If you're game, we could do a bit of cycling over the hills. I can still cycle pretty well even with my bad leg. What do you reckon?'

'All right. I'm not exactly fit and it's been years since I rode a bike, but I could do with the exercise having been stuck in here for so long.'

'Great stuff. I'll speak to 'the doc', and all being well I'll come for you around nine o'clock sharp.' And with that he left.

She noticed how pleased with himself he'd looked, before saying goodbye to her. Immediately she felt apprehensive again, sensing he was attracted to her. But if he ever tried anything she would kick, scratch and scream if need be. Although maybe she shouldn't be quite so negative - there had to be some good people in the world, and after all he was a nurse, a person with responsibility. Maybe she should give him the benefit of the doubt and not jump to conclusions.

<><><>

She was dressed and ready at the arranged time of nine o'clock, wearing faded denims and a light blue top. She had decided to put on trainers and had packed a thin grey blouson in a backpack in case it got cold.

He arrived suitably dressed for the outdoors and it seemed to her he was eyeing her up when he said 'You look very nice.'

'You're joking aren't you? I'm wearing the oldest clothes I could find, we're only going bike riding, aren't we?' She felt uneasy with the amount of attention he was giving her.

'You still look great.'

She raised her eyebrows and widened her eyes, in an effort to show him how irritated she was by these compliments.

The journey to Bodwick Green, an area of outstanding natural beauty, took a little over an hour by car. They had some difficulty finding a suitable parking spot, as the car park was already almost full, and in the end had to settle for a spot quite a way from the park itself. Obviously it was a very popular place to visit.

At the edge of the car park was a small complex, consisting of a log cabin selling souvenirs and grocery, and next door was a small shop displaying a sign 'Cycles for Hire'. There were some people up ahead hiking, whilst others were simply taking their dogs for a walk.

Donna looked at the green hills and the rest of the terrain, feeling a little quiver of dread. There was no way she could cycle up and down those hills. It would kill her. And when Evan suddenly smiled in that boyish way of his, she realised he'd noticed her reservations. 'What you laughing at?' She said.

'You – a bit worried, are you? About all these hills. Listen, by the time I'm finished with you, you'll have legs like a marathon runner.'

'Don't want legs like a marathon runner. I'm very happy with the legs I've got – thank you very much. But seriously Evan, I'll never make it up those hills.'

'Me neither. Don't worry; I know a few tracks around here that avoid the worst of these hills. It's mostly flat, I promise.'

And as they walked towards the hut to hire the cycles she kept telling herself she had to trust him and try to relax in his company.

After hiring the cycles for what she considered a nominal fee, they set off, but she couldn't help wondering if he had exaggerated the bit about 'this flat cycle track that avoided the worst of the hills'. Only time would tell.

The track began behind the two huts and to her relief one of the tracks skirted the bottom of the hills and was very pleasant to cycle on.

Donna viewed the scenery as they rode ever further, and found it breath-taking, indeed the area was unspoilt and even had hides for bird watchers to view rare species. Although enjoying herself, after a time, she began to worry about how they'd get back. Evan seemed to have the energy of a horse, and ignored her constant pleas to turn round.

Eventually, enough was enough, she had to stop. She put her feet down on the ground, allowing him to continue on his own if he wished. He turned his head back to her after only a few seconds.

'Come on Donna, what's the matter with you?' he grinned, seeing she was out of breath, and sweat masked her face.

'Evan, it's no good - I can't carry on any longer. I don't know how I'll make it back. It'll take forever.'

He started laughing again.

'What's so funny now?'

'The look on your face.'

'Something wrong with the look on my face?' she glared at him.

'No, of course not. Tell you what, come and cycle with me a bit further and tell me what you see.'

She wasn't convinced, but had little choice but to do what he said. Then sure enough there below in a valley was a small town, with what looked like lots of houses, a few shops and a park.

'What difference does that make?' She was puzzled and a little irritated.

'Well, that's the town of Mosford. Very pretty, don't you think? There just happens to be a train station there. We hop on the train with our bikes, get off at the second stop, Wydesley, then cycle back to Bodwick Green, about a mile away from where we parked the car. Now do you get it?'

'I suppose, but I'm warning you, if this is a wild goose chase.' She wagged a finger at him.

He just smiled, then continued to cycle. She followed.

Forty five minutes later, after their short train journey from Mosford, they were stepping on to the platform at Wydesley. And as they walked through the village Donna had had enough and decided she couldn't take another step. 'Evan, I'm famished, isn't there anywhere to eat in this damned place?'

'There's a pub around the corner,' he said pointing to his left.

'Doesn't that rather defeat the object?'

'Maybe, but at least we won't put any weight on,' he laughed as they approached the old half-timbered pub. There was a beer garden round the back, where they took their bikes. While Evan went inside the pub to order a meal and get them a drink, Donna found a table with a sun umbrella.

The beer garden was totally deserted and for a few fleeting seconds while she was on her own in a place she hadn't been before, there came a strong urge in the pit of her stomach to run away, as panic swept through her. The memories of her attacker came back vividly and even now feared he might be lurking in the undergrowth.

When Evan came out with the drinks, looking quite pleased with himself, Donna's tension began to slowly melt away into the background.

'Are you all right Donna, you seem quite flushed?'

'Yes I'm fine, just thinking back to something that happened in my past.'

'Well, whatever it was, try and forget it. Don't let it spoil your day – eh?'

She gave him an uneasy smile, but once the meal came they both seemed to be more interested in eating their meal of steak, chips and peas. After that she began to relax in his company.

'So what did you think of the meal?' he asked her finally.

'Very nice, I enjoyed it.' The evidence of an empty plate was there in front of her.

'Want to come back to my house again afterwards? Theresa keeps asking about you - she'd love to see you again. I think she really likes you, you know.'

Donna was quite taken aback. But couldn't help wondering if it was just a ploy on his part to get her to go back to his house.

'Maybe, but I am rather tired. My legs are killing me. And anyway I'm not sure I'm worthy of her friendship.'

'Oh come on - don't be so hard on yourself. A little bird told me you're quite a brainbox, and you have a degree in Mathematics, first class I believe. That's something to be proud of, isn't it?'

'And who's told you that?' It was as if this was a secret no one should know about.

'The doc.'

'Seems to me Doctor Reynolds is very good at revealing things about people. She's even told me a thing or two about you.' An ironic smile formed on her face.

'Has she now? All right, so what did she tell you?'

When she told him, his eyes widened with surprise or was it shock – Donna couldn't be sure.

'Well I never. In that case, maybe I should tell you the full story. Naturally, I was devastated when I knew I'd never play football again, so much so that I turned to drink and drugs, and almost killed myself one night in the process. Only the quick thinking of an off-duty police officer, who found me unconscious in a pub car park, saved my life.

'It took me a long time to get back on the straight and narrow, but I think through the job I have now, I've got back my self-respect. I had to stop feeling sorry for myself.'

'I can see you've had quite a few troubles of your own – haven't you?'

'Not only my troubles, it was dad dying and Cole's problems as well. He was a bit of a tearaway when he was young and went off the rails in a big way. He couldn't keep a job and kept getting into fights, as well as having the police after him. Luckily mum managed to get him into the army, or he might have ended up in prison. In fact, now and then when he comes home on leave, he still goes on a bit of a bender. To let his hair down, he says.'

Donna raised her eyebrows.

'I don't suppose you'll want me to take you out again now you know all this.' Biting his top lip and stroking the back of his head he waited nervously for a reply.

'Evan, everybody's human after all. It just proves you and your family are like the rest of us.'

'Maybe now you can see that I do have an idea of what you're going through, having experienced something similar myself.'

Sitting back in her chair, she went quiet; unable to look at him straight in the eye. 'I don't think you do, Evan. You can't begin to imagine – nobody can.'

'Well, like I said before, if you want to tell me about it, I'm a very good listener.'

Donna shook her head vigorously. 'Think I'd like to go now.'

She noticed he didn't say much after that, probably wary that to pursue the matter would only cause more trouble.

When they arrived back at Evan's house later that afternoon, the weather had suddenly changed to torrential rain. Hurriedly, they ran towards the house. Donna was quite impressed when he gave her his coat to shelter under. He opened the door, allowing her to go in first.

There was music coming from the living room, a keyboard by the sounds of it, which could only belong to one person – Theresa. As Evan opened the living room door, they stood by the doorway, taking in the scene – Theresa sitting at her keyboard playing a melodic tune, their mother sitting on the sofa enthralled. They were captivated by the beauty of the music.

Theresa's face lit up when Donna entered the room, she smiled at her with affection, but carried on playing until the piece was finished, highly delighted with her audience.

At the end of the piece, they clapped and cheered loudly, their eyes and faces beaming with pleasure. When Donna told her how brilliant she was, Theresa looked thrilled to bits, and her eyes sparkled. She even blushed slightly.

Donna felt so sorry for her. If only someone had a magic potion to get rid of her terrible affliction.

'Theresa, you are so talented. Has it always been that way?'

'I've always been interested in music, ever since I was a little girl. I remember having a keyboard when I was about five or six. I used to have lessons, and before long, I only had to hear a tune and I could play it. I stopped playing when dad was ill, and then after he died, I took it up again, to help me get over his death. And lately since I've had to give up work, I've got into it even more. I'd play all day and all night if I could. It's amazing, but it's only in the last year or so that these tunes have been popping into my head. I don't know where they come from, but I'm glad they do.'

'So why don't you do something about it?' Donna suggested, thinking what a shame this talent had only been heard by three people.

'Like what?' Theresa's face was full of uncertainty.

'How about making a tape or a CD, and sending it out to someone. Like to a radio station or a record company or maybe a television programme. We could also include some info on you. You never know what might happen.'

'Hey, that's a brilliant idea, so long as Theresa doesn't mind being in the limelight,' Evan agreed nodding, then looking at his mother said. 'What do you think mum?'

'I don't know what to say.' She looked strangely frightened by the suggestion. 'I don't want lots of people staring at my little girl.'

'I don't mind, honestly mum. Let the people think what they want – I don't care. It used to hurt me, but not anymore. I am what I am and if people can't accept me, then I feel sorry for them. I promise you that deep down inside I have so much music in me. It makes me feel better, and if I can bring a little joy to somebody's life, then it'll be worth it – don't you think?' Theresa's spirits seemed to be lifted by Donna's suggestion.

'Yes, I do. That's if you're game, sis? I know you have a special talent, so why don't we see if we can arrange to make a demo tape of you and then take it from there.'

'But first let's make sure this is what you really want to do. I don't want you to feel you're being pushed into it, like I always did.' Donna was able to see, by the way Theresa was enthused by her suggestion, that this was what she'd wanted all along – it was just that it had needed someone to bring it out in her.

'Think it's a good idea mum?' Evan said turning to her, but she was biting her lip, as if torn between the two options.

'I'm mixed up inside. My heart says yes, but my head says to be very careful.'

Theresa face dropped slightly at her mother's attitude. Which was understandable – it was natural for a mother to worry over her daughter, especially one in such a predicament.

'Look, I know you all want to protect me, but I'm a big girl now. I can take what anybody throws at me. I'm no longer frightened of people staring at me. And I know I'm going to die sooner rather than later, but while I'm still here, I'd like to leave my mark even if it is only a small one. I don't want to die, but I accept it now, even though I hate the pain. As I see it, I'll be going to a better place, my only regret is that I won't see any of you again.'

'Please don't talk like that, Theresa. It does no one any good to think about what might or might not happen in the future,' their mother said, torment and hurt showing on her grey worn face.

Donna felt for Theresa, but at the same time admired her courage and wished she could acquire just an ounce of that. Perhaps she could draw on her bravery for inspiration. She really wanted to help and thereby regain a little self-respect.

As time wore on and after further deliberations, Evan said they should get back to the hospital, but just before leaving, Donna promised Theresa she'd visit again as soon as she could.

Chapter 18

FOR THE FIRST TIME SINCE SHE COULD REMEMBER, DONNA FELT SOMETHING RESEMBLING NORMALITY. Her desire to hurt herself, fatally or otherwise had gradually receded. She told Doctor Reynolds this at one of their sessions, and guessed the doctor would no doubt relay this to her parents, who as of yet had remained discreetly in the background. Donna was glad they weren't around, because before long her relationship with them would become strained, along with her own state of mind. Despite them paying for her stay in hospital, she found it difficult to forget the pressure they'd placed her under in the past, and what a miserable existence she'd endured at times during her early and teen years.

She knew, perhaps thanks to Doctor Reynolds initially, that Evan and his family had made a big difference to her life, and now looked forward to being in his company. While continuing to keep him at arm's length, she considered him a good friend, as were the rest of the family, who'd welcomed her with open arms, without probing into Donna's past. In fact they'd treated her like one of the family. How she wished her own parents could have been a bit like them.

◇◇◇

A couple of weeks later, Evan and Donna were about to drive over to the Derndale Hills for a hike, which she feared would be worse than their recent cycle trip, when, as they walked to the car, Evan said. 'Hey, you'll never guess what?'

'What's that?'

'You know I sent a tape of Theresa to the local TV station –'

'Yes'

'Well, mum told me before I came to pick you up. It seems someone from the TV Company phoned, wanting to send a TV crew round to talk to Theresa, and to hear her play as well.'

'Oh Evan, that's fantastic news!' Donna clapped her hands with glee. 'What does Theresa think about it?'

'She's over the moon, but thinks she'll be extremely nervous. I reckon she'll be all right, but I know she'll worry over what people will say about her when she's pushed into the spotlight. Everyone will be shocked when they see her – hopefully they'll have the sense to see beyond her disfigurement.'

'I agree it's going to be difficult to bear, but knowing how brave she is, I'm sure she'll pull it off.'

'Hope you're right.' He scratched the back of his head, then seemed deep in thought for a moment. 'Er...would you object to being present when the TV guys show up? Theresa wants you with her; I think she feels more secure when you're there.'

Donna was surprised Theresa had asked her to be present, but was also a little fearful as secretly she had an aversion to anyone from the media, remembering what had happened in the past. However, she couldn't let Theresa down; that was unthinkable.

'Of course Evan, I'd consider it an honour.' Was her answer.

<> <> <>

It was three o'clock at 23 Harvest Road. They were all sitting waiting, when the doorbell rang for what seemed like forever. Donna could see they were leaving it to her to get up first and answer the door. So reluctantly she did. Standing there before her was Toby Morton, who she recognised from local television, and a crew of three who would presumably film Theresa.

'Hallo there,' Toby, a tall grey haired man with a sickly smile said to Donna, as he looked her up and down.

'I take it you've come to see Theresa?'

'We have. Pity you're not her, but obviously you're not.' Toby grinned at his companions.

'Well, if I was, there wouldn't be a story, would there?' Was her sharp reply, raising her eyebrows with disapproval. 'You'd better come in.'

Donna felt slightly uncomfortable as she led these typical media type people through into the living room, where Theresa, her mother and Evan were sitting on the sofa together.

Theresa wore a flowered blouse over her jeans. Her long brown hair was freshly washed and worn loose, perhaps a futile attempt to hide her deformity.

'This is Theresa,' Donna said holding out a hand to introduce them, thinking how extremely beautiful she must have been before her illness.

There was a split second expression of shock, then a look of pity appeared on Toby's face.

'Hallo Theresa, it's great to meet you.' He offered her his hand, which she shook delicately. 'Your brother wrote to us, telling us all about you, your condition and your gift for music. The tape he sent us was so beautiful, we had to come and meet you. So I'm here to talk to you, and hear your wonderful music for myself. This is a great human interest story, so are you willing to talk to us, perhaps even play for us as well?'

Theresa nodded unable to meet Toby's gaze.

It was a hive of activity as Toby and his gang set up their equipment, placing the cameras and microphones in readiness. Of course Donna knew any audience Theresa played to, would at some point see her deformity, but hoped and prayed the filming would be sympathetic to her condition.

In the weeks she'd known Theresa, Donna had developed a deep compassion towards her and the last thing she wanted was for her friend to be traumatised by this experience. So she was going to keep a close eye on what happened, and intervene if and when she felt it necessary.

Toby sat next to Theresa on the sofa to discuss what she felt comfortable talking about in front of the cameras. Donna, Evan and his mother got up and stood behind the sofa to listen and give support if need be. Finally at Toby's signal the interview began thus, 'Obviously we've come to talk about your music Theresa, but anyone seeing you can't help to notice your condition. Would you like to tell us a bit about it?' His face was expressionless.

'About five years ago I noticed the left side of my face was swelling up with some sort of hard tissue. It didn't hurt at first, but when it started to get bigger I began to worry. Mum decided to come with me to see a doctor, who after examining me, sent me straight to hospital. They took skin samples of the growth and eventually I was diagnosed as having malignant facial cancer. Although slow growing, it was inoperable, and I was told I had between one to three years to live.

'It's become more painful in the last few months, but they've given me something to help ease this. However, apart from a few dizzy spells, I've been able to live a relatively normal life.'

'It must have been very distressing for you. How have you managed to cope?'

'I don't know, I've had to I suppose. At first, I was so self-conscious. I used to hide myself away from people, but I came to realise that was the wrong thing to do. I have to try to be positive, after all I can still function as a human being and do most of the things other people can do. Although I can't work anymore now, I thought with the time I have left, I'd pursue a lifetime's ambition of mine - to write and play music. So that's what I've been doing.'

'I hear you play the keyboard, piano, and guitar. Having listened to your tape, all the office have commented on how beautiful it is. Any chance of giving us a live sample of your work?' He asked politely which seemed to impress Theresa.

Donna watched as a hint of a shy smile came on Theresa's face, then she went to the back of the room, to help Evan carry the keyboard forward. After a few minute's hesitation, Theresa began to play. It was one of her own compositions starting very slowly with a delicate melody gradually building to a crescendo which left her audience in awe of the beauty of the piece.

'Theresa, that was truly wonderful. Incredible that someone so young has such an ear for music. Anything else you'd like to play for us?' Toby asked.

'Yes, I can play a selection of my favourite tunes, which you will no doubt recognise, and then a few more of my own compositions.' Her confidence was growing.

She played a selection of classical tracks as well as music from popular modern pieces. Then came more of her own melodies, sounding to Donna as good if not better than the well-known tunes. The music went on for well over half an hour.

By the end of it, she had everyone clapping and cheering with emotion on their faces; Evan and their mother in particular.

'Theresa, I'd like to thank you so much for allowing us to hear you play. It was delightful. My sincerest best wishes for your future. I'm sure once the viewers have seen this, they'll realise you have a great talent,' Toby said.

Theresa nodded.

Off camera, Toby turned to Theresa and her family.

'Thanks for your time. Obviously, we'll have to edit all this footage down to about four to five minutes. I'm sure you'll captivate the people in this area. I've been thinking - it might be an idea to set up a Web Site for you, on which we could make lots of your music available to anyone. Hope you'll be able to enjoy whatever success comes your way. And I can say without a shadow of doubt that everyone will adore you.'

The television people left shortly afterwards; Toby told the family Theresa's story would be shown as an item on the regional news the following Friday. Donna and the rest of the family couldn't wait to see it.

There was great excitement in the air as the day drew nearer; Donna had managed to persuade Doctor Reynolds to allow her to go to the Lacey household to watch the television with them.

When the time came there was total silence in the room as the news programme was broadcast. Theresa's name was mentioned by the announcer almost straight away. Tension mounted as they had to wait right until the end when Theresa's little segment came on.

Donna felt for Theresa when the camera showed her deformity, as in reality it was distressing, but as soon as the music began, her talent shone through, putting all thoughts of everything else in the background. The music only lasted four minutes but anyone watching would have been enthralled even in that short period of time.

As the programme finished there were tears of joy and sadness in Mrs Lacey's eyes, Evan too appeared emotional, and they gathered round Theresa to congratulate her.

Donna, as always, was inspired by Theresa's courage, as well as for her God given gift for music. She envied her as well for being so strong in the face of such an awful illness. And although Donna was responding well to her treatment, she felt guilty and ashamed of the way she'd dealt with her problems, and was truly humbled in Theresa's company.

'What did you think Donna? Were you happy with the way I was portrayed?'

'Sure, it was very tastefully done, and it did concentrate on your music.'

'I'm a little worried about what people thought when they saw me. Think they would have viewed me as some kind of horror show?'

'Of course they wouldn't.' Donna put her arm around Theresa's shoulders. 'They'll have seen you as an incredibly talented musician who's tragically been stricken with a terrible illness. But remember whatever success you get will be through your talent and not because people feel sorry for you.'

Theresa smiled, moving across to kiss Donna on the cheek. 'Am I doing the right thing?'

Donna looked her straight in the eye, finding herself glad to have met Theresa and to have had the privilege of getting to know her. 'Most definitely.'

Theresa seemed happier than ever. The joy she felt seemed to glow out of her.

However, on the way back to the hospital, Donna began to have doubts over what had happened. Suddenly she felt responsible and feared if it went wrong she'd be blamed. Evan glanced across at her while he drove, and realised she had something on her mind.

'All right Donna?'

'Yes...' She scratched her brow. 'But...I'm just not sure we've done the right thing by Theresa. Just how would she cope in front of an audience if it came to it? And what if they react in an adverse way?'

'Don't worry. I've had the same thoughts myself, but I've put them out of my head. It's only natural for people to be a little dismayed when they first see her. Although we're assuming someone will promote her and offer to present her to the public via a concert. But that hasn't happened yet and if it does I'm sure any audience will realise there's much more to her - she's such a brilliant musician and composer, I'm positive the music will take over completely.'

'Hope you're right.'

'I am, believe me.'

◇◇◇

A week later Donna was in the doctor's office for their usual meeting, but for once she didn't mind talking to her. Doctor Reynolds seemed to pick up on it and commented 'You seem in a much brighter mood than usual.'

'I'm not too bad.' She tried not to appear too positive.

'Very glad to hear it Donna. No thoughts of self-harm or suicide lately then?'

'None at all. I've quite surprised myself.'

'Wonderful. That couldn't be down to a certain young male nurse, could it?'

Blushing slightly; an awkward look on her face, she said, 'No, not totally, although he has helped. It's the whole family really. They've been through so much together. But it's Theresa I can't help but admire. When you first look at her face, you feel like crying, and then when you hear her play music, you want to cry your eyes out even more. And now through one television appearance it's truly amazing just how many people want to listen to her music. The number of hits she'd had on her website – and the phone hasn't stopped ringing – it's unbelievable. And now she's been invited to appear in front of an audience for the first time. In a few weeks she'll be performing at Dexford Town Hall on her own with only a few musicians for support. I've nothing but admiration for her – she's so brave and nothing seems to faze her.' She stopped there and then added, 'There are times when I wish I could be like her, anything rather than like me, a poor excuse for a human being.'

Looking at her gravely, and shaking her head as if she didn't agree with how bitter Donna felt, the doctor said, 'It's wonderful how Theresa's music has taken off, but I guess she'd trade it all in to be cured of cancer. Theresa is a very special person, but you shouldn't be so hard on yourself. You are very special too, if only you'd realise it.'

'Oh sure I am – 'Donna said screwing up her face in misery.

'You can be anything you want, Donna. If Theresa can do it with what she's got, so can you. Think about it. Oh and by the way, I've been monitoring your progress. Maybe it's about time we reduced your medication. What do you think?'

Donna was quite taken aback, and the thought of it frightened her. Did she want to? That was the question. She thought that maybe she did.

'All right...I'll give it a go, so long as I have your support to go back on a higher dose if I don't feel so well.'

'Of course. Any ill effects, come and see me at once. Now then, since you've done so well recently, in return I'm willing to relax certain rules for you. From now on, although you'll remain at the Hospital for the time being, I'll allow you a limited amount of freedom. You can come and go as you please, and as long as you return here by six o'clock every evening, that privilege will continue. You can visit your parents, or anyone else you wish. All being well, we'll soon have you back living with your parents again - although naturally that will be a gradual process. But it's certainly something to work towards – don't you think?'

Donna shuddered uncontrollably, as if someone had just told her she was going to die. 'I won't go back to live with them. Not ever – I don't care what you say.'

Doctor Reynolds didn't look surprised at this. 'I was half expecting as much. I told your parents the same thing, but they would insist you'd want to live with them. They'll be very disappointed. Isn't there any way you could patch it up with them? They love you dearly, if only you'd give them a chance.'

Donna shook her head vigorously; annoyed that Doctor Reynolds should even suggest such a thing. 'They've had more chances than they deserve already. I can't face living in their house.'

'But – '

Donna got up from her seat, a look of anguish coming on her face. Doctor Reynolds lifted a hand for her to stop.

'All right, no one's forcing you to go back to them. But you have to live somewhere. Any suggestions? A place of your own perhaps?'

'Haven't given it much thought – I never imagined I'd ever leave here. But I'd rather stay here than live with my folks.'

Doctor Reynolds raised her eyebrows, dropping her eyelids slightly. For a moment, she seemed deep in thought, and stroked her chin. 'Actually, I did have an idea. I've already spoken to the person concerned, and she's all for it. You can stay with her family until you get back on your feet again, since you're so friendly with her son and daughter. I imagine you know who I'm talking about?'

Donna nodded but felt embarrassed. 'Mrs Lacey?'

'Exactly right,' The doctor grinned. 'Apparently, although you may not be aware of it, they have a spare bedroom available. It used to be Cole's, her eldest son's room, but he's in the army and is away a lot. The room is empty right now because he's on duty in Afghanistan. So all being well, if you continue to feel better, you're more than welcome to the room, for as long as Cole is away. How do you feel about that?'

She couldn't believe this was happening, felt unsure at first; a lump came in her throat. Then a huge smile filled her face, which she tried to hide by looking to the floor. Although she hadn't considered it, it seemed the obvious solution. 'I don't know. I get on great with them all; but are you sure they won't mind. I wouldn't want to get under their feet.'

'Of course you wouldn't. I've spoken to Evan about you as well, and he says you've come on in leaps and bounds recently. He thinks it'll help you no end with your recovery, and was going to talk to you about it, but I think he was a bit nervous about you taking it the wrong way. Anyway we agreed, if you didn't want to move back in with your parents, I'd run the idea past you. You could go, in say a fortnight's time. How does that sound?'

'Sounds fine.' There was a wide smile all over her face, once again. They were like a second family to her. But she'd have it out with Evan when she saw him next - about why he'd been so frightened she'd take it the wrong way.

When Evan came for her the next morning, she noticed he had a glint in his eye, and looked pleased with himself for some reason. They walked through the Hospital grounds together, talking mainly about Theresa and her forthcoming concert. Finally, they sat on a bench, set in a small alcove at the front of the building, Donna shivering slightly as although it was sunny, the wind was quite strong cooling down the temperature.

Before long, he surprised her by bringing up the subject that was uppermost in their minds himself.

'Err, I gather 'the doc' has talked you into coming to live with us,' he coughed apprehensively.

'Yes, she has Evan.'

'I'd have asked you myself, but I thought - '

'I know, she told me. I'm not sure it's the right thing to do – not if I've got to see your ugly mush at the breakfast table every morning.'

'Err yes, I never thought of that. Well, I admit I'm not at my best first thing in the morning, that's for sure. But you'll get used to me. In fact, you won't see that much of me, I have to leave for work at seven, and then I'm not back home until about six. So I'll be out of your hair for most of the time.'

'That's a relief. Thank goodness Theresa will be there, otherwise I might not come at all.'

'Oh really.'

'Mind you, your mum's really nice too. Such a good cook, which always helps.'

He scratched the top of his head, and seemed put out about it. Surely he realised she was joking. He was quiet for a few seconds, obviously not knowing what to say.

Suddenly she burst out laughing, but then when he realised what she was up to, he joined in. They were both giggling, tears of laughter rolled down her cheeks.

'Got you going then.'

'You think so? Well, just for that I might ask mum if I can cook for you. Then you'd definitely have something to complain about. So there.' He bobbed out his tongue at her.

She did the same back to him.

'You'll come then?'

'Yes, as long as you're sure I won't be in the way.'

'Course you won't – silly. I'll tell you what will irritate you the most, and that's Theresa practising on her keyboard, day and night. I know she's brilliant, but when it's six to eight hours at a time - it'll drive you mad. And she's worse than normal right now with that concert coming up. I don't know where she gets the energy from.'

'It's in her blood, she wants it so much. You can't blame her for that. This concert will be so special.'

'You could be right.'

'Sure your mum doesn't mind me staying with you, Evan. I feel so guilty about it. I should be standing on my own two feet, getting a place of my own - I've got a degree in Mathematics for God's sake.' She lowered her head as if in shame.

'Don't be silly. You've been ill and now you need help to get yourself well again. We're your friends, and that's what we're here for, so I don't want to hear any more about it. Mum said you're moving in a week on Friday - so we might get to spend the weekend together.'

She nodded. 'You'll come and fetch me, then?'

'Of course I will – and don't keep me waiting, or else.'

'Yes sir.' She gave him a mock salute. 'I'll look forward to that.'

However, the more she thought about it the more she worried it might be the wrong move. She'd hate to fall out with any of them after how good they'd been to her. And on top of that, in her present state, that might have devastating consequences for her. Only time would tell.

Chapter 19

STANDING BY THE BED WITH A SUITCASE BESIDE HER, DONNA WAITED IMPATIENTLY FOR EVAN TO COME AND PICK HER UP.

When he came, Doctor Reynolds was with him, all smiles.

'Well then Donna, I see you're ready.'

'Yes, doctor.'

'It's been a long hard journey for you – and no one is more pleased than me that you've finally managed to come through your problems. I did have my doubts about you at one time, but I'm so glad you've proved me wrong.'

'So long as I don't have a relapse.' There were tears in her eyes.

'Why should you? You're staying with a wonderful family. If you don't make it with them, there's something wrong somewhere.'

Donna couldn't help but hug the tiny doctor, who looked close to tears herself.

'Don't forget you have to come and see me every Friday at three o'clock and in the meantime whatever you do don't reduce your tablets any further without reference to me, even if you continue to feel better. And if you feel ill at any time just call me straightaway.'

'OK I will.'

'Your parents still want to see you, I've informed them of the arrangements at Mrs Lacey's house and given them the telephone number, with Evan's mum's permission. All being well I'd advise you to visit them in the not too distant future.'

Donna shrugged her shoulders in reply saying, 'Well I don't know, but I'll see you on Friday.'

Evan picked up the suitcase, and looked to her for the go ahead to leave. She nodded, had a quick look at the room that had been her home for so long, and then was on her way. She'd never been so glad to get out of a place, apart from when she lived with her parents.

'So how you feeling Donna?' he asked as they walked together down the corridor.

'OK, just a bit jittery – that's all.'

'That's only natural. It'll go once you've settled down with us.'

She smiled and hoped this was the case, but realised that this arrangement wouldn't last forever. At some stage she would have to go back to her parents or find a flat of her own.

Evan drove them the short distance to his house. After parking the car they took the luggage from the boot and turning round saw the front door open. Mrs Lacey and Theresa came rushing out to greet them.

'Donna!' Theresa exclaimed, a warm smile coming across her disfigured face. She held out her arms for Donna to go into. They hugged and then it was Mrs Lacey's turn. Donna was so touched by this show of affection. Treating her almost like a long lost daughter.

Inside, Evan took the luggage upstairs to what was Cole's bedroom, placing it on the bed. Theresa had decided to help Donna unpack so she followed them up.

'All right girls, I'll leave you to it, shall I?' Evan said, walking to the door.

But the 'girls' were too engrossed to notice him leave.

Theresa looked admiringly at the expensive dresses and tops as they were hung up, obviously she would have loved to try them on.

'I'm so pleased you're staying with us Donna. You're my very best friend – you know that?'

'I do. And you're my very best friend as well.' She laughed.

'So what are you up to afterwards? If you're doing nothing special, I'd love to play for you. I want to go through what I intend to play at the concert, if that's all right.'

'Theresa, I'd be so honoured if you would. I love listening to all kinds of stuff, although I can't say I know a lot about music or the mechanics of it.'

'You don't need to. After all who in the audience will know anything about how I'm playing the notes. And it's the public at large that counts – not highbrow critics writing for their posh magazines.' Said in such a convincing tone of voice she seemed unfazed by the forthcoming concert.

'In that case, I'm just the type of person you're looking for.'

Donna knew Theresa held her in high regard, but would she still think the same if she found out about the suicide attempts? The family were aware Donna was a patient at the hospital, and therefore had psychological problems, but obviously Evan wasn't allowed to tell them the full extent of her troubles. Did he know exactly what had happened to her previously when she'd been raped? She doubted it.

The two girls came downstairs shortly afterwards. They sat around the television watching an old film. Evan yawned, turning to Donna who was talking to his mother about what she was making for tea.

'Hey Donna, want to go to the cinema tonight after tea?' he asked tapping her on the shoulder.

'What, oh err…' Donna said, not wanting to turn him down, yet remembering what she'd already told Theresa. Then she glanced at Theresa, who was obviously aware of her dilemma.

'It's all right Donna, you carry on, I can always play for you some other time.' A trace of disappointment was evident in her voice.

There was a bewildered expression on Evan's face.

'No, no. I'm sorry Evan, but I promised Theresa I'd listen to her play a full concert programme tonight - and I never break my promises.'

'OK, that's fine,' he said holding out his hands, not looking in the least bit put out. 'In fact if you want I'll come and listen as well.'

'Yes, but you always say I'm good, brother, no matter how I play. Donna's promised to give me an honest opinion, and that's what I value most.'

'But I can still listen, can't I? And I'll tell you what, I'll keep my thoughts to myself. How would that be?'

'Can I listen as well?' their mother asked butting in. 'And I'll keep my thoughts to myself as well.'

Theresa pulled a face. 'I'm going to hold you both to that,' she warned pointing a finger at them.

After tea, they all went up to Theresa's room. Evan and Donna sat on the bed, while her mother sat on a chair Evan had brought in for her. Theresa looked a little embarrassed; and blushed slightly as she sat down in front of her keyboard.

'Ready when you are, sis.'

'Keep quiet will you? I'm just going over it in my mind,' she said staring into space, moving her head from one side to the other, mouthing to herself exactly how and what she was going to play. And then after a few seconds hesitation she began.

For almost an hour without a single break, Theresa had her audience, of three, mesmerised. Donna recognised some of the music from bits she'd played for the television programme, and others presumably new compositions, had been written by her since. But she was taking an almighty gamble since the audience would never have heard any of the music before. Yet in this rehearsal, it had worked perfectly. The emotion and beauty of the melodies were breath-taking. They all seemed transfixed by it.

At the end of the dummy run, Theresa looked exhausted. As she closed her eyes, and slumped back in her chair she began to cough and splutter, and sneezed again and again. Donna and Evan went to her side at once, and handed her handkerchiefs and tissues She sneezed once more, and they were shocked to see blood gushing down her nose. Instinctively she tilted her head back in an effort to stop the flow. They both feared the practice session had gone on too long.

'Oh my God, my head hurts,' Theresa complained touching both sides of her face.

'We'll get you one of your pain killers Theresa,' her mother said. 'Evan, they're in her top draw over there. And Donna would you fetch her a glass of water? There should be some glasses on the window sill in the bathroom.'

Theresa managed to take the tablet with some water, and after lying down for a few minutes, the bleeding subsided. By breathing in deeply, she gradually seemed to recover. Donna was relieved to see her smiling at them again.

'I'm all right now. The pain's gone and I don't feel sick any more. Let's just forget about it shall we? My music is more important than a silly nose bleed.'

But they were all very concerned for her, especially having seen all the blood. It was so upsetting to see this talented young girl in such a bad state of health.

An expression of exasperation came on Theresa's face, as she lay there. 'Stop worrying about me everyone. I get these spasms every now and then. They've been happening for ages. I used to worry, but not anymore – and neither should you.'

'Look sis, these bouts are worse than they used to be, you have to admit that yourself. And you've never lost so much blood before. That's rather worrying. You need to tell the doctor what's happening - maybe he can help.'

Theresa glared at him as if she thought he was crazy. 'Don't be stupid Evan. You know what he'd say as well as I do - and there's no way I'm going through that. What's the point of having any treatment? It won't help much anyway, and if I do I'll never be fit enough to play my music, or compose it? The outcome will be the same no matter what I do.'

'Won't you see him just to make sure there's nothing else he can do? You losing all that blood is worrying me to death,' he replied with moist eyes.

'Stop going on at me, will you? It's up to me what I do. All right, so I'm dying and who knows how long I have left. But while I still can, I intend making the most of it, and nobody is going to stop me – do you hear?' There was passion and determination in her voice and in the redness on her face.

'No one's trying to stop you Theresa. You'll do this for sure, and we'll be right behind you.'

'I know you will, Donna.'

As Theresa got up to pack away her keyboard Evan raised his hand to stop her saying, 'I'll do that sis, I think you have done more than enough for one night.'

So she lay back, her eyes bloodshot, her face suddenly pale. Donna could see, the amount of practice required was obviously too much for her. It seemed to be taking its toll on their mother as well; as during the incident her eyes were full and she had very little to say. But what could Donna do? Theresa was determined to carry on whatever the cost.

They were all lost in thought, until Evan broke the ice by saying 'Shall I get us all a drink?'

'Oh yes please,' Theresa said lifting up her head. 'Playing that keyboard for so long has given me a thirst.'

He was only a few minutes, returning with a tray containing four glasses of diluted orange squash, which he handed around to them.

'So what will you do now you're here, Donna?' Theresa asked, looking to have recovered slightly from her marathon keyboard session. 'I don't suppose you'll want to keep me company every day of the week.'

'Course I would. There's nothing I'd like more than to stay with you here every day, but sooner or later I have to go back into the big bad world and do something with my own life.'

'You thinking about doing some more modelling?' Theresa asked, her face seemingly alive with excitement at the prospect of this.

'Definitely not. To be honest, as I've probably said before, while there might be lots of money and prestige out there on the catwalk, I hate prancing around like an idiot in those stupid clothes nobody ever wears. No, it'll be something else, but what, I don't know yet.'

'What did you do before your illness, dear?' Mrs Lacey asked with interest.

'Believe it or not, I used to be a Statistical Analyst. I've always been quite good at Maths, you see. And my job involved analysing data, forecasting trends and making predictions based on the data,' she explained.

'Wow, that sounds really important,' Theresa giggled. 'You must have done well at school.'

'Well I did get a first class honours degree in Maths,' Donna said, trying not to sound as if she was boasting.

'Hey, so you've got brains as well as beauty,' Theresa said cupping her hands together. 'What a wonderful combination. I never dreamed you were that clever. Hey, I bet you could predict how long I've got to live, couldn't you?'

Donna didn't like the way this conversation was going. 'Well I don't think anyone could make that sort of prediction out of a few figures, but it's much too distressing to even think about. You've got to remember everyone is different, so it would be pointless anyway.'

'Perhaps I shouldn't dwell on what might or might not happen. Best to take each day as it comes, live from day to day. That's all I can do.' She grabbed hold of Donna's arm. Donna felt so sad for her, and put her own hand over Theresa's and squeezed it gently.

'Hey, Evan, did you know your friend was a brain box?' Theresa laughed.

'Yes, I think she did mention it. I knew she was very talented, so maybe she should use that talent.'

'I can't cope with that sort of job right now, I might as well face up to it. I may never get back into that kind of work.'

'What then?' Evan asked.

'If I get myself back to work, it'll have to be something menial at first, anything to get into the swing of things again. Possibly catering. You know something like dishing out meals in some local supermarket restaurant, a job that won't tax my brains, or stress me out.'

'But that'll never satisfy you, will it Donna?' Theresa said shaking her head.

'Maybe not, but if it gets me back on my feet again, it's a start. It'll help boost my confidence, and then once I get that back, there'll be no stopping me.' She was trying her best to sound upbeat.

'From little acorns mighty oaks grow.'

'Yes, Theresa, Something like that.'

Soon afterwards, they went downstairs to watch television. Theresa sat in the middle of her mother and Donna on the sofa. Evan sat on the armchair.

'Your playing was beautiful tonight. Can't wait for this concert of yours, even though I'm still very nervous about it. You'll make your old mum feel so proud.'

Theresa looked happy but also a little embarrassed by this praise.

Donna prayed Theresa would be fit for the concert, although from what she'd seen, was sure her friend would somehow find the courage to pull it off, no matter what she suffered as a result.

'How do you feel about living with us now? Think you'll settle down OK? Mrs Lacey asked, glancing across at her.

'I'm loving it already.' Donna's eyes moved to Evan, who had a warm grin on his face. 'You've all been so kind to me; I don't know how I'll ever repay you.'

'Repay us by keeping yourself well from now on, eh my dear. I imagine you've been through a lot, although my son here, isn't allowed to tell us much about it. Hopefully this could be a turning point for you. A girl like you shouldn't have horrible things happening to her. I don't know what the future holds for you, but I'm sure you're destined for greater things.'

'Honestly, I'm no different from anyone else. It's how people treat me that's the key. If they treat me normally like you have there's not a problem. But I have to get a job of some sort in the future because I need an income. Although I don't know if I can go back to a responsible analytical job at present anyway.'

'You can't do anything about what other people think of you, or what they think you should do with your future. Just do what you believe is best for you. Ignore the comments about what you should do to make lots of money.'

'It's a pity everyone doesn't see life as you do. All I really want is to be ordinary, and to lead a normal life.'

'You've already achieved so much,' Theresa said. 'Getting that degree must have been such hard work. You did that by yourself – and you should be proud. Just as I will be, if people love my music at the concert.'

'I know, but you have so much more courage than me. Wish I could be like that.'

Theresa smiled. She obviously didn't consider herself as courageous. 'I'm not brave. If you knew how I felt inside, you'd have a shock, I'm so frightened of dying, and scared out of my wits over the concert. I dread to think how people will react when they see me. Maybe it would be better if I could just go to sleep and never wake up.'

Donna could have cried as she witnessed the scene in front of her – Theresa being comforted by her mother, their eyes brimming with tears.

'You'll be fine Theresa, and don't forget we'll all be there spurring you on,' Donna said.

'I know, maybe that's what will get me through it.'

For the rest of the evening they all concentrated on the television. Donna noticed Theresa was dozing, which was probably the effect of the strong pain killers. A loud noise on the television suddenly jolted her awake and as she opened her eyes and yawned said 'Think I'll go to bed now.' And noticing they were all staring at her added, 'Before I bring the house down.'

They all smiled at this.

Donna wasn't far behind her. Slipping between the sheets of her new bed, she had hoped to feel relaxed in this new environment. But as various distressing thoughts went through her mind, she found it difficult to sleep. Although she had her freedom, she still had her worries; one of which was what would become of Theresa as her illness progressed - feeling a strong need to be by her side for as long as she was needed. Also she wondered what would happen when Cole came back; something which hadn't been discussed with Doctor Reynolds previously.

As the night wore on Donna did finally fall asleep, but it was anything but restful, filled instead with dreams of her time in that horrible room in the hospital. And then the smiling face of Evan appeared to float over her, looking at her in a way no other man had. Frightening her, almost as much as the man who'd raped her. As the dream went on, she kept seeing Evan coming towards her, again and again, trying to take hold of her hand and when she wouldn't let him, she saw his face gradually disappear into the distance. She woke up with a start and as usual, had no one's arms to fall into.

She lay awake thinking how nice he was. And if he felt the same way... well she just didn't know. They certainly enjoyed each other's company and he'd always acted the perfect gentleman with her. But if she hadn't the ability to return any affection he might give her, sooner or later, he'd get hurt and that may spoil everything.

<><><>

Monday came and off she went to Dexford Job Centre, where she had a lengthy discussion with an advisor about going back to work. She showed him a Statement for Fitness to Work which her own GP had issued, declaring her fit to do an unskilled part-time job. From the information supplied the advisor realised she'd be best suited to a job without responsibility, obviously low paid but at least it would be the first step to getting back to work properly.

Perhaps a job working as a waitress or a kitchen assistant may be suitable the advisor suggested, and Donna agreed she might be able to manage that type of work. There were several vacancies in this criteria and she decided to apply for the three which interested her most.

After filling in all the appropriate forms she left the Job Centre in the knowledge she could claim Job Seekers Allowance. This would be the first bit of money she'd handled since being in hospital and would give her a measure of independence. It would also enable her to give Mrs Lacey enough money to cover her living costs.

Theresa was downstairs practising on her keyboard again, when she got back and seemed so pleased to see her.

'How'd you get on?' she asked pausing from her keyboard for a few minutes.

'All right. It'll be nice to have some of my own money again even if it is just dole money, but even nicer if I can get a job. Shame I can't do what I did before. But it's best to take this gradually, start from the bottom and work myself up – if that's at all possible.'

'I'll miss you when you're back at work. You're great company for me. I look up to you so much after what you achieved at Uni. Like to think if it hadn't been for my illness, I could have studied something worthwhile like you did.' As she said this Donna thought she could see tears in the eyes of her best friend.

'I don't know that I'm someone to look up to. I've done nothing to be proud of. I'm not a very good example to anyone after what's happened to me.'

'Don't say that, silly.'

'You've got more to be proud of than I have. Look what you've done through your music despite your illness.'

'But you're special Donna. Don't think I've ever met anyone as brainy and as pretty as you. Even Evan says so,' Theresa revealed.

'Oh really.' Donna felt slightly embarrassed. 'Well, he's talking rubbish. There's nothing special about me, never has been. My appearance doesn't make me any better than anyone else. People aren't how they look; you of all people should know that.'

'Yes, but you're as nice as you look,' There was an admiring gaze on her face.

Donna felt uncomfortable about being held in such high regard, fearing she may not be able to live up to it.

Over the next couple of weeks Donna attended several interviews and to her surprise a short time later, as they were sitting at the breakfast table, Mrs Lacey came in with the post and handed Donna an official looking letter. She hurriedly opened it and exclaimed, 'Hey, you never guess what!'

'What is it?' Evan beamed having seen how delighted Donna looked.

'I've been offered a job at Dexford Road Primary School as a Catering Assistant. Twenty hours a week, mornings, and the pay isn't too bad either. What do you think of that?'

'Wow, that's wonderful news Donna,' Mrs Lacey commented.

'Brilliant, congratulations,' Evan laughed, putting his arm round her and squeezing her shoulder.

'Glad it's only part-time,' Theresa said in a sort of reserved disappointed way. 'Maybe you can still keep me company in the afternoons.'

'Of course I will. I'll only be working from nine-thirty to one-thirty, so my afternoons are all yours.' Donna widened her eyes at Theresa.

'Only, I need your feedback for my music.'

'Don't worry, you'll get it.' This seemed to hearten Theresa.

'So when do you start love?' Mrs Lacey asked.

'Two weeks today.'

'That's only a week before my concert. Wish you could start after that.'

'Theresa, I do too but I haven't got any choice. Either I start then or I don't get the job. But honestly, when I'm here, I'll support you any way I can. Now stop fretting.'

'Sorry. It's just that I feel so much better when you're around.'

'But I'm not doing anything, except to encourage you, pet. Hey, I heard some of your music on a local radio station earlier. Can't believe how well it's all going. Everyone was praising it. You know, I think you could get yourself a record contract if you've a mind.'

'You really think so?'

'You wait until after the concert, I think the offers will come flooding in,' Donna nodded to her.

'Wouldn't that be fantastic sis?' Evan was obviously trying to imagine what it would be like. 'Think of it, number one in the charts. That would be awesome.'

Theresa seemed starry eyed, with her head in the clouds, hoping no doubt that success would be all she imagined it to be.

◇◇◇

The Friday afternoon before the concert Donna had just returned from work.

'Come and sit down, and tell me how your day's been,' Theresa said.

'Still pretty nerve racking, but as the week's gone on, I've felt a bit better. The kids have been fine, although they can be little devils when they want to be, make no mistake.'

'Think you'll like it there?'

'It should be all right. The more I get into it, the more confident I feel. The teachers and kitchen staff have been so supportive - that's what's made the difference for me.'

'I'm happy for you Donna, you deserve it.'

'And how about you? Are you feeling all right? Looking forward to the concert tomorrow night?'

Theresa shuffled uncomfortably on the sofa. It appeared she was experiencing a few jitters, but who could blame her?

'Don't know. I want to play my music to people but I feel so self-conscious and nervous. Oh God Donna, what if I freeze out there on the stage? That's my biggest fear. I've got to keep telling myself I'll be fine once I can start to play. I'm so glad you, Evan, and mum will be out there at the front of the audience. If I keep looking at you, maybe I can pull it off.'

'We'll all be egging you on. You'll be a sensation, I promise you,' Donna said trying to encourage her.

Chapter 20

THE AFTERNOON OF THE DAY OF THE CONCERT HAD BEEN HECTIC, AND PREPARATIONS WERE WELL UNDER WAY. Donna was already dressed and took one final look in the mirror before leaving her bedroom. She had decided to wear a three quarter length navy blue jacket with matching skirt and plain white blouse Her face had just a touch of make up around the eyes and cheeks and her hair was loose. Overall she had tried to dress conservatively so as not to draw attention to herself, as this was supposed to be Theresa's big night.

As she left her bedroom she knocked on Theresa's bedroom door before stepping inside. 'Are you ready yet?'

'Just be a couple of minutes.'

'OK, I'll wait downstairs for you.'

When Evan and Mrs Lacey told her how lovely she looked, Donna shrugged this off and said, 'You wait till you see Theresa.'

Theresa did appear a few minutes later, and Evan was the first to say, 'Wow! You look gorgeous sis, you really do.'

'Thanks for that Evan. Even if it isn't true, it's the thought that counts.'

'Honestly Theresa, you do look radiant,' Donna said.

'But not as pretty as you.'

Donna frowned. In truth, she could see Theresa looked stunning. She was wearing tight grey trousers and a white blouse, which enhanced her shapely figure. Her hair was long and black with a natural wave, and there was a warmth to her green eyes.

How tragic that she'd been afflicted by such a dreadful disease that had ravaged her otherwise beautiful face. Theresa's mum stared at her admiringly. She'd be so proud of her when she got out there on stage in front of all those people. There were tears in her eyes. Evan too looked emotional. This would be a special night, a night none of them would ever forget.

'It's just a shame Cole couldn't make it. Then I'd have had all my children round me.'

'It doesn't matter, mum. I know being in the army means it's impossible to get away unless it's a wedding or a funeral, or the birth of a child. But Evan has promised to send him a DVD of the concert.'

'He'll probably ring later tonight when it's over,' Evan said.

Donna had never met Cole. In fact, she didn't know much about him except that he was serving in Afghanistan. But she did wonder why very little was said about him.

'Hey,' Theresa said. 'Have you all seen the time?'

'God, you're right,' Donna said looking at her watch. 'It's almost six o'clock. We'd better get a move on.'

'It's all right everyone.' Evan held up his hand to stop them in their tracks. 'Everything is under control. There's a car waiting outside to take us to the theatre.'

And true to his word, pulling back the curtains he showed them the white Rolls Royce parked outside the house, complete with chauffeur in full grey uniform, standing outside the car in wait for them.

Smirking when he saw the astonished looks on their faces, Evan said, 'Come along ladies, your chariot awaits.'

The two girls wasted no time and as they stepped outside began to snigger, in what seemed a surreal situation. As the chauffeur opened the doors to allow them to get in Theresa squealed 'Oh my God, I almost feel like a celebrity.' And she sat back on the leather upholstery looking rather pleased with herself.

'Perhaps that's because you are sis.'

Evan's plan of finding a way to lighten the tension seemed to have worked.

The Rolls moved off, amid a few curious looks from neighbours and passers-by alike. They travelled slowly down the road and out towards Dexford Town Centre, making for the Town Hall situated in the middle of the High Street. The Rolls parked right outside the front of the building. The chauffeur got out to open the doors for them. Evan's mother was out first, followed by Evan and Donna, who took his arm. Then last of all came Theresa.

They were directed to a side entrance and once inside taken to a makeshift dressing room, the door to which was labelled with Theresa's name. Donna was very pleased with the way things were going so far. Theresa opened the door, and they followed her inside. Evan and Donna stood at the back of the room, while Theresa and her mother set about making sure she looked as good as she possibly could, in the circumstances.

In an apparent effort to calm herself down, Theresa started to take in deep breaths, and seemed to avoid looking at herself in the mirror. Tears suddenly started to roll down her cheeks, and for a second Donna feared her friend wouldn't be able to go through with it, even at this late stage.

'It's no good,' she blubbered, taking hold of her mother's hand. 'I...I...can't go out there in front of all those people. Can't bear them staring, sniggering and laughing behind my back, the way everybody else does.'

Her mother cuddled her, as if she was still a little girl. 'Don't be silly. Everyone will love you for what you're doing tonight. All of them will wish they'd got just a tiny bit of your talent.'

'But what about my face? I feel so self-conscious and ugly all of a sudden. Perhaps I should wear a veil or something to cover it up. I'd give anything to be like you, Donna. You always look so fantastic. Why can't I be like that for once in my life?' she cried looking at Donna over her mother's shoulder.

'Come on Theresa, please don't get upset,' her mother said. 'A lot of people have come here to hear you play. They don't care how you look. It's you, the person who writes and plays such beautiful music that matters. You go out there and give them a show they'll remember for the rest of their lives.'

'But I can't face it. I thought I could, but it's just too much for me.'

As Theresa moved away from her mother, she sat down on a stool. Donna stepped forward, bent down, and lifted Theresa's chin up with her thumb. 'Theresa, you can do this. Don't let all the hard work you've put in be for nothing. And what about your audience? Over a thousand people are out there waiting for you. They'll be so disappointed. I know how hard this is for you, but think how you'll feel when it's over and you've given all those people a concert they'll never forget. And us too.'

Theresa suddenly went red in the face, breathed in deeply and looked slightly glassy-eyed. She heaved as if she was going to be sick, and grabbed hold of Donna's arm so hard she winced. But then Theresa appeared to regain control, and her grip loosened.

The door to her dressing room opened. A young man's face appeared to tell her five minutes until she was due on stage. It made her jump and look to Donna again for support.

'Look Theresa I'm not going to let you back down from this, I know how you feel – I used to feel physically sick before my modelling sessions on the catwalk, but this is different. I never wanted to be involved in modelling, and I don't intend to be ever again. But you're not the same, deep down there is nothing you want more than to go out there and play your music. Here, I have a little something that might help you and bring you luck. I've had my gold St Christopher engraved with your name; I inherited it from my grandmother and I'm passing it on to you. I wore it to every examination I took, it gave me the strength to go through with it no matter what my parents wanted for me.'

Theresa was momentarily dumbstruck, and tear drops began to run down her cheeks from closed lashes as she gulped, 'Thank you, Donna – I'll treasure this always. I don't know what I'd do without you.'

By this time they were all crying and Evan moved close to her and said. 'Sis, please... I know how much this means to you – and we'll be so proud.'

Theresa dried her eyes and looked from one to the other of them. Donna's heart beat faster as she tried to work out whether or not Theresa had it in her to go through with it. Then slowly

Theresa's face appeared to look calmer, her mouth was set in a determined straight line. 'OK, I'll be all right,' she said, holding her stomach. 'I'm going out there now, so help me God. Wish me luck.'

She got up, with Donna, Evan and her mother gathering round, embracing and encouraging her too. Then opened the door, walked out, and made her way to the back of the stage.

Donna led the way to their places in the front row of the hall. The curtain was still down. There were rumblings from the audience, as they waited in anticipation.

After a few minutes, a local radio deejay came on to the stage in front of the curtain. Donna only recognised him when he spoke; his voice deep and mellow, and well known around Dexford.

'Good evening ladies and gentlemen. Welcome to an evening of musical excellence from an exciting new talent. Accompanied only by a backing group, this young lady has been an overnight sensation after appearing on TV. Playing a wide selection of musical styles and all her own compositions, could you all please give a warm round of applause to Theresa Lacey.' He lifted his arm as the curtain slowly opened, and then disappeared out of view. The lights dimmed, and the audience began to clap.

Donna felt a tiny flicker of apprehension as the spotlights homed in on Theresa, sitting at her keyboard, her good side facing the audience. She nodded, then the atmosphere went quiet, whilst everyone waited for her to start.

At the back of the stage, a small group of musicians, consisting of bass and lead guitar, drums and violin, waited for her cue. For all of thirty seconds in deadly silence everyone stared up at the stage, wondering what was going on.

Then suddenly Theresa began to play her keyboard. It was quiet and slow at first. People struggled to hear it, but then all at once it became louder and very emotional, gradually building up into something very passionate that ended in a breath taking finale.

This first piece lasted a little over seven minutes, everyone seemed to have been caught off guard, they suddenly looked mesmerised by the sheer beauty and excellence of the playing. At the end of it there was rapturous applause that seemed to go on forever.

Once it had stopped Theresa spoke a little timidly into the microphone, introducing her next piece.

As the audience took to her, Theresa's confidence grew, so that before long she was playing effortlessly with a great deal of skill.

Her set lasted well over an hour and a half, and had the audience shouting for an encore. This must have heartened and thrilled Theresa and then Donna was amazed to see her standing up to face the audience. It seemed she had almost forgotten about her condition, so much so that she began to laugh, tears of joy trickling down her cheeks. She bowed, and looked up at the sea of joyous faces, then down to the first row where Donna, Evan and her mother were sitting. She blew them a kiss. It must have been the happiest moment of her short life.

Then almost in slow motion, everyone watched in horror as Theresa's head went back, her eyes rolled until only the whites showed. This was followed by a high-pitched scream of agony. A frothy red mixture oozed from her mouth, as she collapsed to the ground right there on the stage.

There were cries and gasps of horror from the audience. Donna jumped up from her seat, followed closely by Evan and Mrs Lacey. They climbed onto the stage, making straight for Theresa lying slumped on the stage floor. Other people swarmed round her too, including the backing group and people from behind the scenes. All concerned, and wanting to see if she was all right.

Evan got to her first, with Donna close behind. She watched him cradle her in his arms, aware at once that she was dead as her eyes were wide open and still. Evan hurriedly closed them, whispering 'Oh God, no…' over and over again.

Within minutes an ambulance arrived, but they were too late. A doctor pronounced her dead at the scene. As Evan finally released hold of Theresa's body, allowing the ambulance men to carry the body away on a stretcher, Mrs Lacey became hysterical. Tears came flooding out of her, some dropping off the end of her chin. Instinctively Donna took this dear woman in her arms, amid her own grief.

It had originally been arranged for the same chauffeur-driven car to return to take them home, but now as they got in the waiting car, once the ambulance had gone, the earlier light hearted atmosphere had turned into a melancholy feeling of grief. On the journey home, they sat silent obviously finding it hard to take in the scene they'd actually witnessed, each locked in their own thoughts. Donna had regarded Theresa as a special person, someone she felt privileged to call a true friend. And she'd been taken from her.

Arriving at the house shortly afterwards, Mrs Lacey was inconsolable, perhaps it was the pile of music on the corner of the dining table or the silk scarf over the back of the sofa, but once again the flood gates opened, and she was unable to stop the tears. Donna placed an arm around her shoulders while she sobbed – there was little else she could do. She felt nauseated and uneasy in such a sombre atmosphere. It had always been a happy house, and Theresa had made it that way, despite her illness. She'd been such a positive person in spite of everything, and had brought joy into their lives with her music. Now she was gone how were they going to carry on?

With the atmosphere so sad and grave, Donna thought somehow she must encourage these two people, now so dear to her, to open their hearts. Then Evan suddenly spoke without being coaxed. 'Mum, I'll have to let Cole know about this.'

'I know, but how will you contact him?'

'Through the army. I have a number he told me to ring in an emergency. I'll do it straightaway so that he'll have time to get over here for the funeral. I'm sure he'll be given special dispensation.'

'All right Evan, just do what you think is best,' his mother said, her whole body seeming consumed with emotion.

Evan opened his wallet and pulled out a card. He tapped in the number on his mobile. As soon as it was answered, when he said he needed to speak urgently to Cole Lacey, he was told that would be impossible right now as Cole was in a war zone. He asked for a message to be passed on to Cole, that he needed to contact his family as soon as possible.

A few minutes later the phone rang. Evan quickly got up to answer it.

'Oh hallo Cole, I'm really sorry mate, but something really terrible has happened…' he began.

Donna only heard Evan's part of the conversation, but got the gist of it, that Cole was as heartbroken as his brother.

After about ten minutes, he rang off. 'He thinks they'll fly him over here on the first available flight mum.'

Evan's mother nodded sadly, her eyes squeezing out yet more tears even though there couldn't be many left.

'Should I vacate his room, Mrs Lacey?' Donna asked.

'No, no need to worry about that. He can sleep in Theresa's room.'

'I wouldn't mind. Don't want to cause any trouble. If I'm in the way, I'll move out altogether.'

Mrs Lacey smiled sadly, but shook her head vigorously. 'Don't be silly. I'd be offended if you did, and it would make this whole ordeal much worse. You meant a lot to Theresa, and were almost like sisters. Once you came to live here, she seemed to get a new lease of life. She said you gave her the confidence to do what she did; she looked up to you because of what you've achieved, and were such a good friend to her. She treasured that, so I'll never forget what you did for her.'

'I didn't do much,' was all Donna could say as she started to well up, feeling Theresa had helped her, not the other way around.

'Yes, you did – but to lose her so young is too much to take.' She broke down once again. Both Evan and Donna went to hug her. After several minutes, she finally stopped crying.

'Mum, why don't you go to bed now, try and get some rest.'

She nodded, with Donna at hand to help her to the bedroom.

After hugging and holding her for a few more minutes, Donna came back downstairs to sit next to Evan, who head in hands seemed to be sniffing back tears every now and then. He didn't look at her, obviously lost in his own grief.

They sat in relative silence, barely murmuring to each other. Donna also found it hard to keep her emotions in check, as she'd lost the only real friend she had. But it was nothing to what Evan was going through. Theresa was his own flesh and blood, and from what she'd seen, he'd loved her dearly.

When it came, it was a deluge. His shoulders moved up and down as great sobs came from his lips sounding like he was in mortal pain. It was horrible to see him like this – he was devastated.

As she took him in her arms, her heart stopped momentarily for a couple of seconds, the memory of the rape still fresh in her mind. It was the first time she had embraced anyone male since that awful night. She had to be strong and fight the desire to get away from him. Thankfully, his grief was genuine.

Then as the crying subsided he said in a whisper 'Oh why, oh why, why did she have to die?'

'I don't know. Why does anyone have to die like that? It isn't fair.'

'But she was on the verge of something special. Such a brilliant musician and composer. It takes a genius to write those tunes of hers.'

'Her work will live on, Evan. We have the recordings, all her work is there for everyone to hear and remember. And we must promote that in her memory.'

'I don't know what I'll do without her.'

'Nor I. It will leave a huge gap, no doubt about that. We have to make sure she's never forgotten'

'She may never have been as clever as you, but as a human being I think she was your equal. There was something unique about her; she had a quality few people possess, and I don't think we'll ever see the like of it again.'

Donna was troubled. 'I can only dream of getting anywhere near what she did despite her illness. Being clever and going to Uni is nothing compared to that.'

Evan tried to smile, but it couldn't disguise his true feelings, and she wondered if he had the strength to get over this. Now she dreaded to think what this would do to him.

'We'll all miss her so much –'

'Me as much as anyone. She was the one person I felt I could talk to, the sister I never had.' They hugged one another again. 'We have to help each other to get through this Evan - it's the only way.'

'Yes, I know. I'm so glad you're here. Or I think I'd go to pieces again like I did when I had to give up playing football.'

She smiled, hoping this wasn't the case.

◇◇◇

Late evening the next day, Evan and his mother were sitting subdued on the sofa. Donna kept glancing at them every now and then, worrying over what effect Theresa's death was having on them. There was a knock at the door. Neither of them were quick to get to their feet, so Donna took it upon herself to answer it. She switched on the light in the hall and through the frosted glass saw a dark figure standing there, but didn't think about who it might be. She opened the door to see a young man standing before her. Tall and broad with large shoulders and body. His crew cut black hair and shadow of a beard gave him the appearance of a hard man. His freshly pressed khaki uniform looked smart, complete with a black beret tucked in a shoulder strap, and he carried a large kit bag on his back. Obviously this was Cole, Evan's big brother.

'Who are you?' He looked puzzled to see her answering the door, his ice blue eyes lacking the warmth of his brother's, inspecting her like a soldier on parade. His eyes twitched as if he recognised her from somewhere, although he said nothing.

'I'm Donna,' she told him simply.

'Nice to meet you, Donna. And what are you doing here?'

'I lodge here.'

'Really, that's a pleasant surprise. Well I'm Cole, Evan's brother. So how about letting me in, darling?' he said grinning, revealing a gap between his two front teeth.

'Oh yes, sorry. I was miles away.' As she stood to one side, allowing him to come past, for some reason she shivered.

He put his bag down in the hall, and groaned before stretching. 'That bag's a bit heavy. And I'm totally whacked. I've had a long journey – but I'm here now. I suppose I'd best go and see mum and Evan. I presume they're in the front, are they? Terrible thing about Theresa, wasn't it? It's hard to imagine never seeing her again.'

Donna opened the door to the living room, where Evan and his mother were sitting. The sight of Cole got them both to their feet, and across to him. There were lots of tears as they all hugged one another.

Feeling a little out of it, Donna looked on, but as she wasn't family, she couldn't expect anything else, and just listened intently. Evan told his brother about the dreadful events of the previous day. The whole heart breaking story brought it back home to them again. Having sat down the atmosphere became tense. Cole looked stony faced, mulling over all that had been said, obviously he'd loved his sister a great deal too.

'She didn't have much of a life,' Cole said finally, frowning to show a deep crease in his forehead. 'We all knew she was living on borrowed time, but this still comes as an awful shock.'

'You should have seen her on stage, Cole,' Evan said, remembering back. 'What a revelation. It's ironic really; she was in her element out there, like she was born to it.'

'I honestly think she was too. Wish I'd been there to see it, but you know how it is when you're in the army. Mind you there was no bother about me getting the time off for the funeral, but I only have five days and then I have to go back to the War Zone. Rather harrowing it is over there, I can tell you, and that's putting it mildly.'

'I can well believe it, 'Evan said.

'So have all the arrangements been made?'

'Your brother is sorting it all out,' their mother said. 'She'll be buried in the same plot as your father.'

'Nice touch,' Cole smiled. 'So when is it, mum?'

'Thursday.'

'The day before I have to go back. Perfect. So how well did you know our beloved sister, Donna?' Cole asked, as if he wanted to bring her into the conversation.

'I didn't know her for long, but in the time I did have with her, we were really good friends.'

'She was very unique, but sadly I only saw the beginnings of her talent.' Cole sounded as if he regretted missing out on her moment of fame.

'You don't know what you missed, although I did record it all on a video I was going to send you,' Evan told him.

'I'm not sure I could face watching it yet, if ever, and besides it's not the same as seeing her live. You know, not being there is one of the biggest regrets of my life. But there was nothing I could do about it.' He yawned suddenly. 'To tell you the truth, I'm really knackered. I could fall asleep right here and now. It was a long journey, and I couldn't get to sleep on the plane. I think I'll turn in shortly– we'll talk some more in the morning.'

'Oh Cole, I'm sorry but Donna has your room. You don't mind sleeping in Theresa's old room for the time being, do you?'

'I don't know about that, I don't feel I can mum – it's just too upsetting. Think I'll just kip down on the sofa for the time being.'

Donna felt guilty over this, she bit her lip and knew she had to say something before he left. 'Cole, I don't mind going into Theresa's room tonight, if you want your room back.'

Cole laughed, revealing the gap between his two front teeth again. 'Don't you worry about it, darling. I'll only be here for a few days anyway. It's not worth the hassle. You're more than welcome to it.'

From the little she'd seen of him, Donna thought Cole seemed a larger than life character, who tried hard to be amusing. He was bigger than Evan, and more mature looking. She guessed he must be brave, having been in the 'thick' of the action. He'd certainly know how to look after himself and other people if need be.

The next day the two brothers went to the hospital and arranged for Theresa's body to be taken to the Chapel of Rest at the funeral directors.

When they returned, it was to a very quiet and subdued household. Their mother and Donna had been looking through Theresa's belongings, which they'd both found very distressing.

Evan confirmed the arrangements for the funeral had been finalised and told them the flowers had been ordered.

'Did you have any problems or are there any questions you need to ask me?' their mother enquired.

'No mum, we both think everything will be fine. We even managed to get them to agree to play a piece of Theresa's music when the coffin leaves the church. Oh and by the way Donna, I almost forgot, I thought you might like this back.' Evan pulled out the gold St Christopher from his pocket and placed it in the palm of Donna's hand.

She was utterly shocked 'Oh my God, no. I didn't want you to bring this back. I gave it to Theresa as a keepsake, and I wanted it to remain around her neck.' And at that she burst into tears, left the room and came back dressed to go out, still sobbing.

'Hey, hang on a minute, let me come with you.' Evan offered, getting up from his seat. In the hall he grabbed hold of her arm. 'Please Donna, calm down.'

'I can't believe you did that, you had no right.' She couldn't look at him amid her tears.

'Look, I'm really sorry, I had no idea – I thought you'd want it back. Come on, we'll get this sorted - all right?'

Finally she nodded, but didn't feel better until she actually saw the St Christopher placed back around Theresa's neck, despite how upsetting that was.

Chapter 21

THE WHOLE DAY HAD BEEN FULL OF TENSION AND SADNESS, AND THERE WAS SLIGHT RELIEF WHEN THE FUNERAL ITSELF WAS OVER AND THE LAST OF THE GUESTS HAD LEFT THE HOUSE AFTERWARDS.

'I thought it went off really well,' Cole said, trying to break the subdued atmosphere.

'Yes, I reckon we did Theresa proud – when they played her music at the end, I just broke down,' Evan said.

'We all did. I just wish she was here with us now,' their mother said dabbing her eyes with a tissue.

'That goes without saying, mum,' Cole agreed. 'But that's life for you, isn't it? Always liable to kick you in the teeth, when you least expect. None of us will ever forget her, and she'll always be in our thoughts. What I'll remember most is the happy smile she always had on her face, despite the cancer. She must have been in agony at times, both from the pain and knowledge that her beautiful face had been disfigured, but you never heard her moan about it. I think she was the bravest person I ever met. And I should know – I've seen a few acts of bravery in my time, especially since I've been in Afghanistan. But I've never seen anything to compare with her.'

Evan's face was a mask of pain. 'She was that,' he said sniffing back the tears. 'To get up there in front of all those people and perform the way she did was nothing short of incredible. But why did she have to die like that the first time she went on stage? It's just too much to take.'

'Come on now Evan, don't let it get to you like this.' Cole squeezed his shoulder.

'It's all right for you, you weren't here nor were you living with her.'

'Ok mate, point taken. But she was my sister as well – it's not my fault I wasn't here,' he said protesting his innocence.

'How could this happen? What had she ever done to anyone? Throughout her whole life, she never hurt a soul.'

'Evan, it's no use being bitter,' his mother said. 'That won't bring her back to us – will it? We couldn't have done any more for her, you know that as well as I do. Why did any of the bad things have to happen? I don't know. Don't you think I've asked myself that a thousand times? It won't change anything. We just have to live with it, and console ourselves with the many happy memories we have of her and your dad as well. That's what I'm trying to do anyway – even though it is so very hard.'

'Think I'm going to bed mum,' Evan said getting up.

'Evan - ' Cole tried to restrain him.

'Let him go Cole. He has to deal with his grief in his own way the same as everyone else,' their mum said.

Donna felt bewildered by it all. She'd never seen Evan in such a state before, not even on the day Theresa died on stage, and although it was a sad occasion, she was struck by the warmth and affection and of course love, this family had for one another. She envied them in lots of ways. They were nothing like her family.

'It's been a long hard day, as difficult a day as I've ever faced. I never thought I'd have to bury my own daughter. It doesn't seem fair, but then life can be very cruel.'

Cole hugged her tightly, looking so sorry for her.

'Anyway I think I might as well go to bed myself.' And as she walked towards the living room door she turned towards Donna and said, 'I do so wish this hadn't happened while you're here. This must be so upsetting for you, just when you were getting better.'

'Yes, it has been upsetting, but don't worry – I know it's going to take some doing but we can get over this.'

'You're a good girl, Donna - no wonder Theresa thought the world of you. She always was a great judge of character.'

'Thank you.' She leaned over to kiss Mrs Lacey on the cheek.

Being left alone with Cole made Donna feel uneasy, as always these days, when in unfamiliar male company. And when he said, 'You know when I first saw you with Evan, I thought you two were an item, but now I'm not so sure.' She sensed he was probing.

'We're not an item, but we are friends and we have been out together a few times. But, that's as far as it goes.'

'He's crazy about you; you know that, don't you?'

'I don't flatter myself.'

'Mind you, it's not hard to understand why,' He smiled eyeing her up and down for a couple of seconds, which made her flesh crawl.

'I'm no better than a hundred girls you might see walking down the street.'

Cole chuckled. 'I think you know you're a little better than that, darling. The thing is, I'd hate Evan to be hurt, especially after what's just happened with Theresa.'

'Why should I want to hurt him? That's the last thing I'd do. He knows how things stand with me. In fact, I think it's made our friendship stronger, knowing there won't be any complications.' She raised her eyebrows to bring home the point she was trying to make.

'He's had a few rough deals in his life as well. Naturally, it wasn't anything like Theresa had to go through, but it was bad enough. You might already know he was a very talented footballer. On the verge of breaking through to the first team of a professional club, until he got a horrific injury. A terrible mistimed tackle ultimately ended his career.'

'I know all about it.'

'I couldn't believe it when I found out he was training to be a male nurse. That was the last job I ever expected him to do. What a turnaround eh, although you have to admire the guy for being so plucky.'

'What's it like in the army?' she asked, determined to change the subject.

'Well…mostly it's very dull and the work is routine. But every now and then when we get involved in the action, it can be the most scary experience of your life. I have to admit I've nearly shit myself a couple of times when I've been in tricky situations.'

Donna smiled at this. 'Ever killed one of the enemy?'

'Phew, what a question to ask a guy,' he smiled with glazed eyes. 'No, I haven't but I have shot at and injured one or two of them. It's strange, at first I felt sick in the stomach, but the power of a gun in your hand can be almost euphoric. But also, it shocks you, and allows you to see people at their worst and their most vulnerable. I've seen some awful sights of blown up bits of people's bodies, which left me with nightmares for weeks afterwards.'

'I can imagine it's being in a certain situation that enables you to kill another human being – is that so?'

'Sure, it's a question of kill or be killed, darling. And when someone shoots at you, it sends a rush of adrenalin through your whole body. But it's what you've been trained for, and you react accordingly and somehow you get through it - me included.'

'Will it be difficult to go back?'

'In some ways it will. It's an awful place to be in, you have to watch your back all the time, there's violence wherever you go, although that comes with the job. But on the other hand there's a great camaraderie among the lads – we all look out for each other. Anyway it's no use complaining because I knew what I was letting myself in for when I joined up. Mind you, we weren't at war at the time.'

'You know if something were to happen to you as well it would destroy Evan and your mother. Have you never thought of that?'

He laughed at this remark, but seemed a little agitated. 'Of course I have, but I could get killed crossing the road or in a car accident or any other number of ways.'

'Yes, but the odds are stacked much more against you where you're stationed.'

He seemed to get irritated again; she saw a little twitch of anger in his blue eyes. 'Look, if you're number's up, it's up – there's nothing you can do about it. Don't worry I plan to be around a lot longer yet. And I won't be over there forever either.'

'Let's hope not.'

'Hey, don't tell me a beautiful girl like you is concerned over little old me,' he grinned.

'I'm concerned about everyone who has to go over there – war is a terrible waste of lives – don't you think?'

'I guess so, but sadly sometimes it's the only way to solve problems when all else fails.'

'True, but that doesn't mean I have to like it. So when did you say you have to go back?'

'Well, I was supposed to have five days, so I'll go back tomorrow.'

'That soon?'

'Yep – no peace for the wicked, is there?'

'I wish you all the luck in the world Cole, hope you come through it unscathed.'

'Thanks. You know, it's a shame you're like you are over Evan. Now that is a waste. Seems to me, he's getting close to winning you, so what's holding you back?'

'That's my business, I'm not about to tell you about it, no matter how much you pry,' she snapped.

Holding up his hands in protest he said, 'Don't worry; honestly I don't want to know. But you ought to get help before it ruins your life.'

'Thanks for the lecture Doctor Cole, but I can deal with it myself. I don't need anyone else's help, thank you very much.'

'All right, no need to get on your high horse, I get your drift. Anyway, darling, it's getting late and I have an early start in the morning. Hope you're still here when I next come home on leave.'

'I might be,' and with that she got up to go to bed.

'Good night then.' He walked towards the door to switch off the light, then glancing at her added, 'You know Donna, I keep getting the impression we've met before, but for the life of me I can't think where.'

'I don't think so, I'd remember an ugly mug like yours. Good night.'

He laughed at that and she smiled back slightly sarcastically.

Later that night in a fitful sleep she thought about Cole and couldn't decide whether she liked him or not. Although he was outspoken, streetwise and down to earth there was an underlying strangeness about him, but she couldn't put a finger on what that was. And thought it odd he had the feeling he knew her from somewhere.

Evan on the other hand was kind and considerate, more honest, always willing to help anyone, especially those in his care. They couldn't be more different.

She woke up the next morning thinking of Evan's smiling face and wondered if he would ever try to kiss her and if so what it would be like.

In the kitchen she found Mrs Lacey sitting opposite Evan looking sad.

'Cole gone then?' Donna asked taking a seat next to Evan.

'Yeah, six o'clock this morning,' he replied.

'It's at times like this, having just lost one of my children, that I wish he wasn't in the army. Especially right now with him being posted over there. I worry over him so much, because I know he's constantly at risk of getting himself killed or badly injured.'

'Yes, but mum, it's what he's been trained to do. And it has made a man out of him. He's unrecognisable now compared to what he used to be. He'll be careful – and remember how good he's always been at looking after himself, even before he was in the army. Don't worry.'

'Hope he watches out for himself, because if something happened to him as well... it just doesn't bear thinking about.' As soon as Donna had said this, she realised it was the wrong thing to say. 'Sorry, Mrs Lacey I didn't mean to upset you again.'

'It doesn't matter, I know you meant well.'

But her eyes were soon full of tears. Evan went over to her and put his arms around her obviously trying to make her feel better.

'Mum, want me to have the day off, I'm sure the hospital will understand.'

'No, no, I have to cope with this some time, now is as good a time as any. Although it's going to be horrible here without Theresa, and now you two are going to work, it'll be the first time I've been on my own for a long time.'

'But I'll be back after lunch,' Donna said. 'So you'll only be alone for a few hours.'

'I suppose you're right.'

Sadly, Donna knew she could never replace Theresa. No one could.

◇◇◇

Later that evening while they ate their tea, homemade steak and kidney pudding, Evan asked, 'So how did it go?'

'Not too bad. But I never dreamed there'd be so many kids eating dinners, and some of them are so cheeky, you wouldn't believe it. To be honest I'm exhausted.'

Evan started to snigger, hoping to hide it by putting his hand in front of his mouth and coughing. Mrs Lacey smiled as well. 'I could have told you that Donna. You should have seen my three, and that one over there was the worst.' She pointed to her son.

'Come on mum, I always thought Cole was a lot more demanding than me.'

'He was a lot of the time. Always had a lot to say for himself did Cole? Said what he thought and sometimes that got him into trouble. The number of fights he used to get into, why it must have been nearly every week at one time. In some ways, it was the best thing he ever did, joining the army. Although in other ways, it was the worst because now he's constantly in danger. Hopefully any aggression he has, he'll channel against the enemy, but then again there's a chance he could get himself killed at any time.'

'See I told you I was as good as gold.'

'Sure you were. Quiet at least. But you were always so lively, getting into things. You used to wear me out.'

'And how about you Donna? What sort of child were you?' Evan asked.

'Very timid. I used to do what I was told without question.'

'Were your parents very strict then?'

'You could say that. They used to make me do all the things I hated doing.'

'Oh yes, like what?'

'I don't want to talk about it Evan, so change the subject, will you?' Her face reddened in anger, hating him prying into her past like that.

'OK, sorry babe – I can see it's a sore point with you. If you don't want to talk about it, then the subject's closed as far as I'm concerned.'

After clearing up after tea she went upstairs to her bedroom, shutting the door behind her. Lying on the bed, and mulling over her childhood memories she began to feel distressed again. How she envied Evan and his brother and sister having had a normal childhood. There was nothing normal about her own childhood, being constantly on show, and made to look her best, in front of endless rows of people and cameras. Even now, it turned her stomach – and oh how she resented her parents. All through her life they'd continued going on and on at her – even after the nightmare of her attack. But now she was part of another household, and because of her part time job, had a measure of independence. She was quite determined she'd never go back to that life with her parents again.

A little time later there was a knock at her bedroom door. When she opened it, she was surprised to see Evan standing there with a guilty look on his face. She asked him to come in, and he sat at the end of the bed a little way from her.

'You all right now?' he asked her simply.

'I'll live.' She wasn't able to look at him.

'Look, I'm really sorry if I upset you –'

'It doesn't matter. My childhood wasn't the happiest part of my life. I wish I could forget about it now, but I can't.'

'Don't worry, I understand. I imagine you've had lots of problems in your life. I could see that by the state you were in, in hospital. I'd like to help if you'll let me, but I'm not one to pry, no matter what you think. So I won't push it, but any time you want to talk, I'm ready to listen.' He gave her a warm smile, obviously hoping this would make Donna more comfortable about talking to him.

'I know you are, and I'm really grateful, but I honestly can't talk about it to anyone. Let's drop the subject, shall we? Before I start to cry.' She took out some tissues and dabbed her eyes and cheeks.

'All right. We just wondered if you still want to stay here now Theresa's gone?'

'Well, your mum said I was welcome to stay as long as I liked, unless you've both decided otherwise since then.'

'No, no, it's nothing like that. Mum and me would be devastated if you left. I just thought Theresa was the main reason you came to stay in the first place.'

Donna was stunned by this. Whilst it was true, she was one of the reasons, in reality the whole family had made up her mind for her. They were like the family she'd always wished for. Now she worried over where that statement had come from and where it was leading.

'You know very well it wasn't just Theresa. It was all of you, but if I'm not wanted –'

'I've just told you that's not the case. Just the opposite is true. Have you any idea how we'd feel if you left? You're part of the family now. Perhaps to me more than that.' This made her stomach flutter and whisper, 'Oh God, no' under her breath. She had to head him off quickly.

'Look, I'm nothing special. I'm just a pathetic person with more hang-ups than most. I don't want you wasting your time thinking about me.'

'Donna – for God's sake. You're a lot like Theresa, you know that - there's an aura about you too. It's not about your appearance, it's who you really are underneath all of that, the real you I love so much.'

Donna turned to look at him, seeing that innocent but serious look on his face.

'You've got to be joking, Evan. After all the trouble I've got myself into, and how twice I've tried to commit suicide. I think you're deluding yourself. I'm a failure, pure and simple.'

He shook his head, obviously not agreeing with her. 'You know what I'd like more than anything in the world – for us to be a proper couple. All right, we've been out as friends, and I know we get on really well – so why don't we take it one step further? I mean ever since I've known you, I've never so much as held your hand, or kissed you or anything.'

Although she'd known all along what he really wanted, it still came as a shock to hear him come right out and tell her. It sent shock waves of fear surging through her body, frightening her. She still remembered vividly every minute detail of what had happened to her during her rape ordeal and with Blake afterwards. The repercussions remained, ruining her life.

'Our friendship wouldn't last long if we were a couple. I can't give you what you need me to give.'

'Let me be the judge of that,' he said forcibly, a serious look of determination forming on his face.

She was perplexed, shaking her head from side to side. Couldn't believe this was happening, yet again. If only she could run away from him. But where would she go? 'Evan, you'll get hurt – and it'll be all my fault. You're a real nice guy; you deserve to be happy with someone who'll return your love.'

'Look at me,' he began. 'I don't want to be with anyone else but you. I'd rather take whatever you're able to give, than have a relationship with someone else. You understand what I'm saying.'

Donna reluctantly glanced into his eyes, then sniffed, trying to avoid tears. She so much wanted to return his affection, but couldn't.

'Come on, babe. I don't know what happened to you, but isn't it about time you put whatever it is behind you - or you'll face a life of misery and regret. Is that what you want?'

She shook her head; bit her bottom lip as she took stock of the situation.

'Well then, why don't we give it a try? See what happens. That's all I'm asking,' He sounded almost as if he was begging, she thought.

Grasping her hands tightly, as the torment of it all went through her, she found the whole situation agonising, but realised if she didn't take this opportunity now, her future would be bleak. It would be a risk, but life was all about risk. Was it worth that risk? Potential happiness or an eternity of misery. She had to choose.

'All right,' she said quietly and simply. His blue eyes widened with delight, and his face became a picture of joy.

And for a moment although his mouth opened, he seemed lost for words. Then finally he whispered in disbelief, 'You really mean that?'

'Yes Evan, but don't get the wrong idea. This will be really difficult for me, so don't expect too much and you won't be disappointed.'

'I know what I'm getting myself into. I just want to be with you, talk to you – anything else will be a bonus.'

'Just as long as you're under no illusions.'

'All right if I tell a few people we're going out together?' he wanted to know.

She sighed - had guessed this was coming. 'Evan, I don't care who you tell, so long as you remember I may not be the girl friend you deserve.'

'I know and I respect that. I'll just tell mum, but say it's nothing serious at the moment – all right.'

'OK.'

Evan's mother was thrilled and raised up her arms with joy when she heard the news. 'That's absolutely wonderful, you make a lovely couple.'

'Thanks mum. I think so too.'

Donna just smiled. Already she feared Mrs Lacey would anticipate wedding bells coming soon, but that was the last thing on Donna's mind. She hoped too that Evan wouldn't get carried away.

Chapter 22

THE NIGHT WAS COLD, DONNA SHIVERED SLIGHTLY AS THEY WALKED TOGETHER AFTER ANOTHER EVENING OUT, THIS TIME AT A FRENCH RESTAURANT JUST ON THE OUTSKIRTS OF DEXFORD. It had been an enjoyable night, but as they drove back, Evan seemed unusually quiet, locked in his own thoughts.

After parking the car outside the house, he appeared to hesitate, strangely not making any attempt to get out of the car. Donna was puzzled. Something was going on in his mind, but what?' Then he suddenly gazed into her eyes and said, 'You know something babe. You have the most beautiful sensuous lips. I keep wondering what it would be like to kiss you.'

Donna's heart started to beat faster as he moved across to her. For a second she froze, feeling slightly sick. Seeing the anguish and hurt in his eyes, she began to feel a little guilty. He obviously had strong feelings for her and although she was attracted to him and couldn't imagine life without him, there had been very little physical contact so far.

She did so want to make him happy, yet when their lips met she couldn't move. Sensing her nervousness he took hold of her hand and squeezed it. After only about ten seconds, he moved away again giving her a warm smile. He was very gentle, and for that she was grateful.

'See that wasn't so bad, was it?'

It wasn't. In fact, in the end she had to admit it had been quite pleasant.

Taking hold of both of her hands and looking deep into her eyes, he said, 'We can make it Donna. I know it won't be easy, but we'll get there in the end.'

'You'll need the patience of a saint, Evan.'

'I'll wait for forever if that's what it takes.'

It felt nice to be told this, and she let him kiss her again, although this kiss didn't last quite as long. Donna broke off quickly sensing he was getting carried away.

'Stop it now Evan, you're making me feel strange.' She pushed him gently away.

His eyes dropped, he must have found this upsetting. 'Wish you'd tell me what all this is about. I've heard all about your parents, about how they forced you into the limelight. But something else happened to you, didn't it?'

Donna shook her head vigorously, but knew Evan would need an explanation eventually.

'Please Donna, you have to tell me. If we're ever to make a go of this, we can't have any secrets from each other. You should be able talk to me about anything. And I'll do the same for you. It will help I'm sure, and I promise whatever you tell me, will remain strictly between the two of us.'

'No Evan, no way. You're trying to push me into a corner and if I'm not careful, I'll just go to pieces. I can't talk about it to anyone, not even you – you hear me?' She opened the car door to get out.

Without looking back to see if Evan was following, she made for the front door. Of course, she had a key, but sensed he was behind her, as suddenly he leaned over to put his own key in the lock.

'I'm sorry. I didn't mean to pressurise you. I'll back off, all right. If this thing that happened to you was so awful, keep it to yourself, if that's what you want. I won't mention it again, ever – I promise.' He pushed the front door open.

She was still angry with him for trying to find out about her darkest secret. She couldn't speak about it to him, because it still frightened her so much. Even now, there were times when she had nightmares about the attack, and as no one had ever been caught, she feared her attacker was still out there, waiting in the shadows, ready to pounce, the first time she dropped her guard. That's why when going out, she always felt safer when accompanied by someone.

She ran upstairs to her bedroom, leaving Evan standing in the hall, obviously wondering what he had to do to cure her of this problem. Did he have had an inkling of what had happened to her? She feared he had.

The following morning things were back to normal, the events of the previous day pushed firmly into the background. At some point in the future the truth would come out, or the relationship wouldn't work, but for now it was too much to cope with for her.

◇◇◇

Some months later, Evan was holding Donna's hand as they walked along a pathway overlooking a lake in the glorious Welsh countryside.

'Donna, I wanted to ask you something,' he said suddenly.

'Oh yes, and what's that?' She was looking ahead of her as a red kite seemed to hover before plunging towards the lake, obviously in search of a fish.

She hadn't got a clue what he was going to ask, wasn't even listening as intently as she should have.

'Well...err... this isn't easy for me, you know. In fact, I'm shaking like a leaf. But I've got to do this. It's now or never –'

Donna narrowed her eyes, looked puzzled, then started to giggle. What was he going on about now? Then he put his hand in his pocket, pulled out a small bag. He moved his hand slowly towards her.

'What have you got there, for God's sake - it's not another packet of wine gums is it?' She joked, remembering the last time he'd pulled this stunt.

'Well, not exactly. It's something I've wanted to give you for a long time. In fact, I bought it ages ago, but it's taken me until now to pluck up the courage. Hopefully, you'll wear it for the rest of your life.'

She suddenly stopped in her tracks, the smile vanishing from her face as the situation became clear. She reddened, even more so when he took a small black box out of the bag. With his other hand, he opened the lid to reveal a beautiful diamond engagement ring.

Her eyes widened with astonishment, as she gazed at the contents of the box. The diamond, which sparkled in the sunlight, had a slight yellow tinge. It was held by a band of gold.

'Evan ...no,' she began, her whole body twitching as the enormity of what he was proposing hit her. She moved away from him, feeling afraid again.

'What's wrong? I...I thought you'd be pleased.'

'Sorry – I just can't handle this. Put it away, take it back to the shop and get your money back, because I can never wear it.'

'But I thought –'

She shook her head, realising she should have seen this coming; after all, they'd been going out with each other for almost a year now. They got on really well, rarely had arguments, and seemed happy in each other's company. So long as he kept his distance, just held her hand, and only kissed her occasionally, everything was fine. But this proposal was the natural progression for any couple. The longer they remained together, the more likely something like this would happen. She cursed herself for being so stupid. But he should have known this could never be. Had it not been for the rape, and what she'd suffered afterwards, it might have been possible. Unfortunately it had happened and would be forever ingrained in her memory.

'Why did you have to go and spoil everything?' She looked up at him, through tear-filled eyes. 'Why couldn't you make do with what we have, instead of wanting the earth? I can't give you any more than I'm giving you already – haven't I told you a hundred times? Now it'll never be the same between us again – and it's all your fault.'

Stroking his chin, sighing every now and then, he pondered over what he'd done. He looked stunned. 'I'm really sorry, I never intended to spoil things, as you say. I wanted to make things even better between us, and I thought if I showed you some real commitment, you might finally believe what I keep telling you. If I've offended or hurt you, forgive me. I promise you I'd never harm a hair on your head. Haven't I proved that already enough times in the past?'

Donna looked up at him guardedly. What he'd said was true, so why couldn't she tell him the reason for all this? She was frightened despite how sensitively he'd treated her, fearing someday she might find herself in a situation similar to the one with Blake, especially if they were under pressure or had problems. What would she do then?

'It's me that should say sorry,' she whispered, feeling slightly ashamed of herself. 'You don't deserve this. I've told you before, you'd be better off with someone who can give you the love you need.'

Nervously he began, 'If I went out with anyone else, it wouldn't work – don't you know you're the only person I can be happy with, for God's sake.'

Biting her lip, tears came into her eyes once more as she realised he might actually be speaking the truth. She was as frightened as she'd been when they'd first become a couple. But she'd got through that and he hadn't let her down since – had he? He was a decent honest and caring man who thought the world of her. If only she had it in her to at least try – for his sake.

'Can I have another look at that ring?' she asked suddenly.

A tiny flicker of hope appeared in his eyes. He took it out of the box and placed it on her finger. She held out her arm and stared at it admiringly, as if it was the most precious thing she'd ever worn. For a few seconds it felt good to have on her finger – but then the old feelings of doubt and indecision reappeared. Quickly she took the ring off and gave it back to him.

'You'll like it eventually, Donna – I know you will.'

'Maybe I will. It is gorgeous. I might wear it one day but I won't be rushed. Keep it with you always and when I feel like putting it on for a little while – I will. Be patient with me Evan, and maybe one day you'll get what you deserve.'

'I have so much patience, it'll be coming out my ears before long,' he laughed.

'You'll keep the ring for me then?' she almost begged him.

'Of course I will, wherever I go. And then any time you want to see it or wear it, you can.'

She leaned over and kissed him on the cheek, which she decided would have to be enough for the time being.

'Think there's a chance we might get married someday, Donna?'

'Sorry, but I just can't think that far ahead,' she said looking at him with those sad eyes of hers.

He nodded, but from the look on his face he was obviously disappointed. Nonetheless feeling trapped as she had for most of her life in one way or another, she knew if he didn't stop putting pressure on her, the relationship would fail for sure.

◇◇◇

Only a week later, they were sitting inside Gino's candle lit Wine Bar in Dexford Town Centre; the atmosphere in the room and the wine they'd drunk had begun to take effect, and Donna was thinking about the engagement ring, and how beautiful it was, 'Evan...' She took hold of his hand.

'Yes - what's wrong?' he began, looking straight into her eyes.

'Err...just wondered if you had the ring with you.'

His mouth dropped open a little. 'Of course I have - didn't I say I would?'

She nodded, watching as he took the box out of his inside coat pocket, and placed it on the table in front of her.

Shaking slightly, she opened the little box, and slipped the ring onto her finger staring at it from afar.

'Doesn't it sparkle, Evan? And it's so gorgeous as well.'

'Like everything about you,' he whispered to her.

She glanced up at him, shaking her head slightly, trying to ignore his remark.

'It feels so comfortable on now, not like before. Maybe I could get used to wearing it.'

'That's what I hoped you'd say. If you ever want to wear it permanently, you only have to let me know.'

'Let me wear it for a few days in private, to see how I feel - all right? Maybe gradually I'll find I'm even more relaxed about being engaged, and what people might say.'

'I'll keep my fingers crossed. No pressure babe, you take as long as you want. I just wish you'd confide in me about what happened to you.'

'Maybe I will at some point in the future, but for now the best I can do is to try to wear the ring – because I know how much it means to you.'

'You will, but do it for yourself as well as for me.'

'Don't like to speak too soon, but I have seemed to be a bit better about things just lately. Like work for instance. It's done me good to get involved with the school.'

'I told you it would – didn't I?'

'You did,' she said squeezing his hand.

'And who knows what it might lead to.'

'I'm not thinking that far ahead yet, but it's good to be doing something useful after wasting so much time.'

'That's how I was when I first became a nurse. Helping sick people get well again was great, although it's a shame not all the patients appreciate what you do for them.'

'I can believe that.' She wondered if he was referring to her at a time not so long ago.

Throughout the rest of that evening, Donna couldn't help but constantly stare at the ring, imagining how her colleagues would react. They'd be so thrilled. In her heart, she knew she could trust Evan, and be sure he'd never hurt her. But a tiny voice kept saying that Blake had given her the same impression in the beginning and look how he'd changed. There would always be that small element of doubt in her mind, and if something did go wrong, she feared the pain would destroy her.

The following Saturday they sat watching television in her bedroom, Donna wearing his ring again; thinking how nice it was to have someone who really cared for her again. He'd always been good to her in the time they'd known one another, and she felt safe in his company. Perhaps she would be able to express her feelings to him as it was clear she meant so much to him. It was the very least she could do.

Then out of the blue, she suddenly came to a decision that made her feel giddy with excitement, but also very apprehensive. However, realising nothing ventured was nothing gained, she said 'Evan would you like to show your mum this ring now?'

His eyes widened with shock but also with pleasure.

'Pardon – you serious?' he smiled looking as though this was the best thing that had ever happened to him.

'Yes, very much so.'

'Sure you don't want to think about it. You realise if we show it to her, there's no going back?'

She nodded her head.

'Positive?'

She nodded again, feeling suddenly emotional. He didn't understand what a huge step this was for her.

'Come on then.' And taking her hand said, 'What are we waiting for?'

They went downstairs, still holding hands. Evan pushed the living room door open, to see his mother sitting down watching television. Looking from one to the other, having seen their hands locked together - something they'd never done in her presence - a puzzled expression came over her face.

He cleared his throat before speaking. 'Mum, we've got something to tell you…'

In fact, he didn't have to say anything more. He merely lifted up Donna's left hand and showed his mother the engagement ring perched on her finger. A look of surprise, then joy came across her face.

'It's about time,' was her first comment.

'Donna needed to be sure,' Evan told her. 'And I don't blame her, but I'm so thrilled she's made up her mind at last.'

'This is the most wonderful news. And that ring, why it's absolutely lovely. Must have cost you a small fortune, Evan.'

'It did, but it's worth every penny.' He smiled proudly.

'So when's the big day?'

'We haven't exactly made up our minds yet, but there's no rush mum – we've got all the time in the world.'

She turned to Donna. 'What do you think?'

Slightly taken aback; she hadn't been expecting this sort of pointed question. And with an embarrassed smile quickly said, 'When we can afford it, and when it feels right.'

'That sounds good enough to me. Glad to see you're not rushing into things. Right then, you two. This calls for a celebration! It just so happens I have a bottle of something in the fridge. It was given to me as a present at Christmas, but I never got the chance to open it. Now is as good a time as any. It's such a shame Theresa isn't here to share the good news – she'd have been over the moon for you.'

Evan looked sadly into space. 'She would – I still can't believe she's gone from us.'

'Me neither - she'd have been so happy. I can see her now, with that big grin on her face, hugging us half to death. She'd have loved to be my bridesmaid.'

Evan followed his mother into the kitchen, and the sound of a 'pop' indicated the bottle had been opened successfully. They returned a couple of minutes later, Evan's mother carefully carrying a tray containing three glasses brimming, with what looked like champagne. Donna took a sip of hers, finding it sweet, bubbly and refreshing.

After finishing the bottle they sat talking about the future – saving a deposit for a house and also when they envisaged getting married. Donna had to admit she was getting more used to the idea of becoming Evan's wife and what it would entail. Perhaps she had something to look forward to at last.

Chapter 23

IT HAD BEEN ALMOST TWELVE MONTHS SINCE THE
ENGAGEMENT, AND THE ARRANGEMENTS FOR THE
WEDDING WERE FINALLY WELL UNDER WAY. They had
both been so busy going to work and saving every last penny to
cover the cost of the wedding and a deposit on a house.

With a week to go before the wedding, they had just finished
washing up after tea when there was a knock at the front door.
Donna volunteered to answer it, and was so surprised to see Cole
standing there. He looked very smart in his khaki uniform, his
beret almost covering his left eye. He had a moustache now, but
even that couldn't hide the cheeky grin formed on his face.

'Cole! We weren't expecting you to come home until
Thursday, after all the wedding is still a week away.'

'Thought I'd surprise you all by coming home early. I've
managed to get an extra week's leave – after all it is for my
favourite couple in the world.'

'Oh Cole, you are silly,' she smiled.

They hugged like old friends, and Cole gave her a little peck on
the cheek. After closing the front door behind him, Donna shouted,
'Evan, mum, look who's here.'

They both looked up, and seemed elated upon seeing Cole
enter the living room.

'Cole!' there were tears in his mother's eyes. 'I'm so glad
you're back safe.'

'Hi-ya, mum, brother.'

Cole put his bag down, before embracing first his mother and then Evan vigorously.

'Hey, this is brilliant,' Evan laughed.

'Thought I'd come home early so we can have ourselves a proper stag night – what do you reckon Evan?'

'I wasn't planning on doing anything much – I'm not one for boozy nights out any more.' Evan blushed with embarrassment.

'Oh sure you are,' Cole insisted. 'I bet Donna's going on a Hen night, aren't you Donna?'

She felt herself colour slightly, before replying in an disapproving tone of voice, 'Actually no, I'm not. I don't feel like making a fool of myself, the night before my wedding.'

'Quite right too Donna.'

'But mum, Evan and me – well, we're really close. Couldn't live with myself if I didn't take him out for a bit of a celebration. Don't worry, we'll be good, won't we Evan?'

Donna frowned at them, not believing Cole's promise. But it was only one night after all. 'It's all right Cole; I know it's a man thing. Honestly, I don't mind as long as you don't get yourselves into any trouble.'

Cole grinned, with a mischievous look on his face. 'I'll bring him back in one piece, I promise you – and look after him like a big brother should.'

Raising her eyebrows, she realised there was very little she could do.

For the rest of the evening, they all sat back, listening to Cole's bawdy jokes and stories about life in the army. He was so funny, tears rolled down their cheeks. He appeared to be the complete opposite of Evan, who was quiet, kind and loving.

Feeling tired, Donna told them she was going to bed early. Everyone said good night to her in high spirits. Evan followed her up onto the landing and kissed her goodnight before they went to their respective rooms. She remained in Cole's room while he slept on the sofa, still unable to sleep in Theresa's room he said, because it brought back so many bad memories.

She'd fallen asleep that night feeling content and happy, the only worry constantly popping into her head was the wedding night itself and the fear that she might let him down.

Drifting in and out of sleep, she suddenly woke needing the toilet. Opening the bedroom door, she walked across the landing, making for the bathroom. A few minutes later as she came out of the bathroom she heard a moaning sound coming from downstairs. Standing on the landing, she listened more acutely and realised it was Cole.

What was going on downstairs couldn't be ignored. But now she faced a dilemma. Either she could wake Evan or his mother or she could investigate herself. Since she was already up, there seemed little point in disturbing them.

Tiptoeing downstairs, she stood just inside the doorway, observing Cole lying on the settee, thrashing his arms and legs about. She switched on the light in the hall, so as not to shock him, then moved across to the settee to stand over him. His eyes were closed, and his face was masked in sweat, that tickled down the sides of his cheeks. His hair looked wet and matted down on his head.

'No! No! No! Please don't make ... Can't face ... kill me ... they will,' he mumbled in his sleep. He moved his arms up to protect his head.

Donna watched this in amazement.

'Don't want... to die,' he cried out. 'Can't go back ... not that ... they're animals... can't go ... no ... no ... no!'

With that he jumped, then sat up startled. His eyes opened wide, staring at Donna. But the blank look on his face suggested he was only half-awake and unaware of his surroundings.

'It's all right Cole,' she said softly. 'You're safe now.'

His head gave a little jolt. Then he started to weep, his shoulders shuddering with terror.

Donna was shocked, unsure of what to do, as she'd never seen him like this before. Always he'd been the suave confident happy-go-lucky bloke, everybody's friend, willing to help anyone in trouble. To see this side of him shocked and amazed her.

Sitting on the edge of the sofa, she put her arms around him and held his head against her shoulder, while he juddered continually for some time.

'Sssh, 'she whispered in his ear. 'You're going to be all right Cole; no one will hurt you while you're here.'

'But I have to go back.'

'I know but you'll be with your mates. You'll all look out for each other – you know you will.'

'No, can't do it anymore. I won't go back.' His hands gripped her arm, almost to the point where it hurt.

'You can, Cole. You're stronger than that. Haven't you done this loads of times before?'

'Don't you understand? I'm a mess, a disgrace to the regiment.'

'Cole –'

He moved his head from her, seeming to have come to his senses. 'I don't want you to see me this way. Just go back to bed, and leave me in peace.'

'I can help, if you'll let me. Talk to me about it if you want. I promise I'll never tell another soul.' She looked at him, feeling so sorry for him.

His blue eyes looked afraid as he stared into space, obviously thinking over her suggestion.

'All...all right then,' he said unable to look at her straight in the eye. 'As long as you never breathe a word to anyone, especially not Evan or mum.'

'I already promised, didn't I?'

Taking hold of her hand he sat up on the sofa, allowing her to sit by his side which she felt inclined to do because of the state he was in; although she couldn't help thinking this was getting a little claustrophobic.

'We...we were out on patrol in an armoured car. There were six of us. The streets were full of people, all going about their daily lives. Suddenly there was an almighty explosion. The vehicle must have gone over a device of some sort. Somehow, miraculously I found myself thrown clear into the road. But when I looked back dazed, I saw the most horrific scene I've ever witnessed in my life. There were blood soaked body parts and pieces of flesh strewn all over the place. I looked and saw Alan, my best mate, half his body blown away, his eyes staring at me as if he was trying to beg for help. Can you imagine what that was like? And then I watched a mob, swarm around the burning wreck of our armoured car. They took whatever they could salvage. Then they started kicking the bits of bodies – as if they were like wild animals – and there wasn't anything I could do. Nothing at all.

'Nobody seemed to notice me, that was the strange thing about it. Somehow, I managed to slip away from all that carnage. I ran away when I should have done something for my friends' dignity. But I didn't. I let them do their worst to my comrades. I'll never forget that as long as I live. When I got back to base, I couldn't tell them what happened – I was too ashamed. They thought it was shock, or due to the fact I had a gash on my forehead and had been knocked out. No matter how many times they asked me, the words wouldn't come. When they found the vehicle they must have realised what I'd been through – but they didn't do a thing, except to make me see a doctor and then a shrink, who decided I was fit for duty. Can you believe that? I could have died; and I saw all my mates blown to bits. I was staggered when they said I had to go back. All right, so I only had a few scratches and a bump on the head, but that doesn't mean what I saw didn't do something to me, even though I couldn't tell them the truth. I've never spoken about it to anyone until now. And now I have to go back into that hellhole again. And I don't think I can...'

'Oh Cole.' Donna tried to envisage what this poor man had been through. 'You need to talk to someone more qualified than me about this.'

'No, I can't,' he said shaking his head. 'I don't want them to know. They'll think I'm weak, a coward.'

'They won't. Why don't you ask to see another doctor or a trauma counsellor, a civilian perhaps? There must be other people who deal with this sort of thing, people specially trained in problems such as yours.'

He looked at her as if she was mad. 'Huh, you having a laugh? There's no way I'd ever talk to those quacks. And if I don't go back, they'll lock me up for sure. It's no good, somehow I have to deal with this in my own way. Don't you dare tell Evan or mum - you hear me? If you do, I'll never forgive you.'

'All right Cole, if that's what you want. And it'll stay that way unless you say otherwise. But you're worrying me. You can't sort this out all by yourself.'

He laughed, in a sort of ironic way, as if to say he had no other choice. 'Let's forget this conversation ever took place. In the morning, I'll be my old cheerful self and as far as you're concerned, there's nothing wrong with me. I know I have to cope and I will - but it's just that sometimes it's so hard.' Those last few words were said in anguish, through gritted teeth.

He put his hand on her arm, while breathing in deeply.

'You sure you'll be OK?'

He nodded without looking at her.

'All right, if that's what you want.'

'It is. It's my problem and my problem alone. Go back to bed now – please, and forget about it,' ordering her as if he didn't want her around anymore.

'If you say so.' She reluctantly turned round to go back upstairs to his old bedroom. Halfway up the stairs she looked round to see him lying back on the sofa facing away from her so she couldn't see his face.

As she lay in bed, she was shaking, having found the whole experience unnerving. This wasn't something she'd foreseen at all, and it made her feel so sorry for Cole. Her own hang-ups suddenly seemed insignificant. For although she'd experienced the worst of human nature first hand, it was nothing like the horrors of war that the soldiers in Afghanistan were experiencing. She hoped he'd resolve his problems, and wished she could help more. But sadly he didn't want anyone to interfere.

Slowly Cole's image faded from her mind, to be replaced by Evan's happy smiling face. She knew he loved her and wanted so much to make her happy, and she wanted to do the same for him. Unfortunately, once more her own problems had come to the fore. She needed someone to confide in as well, and perhaps if Theresa was alive she might have spoken to her. Sadly now she felt so alone.

Chapter 24

THE STAG NIGHT CAME ALL TOO QUICKLY FOR DONNA. She should have been thinking of the happiest day in her life, but instead had the worry of the two brothers out on the town, up to no good. She was annoyed with Cole for instigating this, and with Evan for going along with it.

'Ready for the off,' Cole grinned, getting to his feet, when his brother came into the living room at seven o'clock. They were both freshly groomed, their clothes smart and neat, looking forward to Evan's so-called last night of freedom.

'As if I have any choice,' Evan smiled, looking at his brother warily.

'You two had better watch what you're doing. I don't want either of you coming home drunk. Or you'll have Donna and me to answer to – do you hear?' Their mother wagged a finger at them.

'Mum, you're worrying over nothing,' Cole laughed. 'I'll take good care of him, I promise.'

'We'll only have a couple,' Evan said. 'Honestly Donna.'

Donna moved her head to one side and pulled her lips back, wondering if she could trust him now. In all their time together, he'd never let her down once, so surely he wouldn't throw everything away now. 'Just come back safe and sound, that's all I ask.'

'We will – don't you worry about that.' He winked at her, leaning over to give her a peck on the cheek, and then with Cole draping an arm around his shoulder, they left.

After the front door had been slammed shut, the two women looked at one another knowingly, realising exactly what would happen. But Donna hoped they'd be proved wrong.

For the rest of the evening they watched the television together. But Donna found it hard to concentrate on any one programme, constantly fidgeting in her seat, wondering what the two brothers were up to.

'Think I'm going to bed now,' Donna announced a little later, having noticed the time was now close to ten o'clock.

Mrs Lacey smiled. 'You've been very quiet tonight my dear. Something to do with my son's stag night, is it?'

'You could say that.'

'You're not on your own, my dear. I feel exactly the same. Remember, since they were born, I've seen the best and worst of them. They were both in a fair amount of trouble at one time but thank goodness that was some years ago. Mind you since then they have buckled down very well, and in their own way they've made a success of their lives. Let's hope there aren't any lapses just one day before the wedding.'

Donna nodded.

'Evan would be the biggest fool on earth if he did anything to jeopardise your relationship. I think he's the luckiest man alive. You're such a pleasure to have around and so modest with it too. That's what Theresa always used to tell me.'

'Thanks for that, but I'm not that wonderful – honestly.'

'That's exactly what I'm talking about. Your modesty becomes you, my dear. Go on, get off to bed - you have a big day ahead of you in the morning. Try to forget about the lads for a few hours. If there's any bother, I'm more than capable of handling it. They're not too old to have their ears boxed.' She rolled her sleeves up to show the muscles in her arms.

Donna laughed and said 'Thanks. I really do appreciate everything you've done for me since I came to live here. If it hadn't been for your kindness, I dread to think what would have happened to me.'

'You're a really nice girl, so it was easy to treat you the same as my kids. And so good for Theresa, it was almost as if you were sisters. And now by marrying Evan you'll make him the happiest man in the world. A mother couldn't ask for anything more.'

Donna had tears in her eyes wishing, in comparison, her own parents could have been more like this lovely lady. She was determined to make a go of this chance of happiness with Evan, having come through everything else over the years, and now there was just one more obstacle to overcome.

Later, lying in bed, she found it hard to sleep. Imagining the two brothers up to all sorts, out on their pub-crawl, winding up in some seedy night club, having one final fling before Evan became a married man. It was driving her crazy thinking that way. So long as he came back in one piece, that was all that mattered, she kept telling herself.

It must have been in the early hours of the morning that she finally fell asleep, without having heard them return home. And when she was awakened by a knock on the bedroom door, opening her eyes, she was surprised to see daylight flooding in through the curtains. It seemed the day of her wedding had finally arrived.

Mrs Lacey came into her room with a wide grin on her face and a welcome cup of tea.

'Are they all right?' Donna asked, suddenly more alert.

'They're both sleeping like babies.'

'And did you see anything of them when they came back in last night?'

'I did. Waited up for them until two o'clock in the morning. I think they were quite shocked to see me. They seemed OK, perhaps a little unsteady on their feet – but not blind drunk, in fact nowhere near as bad as we feared. Cole said they'd only been drinking beer, so it would have taken a lot for them to get legless. Apparently Cole was a little disappointed in Evan, as he kept on about you the whole time, and how he didn't want to let you down.'

'That's nice,' Donna smiled, sitting up in bed, feeling more secure now. She was touched to know Evan had been thinking about her, and it almost brought a tear to her eye.

'I told you he wouldn't let you down. He's always been a good lad at heart. All right, so he's had his moments especially when he found out he couldn't play football again. But once he got that out of his system, he's been a son to be proud of.'

This put Donna's mind at rest and made her feel much more comfortable about her wedding day.

'What's the weather like?' Donna asked as she put on her dressing gown.

'Very promising, my dear,' And pulling back the curtains to allow in bright sunshine added, 'As you can see it's sunny and the forecast is for a dry warm day. What a wonderful day for a wedding.'

'It certainly is.'

The ceremony was due to take place at St Luke's Church Dexford, an eighteenth century church situated at the top of a hill overlooking the town itself. The couple thought it the perfect venue for the wedding, and the photographs afterwards too.

Donna's heart was racing for most of the morning. It had been arranged that Evan should remain downstairs once he'd taken a shower, and Donna would stay upstairs until Evan had actually left in the wedding car.

That was a little difficult and Mrs Lacey had to constantly make sure the coast was clear before Donna left the confines of her room. Even the hairdresser had to style the bride's hair upstairs in the bedroom.

Once the hairdresser had gone, it was time to put on her wedding gown. There at hand was Mrs Lacey to give her support and guidance. She placed a footstool in front of the mirror for Donna to stand on, so she could arrange the dress and trail to fall without getting creased.

'Think you'll be all right to stand for a while, until the car arrives?'

She nodded.

Moving back to see how the dress looked, she gasped, took Donna in her arms and cried.

'You look so wonderful my dear. The photographer will have it easy taking pictures of you.'

'Oh come on - that's a bit of an exaggeration,' Donna grinned, feeling embarrassed.

'It's such a shame about your parents. You ought to have forgiven them, you know - it is the biggest day in your life after all.'

Feeling her face flush again, and not wanting an argument with her soon-to-be mother in law, she said. 'I'm sorry, but I can't help how I feel. They should never have treated me like that, forever making me do things they knew I hated doing. I never wanted to be thrust into the limelight at all - I kept telling them, and yet they still carried on and on at me - so they only have themselves to blame. And then of course there was their attitude over Evan. Just because he's a male nurse, for God's sake.'

Mrs Lacey looked sad. It would seem she hated family bust ups, but as far as Donna was concerned, it was impossible to resolve any differences she had with her folks.

'Well, I suppose that's between you and them, my dear–'

'I won't change my mind.'

Having stayed in her room all morning, she was eager for the wedding to start, especially now she had her wedding dress on. She was all for sticking with tradition, but this was ridiculous. As it had been agreed for Evan to leave half an hour before her, she felt sure it would soon be time for the boys to depart.

Just as she looked at the clock on the bedside table for the umpteenth time, there was a gentle knock on her bedroom door. She was on her own. Who on earth could that be?

'Come in,' Donna replied, sure it couldn't be Evan. Much to her surprise, it was Cole, admittedly looking very smart in his army uniform, but he seemed a little ill at ease. He kept adjusting the collar of his shirt, and couldn't look her straight in the eye.

'Err…could I have a quick word with the bride?' He closed the door behind him.

'Why – what's wrong?' There was a sudden dread in the pit of her stomach that Evan had changed his mind. Surely not.

'Oh nothing much.' He seemed awkward, and sat down on the bed, then brushed away some fluff off his lapels with his hand, hesitating, as if he was trying to summon up the courage to tell her something.

She was bewildered, and not for the first time, noticed a peculiar expression on his face. A smirk seemed to over emphasise the gap in his teeth, making her blood run cold. It seemed odd he'd made her shudder as if someone had just walked over her grave.

What was going on now? Was she over reacting to everything because of the anxiety of the day? What if Evan really had had a change of heart? Oh dear God, if that happened, she couldn't bear it.

She watched Cole breathing in deeply, obviously finding it difficult to reveal what he wanted to say.

'What is it Cole? He's not ill, is he?'

'No, he isn't. Donna...Look I...I don't know quite how to tell you this... but I think you'll be making the biggest mistake of your life if you marry him.'

'Pardon?'

'I said – for God's sake, don't go ahead with this wedding.' His hands were shaking slightly.

'Cole, what the hell do you mean by that? I'm supposed to be getting married to him within the hour, so why are you telling me this now of all times. You'd better explain yourself – and double quick.' She glared at him angrily.

'I'm sorry but I can't tell you why. Evan's my brother and I don't want to do this to him, but there's no other way. Take my word for it – this marriage will never work. I'm warning you, it'll end in heartbreak, and when it does, I can't begin to imagine what it'll do to you.'

'Don't do this to me.' She walked across to the window with her back to him.

'I'd have told you before, but I wasn't sure, not until last night. Now that I am, I feel it's my duty to try to stop you before it's too late.'

She was suddenly outraged at what he was implying. What right had he to come here and tell her this? She dreaded to think what Evan would do, if he knew. There'd be a massive argument.

'I'm going through with this, whatever you say or do. So unless you can give me good reason not to, or can show me some proof, I'd be grateful if you'd shut up about it. In fact, I'm not sure I want you at my wedding now. And what's more, maybe I should tell

Evan what you've been saying to me. Let's see what he has to say about it.'

Cole scratched the back of his head with his fingernails. Donna guessed he realised he shouldn't have said any of this.

'All right. Suit yourself, but don't say I didn't warn you.'

There was another knock on the door then. Mrs Lacey popped her head around the door, surprised to see Cole sitting on the bed.

'Your brother's looking for you. You'd better get downstairs; he wants to get on to the church as soon as the car arrives.'

'All right, I'm coming mum.'

Donna glanced at him as he left, not liking the concern he tried to display on his face. She immediately felt like crying. What had got into him all of a sudden? She'd always thought of Cole as a hero, the life and soul of the party, willing to put himself out for anyone. And when he'd told her how he'd suffered in action, his dread of going back to the front line, she'd really felt sorry for him. Now it was difficult to know what to think.

'Is everything all right Donna? What did Cole want?' Mrs Lacey asked, although clearly she didn't suspect anything was amiss.

'Oh nothing much. Wanted to wish me luck. Really nice of him, I thought. Anyway, they should be going soon. We'll just give them a few minutes, then we'll finish getting ourselves ready, and hope the other car comes on time.'

'It will.'

They stood there together for a few minutes, musing over what was to come. Donna had already been nervous, but now after Cole's revelation, she felt even more jittery. He'd upset her. But why had he done it? She couldn't answer that one, unless it was because he was jealous and secretly wanted her for himself. Although up until now that thought hadn't crossed her mind.

Mrs Lacey went across to the window.

'They've just gone out. They're getting into the car, and now they're driving off. Both of them look so handsome and debonair. Oh, I do feel so proud of them, and you too. You'll make a lovely couple – and with the weather the way it is, the photos should come out a treat.'

Donna kept glancing at her watch. She'd hardly heard what Mrs Lacey was saying. And was now trembling, daring to doubt Evan. What if there was some truth in his accusations? Yet what exactly had he said? Very little except to run his brother down. Surely she knew Evan better than that, didn't she? Then for a few seconds she had a terrible urge to tell Mrs Lacey just what had happened. She was in a quandary, unsure of what to do for the best. In the end she thought it best to keep this to herself, Evan had always treated her with respect, and was so patient and understanding, it bordered on the sublime.

'Come on then Donna. Are you ready now?'

'As ready as I'll ever be.'

'Good, the wedding car is pulling up outside.'

It was difficult for Donna to move in her long white wedding dress, especially coming down the stairs. But she made it, with Mrs Lacey following behind holding the trail, before opening the front door for them to go out.

Although this was supposed to be the biggest day of her life, Cole's outburst was putting a damper on things. And sitting in the back of the wedding car her mind began to ponder again about the possibility of not going through with the wedding. Her brain wouldn't function properly, but then again she didn't feel it fair to let Evan down purely on hearsay. The more she thought about it, the more it seemed to her Cole was doing this out of spite and jealousy. As the car travelled towards the church, she considered telling Evan about her conversation with Cole, before the ceremony began, but if she did it would almost certainly ruin the whole wedding.

As the car turned left into the entrance of the church grounds, she felt the tension mounting, and had the urge to run away again. Then looking up she saw the photographer waiting for the car to pull up in front of the church, and realised she had to go through with it now. She knew Evan as well as she'd ever known anyone; and he'd helped turn her life around whilst in hospital. And hadn't he been her rock ever since? Never complained or pressurised her into revealing the dark side of her past which he knew of, but not about. Surely that meant he loved her a great deal.

The car stopped and the driver quickly got out and opened the door for the bride and the soon to be mother-in-law.

It was at this point Donna thought about her parents, normally the father of the bride would have travelled with the bride to the church and then escorted her into the church and down the aisle, but weeks before the wedding was due to take place her parents had made it quite clear, in their opinion, she was marrying beneath her. The fact that Evan was only a male nurse and had encouraged her to work as a menial kitchen assistant hadn't gone down well with them. The meeting had ended with a furious altercation, resulting in Donna telling them to stay away from the wedding ceremony and reception.

Mrs Lacey squeezed Donna's arm, noticing how distracted and quiet she had become.

'Try not to worry dear – everything will go off fine, I promise you. Nothing to worry about. Enjoy it as much as you can, it's going to be the best day of your life, but it'll pass all too quickly – believe me.'

'I know, I'll do my best.'

As Donna looked around and took in the picturesque setting of the eighteenth century church, situated above the town of Dexford, she heard footsteps on the gravel pathway. Looking up she saw her father rushing towards her. He was smartly dressed, his face flushed and he was breathing heavily from exertion. She suddenly felt very emotional.

'Please Donna, would it be all right if I gave you away?' He appeared to be pleading.

This brought tears to her eyes - despite what had happened between them, she didn't have the heart to say no. Nodding in agreement she looked at Mrs Lacey, who seemed pleased at how this had unfolded. And as they walked towards the entrance to the church, the strains of Love Divine could be heard.

Stepping into the church, after a few minutes, the wedding march started, and taking hold of her father's arm, they walked slowly down the aisle to the front of the church, which was packed with well-wishers. She recognised some of the staff from the hospital, and her colleagues from the school where she worked.

Gazing to her left she noticed her mother standing a few rows back from the front. It seemed she too had decided to come, despite being told to stay away, and gave Donna a warm smile although her eyes seemed tearful, as if to say everything was all right now. Whether they would ever have any sort of relationship again, she didn't know. But at least her mother had made a start, and for that Donna was grateful.

Evan was waiting at the front pew for her. He wore a dark blue suit, with a pink carnation in his buttonhole, his black hair freshly groomed and brushed back. He looked elated. Next to him stood Cole, all smiles, acting as if nothing was wrong.

At last, the happy couple stood side by side ready to make their vows. Evan kept smiling at her reassuringly.

The bald-headed vicar in his white robes stood in front of them, smiling too, happy it seemed, to be conducting this marriage service. In his hands, he held an open bible. After a quick glance at both of them, to ensure they were both ready, he began.

'Dearly beloved, we are gathered here today to join this man and this woman in Holy Matrimony…'

To Donna the ceremony seemed to pass in a blur. She could barely remember repeating the words after the vicar except to say ' I do.'

Finally, the couple kissed clumsily, before making their way back down the aisle amid the music and out of the church, where everyone would soon congregate.

After the photographs had been taken, Donna's mother and father moved closer to her. Her father slipped an envelope into her hand with instructions not to open it until later. Donna was intrigued but resisted the temptation.

'Well, Mrs Lacey, I suppose we'd better lead the way to the reception,' Evan said grinning.

'Yes, Mr Lacey, I think we better had.' She smiled, and the guests walked over to their respective cars.

From there they travelled to the Red Lion Inn, quaintly situated in the country just outside Dexford. At the back was a function room, where the wedding reception was to take place, followed later in the evening, by a buffet and disco.

The bride and groom sat at the top table, in the middle of guests from both sides. Once the meal was over it was the bride's father, surprisingly, who got to his feet to make a speech.

'We are here today to celebrate the marriage of my daughter Donna to Evan. Obviously they are very much in love, as Donna's mother and I were too many years ago for us to care to remember…'

Donna felt so proud of her father, as he made his speech, it was just what was needed to lighten the atmosphere. Experienced in this sort of thing, he had only positive things to say about them which was nice to hear; in fact at one point she became quite emotional. Once again glancing at her mother, she was surprised to see more tears in her eyes.

'… so, it just remains for me, along with everyone else here, to toast the happy couple and wish them a long and joyous future together.'

Then it was Cole's turn. He had all the guests in hysterics, with his funny anecdotes, most especially about when the two brothers were young. Then came a moving tribute to his sister Theresa, which was very poignant and there didn't seem to be a dry eye in the room. But the moment passed, and then on he went with more of his funny stories.

When all the speeches and well wishes had been made to the couple, the tables were cleared away in readiness for the disco.

Cole was on his feet again and said, 'Now I gather there's a disco laid on, so I would encourage you all to get on to the floor – and let's start boogieing. But first to start the proceedings, Mr and Mrs Lacey will take the first dance.'

The main lights were dimmed, and replaced by flashing lights of blue, red and yellow; everyone waited for the happy couple to appear on the dance floor.

'Well, Mrs Lacey, shall we?' Evan invited holding out his arm.

'Why not?'

After a while they were joined on the dance floor by the younger guests. And as the night wore on, following a number of requests from the older generation, the music slowed down, in order to cater for all age groups.

It was a struggle for Donna to dance in her wedding dress, she must have looked comical, perhaps the reason why Evan kept smiling at her. However, once the music was toned down it was easier for the couple to dance together. Donna was happy and at long last experiencing the 'glad to be alive' feeling. How wonderful it was to be able to spend the rest of her life with the person she loved. She wasn't going to let Cole get her down; after all once the wedding was over he would return to Afghanistan and wouldn't be home on leave again for many months.

A short time later they sat down, exhausted from their endeavours. They held hands, watching what was going on around them.

'I wish Theresa could have been here to see this,' Donna said suddenly.

Evan squeezed her hand. 'Me too. She would have brought the ceremony alive with her music. Maybe she's looking down on us right now, enjoying our special day with us.'

Donna felt sad for a moment. Everyone had been devastated when Theresa had died; and none of them would ever forget it.

'Come on now love, don't be sad. Theresa wouldn't want you to be like this. She'd want you to be happy, so let's try to be that in her memory.'

'I know, I'm sorry. I was just being silly.'

'Don't worry, I understand. I feel the same myself, but we can't change what happened. We'll never forget her, but it's time to move on, and get on with our own lives.'

Evan pulled Donna towards him and kissed her lightly on the lips.

Suddenly Cole leaned over towards them. 'Hey, what's the matter with you two? The honeymoon hasn't started yet, and you're all over each other already. Have you no shame?' he joked, his beaming face only inches away from them.

'Cole, get lost will you,' Evan told him in a humorous tone of voice.

'Well, that's a nice way to treat your one and only brother. You know, I came over here to ask your darling wife for a dance, but if that's how you're going to treat me, I don't think I'll bother.' A half-smile appeared on his face as he winked at Donna.

'Cole, have you thought she may not want to dance with you. She's a married woman after all, and married women don't dance with strange men.'

'Strange - is that what I am? Well I reckon she won't say no to the groom's brother, just for old time's sake.'

As Donna took in the situation, she wondered what was going on in Cole's mind, despite his joking with Evan.

'Cole, if she wants to accept your invitation to dance, then that's fine with me. I can stand the competition now you know,' Evan laughed, showing his perfect snow white teeth.

'Right, how about it Donna? May I have the pleasure? Let me show my little brother how to really dance.' He held out his hand for her.

Donna tried to look amused, but her stomach fluttered alarmingly, remembering what he'd said to her earlier.

The music was fast and loud when they got up. At first, they danced opposite each other, laughing and smiling as if their previous conversation had never happened.

But then after a few minutes, Cole moved towards her, as if he wanted to whisper something in her ear.

'You should have heeded my warning earlier, darling – please, you've got to believe me. I can't tell you how worried I am. You're in great danger.'

She was astounded, and glared at him angrily. 'Oh for God's sake – not that rubbish again. This has to stop right now before I fall out with you. Evan will be a wonderful husband to me. I love him and he loves me. So why are you doing this?' Gently pushing his shoulder with her hand, she continued, 'Enough Cole, or I'll tell him what you've said.'

Then as she moved away he said, 'Tell him if you want to. Of course, he'll deny it. But look him in the eye when he does, and then tell me if he's telling the truth. Look, I've had to come clean about him, even though he made me swear not to. I don't want you to get hurt.'

Donna had had enough of Cole's lies. She stormed away from him; about to tell Evan what he'd said, then realising it would spoil what had otherwise been a perfect day, and changed her mind. Deciding instead to ignore what Cole had said for now. After all, he'd soon be back with his army mates on another tour of duty. But why was he suggesting his brother had done something wrong? Almost as if he hated Evan, and wanted to spoil his happiness. Whatever the reason, she couldn't think about it right now, and would make up her mind later as to whether or not to tell Evan. Nevertheless it made her feel anxious again, bringing back those horrible feelings similar to when she'd been raped.

'Hi love,' Evan said, smiling at her as she went back to sit down beside him, unaware it seemed, that she'd walked off from Cole.

'Evan...' she said taking hold of his hand, before kissing him lightly on the lips.

'That dance didn't last long.' He sounded almost pleased his brother hadn't hogged her any longer. 'What's happened to Cole?'

'Oh, I think he spotted an old girlfriend, who's been giving him the glad eye all night - and decided to go after her.'

'He's a randy sod, my brother – always has been. Mind you, I reckon he's entitled to some release considering his job in the army.'

'I suppose. So what time do we have to make our way to the airport?'

Evan raised his eyebrows, almost as if he'd forgotten about it. 'Oh damn! What time is it?' He looked at his watch. 'It's just after midnight now, so that only gives us a couple of hours. My God, we'd better get a move on or we'll be late. Come on, let's go upstairs to get changed'

Donna was relieved, as it meant she could get away and avoid any further awkward scenes with Cole, should he suddenly decide to join them again.

'Lead the way then, husband.'

'Let's try and slip away unnoticed, eh.' He got up holding onto her hand.

But their plan to make a discreet exit was soon shattered and when they reached the bottom of the stairs, the lights flooded on.

'Hey – we know where you're going,' a voice shouted at them.

They both froze momentarily. Then the clapping and cheering started. Donna had never felt so embarrassed in her life. As Evan dragged her up the stairs; they waved without looking back, glad of the relative safety of the room designated for them to change in.

While he went to the bathroom to freshen up, Donna started to get out of the dress. She jumped when he came back, and felt his eyes on her. Never before had she allowed him to see her like this, even though she was still in her underwear. She felt flushed.

'You are so gorgeous. You've no idea how much I've been aching for you these past few months.'

She smiled as he moved closer and put his strong arms around her. Kissed her delicately and sweetly on the lips as if he loved her more than life itself.

Donna closed her eyes in a dreamy sort of way, sure now more than ever that Evan was the man for her, and that Cole couldn't be more wrong. He was just out to make mischief and obviously jealous of what she and Evan had. Maybe at some stage during the honeymoon she might tell Evan all about his wonderful brother. Let him know exactly what Cole was really like – so much for being the all action war hero. When they parted Donna smiled warmly at Evan, the love of her life, the man who'd saved her in more ways than one.

Chapter 25

HAVING QUICKLY CHANGED INTO JEANS AND TEE SHIRTS, EVAN SAID, 'COME ON THEN, WE'D BETTER SHOW OUR FACES, BEFORE THEY START WONDERING WHAT WE'RE UP TO.'

He slapped her playfully on the behind.

She gave a little yelp and slapped him back, then saw him raise his hand again. 'Don't you dare, or I'll scream for help.'

'Oops, think I'd better behave myself then before I get into trouble. So are we going down or what?' And took hold of her hand smiling.

She hesitated. 'I'm not looking forward to this,' she said as he opened the door.

Evan held onto her hand tightly, maybe too tightly, amid more clapping and cheering as they came downstairs. People were shouting good luck and all the best. Donna tried to put a brave face on it but all the time she just wanted to get on with the honeymoon and be alone with Evan. Just before they reached the front entrance, she caught sight of Cole with a worried look on his face, acting as if he really did fear for her. She didn't want to look at him, and was glad when those few fleeting seconds were gone, and they were outside making their way to the taxi parked in front of the Inn. As they got inside Donna's mind suddenly seemed in a whirl.

She was aware of the guests gathered around the car to see them off, but was a little overcome with emotion. Evan rolled down the window and responded to the good wishes, at which point he indicated to Donna to throw the posy out into the crowd, and as soon as she did this, she seemed to come round and finally managed to wave goodbye to all the well-wishers. The car slowly moved forward with the happy couple continuing to wave frantically until finally the guests disappeared from view.

Sitting back in her seat, shaking ever so slightly, relieved now they were on their way, she tried to forget all about Cole and concentrated on what should be a wonderful honeymoon. Just the two of them away from the hustle and bustle of people, the first time they'd been truly alone together.

She felt his warm hand on hers, and turned to look at his smiling face, seeing the joy he felt at having her as his wife.

'How you feeling, love? Happy?'

She nodded, looking content. 'Couldn't be happier.'

'Me too – can't tell you how much I've dreamed for this day to come. And even now that it has, I still can't believe it.'

'Neither can I.' She leaned towards him to give him a quick peck on the cheek. 'I never thought I'd meet anyone who'd love me for myself, rather than just for how I look.'

He smiled again, his eyes almost sparkling in expectation. 'We're going to have the best honeymoon ever. We won't want to come back.'

'I hope we don't. It's a shame the only flight available was at two o'clock in the morning. Means we have to spend our first night together on board the plane.'

'Well, it's just one of those things. We'll more than make up for it later, I promise you,' he grinned mischievously, which made her feel uncomfortable, still fearing their wedding night, which she did so want to be special.

'I suppose we will.'

A little over an hour later they reached the Airport. Luckily, the traffic had been light, enabling them to get there quickly.

The taxi stopped right outside the Airport Terminal. They got out with only their essential luggage that was light and easy to carry. The taxi driver took the rest of their belongings into the Airport to a baggage handler.

When Evan presented their tickets at the ticket barrier and passport control, they were told their plane for Torrelino, a small Spanish island close to the island of Majorca, would be leaving within the next hour. Donna sat waiting with Evan, wondering if his choice of venue for their honeymoon had been deliberate – perhaps he wanted them to get to know each other, so that they'd talk about things they'd kept to themselves for so long. Maybe she'd finally feel able to tell him about being raped.

After about forty-five minutes they got the call to board the plane, which set their excitement going at full speed again. Once they were on board, they were ushered into their seats by a pleasant blond-haired stewardess. Evan allowed Donna to go in first, so that she could sit by the window, and look out if she wished. Very noble of him, she thought.

He sat back in his seat, closed his eyes and yawned as if he was tired, then squeezed her hand tightly. She squeezed his hand back, then when he leaned over to kiss her again, she began to feel better. Maybe at last she could put the past behind her and live a normal life.

Not long after take-off, a film, The Island, starring Ewan McGregor was put on for their entertainment. Evan seemed to be enjoying it and could hardly take his eyes off the screen. They continued to hold hands and occasionally he looked across at her, as if he wanted to make sure she was all right.

Shortly afterwards, she realised she must have been dozing, as when she turned her head, she saw that Evan had dropped off to sleep, probably dreaming of their honeymoon. The brightness of the film made it difficult for her to sleep. All she could think and worry about was their first night together.

Needing the bathroom, she moved his hand delicately away, and with some difficulty managed to climb over his legs without waking him.

It felt such a relief to be able to stretch her legs, but she would be so glad when the plane landed and they could step out onto the beautiful island of Torrelino.

Within fifteen minutes, she returned to her seat, noticing Evan quietly fidgeting in his sleep, dead to the world. When he started to snore, his top lip vibrated, causing Donna to snigger with amusement. He could be quite funny when he wanted to be, even in his sleep.

Leaning against his shoulder, she snuggled up close to him, and eventually drifted off to sleep hoping when she woke they'd have reached their destination.

She woke with a start. Bright light made her squint and then remembered what she'd been dreaming about. Of a time not so long ago when her worst nightmare had come true. The dream had come all too often of late, and this time it was so vivid and real – it was almost as if she'd relived every second of the horrendous ordeal.

Then the first thing that hit her as Evan moved in his seat was that she was a married woman now, and had someone to share her life with, someone who could help soothe away the bad memories of her past.

With Evan's seat adjusted to almost a lying down position, she was able to look at him fully, and believe she really had married him. After all the events of the last few years, to have actually found happiness seemed to her incredible. What a shame Cole had almost spoilt what had otherwise been such a joyous occasion. Thank God she hadn't listened to him. If any of his family ever found out about what he claimed Evan had done, there would be hell to pay.

She was amazed the two brothers got on at all, as they couldn't be more different in character. Although if what she thought to be lies came out, they'd most definitely be at each other's throats. How could Cole infer Evan wasn't worthy of her, without specifically saying what his brother had done wrong. He was a nurse for God's sake; in a position of trust, dedicated to saving lives, not taking them. Hadn't he even stopped her from jumping off the top of the Hospital building? And how many other people had he helped in his time? People who might have otherwise died. And he'd always been so good to her, never wavering despite her tantrums and mood swings.

She watched his eyes flicker open, and smiled warmly at him when their eyes met.

'Hallo darling,' he whispered. 'We anywhere near Torrelino yet?'

'Don't know. They haven't said, but it can't be far away because it's getting light.'

'I'm getting so excited about this Donna. Just think of it, our very own Villa for a fortnight. Miles away from anywhere, with a private beach close by. We'll feel like we're in paradise, for a while at least. And no one can contact us, seeing as we left our mobiles with mum.'

'That's true.'

'What's the time?' he yawned.

'Just after six.'

'Still early then. I wish we'd hurry up and get there. I'm dying to get on that beach, and swim in the cool clear blue sea.'

'We'll get there soon enough.'

Just then a message came over the loudspeaker system. 'Good morning ladies and gentlemen. We are now approaching Santonio airport. I would ask you all to return to your seats, and fasten your safety belts…'

'Oh yeah! Think someone must have heard me.'

'They must have, Evan.'

Looking down out of the window, having just fastened her safety-belt, she could only see blue sky and fluffy white clouds. Watching the plane descend through the clouds, she noticed below stretches of hilly brown land interspersed with bits of vegetation. Then the white buildings of the one large settlement came into view. Further afield were the golden sands that encircled the island, and beyond that, the blue sea looked calm.

Soon everything became larger and larger, until the plane finally touched down on the runway with just a slight jolt, before taxiing towards the white terminal building.

'Welcome to Santonio, the capital of Torrelino. We hope you had a pleasant journey and will enjoy your stay…'

At last, it was time for them to leave the plane. The door opened, and waiting their turn holding hands, Donna and Evan walked down the steps, before making their way across to the terminal building.

They breezed through customs, then went outside, with their luggage in tow, to wait for a car with the words Villa Mortes painted on its side.

Donna felt extremely nervous but also excited, and knew once they were inside the car it wouldn't be long. She was aware of Evan constantly staring at her with longing; obviously looking forward to what should be the happiest time in their lives. When their love would finally be cemented. She tried to look forward to their first night together, but didn't except too much from it. So long as he was gentle with her, and was understanding, that's all she asked.

Nudging Donna, Evan pointed to a car approaching in the distance bearing the appropriate wording. They both waved.

The car stopped close by and a thin dark haired man with a droopy moustache, and muddy brown eyes got out and walked towards them. There was a warm expression of friendliness on his face.

'Welcome.' He stretched out his hand, which Donna took but found hot and clammy. 'I am Juan. I own Villa you live in for next two weeks. You must be Evan and Donna. Congratulations on your marriage – I hope you have very happy time in my Villa.'

'Thank you, I'm sure we will,' Evan said smiling.

Donna just nodded.

'I put your things in boot, and then we go – yes?'

Evan nodded; bending down to help Juan with the suitcases.

'OK, we have everything - yes? Good – now we go to my Villa. Please get in and look as I drive through at my beautiful island.' Juan talked as if he owned the island, which of course he didn't.

Driving out of the main town, Juan took the car down a coastal road, then went up into the hills filled with parched yellowing vegetation and spectacular views, that were rather too hair-raising at times. He then drove off the beaten track over bumpy and occasionally dangerous looking terrain with ease. He explained they were travelling through to the other end of the island, which apart from a few small areas of development was largely unspoilt.

Suddenly without warning, as the car descended, Juan pointed to a white washed Villa, behind which were white sands leading to the calm waters of the sea. It was certainly out in the wilds, she thought. He drove to the front of the Villa, stopping on a tarmacked area outside the building.

'I help you with your things, show you my Villa, then I leave you in peace.' He smiled at them.

First, he opened the door, allowing them into a spacious living room with light coloured furniture and abstract pictures on the walls. The kitchen appeared to be modern with every convenience. Upstairs were two bedrooms, the main one to the rear of the property, opening out to a balcony, and from this vantage point it was easy to make out the beach with palm trees, their leaves swaying in the breeze. At the back of the Villa was a large swimming pool in an enclosed garden area.

'Here you have peace, quiet and privacy. No one to disturb you. There is plenty of food in fridge and freezer. I try to think of your English tastes, but you have car in garage if you want to go into town for some supplies. I hope you have very nice honeymoon, and many happy years together. If you need anything you ring me on this number.' He handed them a little card with his name, address and phone number. 'And now if there is nothing else, I leave you to enjoy yourselves.'

He gave them both a little wave with a slight knowing smile on his face, before he left. They both waved back. Donna was glad he'd gone, as she thought he was slimy and reeked of garlic. She hadn't liked the way he looked at her either, and hoped they wouldn't need to call upon him. If they did, she might decide to go out for the duration.

They watched from the window of the living room, as Juan drove off, a dust cloud gathering where the car had been. Then Evan turned round and took her in his arms, hugged her so tightly it almost took her breath away. He kissed her with so much gusto, she began to realise just how much she meant to him. She hoped he wouldn't be disappointed.

'So what do you think?'

'Wonderful Evan – the place is idyllic. I never dreamed I'd be spending a honeymoon somewhere as beautiful as this.'

'Isn't it just perfect? It has everything we need, and most of all we're on our own, away from people. To be with you like this Donna, is my ultimate dream come true.' He laughed.

She laughed too, trying not to sound too happy, or it might well blow up in her face. 'So what shall we do first? Maybe unpack our things, then go for a dip in the pool, or even go down to that private beach.'

He shook his head vigorously, stared at her, his blue eyes widening in all seriousness. Shudders of fear went through her whole body. Please not already, she thought. Then he began to snigger. She couldn't see what was so funny.

'Evan, I'm beginning to think you're sex mad,' she tried to joke.

'Oh come on Donna, what's the matter with you? Surely, you don't want to just hold hands now we're married. You wait till you know what I've got planned for us– it's going to blow your mind.'

'I don't think so. I'm not into all those horrible things, people get up to.'

'Well, we'll see about that.' Raising his eyebrows up and down, she began to realise he was pulling her leg, which made her giggle.

'Don't you know, a girl likes a little romance with candlelight, soft music and so on.'

He grinned, thinking for a minute before raising a finger. 'Of course. You're right. Don't worry, I was only kidding.'

'You'd better be, or you'll be sleeping in the spare room tonight. Come on, we'll unpack, have a bit of a rest, then go out somewhere.'

'All right, if you insist.'

It took them an hour or so to unpack most of their belongings, then freshen up and change into something more casual. Donna went into the bathroom first, had a shower and when she came out she had a swimsuit on under a thin blouse and khaki shorts. She smiled at him as he walked towards her, carrying a bag of toiletries and his shaver, and hoped he wouldn't be too long or the day would be over.

Sitting on a deckchair on the veranda, she waited for him. She sipped the ice cold drink she'd just made, placing it back on the table next to his. From this position she could take in the view of the beach from their Villa. Putting on her sunglasses and closing her eyes, she dreamed of their two weeks of bliss. She wanted the honeymoon to be a time they'd both treasure forever.

She never heard Evan approach her from behind, and instinctively jumped when as he placed his hands around her sunglasses. Then when he moved his face close to her own, she shuddered slightly. For a fleeting moment she glimpsed a face masked with a balaclava helmet. Then it vanished, and she saw his happy smiling love struck face. They kissed.

As he sat down beside her, he gave her what was intended to be a reassuring smile, but she felt uneasy, even frightened in case she couldn't be a good wife to him.

'Cheers,' he picked up his drink to clink against hers. 'To us, and a happy fruitful marriage.'

'To us.'

He lay back, took in the scenery and sea, and breathing in deeply, seemed so contented. If only she could find the courage to tell him the truth about the rape.

'Shall we take a walk down to the beach now?' he said after they'd rested for a while.

'What?'

'Come on Donna, get with it. I said, let's go down to the beach.'

'Oh, all right. Sorry I was miles away. It'll be nice to get a feel of the place.'

Hand in hand, they walked down to the beach, which was only about a hundred yards away. The white sandy beach formed a cove approximately five hundred yards long, and had palm trees at the head of it.

When they reached the water's edge, Donna dipped her bare feet in, and found the water cool and refreshing. Evan did the same, then suddenly began kicking water onto her. She yelped, responding in a similar manner, so that soon they were both soaked. They fell about laughing, both so happy in this little cocoon they'd created for themselves. All thoughts of Cole, the rape and everything that had happened to her, were momentarily pushed to the back of her mind.

They lay on the sands, in their swimwear, relaxing in the sun.

'Isn't this just the best?' Evan remarked turning to her.

'Yes it is - let's savour it while we can.'

'Let's.' He grabbed hold of her hand.

They'd brought a packed lunch with them, consisting of sandwiches of tongue and ham kept in a cool box, along with a bottle of champagne which they drank from plastic cups. Donna only drank a small amount, while Evan knocked it back like there was no tomorrow, much to her dismay.

'Hey, I could get quite a liking for this stuff. Phew, and it's got a bit of a kick to it as well.' He wiped his brow with the back of his hand.

'Take it steady then Evan, you don't want to be ill on our first night together.'

'Don't you worry about that? I'll be more than capable - you can bet your life on it,' he told her forcefully.

Donna smiled, yet deep inside she was apprehensive, but made no comment.

'You know something?' He suddenly sat up, his elbows deep in the hot sand. 'I still can't believe this has happened. For an ordinary guy like me, to win the heart of such a girl as you is the stuff dreams are made of. But it's not only your looks that attracted me - it's the real you, the girl I met in hospital and only glimpsed at until recently. I knew I was right to persevere with you. Just wish someone would tell me what I've done to deserve all this happiness.' He had a soppy grin on his handsome face. 'When I think back to how I used to be, and the things I got up to when I was a teenager and beyond – well, I could never hope to be in the same league as you.'

She cleared her throat nervously, wondering what was coming next.

'I was bad, when I was young and found out I'd never be able to play football again - it almost finished me. I went way off the rails completely, and anyone in my way was a target. I could have ended up in prison or even dead. Then when I was at my lowest ebb, I think God in his infinite wisdom saw something in me, something I didn't know was there. Somehow, I got a job in the hospital, saw so many horrific sights, people so much worse off than me, and that made me realise how lucky I was – and I haven't looked back since. Then the icing on the cake came when I met you. Although I didn't know it at the time, I thank God I managed to get there in time to stop you jumping off that roof, or we wouldn't be here on this beach now.' At that he stopped for a minute as tears filled his eyes.

She touched his naked shoulder. 'I think you've let the drink get to you, Evan. Maybe we ought to go for a swim, it might cool you down a little.'

'You may be right. Come on then, I'll race you.' He was quickly on his feet running across the scorching sand into the sea. She was right behind, but couldn't run as quickly as him.

The water was cool and Donna shrieked as she dived in, but they soon got used to it. Evan was already swimming, waving to her as he did so, eager to show off his prowess, she thought, slightly amused.

Although she was touched by his admissions, it didn't alter the situation she was in and this was just killing time.

When they came out of the water, he appeared to be a little more restrained, resorting back to being his normal self, helping her to get dry, and was eager to do anything for her again. This brought about a feeling of hope that he'd be understanding and sympathetic with her when the time came, and that maybe she'd be able to tell him the full story of what had happened to her and its repercussions.

They remained on the beach for a while, getting their breath back, but with the sun lower in the sky, as time went on there was a drop in temperature and Donna felt they ought to get back to the Villa.

'Shall we go now, Evan?' She shivered slightly. 'It's getting cooler, don't you think?'

'Sure, why not. There'll be plenty of time for the beach over the next couple of weeks.'

'Why don't we dine out tonight, maybe in the town. Save us cooking?'

Evan's jaw dropped open. 'You've got to be joking, haven't you? Wouldn't it be better to dine in, just the two of us, so we don't have lots of other people all around us? I'd planned to cook something special, a steak maybe, then eat it outside, and see the sun setting.'

'Oh come on Evan, neither of us wants to go to that much trouble on our first night here. Not when we could just pop into the town, and have it ready prepared. We're supposed to be enjoying ourselves – aren't we? So why not do just that?'

Evan looked on edge; his eyes were moving from left to right. 'Donna, what's wrong with you? I thought you wanted a bit of romance, soft lights, music and so on? That's all I'm suggesting. Please babe, I want to do this for you. And you won't have to do a thing. No more arguments - all right?'

What could she say? She could hardly refuse, not when he was so insistent. She nodded, reluctantly giving way to him. They walked back to the Villa, hand in hand. And as soon they got back, he insisted Donna sit down outside on the veranda while he got on with the dinner. She heard him busily cooking the food, attempting a rendition of 'She' terribly out of tune. Then after a time she smelt the delicious aromas of some sort of sauce, containing herbs and spices, and of course the sizzling steaks cooking under the grill.

As she sat back relaxing, turning her head to the right, she could just about see what was going on in the kitchen – she'd never known he could cook – perhaps his mum had given him a few lessons, she thought smiling.

Jumping slightly when she heard a knock on the window, she turned round to see Evan waving at her. He was encouraging her to come in, as evidently the dinner he'd spent so long in preparing and cooking was ready.

She got up and walked to the French doors, opening them to the delicious smells of the cooking. He wore an apron, had a spoon in his hand, as if he'd just tasted the sauce he was making.

'Smells really nice.'

'Let's hope it tastes as good as it smells. If you're ready, I'll dish up. I think everything's done now. Would you like to eat inside or out on the veranda?'

'It would be nice on the veranda. It's still warm and not as hot as in here. Want any help?'

He shook his head. 'Just lay the table for me, and I'll do the rest.'

She nodded, went to a draw and found out knives, forks, and place mats, then set the table outside on the veranda, and task done, sat there waiting for him to come out. Within two minutes he came out carrying two steaming hot plates containing the steaks, new potatoes and an assortment of vegetables covered in a creamy sauce.

After placing the plates on the table he went back to the kitchen for a bottle of wine and two glasses.

Having poured the wine into the glasses, he sat down at the table, his face flushed from the heat of the kitchen. They clinked their glasses together, before starting on the meal. Donna couldn't help but be impressed – it tasted as good as it looked. The steak was succulent and tender, the sauce creamy and cheesy with a tang to it.

'I never dreamed you could cook this well.'

'I'm a man of many talents babe, and now you're my wife you'll soon find that out,' he grinned.

'Well, I think we've both got a lot of finding out to do.' She raised her eyebrows to emphasise the point.

'Oh really.' He smiled in a knowing way.

'Isn't that what being married is all about? Learning what your partner is really like, warts and all.'

'Yes, I suppose it is. And I for one can't wait to know all there is to know about you.'

'You might wish you hadn't.'

'I don't think so, babe.' He stared straight into her eyes, making her finally look away embarrassed.

They finished their meals, eating every last morsel, then had a ready-made gateau for dessert, before sitting back with their glasses of wine in front of them, to see the final shafts of sunlight disappearing from sight.

Sitting in the twilight, apprehension began to creep up on her, her thoughts only on the night ahead. To make things worse again Evan seemed to be drinking more than normal.

'Evan, aren't you knocking back a bit too much of that wine? You'll be spark out before you know where you are – you don't want to spoil everything, do you?'

'Sorry Donna. I need a bit of Dutch courage.'

'Why should you need that?'

'Because I keep getting the feeling you'll freak out if I so much as lay a finger on you – and that would really hurt, especially on our honeymoon. I'm drinking in case that happens, to soften the blow.'

Donna's mind began to work overtime – already feeling guilty, now she felt pressurised as well. Not the ideal start for their first night together.

'Evan...I wouldn't have married you if...' she replied, trying to appear normal.

'Tell you what babe, let me have a quick shower first, then you go and do the same, make yourself beautiful, and I'll wait in bed for you. I'll even dim the lights if you like. Take as long as you like, I don't mind. After all I've waited this long, another half an hour or so won't make much difference.'

As their eyes met, she trembled, hoping he wouldn't notice her fear of failure.

'Hope I'm worth the wait.'

'Believe me, you are,' he said giving a little haughty laugh.

While he went into the bathroom, she lay on the bed in the main bedroom, closing her eyes, aware that very soon she would find out whether or not she'd finally managed to put the past behind her.

She was dozing, when suddenly she smelt a familiar pungent aftershave. Her eyes sprung open, and there standing over her was Evan. He was grinning, and wore only a terri-robe. But it was the smell that concerned her most. That horrible repulsive odour she remembered so well. She began to shake, her fear suddenly intense and deep. It seemed unbelievable, and every time she breathed in, it was there worse than before. Dear God – it was Evan. He was the man who'd raped her, and almost ruined her life. Cole had been right all along. And now she was trapped. Did he know who she was? He must do. He'd lured her here, and was sure to be intending to silence her now for good.

'I've finished babe – the bathroom is all yours.' He kissed her softly on the lips.

'OK.' She got up off the bed, fetched herself a towel, her thin negligee and dressing gown, and walked towards the bathroom.

'Don't be long,' he laughed, sending a cold chill down her spine.

She didn't reply, and hurriedly went inside, locking the door behind her.

In the relative safety of the bathroom, she leaned against the door, her breathing laboured, her heart pounding. Contemplating what the next half an hour might bring.

And after deciding to remain there for as long as she could, she shed her clothes and stepped into the Jacuzzi, praying in the meantime he might drop off to sleep. Maybe it was a good thing he'd drunk all that wine.

Finally, she realised the time had come to get out of the water. She'd heard nothing from Evan, not even a shout for her to hurry up or a knock on the door. Could he really have fallen asleep, or might he be waiting behind the door, ready to strike.

Donna dried her lithe shapely body thoroughly with her bath towel, sprinkled on some talc, before putting on the negligee, which she knew showed up more than she would have liked. She must try to act normal in case he was awake. She stared at herself in the mirror, observing the face and body that had caused her so much trouble. Having brushed her teeth, she knew there was no choice but to find out what lay behind the door.

Feeling anything but relaxed, she cautiously pushed back the lock on the door, opening it as quietly as possible, surprised to find the Villa in complete darkness. Standing in the doorway she couldn't make out whether Evan was asleep or not, and at that moment knew there was only one thing to do - to visualise the position of the furniture in the bedroom in relation to the window. She walked slowly forward stepping carefully in case she bumped into anything. If he was still awake, he could grab hold of her at any moment, surprise her, then rape and kill her very easily.

After only a matter of seconds she jumped as she touched something soft which lay in her path - the bed. Please God, don't let it wake Evan. Standing still, the silence was almost deafening. But she had to force herself to carry on, and try to make good her escape, in order to get away from him.

Once more she became aware of that overpowering smell; it was as if he was taunting her with it. The stench of the awful sweet sickly aroma was too much, and almost made her throw up. But she had to keep calm, freedom was only minutes away.

Satisfied he was asleep, she moved slowly to her left. With her jeans, tee-shirt and trainers tucked under her arm, she slipped quietly out of the room. After dressing quietly on the landing, she tiptoed downstairs but then halfway down her heart leapt in horror. One of the steps creaked loudly as she trod on it. Shit, she whispered under her breath, feeling sure this was bound to wake him. She could have died.

'Donna – is that you? What on earth are you doing?'

That was it for Donna. Any thought of searching for the car keys was abandoned. Panicking, she dashed across the hallway, making for the front door.

A shaft of light lit the hall from the bedroom lamp.

'Oh my God,' she whispered, then heard what sounded like a thud, that meant he must have been getting out of bed.

Fumbling with the door knob she finally managed to open it and ran out into the night.

'Donna! Donna! Come back here, damn it! Where are you going?' he shouted after her.

She wasn't having any of it, and ran because her life was at stake. Thankfully the moon came from behind the clouds, enabling her to see where she was going, First she went alongside the dirt track, thinking she'd make better time this way.

'What are you running away from – you idiot? There's nothing to be frightened of – You know I'd never hurt you...'

Her pulse raced and she trembled with fear.

Suddenly she heard the sound of a car starting up - Evan in the hire car, out to get her no matter what the cost.

Leaving the track, she rushed onto the rough uneven terrain that consisted of parched grassland and just a few scraggy bushes, running as fast as her legs would carry her, diving down to the ground when she caught sight of a beam from the headlights of the car.

Once the lights had passed, she got up and carried on running again. Although she didn't know where she was, it was imperative she got as far away from him as possible. Her lack of fitness forced her to stop a number of times, she even fell over once or twice, but saw no sign of the car or Evan. Thankfully she knew, despite the moon, she'd be difficult to find in the dark.

Later, when she came across a clump of prickly bushes she stopped, and lay down behind them, exhausted. This would be just the place to hide.

Keeping as quiet as a mouse, and from the sanctuary of the bushes, she could see a beam of light shining in the distance as Evan frantically tried to find her. But the shaft of light appeared to be moving farther away, and after a time it extinguished.

Had he given up? Somehow she doubted it, but at least she had something of a respite for the remainder of the night. It would be like looking for a needle in a haystack in the dark, and as long as she kept off the road in the daytime, she would be hard to find.

She must have slept for a while, and woke to the sound of birds screeching above her. As her eyes grew accustomed to the bright sunlight, from beneath the bushes she could see clear blue skies and feel the heat building from the sun.

Hurriedly she got to her feet, and brushed the dust off her clothes. Moving from the cover of the bushes, she felt a stiffness in her legs and body, probably due to sleeping on the hard ground, and from all the running she'd done the night before. She wondered how she'd survive, as another scorching day seemed in prospect.

Being unsure of which direction to take, she glanced around, and saw the sea and the Villa, tiny dots in the distance. There was only one thing to do, and that was to walk further inland, in the hope of finding someone to help her. The countryside could be seen more clearly in the daylight and was indeed barren scrubland.

As the morning wore on, she developed a terrible thirst but had no means of quenching it. She carried on at an even pace, trying to conserve her energy in the searing heat, but realised it wouldn't be long before this and the lack of water would take its toll. This desolate land appeared to go on forever, and she seemed no nearer civilisation. Wasn't the island supposed to be small, perhaps twenty-five miles or so across? Then why did even this distance seem like an eternity?

The morning passed slowly, and gradually she found it more and more difficult to carry on, pausing several times to rest and catch her breath. Each time she began to walk again, she feared just how much more she could endure. Her throat was so dry she hardly had any spit.

With the sun high in the sky, and the heat so intense, she suddenly began to feel very weak and lightheaded. Her legs became like rubber, and she fell to her knees. Then looking up ahead, she saw what appeared to be a figure coming towards her.

The figure seemed to be a well-built man carrying some sort of rucksack on his back.

She desperately tried to shout out in order to gain his attention, but the closer he got, the more his face seemed to be out of focus. For a few awful seconds she imagined it was Evan. And now had no means of escape. As these terrifying thoughts went through her mind, she collapsed to the ground from sheer exhaustion.

Had she passed out for a few seconds or longer? Or was this a dream? Then suddenly someone in a very English accent said, 'You shouldn't be out alone in this sort of terrain, it's dangerous in this hot weather – darling.'

Looking up, from his lilt, she realised who it was, and was unable to believe her ears. 'Cole! Is…is it really you? How...why... .' He gathered her up in his arms and put a water bottle to her lips. She gulped some of the liquid down but then suddenly blackness overwhelmed   her.

Chapter 26

IT WAS DARK WHEN SHE WOKE SOME TIME LATER. Close by she could see a fire flickering away. Looking down, she saw she was lying in some sort of sleeping bag. Cole had his back to her, and was sitting on a large boulder. He must have heard her moving behind him, because he turned his face towards her smiling and said, 'Aah, sleeping beauty awakens. How you feeling?'

'Tired, weak and very thirsty and hungry.'

He moved across to her, picked up a water bottle, and handed it to her. Then watched as she gulped down the precious liquid, spilling some of it down the sides of her mouth. She coughed and spluttered, before drinking some more, wiping her mouth with the sleeve of her top.

'So what were you doing out in the open on a day like today?'

'You don't want to know.'

'Ah, think I've an idea already, Donna. It's Evan, I'll bet. You've found out I was telling the truth about him – haven't you?'

She felt embarrassed. 'He... well, he'd had too much to drink for a start, and was shouting at me. I made a run for it after I'd smelt his aftershave. That horrible pungent smell I still have nightmares about.'

'What do you mean, the smell?'

'Well, I haven't told anyone this before but someone attacked me a while ago, and he had that same smell on him.'

There was an eerie silence for a few seconds, as Cole appeared to deliberate over what he'd been told.

'Well I did warn you darling, but you wouldn't listen. I wouldn't lie to you, Donna. And that's why I decided I had to come after you, to save you from him.'

'I don't know what to do.'

'Don't worry. Now I'm here, there's no need for you to do anything. I'll protect you, and believe me once he sees you're with me, he won't touch you; because he'll know if he does I'll kill him. In the morning, we'll make our way out of here and get you back to civilisation.'

'That would be great.'

'Like I said, that's not a problem. Ever since I found out you were going with him, I've feared for you. And as soon as he told me what he'd done, I knew I had to come here to help you.'

'What are you talking about Cole?'

'It was on his stag night. He'd had too much to drink then too, and he started talking about how he'd lusted after this girl. It was some time ago after he'd been forced to stop playing football, he said he had to have her even though she'd said no. I didn't want the same to happen to you.'

'Oh my God…no,' Donna began, her heart beating fiercely against her chest.

'Don't worry, I'm here to take care of you and stop him from hurting you.'

She smiled at him, suddenly feeling she owed him a great debt. 'That's good to know. I still can't believe you're here, Cole. How did you manage to get away?'

He put his hand on her arm. 'Pure luck love. By some strange but wonderful coincidence, my unit are over here on manoeuvres. We use this place to play at what we're doing for real over in

Afghanistan. The area here is very similar to what we encounter over there. As soon as I got back, I slipped away from my mates and was trying to get to the Villa, when I saw you out there. It's almost like I was meant to be here to save you.'

'Can't tell you how relieved I am to see you.'

He glanced at his watch and gave her a little smile. 'When did you last eat?

'It must have been roughly this time last night, when I escaped from Evan.'

'No wonder you're starving. I'll heat you something on the fire. It's only out of a can, but it's better than staying hungry.'

After opening a can of stewed beef, he tipped the contents into a saucepan, and stirred it whilst holding the pan over the fire. Before long it was bubbling away. Half he poured into a metal dish for Donna, the remains he ate from the saucepan himself.

She ate slowly, enjoying it as much as a meal at a top restaurant. Then once she'd finished he handed her a flask containing ice-cold water. She drank it greedily soon quenching her thirst.

'That better?' he asked her smiling.

'Much.'

'You've done really well to get away from him. That must have been difficult.'

'It was,' she said, her hand shaking as she gave the flask back to him.

Then she began to tell him what had happened.

'You know, you're the luckiest woman alive. You've no idea how much I've worried over what he might do to you.'

She put her hand on top of his. 'I'm sorry Cole – I didn't want to believe it, after how good he'd been to me, not until I had it clear in my own mind.'

'No worries – at least you realised before it was too late. So what did he try to do?'

'Nothing. I never gave him the chance. As I've just said, I knew it was him as soon as I smelt his aftershave. I shall never forget that horrible aroma as long as I live. I had no choice but to make a run for it.'

'I don't blame you. Listen, you've already mentioned about that smell. What exactly do you mean by that?' he said looking suddenly interested and concerned.

'When I said I was attacked...actually I...I was raped and nearly killed. I'd left work late one night and it was getting dark. I took a shortcut to the station when someone grabbed hold of me. I pictured him more heavily built than Evan. But... I'm...I'm sorry but I can't talk about it. Except to say I now know he was the one who did it.'

'Jesus, I just knew it,' Cole exclaimed. 'Even before his injury he was always so full of himself being a footballer, in fact I remember one time, he beat up a girl when she cheated on him with another player from the same club. Luckily, that day I was there to get him out of it. I should have known he'd been up to something else. Should have realised he hadn't changed. If only I could have kept an eye on him, but being away made that impossible. I should have told mum, but I just thought she's been through so much lately with dad and Theresa... although he didn't tell me he'd been up to his tricks again more recently, but he must have been, and you were the one in the wrong place at the wrong time. My God, how ironic – it's unbelievable, you've married the man who raped you!'

'We need to call the police Cole – get him arrested, before it's too late.'

'I agree, but first I have to get you out of here and back home. While he's out there on the loose, there's still danger. Even though I'm here with you, he could still surprise us.'

'Oh God!'

'Don't worry, I'll look after you. My army training has made me an expert in defending myself. But no one's infallible - that's why I don't want us hanging around waiting for something to happen.'

'So what are we going to do?'

'I've had an idea. It's what he'll least expect. I won't tell you the exact details yet, but when the time comes, believe me, you'll be surprised. Trust me, that's all I ask.'

She smiled, squeezed the back of his hand. Felt relief now after all the anxiety of the past couple of days. If only she could have met Cole before she'd met Evan, her life might have been so different. He was twice the man Evan would ever be, despite Evan saving her life one time.

A few hours later at dawn, Cole woke her, and gave her tinned fruit to eat and a drink of tea with powdered milk. He explained they had to make an early start before the sun got too powerful.

Cole hurriedly packed everything up, reassuring Donna she'd be all right. It was already humid, and she didn't relish the idea of a long walk, but she had to go along with what Cole said, after all he was the expert, and would take good care of her.

'You ready then?'

She nodded with a sad smile.

They walked the best part of the morning, stopping every now and then for a drink and something to eat. He seemed to know where he was going, but to Donna, all the countryside looked very much the same, scorched and with very little vegetation save for the odd clump of bushes here and there.

At last, Donna could make out the blueness of the sea in the distance. It looked strangely familiar and then it became clear to her exactly where they were.

She glanced across at him; saw the grin on his unshaven face.

'You're taking us back to the Villa.' There was a worried tone to her voice, and a lump formed in her throat, as she suddenly feared Cole was Evan's accomplice to kill her. Various terrifying images went through her mind, and she almost decided to run away again, but knew in her present state, she couldn't run anywhere.

'Calm down Donna, this isn't what you think. Believe me, this is the best option. You'd never make it back to civilisation – it's much too far to walk. And if I know Evan, he'll still be out there looking for you – shitting himself, in case you get away. I reckon there's a good chance the Villa's empty. There has to be a phone in there; so we can call the police and get some help - mobiles don't work around here unfortunately. We might even strike lucky and find the car still there, although, knowing him I doubt it. But the beauty of it is, it's the last place he'll ever think of looking for you. And if he comes back, boy will he get the shock of his life - cos I'll be waiting for him. And, darling, that's where brotherly love ends.' The corners of his mouth turned up into a crude smile.

Donna felt a bit puzzled by the look on his face, as if he was actually enjoying this. 'Well, if you're sure that's the right thing to do?'

'Of course I'm sure.'

'But what if he's back already?'

'Come on now Donna, he won't be. He'll be going crazy looking for you, and won't come back until he's searched everywhere he can think of. But even if he is there,' he nodded in the direction of the Villa. 'We'll have the element of surprise on our side. And we won't go over there until it's dark.'

It wasn't long before she made out the Villa clearly in the distance. He told her to keep down. They crawled across to some large rocks to hide behind, and remained there until dusk approached. During this time, Cole kept a constant lookout for his elusive brother, finally using binoculars to home in on the road leading to the Villa.

'The car isn't there, here look for yourself.' He handed the binoculars to her. 'But we can keep an eye out for him from here.'

It seemed he was right, and indeed the Villa did look empty. Maybe they ought to go over there straight away, she thought, getting up from behind the rocks.

'No, get down. If he's hiding somewhere, we'll be an easy target. I have some night goggles, which will help me see a way to the Villa when its dark. When the time comes, just grab hold of me and stay close.'

The wait was long and monotonous, but there was no other way. At last it was completely dark, except for short periods when the moon kept coming in and out from behind scudding clouds. Cole tapped her on the shoulder, indicating they should make a move, and keep their heads down; so for the most part they crawled their way towards the Villa. When they got there, he told Donna to wait by the side of an outbuilding to the right of the Villa, while he checked the property over. After peering into every window to make sure there was no one inside, he went back round to the front and tried the front door, but as expected, it was locked. As Donna went over to him, she could see he had a long thin metal rod, presumably to pick the lock. For several minutes, he messed about with it until at last there was a click. The door opened and hurriedly they went inside. He shut the door behind them. Adrenaline pumped through Donna veins. She glanced at Cole, who reassuringly squeezed her arm.

'All right darling, you stay by the door while I have a look around. If I'm not back in five minutes, or you hear any noises, get the hell out of here.'

She nodded, allowing him to go, but felt extremely nervous at being left alone. So tense, she kept her hand on the front door handle just in case. Hopefully Cole would hurry up and come back. Then she had a terrible dread in case Evan was waiting in the shadows, or behind the furniture ready to attack her, the first chance he got. But everywhere seemed quiet and within five minutes, Cole returned.

'The place is as clean as a whistle, Donna.'

'Thank God for that.'

'Best keep the lights off though and lock the front door, or he'll know we're here for sure. Then I need to get down to business. Know where there's a phone?'

She had to think for a minute. 'In the living room by the television, I think.' Donna pointed in that direction.

Wearing his goggles, Cole went into the living room, finding the phone exactly where she'd told him. Donna stayed where she was, by the window, in order to keep a look out for Evan.

'Excuse me while I make a couple of calls. This should only take a few minutes, I promise you.'

She nodded, not taking too much notice of what he was saying - wishing instead that the full moon would come out so that if Evan did turn up she would be able to see him, as at present it was almost impossible to see anything. In the quietness she felt as if her heart beat could be heard clearly in the room.

Finally, Cole put the phone back on its cradle, then sat down on the sofa opposite the front door, and told her to do the same.

'Right, I've phoned the police. I told them what's happened and they're sending someone up here as soon as they can. The only problem is the distance involved. Although it's a relatively small island, the roads aren't very good, and the visibility is poor at night, so it could take over an hour to get here. In the meantime all we can do is to sit tight and wait. And if Evan comes back, so much the better.'

As she squirmed in her seat, and bit her fingernails, she sensed Cole could tell how she was feeling because he squeezed her hand. Looking up in his direction, shaking slightly, she wished the police were here, so that an ugly confrontation could be avoided.

Then suddenly Cole got up and prowled around the room like a lion waiting for his prey. He kept looking out of the window too, breathing in and out deeply, sniffing and flexing his muscles as if readying himself for any eventuality.

After some time, she could stand it no longer. 'Why doesn't that police car hurry up?'

'It'll be here soon enough. Don't worry everything is under control. Remember even if he does come back now, he has no chance. We'll hear him coming. Can't wait to see the look on his face.'

'Yes, but I'm still scared.'

'I'm nervous myself, darling. But that helps me keep in tune with anything that might happen, and I assure you my reflexes are razor sharp. The fact that he's my brother doesn't come into it. He'll get what he deserves, I promise you.'

'Why does it have to be him?'

'I don't know. I'm as saddened as you are. When you think he could have had it all with you, yet he blew it before you even met.'

She shrugged her shoulders. Really, it was unbelievable that this should have happened to her. Thank God Cole was there to help her.

As he came back towards her, she was aware of him pulling something out of the inside pocket of his jacket. Donna could barely see it, but knew instinctively it was a gun. Then when she heard him unclip the safety catch, she had this confirmed, and suddenly felt very frightened again.

'Don't worry it's just a precaution. If he does show his face, it'll keep him quiet until the police arrive.'

'But is that really necessary?' She commented, thinking not for the first time that Cole was viewing the whole situation through different eyes. After all she wanted to stop Evan and thought he should pay for what he'd done, but she didn't want him to die.

'It is if you want to stay alive. The man's desperate – he'll do anything to cover his tracks, now he knows you've probably recognised him.'

As Cole sat back down beside her, Donna was so tensed up, she felt she might pee herself.

Putting a reassuring hand on her knee, he said, 'Stop worrying – it won't be long now – very soon it'll all be over, and you can start living a normal life again.'

As she pondered over what 'a normal life' might be, she heard the sound of a car. It had to be the police. Or Evan. She made to rush to the window but Cole restrained her with his hand.

'We'll find out who it is soon enough,' he whispered.

Her nerves were jangling, her breathing quick and deep. If it was the police, they'd knock on the door. If it was Evan, he'd try to unlock the door.

She quivered all over, her legs like jelly, willing it to be the police. But then to her horror she heard a click, the door opened. A scream almost left her mouth. Evan.

She heard him put down the car keys, walk to where they were sitting, then switch on the light.

'Donna!' he shouted, his eyes widening with shock and then revulsion at the sight of her and Cole sitting on the settee, Cole with his gun pointing straight at him. Evan's eyes bulged with hate at his brother. 'What the hell is going on here? What's with the gun, brother? Why, you… no wonder you didn't want me to touch you, Donna. And with my big brother too. That really is the pits.'

'He's over here on manoeuvres – thank God!' Donna said.

'And you believe that? Well, there's one born every minute, babe,' Evan laughed.

'It's true. Why else would he be wearing his uniform?'

Evan shook his head. 'Come on, Donna, think about it rationally, is that really feasible?' He came towards her, and for a second she thought even the threat of Cole's gun wouldn't stop him.

'Stay where you are Evan, or so help me God, I'll shoot you, you fucking rapist.'

Evan did stop where he was. 'You what? You're off your head, mate. There you are shagging my missus, and you're calling me a rapist. What's that all about. It's the biggest load of crap I've heard in my life. I've never raped anyone. And you Donna, after all we've been through together. Maybe I should have let you jump off that bloody roof.'

Donna shook her head. 'We're not sleeping together – I... I can't after what you did to me.'

'Eh, after what I did to you. I've never done more than kiss you, never so much as touched a hair on your sweet head. How can you say that to me? You're no better than him – you bastard.' He screamed, and without warning he dived for Cole. Donna had quickly managed to dive out of the way, just before the settee toppled over and Evan landed on top of Cole.

Getting up from the floor, she watched in horror as the two of them grappled with each other, Evan tried to prise the gun away from Cole, but Cole resisted. The gun went off. Donna's heart jumped. A hole appeared in the ceiling, bits of plaster dropped down and then the gun flew out of Cole's hand.

Donna shivered like a frightened rabbit, as Cole pushed Evan off, hit him in the face, then in the stomach, and on the chin.

Evan fell to the ground, half got up before Cole punched him down again. Blood spurted down Evan's nose. He coughed and spat out blood, then went for Cole, his head down straight into Cole's midriff. Cole gasped, fell back against the wall, then bounced forward, and hit Evan hard on the cheek. Evan went down again, and before he could get up, Cole began to kick him repeatedly in the stomach, the legs, his arms, and his head.

'Stop it, both of you,' Donna shouted. She had the gun in both hands, and was pointing it at both of them, although it wavered alarmingly. She managed to fire a shot, that whizzed over Cole's head, forcing him to stop and duck, and look directly at her, his eyes ablaze with anger.

'Come on Donna, you saw how he went for me. If he'd got the gun off me, he'd have killed us both. I was only defending myself. Give me the gun, so I can hold him here until the police arrive.' He held out his hand for her.

'Don't fall for it Donna –' Evan coughed.

'Come any closer, either of you and I'll shoot you both.' She pointed the gun at the two of them.

'Donna, you know he's the one that raped you, the man who almost ruined your life - and he'll be a murderer as well, if you give him half a chance. We've got to stop him before it's too late,' Cole said. 'Come on, hand me the gun before somebody gets hurt.'

She shook her head. Fired another shot, that just missed the top of Cole's head. He looked stunned. 'Have you gone mad? For God's sake, don't let him fool you again.'

Behind him, Donna saw Evan get to his feet.

'We'll wait for the police to arrive, let them sort this out.' Her eyes moved one to the other, as terrified as she'd ever been in her life.

'Well, if you've phoned them from here you'll have a long wait,' Evan said wiping blood from his mouth onto his sleeve.

'The landline's dead, and there's no signal for mobiles around this place.'

Narrowing her eyes for a few seconds, she stared at both of them, then went across to the phone, picked it up and heard that the line was indeed dead. She threw it down in a panic as if it was contaminated. Didn't know what to think anymore. But the police weren't coming, that was for sure.

'You cut the line,' Cole shouted.

'No, I didn't, but it was dead when I tried it earlier. Sounds to me as if you've been telling Donna a few porkies – haven't you? And that's not the only fib you've been telling, is it Cole?'

'Well, I didn't want to worry her, with you out on the prowl.'

Donna winced. Unable to decide who was telling the truth as tears streamed down her cheeks. She trembled with fright, the gun shaking in her hand. She was on her own, and feared she'd have to shoot them both, but could she kill someone in cold blood?

'Please Donna, before you do something stupid.' Cole started to step a little closer to her.

'Don't listen to him,' Evan shouted. 'He's lying through his teeth – can't you see that, babe?'

Cole shook his head. 'Let me have the gun Donna, and I'll keep him covered while you drive us into town. It's the only choice you have. You can still send him to jail for what he did, darling – if only you can find the courage.' He edged ever closer.

'I didn't do anything to her, you bastard. I'd never hurt a hair on her head – I love her for God's sake,' Evan pleaded.

'You admitted it to me, that you forced yourself on someone – well it was her. You know it was. That's why you bought her here, to kill her and pretend it was an accident.'

'You're talking rubbish, and lying through your teeth, Cole. I don't know why you're doing this – unless it's because you want her for yourself. Is that what it is?'

'No, that's not true. You remember what you told me Donna, about the one thing that made you absolutely certain it was him.'

'Yes...but I...I don't know what to think any more. I'll have to take you both in.' And as she hesitated Cole moved a shade nearer. She panicked, and accidently fired a shot which just clipped the side of Cole's cheek.

A piercing high pitched giggle came from the back of Cole's throat 'Nearly got me there darling. Try and shoot a bit straighter next time.' He wiped the blood off the side of his face with the back of his hand.

Donna gasped for a second. It was his high-pitched snigger, his eyes widening, his mouth opening, that seemed to accentuate the gap in his teeth. The events of that awful night came rushing back into her mind in flashbacks. And then it suddenly came to her – and she realised who the rapist actually was.

As she hesitated, Cole suddenly made a mad dash for her, in a desperate effort to get the gun. Another shot rang out and a penetrating scream came from the back of Donna's throat.

Cole stood motionless for a few seconds, before gazing down at his left thigh which was now saturated with blood.

'You bitch...'he mouthed, slipping down to the floor.

Donna released the gun, allowing it to fall from her grasp. She began to cry, and somehow Evan managed to get to her, and held her in his weakened arms.

Finally, they parted; both staring down at Cole motionless on the ground. Clearly in a state of shock, Donna allowed Evan to move her chin up with his thumb. As they stared at each other, she bit her lip feeling shame and guilt at judging Evan wrongly.

'I'm so sorry Evan – can you ever forgive me for doubting you?'

He smiled. 'Of course I can. I know how persuasive Cole can be – don't forget I'm his brother.'

'I should have known it was him...how could I have been so stupid?' she began, spilling out the whole grisly details.

Evan listened, open-mouthed, shocked it seemed, by these revelations that she'd never found the courage to tell him before.

'It was the smell that made me think it was you, Evan. That aftershave you wore was the very same one I smelt the day he raped me. I'll never forget it. But then when I saw the rage in him just now, the manic giggle, those creepy eyes of his and the gap in his teeth - it suddenly dawned on me, and I knew for certain he was the rapist.'

'He bought the aftershave back from the Far East for me. Said it was some kind of aphrodisiac. I thought because... you know... you couldn't. I was willing to try anything even though the smell was a bit over the top.'

'Oh Evan, you should know I don't need anything like that. As long as you love me for who I am, and don't try to push me into anything, everything will turn out just fine.' She rested her head on his shoulder.

As they parted Evan looked down at his brother. 'I feel like leaving him here, after what he's done, he should be made to suffer, like he made you suffer. But we have to get him to hospital and make sure he stands trial for his crimes.'

'Good, I intend to make sure he's brought to justice. I hope he gets put away for a very long time'

'Don't worry he will be, and if he ever gets released he won't dare show his face around us again.'

Donna hugged him tightly and instinctively knew in her heart she was safe at last and that everything between them would come right. Perhaps happiness wasn't as elusive as she thought.

THE END